Table of Content

Consciousness
and
Awareness

Truth Love Light
Path to the End of Human Suffering

Author: Ram Shah

Author's Note

I was born in the city of Tehran in 1984, during the eight-year war between Iran and Iraq. At the tender age of 3, I was often abruptly awakened in the dead of night by the piercing wails of citywide alarm. This was far from an isolated incident; it had become an unwelcome routine in our lives.

One night, as the shrill alarm pierced the silence, I awoke and noticed my sister stirring beside me. Together, we anxiously awaited what would come next. It felt like an eternity, but within moments, our mother rushed into the room. She illuminated the darkness by switching on the light and urgently told us, "Wake up, kids. We have to go." With remarkable agility, she effortlessly lifted me with one arm and firmly grasped my sister's hand with the other.

Meanwhile, my brother had already sprinted ahead, racing up the stairs to the rooftop. We quickly followed suit, and as we gathered on the rooftop, our father emerged from the shadows to join us. In that precarious moment, our entire family huddled close, drawn together by the shared challenges of our time, united in the face of uncertainty.

The city alarm continued to echo through the night, a constant reminder of the looming danger. Then, abruptly, the entire city plunged into darkness. The electric power grid had been deliberately switched off to eliminate any visibility for enemy bombers. This moment, above all others, filled me with dread—the darkness, the unbearable anticipation.

Cradled securely in my mom's arms, I could sense the fear hanging thick in the air, almost palpable. It seemed to seep into every fiber of my being, filling me with an overwhelming sense of unease. I felt my mother's grip on me tighten, as if she believed that holding me close could somehow shield me from the ominous unknown that lurked in the blackened void.

The city laid shrouded in darkness, rendering the enemy bomber planes blind to their intended targets. In this unsettling blackout, the stakes were high, for a missed target would likely result in bombs falling on civilians, including our home.

1

Conventional wisdom dictated that, in such dire times, people would seek refuge in their basement shelters. Yet, my parents' reasoning ran in the opposite direction. They were determined to avoid the horrifying fate of being buried under the rubble if bombs were dropped on our home. In the midst of this war, help was a remote possibility—one that might take days to arrive. Even for those lucky enough to survive under the rubble, death could still claim them before help arrived. This harsh reality meant that some among us would perish, while others might endure.

For those who would survive, the burden of grief and loss would be a heavy cross to bear. The prospect of such unbearable pain drove my parents to opt for a swifter death, one that would spare us from suffering. So, while the majority sought refuge underground, our family gathered on the rooftop, our gazes fixed on the sky, bound together in our silent yearning for a swift and painless exit from a world consumed by conflict.

As we huddled together on the rooftop, we were acutely aware of the ominous symphony playing above us—the distant hum of enemy aircrafts passing overhead, accompanied by the eerie whistling of bombs hurtling toward their targets. Inevitably, the whistling was drowned out by deafening explosions and blinding flashes of light. The overwhelming sensory assault pushed me past my breaking point. I broke down, tears streaming down my face as I screamed, repeatedly asking, "Why has here become a battleground?"

Undoubtedly, the war had left me deeply scarred, not to mention the daily struggles with scarcity—the constant shortage of food, the absence of warm water, and the inability to heat our home during freezing winters. The memories of war etched a lasting trauma in my mind. The fear that gripped my body whenever the city plunged into darkness resurfaced whenever I found myself in dimly lit places. Throughout my entire childhood, I left the light on during the nighttime sleep, never daring to stay up late or venture alone into the dark. I abhorred darkness and avoided it at every opportunity.

As I transitioned into young adulthood, it seemed like I had successfully managed to overcome the traumas of my past. I could now comfortably sleep in a darkened room and confidently tread the dimly lit streets alone in the dead of night. However, as I reached the end of my twenties, I encountered a new form of darkness—one I had spent my entire life evading: the darkness within myself.

Whenever I dared to peer into the depths of my own being and confront my naked truth, when I came face to face with my own inner darkness, demons, and imperfections, I would be seized by panic. It resembled the overwhelming fear I had experienced as a three-year-old, only this time, the darkness I grappled with more than two decades later had nothing to do with the external world. It was the profound darkness dwelling within my own being, capable of sending shivers down my spine.

Escaping from my own inner darkness was no longer an option, for I carried it with me wherever I went. No ordinary light bulb possessed the power to cast its glow into the depths of my darkened soul. Consequently, I made the choice to confront my inner demons, to understand them, to find comfort in their presence, and ultimately, to strive for their eradication. I cannot claim to have reached the journey's end, but I have embarked on the infinitely long path of self-discovery.

This newfound pursuit inspired me to write the second half of this book, commencing with Chapter 8. Venturing along the path of inner enlightenment has proven to be the most challenging endeavor I have ever undertaken, and I am eager to share with you the lessons and insights I have gathered along the way.

Another motivating factor behind my decision to write this book can also be traced back to my childhood memories. As the youngest of three siblings, I had a brother and a sister who were a few years older than me and naturally possessed more knowledge. When I was 5 years old, I didn't realize that an age gap also meant a gap in understanding among children. Instead, I internalized my lack of knowledge as intellectual inadequacy.

Throughout my upbringing, I carried a heavy burden of self-doubt, deeming myself unintelligent, foolish, and inferior. Whenever questions arose within my family, it seemed my brother or sister always had the answers, while I remained in the dark. I distinctly recall that by the time I turned 15, my most fervent aspiration was simply to acquire knowledge.

I yearned for it with every fiber of my being. In every social gathering, it felt as though I was consistently the least knowledgeable person in the room, a sentiment that weighed heavily on me.

My sense of inadequacy intensified when I relocated to the United States at the age of 17. My feelings of being intellectually behind, combined with my unfamiliarity with the language, culture, and society, brought back the childhood wounds of feeling inadequate. I harbored a deep resentment toward myself for not measuring up to the intellectual prowess of those around me, perpetuating a cycle of self-loathing.

The self-hatred I harbored drove me relentlessly to prove to myself that I could eventually attain a sense of normalcy, just like others. Gaining knowledge, accumulating facts, and the quest for wisdom became an all-consuming obsession during my young adulthood. My quest was fueled by the desire to reach a point where I would no longer label myself as intellectually challenged.

I dedicated countless hours to watching documentaries on various subjects, voraciously reading books, and engaging in self-study of any topic that piqued my interest. The insatiable thirst to acquire knowledge propelled me through my adulthood. During this journey, I came across the most profound question I had ever encountered: Why are we alive? What is the meaning of life? And what is the purpose of living?

This inspiration led me to embark on writing the initial half of this book. It stands as an amalgamation of the knowledge I've accumulated over the years, offering my own perspective on the fundamental nature of our universe and the very essence of existence itself. Originally, I wrote this book as a personal endeavor, a means to solidify my own comprehension of the topics explored within. Now, I am revising and rewriting this book with the intention of sharing my perspective with you.

My intention is not to persuade you to adopt my viewpoint. On the contrary, I encourage you to think independently, form your own thoughts, and challenge aspects of this book that may not resonate with you. I hope that the portions of this book which do resonate with you provide insights that empower you to enhance your thinking in your own unique way.

In this book, you will read about my model of reality that works for me and has made my life infinitely better, providing me with a greater sense of peace and a more lasting sense of happiness and joy. It is true for me and works for me, but it may not necessarily work for you. Everyone's perspective is unique, shaped by their individual experiences, beliefs, and values. My aim is not to impose my viewpoint on you but to share insights that might help you develop your own model of reality. Any model that enables you to achieve a more permanent sense of peace and pure happiness is a good model.

I hope you discover the purest form of peace, love, joy, and happiness throughout your life journey. If anything within these pages helps you get there, then the purpose of this book has been fulfilled.

Within these pages, you'll encounter complex theories that diverge significantly from widely accepted belief systems. It will take reading the entire book to construct a clear and complete picture of the concepts I'm trying to convey. If you appreciate delving into uncommon perspectives on life and enjoy exploring unconventional theories and philosophies, this book may captivate your interest.

Chapter 1: Apple Tree

In the vast expanse of the universe, everything follows a natural cycle of birth, growth, and death. It's the rhythm of life. You and I were born, we age and grow over time, and someday, we'll reach the end of our life journey. But this cycle isn't just about living beings. The entire universe follows the same pattern. Stars, for instance, are born from clouds of dust, grow by burning their internal fuel, and eventually perish in violent explosions. Even the universe itself, born from the Big Bang, keeps expanding and evolving. One day, far in the future, it too will come to an end—either by collapsing back into itself or completely depleting its hydrogen fuel and freezing into complete darkness. This cycle of birth, growth, and death is woven into every facet of the universe.

For now, let's focus on growth—the magical process that happens between the start and the end. Take an apple tree, for example. Isn't it incredible that an entire tree can grow from a single seed? That little seed contains all the information it needs to grow into a full-fledged tree. It is a tiny package of instructions, ready to unfold when the time is right. The seed holds a blueprint that dictates every stage of its development. It knows exactly how to transform into roots, branches, leaves, and fruits.

Of course, the seed doesn't grow on its own. It needs help from the world around it—sunlight, water, and rich soil. The sun provides energy, water helps carry nutrients, and the soil gives the minerals that the tree needs to thrive. But here's the amazing part: the seed already knows how to take these resources and use them. Within its tiny core, the seed holds the hidden wisdom—the know-how required to grow into a majestic tree.

You, too, began your life's journey as a single cell, formed by the fusion of a sperm and an egg—just like an apple tree that sprouts from a single seed. Even as a tiny little cell, you carried within you a marvelous blueprint, a subconscious intelligence that knew exactly what to do to become who you are today. From the very beginning, growth took over automatically. As a single cell, you multiplied again and again, forming tissues, organs, and eventually the trillions of cells that make up your body.

At no point did you need to consciously direct this process—it unfolded seamlessly, guided by the natural wisdom embedded within you. Just as an apple tree doesn't need instructions from the outside world to stretch its roots into the soil, push its branches toward the sky, or bear fruit, your body evolved without external guidance, following an invisible roadmap that nature has woven into you. Growth, whether in a tree or a person, is nothing short of a miracle—an unstoppable force, an innate unfolding of potential, a testament to the profound intelligence and wisdom woven into the fabric of existence.

Moreover, the natural world is incredibly intelligent and rarely makes mistakes. During the development of a human fetus, even a small error in the process can lead to significant health conditions, such as the production of abnormal proteins that can result in conditions like Down syndrome. If you are healthy, it's because more than 30 trillion cells in your body have been constructed almost flawlessly. Conversely, if you have Down syndrome or another health condition, it could be due to a single type of protein experiencing a misstep in its growth process. Even if you suffer from a disability, you are still remarkably close to perfect in the grand scheme of nature's design.

Everywhere we look, we observe that the growth processes of all living organisms, whether it's an apple tree sprouting from a seed or a human maturing from a fertilized egg, are inherently automatic, meticulously precise, and, for the most part, remarkably error-free.

But what about non-living entities? Are their growth processes as precise and flawless as those of living organisms? To answer this question, we can turn our gaze to the sky. When we look at the Sun, we are not seeing it as it is now but as it appeared about 8 minutes and 20 seconds ago due to the time it takes for light to travel from the Sun to Earth. The stars we see at night are much farther away, their light having journeyed across space for years, centuries, or even billions of years before reaching us.

When we gaze at the night sky, we are essentially traveling through time—moving forward into the past to witness events that occurred long ago. This reverse perspective of time allows us to witness the growth and development of the universe and everything within it.

One fascinating discovery in astronomy is the light emitted from tightly gathered groups of matter, composed of gas and dust, known as "protoclusters," which existed billions of years ago in the early universe. These protoclusters were the seeds from which galaxies were born. Over time, the cosmic forces within these protoclusters, caused the matter to coalesce into larger structures, eventually forming the galaxies we see today. It's an awe-inspiring dance of particles and molecules coming together to form something far greater than themselves—a process that reflects how living cells join forces to create a more complex life form.

These protoclusters carried an inherent sense of purpose, a cosmic blueprint for what they were destined to become. Like a fertilized egg that instinctively grows into a human or an apple seed that transforms into a towering tree, these clusters seemed to "know" their path. Step by step, they evolved into magnificent galaxies, each brimming with billions of stars, planets, and celestial wonders, all working together in perfect harmony.

Unlike living organisms, protoclusters don't have DNA to dictate their journey. Yet, they act as though driven by some mysterious, built-in plan. In place of genetic codes, forces like dark energy, dark matter, and gravity orchestrate their transformation. These cosmic forces are the architects of galactic evolution, shaping and molding the protoclusters into majestic galaxies.

Discoveries like protoclusters reveal just how remarkably precise the universe's evolution truly is. Consider, another example, the "molecular clouds" or "stellar nurseries"—vast regions of gas and dust which give rise to stars in highly predictable ways. Just as we can look at an apple seed and know it will grow into an apple tree; we can observe these clouds of dust and predict how they will transform into stars.

Whether we examine the development of living organisms or the formation of cosmic wonders, the level of precision and predictability are truly astonishing. On Earth, life unfolds according to the genetic instructions encoded in DNA, transforming single cells into complex life forms. Similarly, across the vast expanse of the universe, cosmic laws act like a universal blueprint, guiding the evolution of simple particles into majestic stars and sprawling galaxies.

At the time of the Big Bang, the universe was an empty canvas—there were no galaxies, stars, planets, or even the basic elements we know today. Yet, from the very start, everything we see now was set into motion, as if the universe carried within it a cosmic "genetic code." This blueprint directed its growth and expansion with astonishing precision, ensuring every stage unfolded in a purposeful and deliberate way.

Much like an apple seed inherently knows it will one day grow into a towering tree, the universe seemed to be programmed with an intrinsic understanding of its predetermined destiny. Its evolution was not a series of random events but a carefully orchestrated process, each phase building upon the last to bring about the grandeur we witness today. Far from being a chaotic accident, the universe reveals itself as an organized, purposeful entity—a vast cosmic design moving steadily toward its ultimate goal.

Consider the analogy of the sperm and the egg—a single cell giving rise to over 30 trillion cells, comprising your body, each harmoniously collaborating to bestow upon you the profound essence of life. In a parallel vein, the colossal event of the Big Bang spawned trillions, perhaps even more, galaxies and stars, harmoniously intertwined to create conditions suitable for life on our tiny planet. Trillions upon trillions of cells and galaxies coexist harmoniously, working nonstop around the clock so that you and I can enjoy the simple beauty of existence. This cannot all be the result of luck. It seems far too intricate, elegant, and purposeful to be dismissed as mere chance.

This harmony is a fundamental pattern woven throughout the cosmos. Every entity dwell within something larger, contributing to a grand design that connects all things. The universe itself is expanding and evolving, an immense entity giving rise to countless galaxies that grow, merge, and transform over time. Stars form within these galaxies, burning their internal fuel to light up the cosmos. These stars give birth to solar systems, where planets and moons take shape. On planets like

Earth, living organisms emerge and grow, with countless cells within our bodies living, dying, and regenerating as we tread the journey of life.

Within those cells, viruses and bacteria grow and multiply, subtly influencing the course of genetic evolution. And everything that exists in the material world is composed of particles and atoms. At the heart of atoms, subatomic particles like protons and neutrons interact, held together by fundamental forces. Delving deeper, these particles are made of even smaller elemental components—vibrations in perfect harmony that create matter itself. Beneath it all, dark energy and dark matter permeate the universe, shaping its structure and guiding its destiny. The entire universe adheres to a cosmic symphony of growth and transformation, orchestrating a harmonious dance of interconnectedness on a scale beyond comprehension.

Everything in existence unfolds through an automatic and harmonious growth process, bound together in a web of deep interconnectedness. This universal unity allows us to draw parallels between seemingly distinct structures, revealing a shared pattern beneath their forms. The phrase "tree of life" beautifully symbolizes the essence of interconnectedness, a metaphor for the way all things are elegantly linked.

If we were to compare the universe to the tree of life—often depicted as an apple tree—their structures would align seamlessly. According to current scientific theories, the entire universe sprouted from a tiny, dense core known as the singularity at the moment of the Big Bang, much like an apple tree sprouting from a single seed. Just as the seed holds the genetic codes for its transformation into a tree, the Big Bang contained the blueprint for the vast and complex universe we see today.

Scientists also claim that the stability of the universe relies heavily on the invisible forces of dark energy and dark matter, holding everything in place. In a similar vein, the unseen roots of a tree provide essential support and stability, anchoring the tree firmly in the ground. Dark energy and dark matter are invisible forces, lying beneath, supporting the visible aspect of reality, just as roots, hidden beneath the soil, provide stability for the visible parts of the tree. One is the concealed underpinning of the universe; the other is the concealed underpinning of the tree.

At the center of galaxies, supermassive black holes act as gravitational anchors, around which all other celestial objects orbit. This mirrors the role of a tree's trunk—a central support from which branches, leaves, and fruits emerge and grow. The trunk provides stability, enabling the tree to balance itself and extend its branches outward. Similarly, black holes maintain the gravitational order that upholds the structural integrity of galaxies. Their immense pull ensures the balance and movement of stars, planets, and other celestial bodies.

Stars can be compared to branches. Just as branches are made of the same material as the trunk of a tree, stars are fundamentally the same as black holes. Black holes were once massive stars that underwent a transformation over time. Similarly, a tree's trunk begins as a branch growing out of the ground, eventually maturing into the trunk over time. Additionally, branches provide the structure from which leaves and fruit grow, offering support and nourishment. Likewise, stars support the formation of planets and moons, supplying them with energy and stability.

Moreover, the death of stars can be likened to the dead branches of a tree. When a tree loses a branch, it falls to the ground and decomposes, enriching the soil for new growth. Likewise, dying stars release essential elements into space, providing the universe with the building blocks for new stars, planets, and even life. In this way, dying stars contribute to the cosmic recycling of matter, just as dead branches are recycled within the biological world.

Moons resemble leaves, and planets can be likened to the flowers of a tree. In the natural world, leaves play a vital role in supporting the growth of flowers on a tree, converting sunlight into energy through photosynthesis. Similarly, moons reflect starlight, stabilize planetary orbits, and influence conditions like tides, contributing to the stable environment within their planet. Moons ensure that the planets they orbit receive adequate light and stability, much like how leaves ensure that flowers get the nutrients and energy they need to blossom.

Planets are the flowers of this cosmic tree, each holding the potential for life. And life itself is the cosmic fruit of existence. Just as flowers on a tree may blossom into fruit under the right conditions, planets can foster life if they have the right atmospheric conditions. However, not all flowers bear fruit, and not all planets harbor life.

Finally, the fruit of an apple tree contains seeds that carry the promise of new life. Similarly, life is the cosmic fruit, creating and nurturing new life. Just as an apple represents the culmination of a tree's growth, the emergence of life signifies the apex of cosmic evolution.

This analogy, from roots to fruits, illustrates how everything in existence follows similar principles of growth and interconnectedness. Our ability to draw these comparisons stems from a natural human tendency to seek patterns, a phenomenon known as *apophenia*. It is scientifically proven that when we actively seek patterns, we tend to discover them abundantly everywhere. While this pattern-seeking is a human cognitive ability, it also hints at a deeper truth—that the universe operates under one grand design, governed by universal principles that echo across the vastness of existence. These universal principles are what give meaning to the concept of apophenia itself, enabling us to perceive patterns everywhere we look.

Up to this point, we have explored the universal concept of automatic growth processes and the similarities inherent in these processes. Now, let's shift our perspective to the other end of the spectrum and seek out distinctions. Let's use the concept of apophenia to detect patterns that emerge when we focus on differences rather than similarities.

One striking observation is the uniqueness inherent in everything that exists in the universe. While everything follows a predictable growth pattern, every entity also possesses a distinct and individual character. Even identical twins, who share almost the same genetic blueprint, grow to possess their own distinct personalities. To date, scientists have not encountered any two entities that are exact replicas.

This principle holds true from the celestial realm to the microscopic level. No two stars, planets, animals, or even bacteria are identical. A particularly captivating example is the snowflake. Despite its seemingly simple structure, each snowflake is entirely unique and unlike any other.

As a snowflake takes shape and descends from the sky, it interacts with countless air molecules, with each collision subtly altering its form. Additionally, environmental factors such as humidity, temperature, and atmospheric conditions influence the shaping of each snowflake. The likelihood of two snowflakes undergoing precisely the same series of events to become exact replicas is practically impossible. Despite decades of searching, scientists have yet to find identical snowflakes. It is safe to say that every snowflake that has ever fallen or will ever fall from the sky is unique in its appearance.

Consider yourself for a moment. You are utterly one-of-a-kind. Your fingerprint, eye pattern, ear shape, and the intricate patterns of connections within your brain are all distinct to you alone. Every cell within your body holds your genetic code, bearing the mark of your unique identity. No one has ever existed with your exact identity, and none will ever come into existence as your exact replica. Everything that will ever come into existence in the universe will possess its own unique combination of attributes, differing from all that has come before it.

Now, let's combine the ideas of similarities and differences with the concept of the automatic growth process to explore a fundamental question about the nature of the universe. Is it possible that we inhabit a universe governed by an entirely automated system with a fixed growth pattern? And if that were the case, would it imply that everything in our lives has already been predetermined? In my perspective, the answers to both questions reside in a paradoxical interplay of "yes" and "no."

On the one hand, the affirmative response, the "yes," suggests that everything is predetermined, and our future is fixed, leaving no room for change. This concept aligns with the idea that the universe operates through automatic growth processes that are precise, meticulous, and error-free. In a broader sense, many aspects of existence were set in motion and determined long ago.

On the other hand, the negative response, the "no," is rooted in the unique and unpredictable nature of everything within the universe. Every entity, no matter how simple or complex, undergoes a profoundly complex journey, resulting in outcomes that are inherently uncertain and unique. The sheer complexity of these processes makes the final result unpredictable and undetermined.

In essence, when we juxtapose similarities and differences, we arrive at a profound understanding of the universe—a place where the certainty of overarching patterns coexists with the unpredictability found in the intricacies of each individual entity and event.

Consider the apple tree. It is certain that an apple seed will grow into an apple tree, and we can predict the general shape of its overall structure, branches, leaves, and even the type of fruit it will bear. Yet, as the tree develops, the path each branch takes, the number of leaves it grows, and the precise taste and texture of each apple are shaped by unpredictable environmental forces.

Look at your own life, you can anticipate the general rhythms of your life: eating, working, sleeping, living, and dying. These aspects are highly predictable. However, when you delve into the finer details, many factors make things unpredictable. Random conversations, unexpected encounters, and many small details all influence your experiences in ways you can't predict.

From a broader perspective, the universe is incredibly intelligent and aware of everything that unfolds within it. From the moment of the Big Bang, the universe may have been aware of its potential to create life. Perhaps it even foresaw the emergence of humanity, knowing that you and I would one day exist. It's possible that the universe has already determined the arc of your life—how and when you will die, the pivotal events that will shape your journey, perhaps even the identity of your soulmate, the person you will marry, and the children you might have. This could be your destiny, a script written by the cosmos, unchangeable in its broad strokes. Much like a snowflake cannot control the atmospheric conditions that shape its form, you cannot alter the major events the universe has set in motion for you.

Yet, within this predestined framework, there lies freedom. How you arrive at these major events in your life, the attitude you harbor toward them, the decisions you make along the way, and the character you build through these experiences—all of this remains entirely within your power.

Think of it this way: you are destined to travel from point A to point B. The path is set, and you will reach point B eventually. But *how* you journey from point A to point B is up to you. You can walk with grace or stumble with resistance; you can learn and grow or remain stagnant. The path may twist and turn, but your response to its challenges and your growth along the way are uniquely yours to determine. In this, you find your free will, even amidst the inevitability of predetermined destiny.

It seems contradictory to suggest that you have absolute free will and control over your life amidst an utterly unchanging, predetermined destiny. Yet, this paradox—where the big picture unfolds with absolute certainty, while the finer details overflow with infinite variety and free will—beautifully captures the essence of duality at the heart of existence. This isn't chaos or randomness; rather, it's a perfect balance that governs reality.

Contradictions are woven into the fabric of existence, not as errors but as essential threads that create harmony through their interplay. This is the essence of duality—a principle that embraces opposites and allows them to coexist in a captivating dance. The predictable and the unpredictable, the known and the unknown, predetermination and free will merge not in conflict but in a mesmerizing rhythm that defines existence. While reality may appear contradictory, it is never illogical; it simply operates on a level where contradiction and harmony unite as one.

Let's take a closer look at how contradictions coexist beautifully and harmoniously in the world around us. During the course of human evolution, we developed a heightened sensitivity to bitter tastes, as they often signal toxins or harmful substances in plants and fruits that could make us ill or even kill us. If you were lost in a jungle with no knowledge of edible flora, avoiding bitter-tasting plants and fruits might save your life.

Yet, paradoxically, the bitter taste is also associated with healing properties. Notice how many medicines have a bitter taste. Herein lies the contradiction: the bitter taste has the power to either kill you or heal you, depending on which bitter substance you choose to consume.

On the other hand, sweetness, the flavor of life, offers another intriguing paradox. Sugar, in the form of glucose, is the most fundamental energy source for the cells in your body and is considered the single most important nutrient. Nevertheless, excessive sugar consumption has been linked to a range of health concerns, such as diabetes, obesity, heart disease, cancer, and even neurological disorders as well as anxiety and depression. Here, the paradox lies in the dual nature of sweetness. Sugar serves as a fundamental source of nourishment for your body, yet it's also the taste most strongly linked to a myriad of health concerns.

These contrasts—bitterness that can kill or heal, sweetness that can nourish or harm—echo the symbolism of the Yin and Yang, the ancient representation of duality. The Yin and Yang symbol features two complementary halves: one half features a black section with a white circle at its center, while the other half shows a white region with a black dot in its core. Now, let's integrate the concept of taste into the Yin and Yang symbol. The taste of sweetness, typically associated with goodness, harbors a negative aspect at its core, akin to Yang, the white area with the black dot in its center. Conversely, the taste of bitterness, often considered unpleasant and harmful, can have a healing effect when consumed thoughtfully, resembling the Yin, the black facet of duality, with its inner goodness denoted by a white circle.

Understanding the paradoxical nature of reality, with its inherent contradictions, embodies the essence of duality symbolized by the Yin and Yang symbol. When you fully comprehend this concept, you begin to see countless examples of it all around you, in every direction you gaze.

Let's delve into another example of paradoxical duality: the interplay between light and darkness. We commonly link light with illumination, clarity, and the ability to understand our surroundings. However, during the day when light is abundant, it is impossible to see the stars and the vastness of the cosmos in all its celestial splendor. This paradox highlights how, while light offers clarity of sight, it can also make us somewhat shortsighted, limiting our perception of the wider universe.

On the other side of the spectrum, darkness is often associated with the unknown and uncertainty, hiding what lies ahead in the shadows. Yet, it is precisely during the darkest nights that we are granted the most unobstructed view of the cosmos, with stars and celestial wonders shining brightly. The paradoxical nature of darkness reveals that, while it conceals what lies before us, it bestows upon us the ability to gaze into the far reaches of the universe.

In this way, the relationship between light and darkness represents a dichotomy, where the benefits and drawbacks of each are intrinsically intertwined, as represented in the Yin and Yang symbol. The black side, Yin, signifies the darkness of the night, with a white dot at its core representing the radiant lights of celestial objects in the night sky. Conversely, the white area, Yang, symbolizes the brightness of daytime, with a black dot at its core signifying the obscured sky where all celestial objects remain concealed from sight.

Let's explore another example of duality, this time within the contrasting elements of water and fire. Water is a symbol of life and vitality. Water is indispensable to all living beings, nourishing plants, sustaining animals, and quenching human thirst. Its gentle flow sustains ecosystems, and its abundance is often equated with prosperity and health. However, the paradox unfolds when we consider that the very abundance of water, as seen in the vast oceans, can be detrimental to us. Ocean water is undrinkable due to its high salt content, as it dehydrates the human body and exacerbates thirst. Furthermore, it is not suitable for cleansing, as the salt residue can leave the skin dry and uncomfortable. In an ironic twist, in the days before the convenience of GPS, sailors, while lost in the ocean, found themselves surrounded by water, yet perished from thirst and a lack of drinkable water.

Water's paradox deepens when we consider its dual role as both creator and destroyer. While it sustains life, it also has the capacity to take it away. Tsunamis, hurricanes, and floods showcase its raw, untamed power, causing widespread devastation and loss. Entire communities can be swept away by this force that otherwise nurtures crops and quenches thirst. Water, for all its benevolence, can wield a destructive force that shapes and reshapes the world around us.

Now, turning our attention to fire, it is considered the embodiment of destruction. It consumes and engulfs everything it comes into contact with, leaving behind ashes and ruins. Yet, fire is also a symbol of transformation and progress. When humans learned to harness and control fire, it became one of the most pivotal milestones in our history.

Fire provided the means to cook food, enabling better nourishment. It offered warmth, allowing humans to adapt and thrive in colder climates. Fire also provided illumination at night, enabling activities beyond daylight hours. In ancient times, the mastery of fire bestowed upon us the status of the apex predators. The power to wield fire deterred other predators from approaching us, granting safety and dominance in the natural world. Fire became a tool of survival and progress, helping shape civilizations.

When viewed through the lens of duality, water and fire form a perfect pair of opposites. Water, with its nurturing and life-sustaining essence, symbolizes Yang—a gentle force that, despite its softness, can also become a source of immense devastation. Fire, with its destructive and consuming power, symbolizes Yin—an intense force that, despite its chaotic nature, also brings transformation and progress. Together, they represent the balance of opposites, each indispensable to the harmony of existence.

Now, consider the common saying, "hot air rises." If you've lived in a multi-story house, you've probably noticed that the lower floors and basements are consistently cooler than the upper ones. This makes sense—heat tends to rise, always warming the upper floors. But if heat naturally ascends, why are mountain tops always colder than their bases? I'll leave you to contemplate this one.

The key insight here is that contradictions, when properly understood, make perfect sense. This is the essence of duality, and the universe is replete with such wonders and apparent paradoxes.

Everything we've discussed thus far has been leading us to the fundamental concept of duality. This concept is so deeply woven into the fabric of the world that as humans, we find it nearly impossible to grasp or understand anything without its complementary counterpart. Think about it: how would you recognize and define "light" if there was no "darkness" to contrast it with? How would you grasp the concept of "good" without its opposite, "bad"? "tall" without "short"? "hot" without "cold"? Duality provides us with the necessary contrast, difference, and opposition that enables us to discern and distinguish between different concepts.

Imagine a universe where everything—the air, the water, the fire, every solid object, gas, and liquid—exists at the exact same temperature as your body, 37 degrees Celsius. Day and night, nothing ever fluctuates. Your skin might still have the sensitivity to detect temperature, but if there were no variations—no hot or cold—you would never experience temperature as a sensation. In fact, the very concept of temperature would be meaningless to you. Without the duality of hot and cold, the idea of temperature would simply not exist.

This principle applies to everything in the universe. Through duality, concepts arise, giving us the framework to experience and interpret existence. It is only through contrasts—light and dark, sound and silence, pleasure and pain—that we come to understand and interact with the world. Every experience you've ever had is rooted in the interplay of dualities, allowing you to perceive, feel, and make sense of existence. Duality is the foundation that shapes your awareness, giving depth and meaning to your life.

Even one of the cornerstone laws of physics, Newton's Third Law, highlights this principle. It states that "For every action, there is an equal and opposite reaction." This idea extends to mathematics, where every number has an equal negative counterpart, and to particle physics, where matter is mirrored by antimatter. In fact, there is nothing in the entire universe that lacks an opposite or counterpart. Duality, with its interplay of contrasting and contradicting elements, stands as an indispensable foundation for our understanding of the world.

Before we transition to the next chapter, let's contemplate a few more questions about the universe. How vast is the universe, truly? Have you ever pondered when humanity might pen the final book of mathematics, physics, chemistry, or any other scientific discipline? Is there a conceivable future where the creation of new songs, dances, drawings, or any other form of art reaches a point with no further variations?

Have you ever considered when we might fathom the limits of scientific and artistic boundaries? The resounding answer is that such limits will never materialize. Our existence is entrenched in a realm of infinity and boundless potential. The laws governing our universe exhibit an unending tapestry of complexity. Every new scientific revelation unfurls more complications rather than simplifications. Whether we peer through telescopes or microscopes, the universe consistently unfolds into exponentially greater complexity. The trajectory of artistic and scientific progress invariably propels us toward heightened complexity, never toward simplicity.

What is also extremely captivating and interesting is the unwavering laws and regulations found in every aspect of science and the totality of existence. It is as if everything adheres to precise rules without exception. In this world, the concept of randomness seems nonexistent; rather, randomness is a label we assign when faced with complexities beyond our comprehension. As our intellect advances, we unveil patterns and laws that demystify what we once perceived as random occurrences.

Science rigorously studies randomness through various disciplines such as stochastic processes, probability theory, chaos theory, and random matrix theory, among others. However, all these studies highlight the current limitations of human knowledge and the infancy of science in our era. This presents yet another paradox we encounter. While most scientific advancements are grounded in logic, repeatable experiments, and meticulous measurements, science must also venture into realms of complexity that currently elude its understanding, labeling them as randomness. The term "randomness" is used to describe phenomena that appear to lack order or predictability, but this simply reflects the limits of our current knowledge. As science progresses, what once seemed random will be revealed to follow specific rules and patterns that were previously hidden from our understanding.

For instance, chaos theory has shown that systems which appear chaotic and unpredictable are governed by natural laws, but their predictable behavior is highly sensitive to initial conditions. This means that as we develop more advanced tools and gain deeper insights, we will uncover the underlying order within what we now perceive as random.

Let's summarize the key points covered in this chapter:

Automatic Growth Process: We started by discussing the automatic growth process. We highlighted how every entity in the world, both living and non-living, adheres to this growth process with remarkable precision and minimal error.

Ubiquitous Similarities: We also discussed the prevalence of similarities throughout the world. Regardless of where we look, we can find similarities, noting the human cognitive ability to find patterns, a phenomenon science refers to as apophenia.

Uniqueness and Differences: Delving into the topic of differences, we uncovered the idea that every existence is inherently unique and lacks perfect replicas. This emphasizes the diversity and individuality present in the world.

Contradictions and Paradoxes: Through the exploration of both similarities and differences, we uncovered contradictions that, upon closer examination and proper explanation, revealed themselves as paradoxes with logical resolutions.

Duality as a Fundamental Principle: We introduced the notion of duality as a fundamental and pervasive concept in existence. It emerged as a means of understanding and categorizing the entire universe with opposing characteristics.

Complexity in Scientific Progress: We noted the trend in science where discoveries consistently reveal more complexity rather than simplicity. This concept highlights the infinite complexity of the universe and the ever-evolving nature of scientific knowledge.

Scientific Laws and Regulations: Lastly, despite the vastness of the universe, all aspects of existence adhere to precise laws and regulations that can be uncovered and understood over time. We noted that perceived randomness is a consequence of our limited understanding rather than a fundamental law of nature.

You might wonder about the purpose of these seemingly diverse ideas. Consider each of these concepts as pieces of a larger puzzle that, when assembled, will unveil a more comprehensive picture. In the upcoming chapter, we will explore a fresh set of ideas, distinct from our current discussions but interconnected in their own right, further contributing to the mosaic of knowledge being constructed.

Chapter 2: Consciousness and Awareness

Everything in the universe, at its core, is a form of information. From the tiniest subatomic particles to the vast expanse of galaxies, every element of existence can be understood as a collection of data encoded within the fabric of reality. On the biological level, you are the embodiment of information stored in strands of DNA—a molecular code that holds the blueprint of your unique identity. These genetic sequences determine your physical traits, such as the color of your eyes, the texture of your hair, and the way your cells function and interact.

Stepping beyond biology, particles and subatomic particles—the building blocks of the material world—interact with one another in precise and harmonious ways. Within each of these entities lies the encoded information that defines their identity and governs their behavior, enabling them to weave the fabric of the cosmos. Every particle, photon, and form of energy carries data about its properties.

From a broader perspective, even the intangible aspects of existence—thoughts, feelings, imaginations, and ideas—can be understood as forms of information. The thought of a solution to a particular problem is an information exchange between brain cells. A feeling of joy can be understood as biochemical signals in the body, while the creative imagination of an artist manifests as vivid mental constructs. All of these are expressions of information, each manifested in different ways.

Information permeates throughout the entire world, even in the darkest and seemingly emptiest spaces. In every corner of the universe, we can observe the interplay of time, space, matter, antimatter, strange matter, dark matter, dark energy, the force of gravity, and a multitude of other phenomena. No place in the entire universe is truly empty; some form of information persists everywhere.

The absence of information implies the absence of existence. Without information, there would be no time, no space, no material world, and no discernible reality. Time, space, and dimensions are too forms of information. If information does not exist, nothing else can exist.

As we mentioned in the last chapter, every entity in existence has a definite purpose, guided by an inherent knowledge of how to grow and evolve. When we layer this understanding onto the concept of information, a new idea emerges: the entire universe is composed of information, and every piece of information is imbued with the knowledge necessary for growth and evolution. In other words, existence itself is a vast system of interconnected information, with each piece carrying the wisdom of its purpose and the blueprint for its transformation.

Now, imagine compiling all the information in the universe—including potential parallel universes and the full spectrum of broader reality—and encapsulating it into a single entity. I refer to this unified capsule of universal information imbued with knowledge as *consciousness*.

Let's unpack the etymology of the word consciousness. In Latin, *con* means "with," while *scious* denotes "having knowledge." Adding *ness* at the end signifies a state of being. Thus, from Latin to English, consciousness translates to "being with knowledge." However, this translation hints at something deeper: the relationship between knowledge and information.

For knowledge to exist, information must first exist. Information is the raw material—the essence—from which knowledge is formed. When you uncover the meaning within a piece of information, it transforms into knowledge, and in that moment, you become more conscious.

Consciousness, which means being with knowledge, points to something that holds and carries knowledge—and that something is information. Every piece of information contains its own embedded knowledge. Therefore, when all the knowledge from every piece of information in the entire existence comes together, it forms the concept of consciousness, where knowledge and information unite as one.

Now, consider every action you've ever taken, every word you've ever spoken, every feeling you've ever felt, and every thought that has ever crossed your mind as distinct forms of information interwoven within the fabric of consciousness. These actions, words, feelings, and thoughts define who you are and shape how you perceive the world. They are data points that contribute to the continuous stream of information within the construct of consciousness.

Now, rather than thinking of consciousness as something you possess, imagine it the other way around. Envision yourself as a packet of purposeful information, with consciousness as the entity that encompasses you. Consciousness is not a byproduct of brain activity but a fundamental aspect of reality. Your individual consciousness is a thread in a much larger, universal tapestry of consciousness.

By viewing yourself as an integral part of the vast consciousness, you begin to realize that you are part of a much larger, interconnected system of information exchange. This system is not limited only to human experience but extends to all forms of life and even to non-living entities in the entirety of the world.

Consciousness bears a resemblance to the concept of God, for it is omnipresent and all-knowing. However, consciousness and God are not interchangeable. While they share characteristics, they differ fundamentally in their roles. Unlike God, who creates, consciousness remains passive. It doesn't actively engage in creations; rather, it exists as meaningful information, silently shaping the universe's tapestry.

Think of it this way. Everything that we have ever known, have ever done, have ever thought, have ever imagined, and have ever felt is within the boundaries of consciousness. The whole existence is interwoven using the fabric of consciousness. Consciousness is where boundaries cannot be seen or measured. Even infinity fits within it. Consciousness holds all that ever was, all that is, and all that ever will be. Boundaries of consciousness extend far beyond time and dimensions and everything else we consider as existence.

Now that we have redefined the meaning of consciousness, let us also redefine awareness. Awareness is the cognitive faculty that enables us to perceive, understand, and analyze the vast information contained within consciousness. To simplify, if consciousness represents the repository of meaningful data, awareness serves as the tool for accessing and harnessing the meaning of that data. Awareness is the essential tool that empowers us to become more conscious. It serves as the lens through which we perceive, process, and engage with the world around us. By connecting individual entities—like you and me—to the boundless expanse of consciousness, awareness serves as a bridge, linking our personal experiences to the universal flow of knowledge.

Every time you attempt to understand the world—which is essentially a manifestation of consciousness—you must utilize the power of awareness. Awareness enables you to tap into consciousness. When you are aware, you can understand the world around you and become more conscious.

Think of awareness as a conduit or a wormhole through which information flows between consciousness and yourself. Awareness is the medium for the exchange of information. Much like fish navigate through water, information traverses through awareness.

Awareness is accessible through your sensory faculties like sight and smell. It can also be accessed through your thoughts and imaginations. Furthermore, awareness is attainable through your feelings and emotions, as well as through accumulated experiences and honed skills. You utilize your senses, thoughts, imaginations, feelings, experiences, and skills as the components of awareness to gain access to the knowledge stored within consciousness. In this framework, consciousness, awareness, and all individual entities—such as you and I—are deeply interconnected.

Just as everything in existence is a part of consciousness, every entity possesses some form of awareness that connects it to totality of consciousness. Let's briefly explore how science has identified the existence of awareness within even the simplest particles in the universe. In 1935, Albert Einstein, along with his colleagues, published a paper discussing a phenomenon he famously referred to as "spooky action at a distance." This term expressed the idea that particles can be aware of one another across vast distances. Shortly after, another German scientist, Erwin Schrödinger, coined the term "entanglement" to describe this quantum phenomenon.

Today, this phenomenon is called "quantum entanglement," which means that particles that have interacted or share the same origin can become entangled in such a way that the state of one particle instantaneously influences the state of the other, regardless of the distance between them. If one particle's state is modified, the other particle's state will correspondingly adjust. For example, if two photons (particles of light) were entangled billions of years ago and one photon reached Earth while the other is in a distant galaxy, modifying the photon on Earth would instantaneously affect the state of the photon in that distant galaxy. As long as the two photons remain entangled, they remain aware of one another and interact with each other in meaningful ways.

Quantum entanglement is a mysterious phenomenon that reveals a deep interconnectedness within the universe that surpasses the limitations of time and space. It shows that even the simplest particles possess a form of awareness, interacting with one another in ways that defy conventional laws of physics.

Just as we can become entangled through our interactions and affect each other's lives, simple particles in the universe can also be entangled and influence one another in meaningful ways. As science evolves, we increasingly realize that the world is more interconnected than we previously thought.

In a broader sense, every entity in existence, whether living or non-living, possesses some level of awareness, continuously connected to the totality of consciousness. This creates a triangular relationship between consciousness, awareness, and every single entity in existence. This is what gives meaning to the age-old concept known as the *trinity*, symbolizing the notion of three. While trinity may initially seem like a religious concept, its deeper meaning transcends religion, representing a universal principle much like duality. Having explored duality in the previous chapter, the focus for the remainder of this chapter will be on delving into the concept of the trinity.

The word trinity comes from the Latin term *trinitas* and the Greek word *triás*, both of which means "a set of three" or "triad." Trinity has a unique attribute; it is always related to three distinct entities that come together as one.

The deeper meaning of trinity lies in its inherent process: something at a lower level interacts with an intermediary to ascend to a higher level. When this process succeeds, all three unite seamlessly. Trinity is the force of nature that brings about unity, guiding the lower toward integration with the greater.

The concept of trinity is woven into every aspect of life. Anytime you see a triad—three components working in harmony—you're witnessing the trinity in action. Much like duality, trinity is a universal principle that runs through all of existence. But while duality creates separation and balance between contrasting concepts, trinity works in the opposite way—it bridges gaps. Instead of maintaining tension, trinity fosters connection and integration, uniting what was divided and guiding the lower toward harmony with the higher.

Let's explore some examples of the concept of trinity in our daily lives, starting with music. The entire realm of sound and music, with all its wonders, represents a form of universal knowledge and a segment of consciousness, forming the upper tier of the musical trinity. Musical instruments, which allow us to produce, practice, and understand music, constitute the middle tier of the musical trinity. The musician, who diligently strives to acquire musical knowledge, embodies the lower tier of this trinity. When you witness a talented musician performing, it appears as though the musical instrument is an extension of their body and the music they create is an integral part of their being. In this way, the musical realm, the instrument, and the musician become one during a performance. The more harmoniously and coherently this triad merges, the more exquisite musical wonders are produced, enhancing the unity between the musician, the instrument, and the entirety of the musical realm.

In the realm of science, the primary objective is to acquire knowledge, which corresponds to gaining access to consciousness, forming the apex of the scientific trinity. The developing sciences, such as chemistry, physics, and mathematics, represent our scientific awareness and provide the means to attain scientific knowledge, thereby forming the middle tier of this trinity. Each scientist, as an individual entity striving to unravel the mysteries of the universe, comprises the lower tier.

When a scientist applies scientific disciplines, such as mathematics and physics, they tap into higher realms of consciousness to uncover the deep mysteries of the universe. This triad—scientists, scientific disciplines, and universal scientific principles—collectively forms the scientific trinity. Each component plays its role: scientists represent the seekers of knowledge, scientific disciplines serve as the tools of exploration and awareness, and universal scientific principles embody the universal truths in existence.

The concept of the trinity is most widely recognized in the context of religion. While it is predominantly associated with modern Christianity, its roots can be traced back thousands of years before the emergence of Christianity, appearing in various forms in ancient religious and philosophical traditions.

The concept of a trinity is fundamental to Zoroastrianism, one of the world's oldest monotheistic religions. This ancient faith places a strong emphasis on the worship of Ahura Mazda as the supreme and singular deity. Ahura Mazda, the Wise Lord, is seen as the creator and the source of all that is good, embodying the apex of this trinity.

In Zoroastrianism, the Amesha Spentas, often referred to as the "Holy Immortals," represent the middle tier of this trinity. These divine beings serve as manifestations of Ahura Mazda's divine attributes, such as righteousness, truth, and dominion. Each Holy Immortal embodies a particular aspect of Ahura Mazda's nature and assists in guiding the faithful toward the path of righteousness.

Devout followers of Zoroastrianism, through their interactions with the Holy Immortals and their connections to Ahura Mazda, form the lower tier of this trinity. By adhering to the principles and virtues represented by these Holy Immortals, Zoroastrians endeavor to elevate their spiritual understanding, thereby forging a deeper connection and unity with the divine. This is the spiritual Zoroastrian trinity.

Central to Zoroastrian teaching is another triad encapsulated in the slogan "Good thoughts, good words, good deeds." This ethical triad forms the cornerstone of Zoroastrian philosophy. Zoroastrians believe that when one's thoughts and words are aligned with moral integrity, they naturally lead to constructive and harmonious actions. This alignment fosters inner unity, creating a sense of peace and purpose within.

The trinity of good thoughts, good words, and good deeds, though grounded in the ethical realm, transcends to a higher spiritual order. Through this practice, Zoroastrians harmonize with the divine essence of the Amesha Spentas (Holy Immortals) and ultimately unite with Ahura Mazda (the Supreme Deity). In this way, the ethical trinity becomes a bridge to spiritual trinity, linking humanity to the divine.

This dual concept of trinity, which includes both the divine hierarchy of Ahura Mazda, the Amesha Spentas, and the faithful, as well as the ethical trinity of good thought, good word, and good deed, forms the core of Zoroastrian faith and teachings.

In Kabbalistic texts such as the Sefer Yetzirah and the Zohar, literature of Jewish mysticism, traces of trinity structures are abundantly evident. Keter, referred to as the "Crown," holds the position of the highest Sefirah within the Kabbalistic framework. It symbolizes the divine will and the boundless light of God, signifying the uppermost tier of this triadic structure.

Chokhmah, meaning "Wisdom," is the second Sefirah and represents the first spark of divine insight and wisdom. It acts as the intermediary step toward understanding Keter, serving as the gateway to the divine will, forming the middle tier of this kabbalistic trinity.

Binah, known as "Understanding," is the third Sefirah and represents the process by which the wisdom of Chokhmah can be comprehended. As the foundation of wisdom, Binah forms the lower tier of this trinity.

Kabbalists believe that when understanding (Binah) is combined with wisdom (Chokhmah), the divine will (Keter)—the light of God—shines forth. In this way, the three Sefirot—Keter, Chokhmah, and Binah—coalesce, representing a unified process of divine emanation where the light of God is revealed through the integration of wisdom and understanding.

In Kabbalistic teachings, another triadic structure is that of Chesed (Kindness), Gevurah (Judgment), and Tiferet (Beauty), which are the fourth, fifth, and sixth Sefirot. The triad illustrates that when one balances Chesed—unbounded kindness and compassion—with Gevurah—disciplined judgment and restraint—they achieve Tiferet, the true beauty of harmony and balance. This is the triad of inner spiritual beauty, the unification of mercy and justice. This triad forms the second major trinity within Kabbalistic teachings.

Netzach (Eternity/Victory), Hod (Glory), and Yesod (Foundation), which are the seventh, eighth and ninth Sefirot—form another significant triad within Kabbalistic teachings. Each represents a vital aspect of spiritual and practical balance. Netzach embodies enduring ambition, and the perseverance needed to achieve victory. Hod reflects intellectual splendor tempered by humility and gratitude. Yesod serves as the foundation, the channel through which the energies of the higher Sefirot are channeled into the physical world. When one harnesses the enduring ambition and raw energy of Netzach alongside the glory of intellect and disciplined analysis of Hod, they create a strong foundation in Yesod.

These three trinities—Keter, Chokhmah, Binah; Chesed, Gevurah, Tiferet; and Netzach, Hod, Yesod—together form another larger triadic concept, a "trinity within a trinity." Within this larger triadic concept, each trinity becomes one component of a higher triad, embodying the full spectrum of divine emanations. Each triad represents a unique layer of divine attributes, and together they create a cohesive framework that reflects the unity of creation.

These nine Sefirot collectively manifest the divine attributes through which the world was created. This unified structure of trinity within a trinity gives rise to the tenth and final Sefirah, Malkhut (Kingdom), which represents the physical realm—the materialization of divine presence in the world. Malkhut serves as the culmination of this spiritual hierarchy, where the divine flows into tangible reality.

This forms the ultimate and divine trinity: "trinity within a trinity within a trinity." In this structure, the tenth Sefirah, Malkut (Kingdom), represents physical reality and the lower tier. The remaining nine Sefirot embody spiritual reality and the middle tier, while God occupies the apex, completing the divine hierarchy.

For devout practitioners of Kabbalistic teachings, the ultimate goal is to harmonize all elements of the nine Sefirot of "trinity within a trinity." By achieving this harmony, they seek to manifest the light of God in the physical realm and attain a profound union with the divine. At the culmination of time, when all devoted Kabbalists achieve this union with the light of God, the physical world will dissolve and merge fully into the spiritual realm, becoming one with the infinite essence of God. This process will fulfill the purpose of divine emanation and complete the "trinity within a trinity within a trinity."

Nearly 2400 years ago, another mystical concept emerged in China known as Taoism, attributed to Lao tzu, which translates to "old boy." In the book Tao Te Ching—meaning "The Way of Virtue"—Tao is described with the famous words: "The Tao that can be told is not the eternal Tao; the name that can be named is not the eternal name."

In Taoism, the Tao is portrayed as "the way" or "the path." It is considered ineffable and beyond precise definition or description. The Tao is recognized as the source and essence of all that exists. It is the unchanging, eternal principle that governs the natural order of the universe. As the harmonious origin from which all things emanate, the Tao serves as the guiding force leading Taoist toward unity and equilibrium with the world around them. Tao resembles the concept of God in Western traditions, occupying the apex of the Taoist trinity as the beacon of universal harmony.

In Taoism, two other key principles complement the Tao, forming a triadic framework. The middle tier of this trinity is represented by Qi, the vital energy believed to flow through invisible channels within the body and throughout existence.

The third principle, Wu Wei, often translated as "non-action" or "effortless action," occupies the base of the Taoist trinity. Wu Wei is about a way of life that aligns one's actions with the natural flow of existence, without force or resistance.

In this way, the effortless action of Wu Wei aligns with the natural flow of Qi, harmonizing seamlessly with the Tao. Together, Tao, Qi, and Wu Wei form an interconnected trinity.

In Taoism, there exists another triad called the Three Treasures, or Sanbao, which aims to unify the physical, mental, and spiritual aspects of a person. The Three Treasures are: Jing (Essence), Qi (Vital Energy), and Shen (Spirit).

Jing is deeply associated with the physical body and is responsible for growth, physical health, longevity, and overall vitality of the individual. It represents the essential physical energy that sustains life.

As mentioned before, Qi energy is the dynamic force flowing through the body's meridians. It is derived from the air we breathe, the food we eat. The quality of Qi represents our mental and emotional states. Qi energy also connects the physical body with the spiritual body.

Shen translated as "spirit," is the most mystical of the Three Treasures, associated with the spiritual awareness. Shen is the human spirit that is influenced by the quality of Jing and Qi.

The Three Treasures are deeply interconnected and interdependent. Jing influences the quality of Qi energy, which in turn nourishes and sustains Jing, while Shen relies on both Jing and Qi to flourish. These Three Treasures represent physical health, emotional balance, and spiritual well-being. For the Taoist, the goal is to harmonize and unify the Three Treasures to attain enlightenment.

Both the Taoist Trinity (Tao, Qi, and Wu Wei) and the Three Treasures (Jing, Qi, and Shen) reflect the Taoist emphasis on balance and interconnectedness. These double trinities guide Taoists toward unity with the universe and internal harmony.

Within Buddhism, there exists the Sanbao triad as well, but different from the Taoist Sanbao, which consists of Buddha, Dharma, and Sangha. At the summit of this triad stands Buddha, the supreme teacher. In mystic Buddhist practices, Buddha is not merely the historical figure sitting under the Bodhi tree; rather, Buddha represents the state of being attuned to the essence of the entirety of life and existence, an ultimate achievement of the pure heart. In this perspective, the supreme teacher, the Buddha, forms the apex of the Buddhist trinity.

In the center of this triad, we come across Dharma, the Buddhist teachings and wisdom. It also represents the pinnacle of moral virtues and ethical values. Dharma acts as the conduit through which the

Sangha, the community of followers, accesses the wisdom expounded by Buddha. When the Sangha, through the practice of the Dharma, attains the state of Buddha, the state of unity and bliss is achieved.

In Mahayana Buddhism, there exists another triad that encapsulates the nature of existence and enlightenment: the triad of Dharmakaya, Nirvana, and Samsara. Dharmakaya, or the "Truth Body," resides at the apex of this trinity. It represents the ultimate, ineffable reality that underlies and pervades all existence. Comparable to the Tao in Chinese tradition or the concept of God in Western traditions.

Nirvana occupies the middle tier of this triad. It signifies the state of ultimate liberation, where suffering dissolves entirely, and one transcends the cycles of physical reality—a concept akin to heaven in Western traditions. Samsara, at the base of the triad, symbolizes the cyclical nature of birth, death, and rebirth. It is the realm of physical reality, characterized by impermanence, suffering, and the illusion of separateness.

Therefore, the Buddha, Dharma, and Sangha represent the trinity within physical reality. Through the unification and harmonious integration of this trinity, one can transcend the confines of Samsara—the cyclical realm of suffering and illusion—into the state of Nirvana, where suffering ceases, peace prevails, and the essence of Dharmakaya is understood.

Furthermore, during the Roman Empire, around two thousand years ago, an ancient religion known as Mithraism resurfaced and thrived, becoming one of the most widely practiced faiths in Europe with a vast number of followers. Mithraism was centered around the worship of Mithra, a deity associated with the sun. While Mithra was regarded as a god, he occupied a subordinate position beneath the supreme deity, called Sol Invictus, which translates to "the unconquered sun". In the context of Mithraism, Sol Invictus represents the highest divine power, forming the apex of the Mithraic trinity.

Mithra's role was seen as a mediator, connecting humanity to the divine realm and forming the middle tier of the trinity. Followers who, through Mithra, become one with the ultimate divine, Sol Invictus, form the lower tier of this trinity.

Couple of interesting facts about Mithraism. Mithra was often depicted as a youthful figure engaged in the act of slaying a bull, an important ritual within the Mithraic tradition. The practice of bull-slaying in a ceremonial context continues to be practiced in various smaller towns in Southern Europe to this day, carrying forward elements of this ancient religious tradition.

Additionally, in ancient Rome, the Dies Natalis Solis Invicti (the birthday of the Unconquered Sun) was celebrated on December 25. This holiday honored the rebirth of the sun during the winter solstice, symbolizing the triumph of light over darkness as the days began to grow longer. This festival was deeply rooted in Roman culture and continued to thrive until the rise of Christianity, when Dies Natalis Solis Invicti was gradually replaced by Christmas. In this transition, the celebration of the birthday of the sun evolved into the celebration of the birthday of the son.

Many traditions from Dies Natalis Solis Invicti were absorbed into Christmas celebrations as Romans shifted their beliefs from Mithraism to Christianity. Customs such as feasting, gift-giving, decorating evergreen trees, burning candles, and illuminating the long winter nights carried over, blending seamlessly into the newly established holiday of Christmas.

Then came Christianity, bringing about the widely recognized concept of the trinity, characterized by the triad of the Father, the Son, and the Holy Spirit. Regardless of whether Jesus is viewed as a man, an angel, or the Son of God, he is believed to have sought unity with the Father through the Holy Spirit. This pursuit of divine unity represents the essence of the Christian Trinity.

In Islam, Muhammad established a connection with Allah (God) through the angel Jibril (Gabriel). The examples of trinity concepts in various religions are numerous and seemingly endless. However, the concept of the trinity, wherever it has appeared in various religious traditions, serves as a means of unifying believers with the divine.

The concept of trinity is not confined to art, science, and religion alone. Modern psychology was born from the seed of trinity. Sigmund Freud, the founding father of psychoanalysis, set the groundwork for understanding human behavior. Freud is renowned for his trinity concept, which comprises the id, ego, and superego.

Freud asserted that the human psyche can be divided into three distinct parts. The first part, referred to as the id, is the most primal and instinctual aspect of the psyche. This region predominantly houses our basic desires, encompassing hunger, thirst, sexual impulses, and the yearning for social connection.

The meaning of the word "ego" has evolved over time. When Freud used the term, it differed somewhat from its common usage today. In Freudian theory, the ego represented the rational component of the psyche—the part responsible for logical and emotional decision-making processes within the mind. The ego functions to fulfill the desires of the id while ensuring that actions comply with social norms and moral values. In essence, ego acts as a mediator, bridging the primal desires of the id with the moral guidance of the superego, representing the middle tier in this Freudian trinity.

The apex of this triad, the superego, represents the internal code of conduct of an individual, encompassing human morality, intelligence, as well as socially and culturally accepted behaviors. The superego sets moral and ethical standards, striving for perfection and adhering to a sense of right and wrong. Freud believed that when one harmoniously unifies the triad of id, ego, and superego within their mental landscape, they will achieve a sense of serenity and tranquility.

The concept of the trinity does not stop there. In recent decades, new age spirituality has been filled with many trinity concepts for its followers. One of the most famous is the triad of the inner child, the intelligent self, and the higher self.

The inner child represents the childlike and youthful aspect of a person's psyche. It refers to the emotional, vulnerable, part of the person that senses feelings, memories, and experiences like a child within.

The term intelligent self typically refers to the aspect of an individual's personality or psyche that is characterized by cognitive and intellectual abilities. It represents the rational, analytical, problem-solving, and logical dimensions of a person's mind.

The higher self is considered the spiritual aspect of a person's existence. It represents a deeper and more profound level of self-awareness and connection to the universe or a higher power. The higher self is associated with qualities such as wisdom, intuition, and a sense of unity with all of existence.

In this context of modern spirituality, spiritual growth entails the process of understanding the struggles of the inner child, using the wisdom acquired through the intelligent self to establish a connection with the higher self.

The concept of the trinity is a pervasive idea that spans across every facet of our existence. Whether it appears in art, science, religion, psychology, philosophy, or any other domain, all examples of trinity share a common principle. This common principle involves establishing a connection between the lower level and the higher level through a medium, with the ultimate aim of attaining fulfillment, a deeper understanding of oneself, or unification with the divine.

In the earlier section of this chapter, I introduced my own interpretation of the trinity concept by redefining the meaning of consciousness and awareness. Let's briefly review this triad. Consciousness, serving as the repository of meaningful information, occupies the highest position within this trinity. Awareness, functioning as the conduit for accessing information, serves as the connecting element of this trinity, while all individual entities in existence, such as you and me, reside at the lower tier.

In this trinity framework, you and I use our faculties of awareness—our senses, feelings, imaginations, and intellect—to become more conscious. However, consciousness itself encompasses everything that exists, including you and me. We are all integral parts of this vast consciousness, each of us representing a fragment of the greater whole. In this way, the upper and lower tiers of this trinity are essentially the same—the upper tier embodies the wholeness of consciousness, while the lower tier reflects its fragmented nature.

This mirrors the structure of the brain: each brain cell exists as a unique individual, seamlessly interconnected with other cells to collectively form the entirety of the brain. Similarly, you, I, and every other entity in existence are like individual brain cells, fragments of consciousness. Everything you know, every experience you have, and every thought that arises in your mind is made possible through your awareness—the thread that connects you to the fabric of existence. Now, consider all living and non-living things, all energies, and all forces of nature—along with the connections between them—as forming the totality of consciousness itself.

Therefore, when we interact with one another, it is akin to one facet of consciousness interacting with another facet of itself. Consciousness experiences itself in different ways through human awareness. In this way, there's no real separation between you and me—just different expressions of the same universal consciousness. We're like unique facets of the same whole, each reflecting a different perspective of the same essence.

In a broader perspective, every interaction you have—whether with another person, an animal, or even an inanimate object—is an interaction with consciousness itself. When you speak to an animal, you are engaging with another fragment of the same unified consciousness that forms you. When you kick a rock, you are, in essence, kicking a part of yourself. The apparent separation between you and the rock, or between you and another being, is merely an illusion—a byproduct of fragmentation.

This perceived fragmentation serves as the mechanism through which consciousness experiences itself in different forms, but it is not real separation. At the deepest layers of reality, the boundaries dissolve, and what remains is unity. Everything you see, touch, or feel is a reflection of yourself.

The illusion of separation is akin to waves on the surface of the ocean. The waves appear distinct, rising and falling individually, but they are all part of the same ocean. Similarly, everything is you, and everything is me. At the deepest level of existence, there is no "other." There is only oneness, where all beings and all things are expressions of the same infinite consciousness.

Now, let's momentarily shift our focus to a new concept. Picture yourself aboard a space shuttle, journeying to the moon. As you stand on the moon's surface and gaze at Earth, you see a serene blue planet. From that distance, all the bustling activity within Earth's boundaries—the lives of billions of humans, the movements of countless creatures, and even the powerful forces of storms and earthquakes—remains invisible. The surface of the Earth appears calm and almost motionless, a stark contrast to the vibrancy of life it holds.

Let's keep this new perspective in mind and return to the topic of consciousness. If consciousness were to look at itself in its entirety, it would be similar to gazing at Earth from the moon's surface—unable to see all the details within. Consciousness fragmented itself into smaller pieces to closely examine the world within it and experience existence.

This ironic twist indicates that the totality of consciousness resides within you. The Persian poet Rumi beautifully expressed this idea when he said, "You are not a drop in the ocean. You are the ocean in a drop." I would rephrase it by saying, "You are as much a drop in the ocean as you are an ocean in a drop."

Consider another example: Without the progress of medical science, we would remain in complete darkness about the intricate workings of our own bodies. Even now, we do not fully understand how everything in our body functions. However, thanks to advancements in medicine, we have gained a better understanding of the inner workings of our bodies by examining ourselves from an external vantage point through the lens of medical devices.

Similarly, consciousness benefits from examining itself from an external standpoint through the lens of human experience to better understand itself. By perceiving the world as something external to us, we allow our inner consciousness to experience and explore itself. In this way, consciousness gains insights into its own nature, much like how medical science provides a clearer understanding of the human body.

Now, consider life from the perspective of a single cell in your body. Each cell is a living entity, perceiving itself as an individual, distinct from other cells. The harmonious collaboration of trillions of cells and countless many non-living molecules, such as water and oxygen, gives rise to a completely new life form, which you recognize as yourself. You are a complex amalgamation of trillions of individual living organisms and non-living entities. Consciousness, too, is an even more complex amalgamation of countless living organisms like us and non-living entities like stars and stones, viewed from a much broader scale.

Furthermore, while we are aware of having cells, the cells themselves lack awareness of us. A cell recognizes that it is part of something larger as it interacts with its surroundings, but it cannot comprehend the true nature of the greater whole it serves. Your cells do not "know" exactly who you are, even though they are integral building blocks of your existence.

Similarly, while consciousness is aware of our existence, we, as fragments of consciousness, are unable to fully grasp the vastness of the whole of consciousness. However, when we take a step back and observe how every object and entity in existence coexists in harmony, we catch a fleeting glimpse of the truth—we are part of something far greater than ourselves, an integral part of universal consciousness.

Just as the collaboration of cells and molecules gives rise to the unified human experience, the seamless interconnectedness of all things in existence forms the essence of consciousness itself. The entire world is interconnected and layered in a way that each part contributes to a greater whole.

In a nutshell, we, as fragments of consciousness guided by the conduit of awareness, strive to reconnect with the entirety of consciousness. This represents the trinity concept in action. As humans, we have developed various ideologies and practices to achieve this connection. Ultimately, deep within, we are fundamentally one entity, yearning to reunite with the whole.

All trinity concepts endeavor to transform you into the ultimate version of yourself, which is essentially the quintessence of consciousness dwelling within you. These trinity-like concepts serve as roadmaps to reveal the grand tapestry—the entirety of consciousness—from a fragmented viewpoint. Regardless of whether you seek to attain the zenith of the trinity through art, science, spirituality, religion, psychology, philosophy, or any other method, you ultimately arrive at the same destination: discovering the essence of your existence. These myriad pathways, if understood properly with a pure heart, converge into a singular point leading to the same destination: unification with oneself and the divine.

Now think of it this way: the more deeply you understand yourself, the better you can navigate the ebbs and flows within you. This self-awareness and self-control represent a deep connection with your true essence—your inner consciousness—which brings a profound sense of satisfaction and fulfillment. Why? Because at your core, what you most deeply desire is to align with your truest self. The closer you come to this essence, the more you experience bliss and genuine happiness in your life. You are designed to strive for this connection, an intrinsic drive woven into the fabric of your being.

But this journey of understanding and harmony doesn't stop with yourself. True inner peace expands outward. To fully embody it, you must also nurture meaningful connections with others, recognizing that they, too, are made of the same essence as you. Each of us, as fragments of a greater consciousness, becomes more as we deepen our connection with ourselves and with one another—just as water drops together become oceans. In a broader context, the highest sense of fulfillment, satisfaction, and peace in your life can only be realized by deepening your connections with yourself, with others, with nature, and with the entirety of the world itself—physically, emotionally, and spiritually.

When you reach this state of connection true happiness naturally follows. Happiness becomes the byproduct of the inner peace you cultivate. It isn't something found in isolation but arises from meaningful connections and a sense of unity. Later in this book, we'll dive deeply into the concept of attaining lasting happiness and explore how it can be nurtured and sustained in your life.

In the first chapter, we touched upon the concept of duality before transitioning to the concept of trinity. In the following chapter, we will delve into a relatively obscure and lesser-known idea known as the quaternity. From my perspective, quaternity is one of the most powerful concepts in the domain of philosophy and mysticism. Its complexity and abstract nature make it a challenging concept to grasp. I hope I can present quaternity in a manner that will be easy to understand, despite its elusive and exceedingly complex nature.

Chapter 3: Types of Consciousness

In the first chapter, we explored the idea that scientific progress tends to move toward increased complexity rather than simplicity. In other words, advancements in science always lead to more complex and abstract concepts. Consider the progression of education: as students advance through each grade, the material becomes more abstract and challenging. The educational system mirrors the trend of scientific advancement, where each new discovery becomes more complex and abstract than the last. That is why students must learn increasingly difficult concepts year after year during their educational journey.

Additionally, the nature of the world is limitless, infinitely vast, and without an end. As we delve deeper into the mysteries of the universe, each discovery leads to new questions and unexplored territories. The more we learn and discover, the more we realize that there is still so much we do not know. The pursuit of knowledge is an ever-expanding journey into the depths of the unknown, where every answer paves the way for further questions.

The point being made here is twofold: First, as human intelligence advances, new concepts become more complex and abstract. Second, the world is infinitely vast, and we will never reach the end of scientific inquiry. Each discovery opens the door to new scientific problems, each more challenging than the last.

Let's take a look at plant life and see how complex they truly are. You might think we know a lot about plants. After all, they do not appear to do much. While we understand key processes such as reproduction, respiration, and photosynthesis, our knowledge barely scratches the surface of plant life.

Around the turn of the 21st century, scientists discovered an underground network of fungi that spans across vast expanses of the Earth's soil, enabling the transmission of chemical and electrical signals from one plant to another. These fungi, known as "mycorrhizal fungi," engage in a mutually beneficial relationship with plants. The fungi receive carbohydrates and other organic materials from the plants, while helping the plants communicate and share resources with one another.

Think of this network as nature's internet. Scientists named this fungal network the "wood wide web," inspired by the term "world wide web." Humanity created the internet just a few decades ago, but the natural world had already established its own biological internet long ago.

This fungal network allows for the exchange of nutrients, water, and even information among plants. Mycorrhizal fungi transport nutrients, particularly phosphorus and nitrogen, from areas with an abundance of these nutrients to areas where they are scarce. In times of stress or resource limitation, healthier and more established plants provide nutrients to neighboring younger or weaker plants. The fungal network also facilitates the transfer of chemical and electrical signals between plants. This communication allows trees and other plants to share information about threats and environmental changes.

For example, if animals begin to eat the leaves of one tree excessively, that tree sends signals to neighboring trees and plants, alerting them to the attack, utilizing the mycorrhizal fungi. In response, the other trees and plants then produce chemicals in their leaves that are bitter or unpleasant to the animals, deterring the attackers from approaching them. This form of communication allows plants to collectively defend themselves against threats. In a jungle, you might see one tree or plant dead among many healthy ones; this could be because it was the first to be attacked by insects or animals and it sent out warnings to other plants, helping them to fortify their defenses and avoid the same fate.

Plants also release chemical materials into the air and soil, referred to as phytochemical signals. These signals serve various purposes, such as deterring herbivores, attracting pollinators, or signaling other plants to bolster their defenses against pests. Similar to the last example, when a plant is attacked by insects or animals, it emits chemicals into the air and soil that alert nearby plants to activate their defensive mechanisms. Plants literally talk to each other in their own biological language.

Imagine this: you want to connect with a friend. First, you might send a quick message over the internet—essentially a burst of electrical signals—to let them know you'd like to talk. Then, to deepen the connection, you meet in person for a more intimate conversation. Plants, in their own extraordinary way, do something remarkably similar.

When one plant is attacked, it uses its biological internet—mycorrhizal fungi networks—to send fast electrical signals, alerting neighboring plants to potential danger. This initial message is like an emergency broadcast, delivering an immediate warning to prepare defenses. However, communication doesn't stop there. The plant then releases phytochemicals into the air, a kind of biological language that carries more detailed information about the nature of the threat. This slower, more nuanced form of communication allows nearby plants to understand and adapt to the situation in a more specific way.

Just as we use quick digital messages for immediate contact and face-to-face conversations for richer, deeper exchanges, plants use a similar two-tiered system of communication: the fungal internet for speed and airborne phytochemicals for detail.

Additionally, plants respond to touch through a phenomenon known as thigmotropism. When plants are touched or exposed to wind or movement, they adjust their growth patterns. For instance, climbing plants sense their environment through touch and wrap around supports as they grow. Other plants develop shorter and sturdier stems when regularly exposed to wind, ensuring their stability in harsh environments.

Plants also respond to sound waves. Birdsong before dawn, known as the "dawn chorus," helps open up the pores in plant leaves called "stomata" to absorb moisture and nutrients during the early morning dew. Birdsong acts like a musical alarm clock that dilates the stomata, allowing the plants to absorb nutrients more effectively for a healthier start to the day. Plants provide housing for birds. In return, birds wake up plants every morning, helping them with having a good breakfast.

Today, thanks to scientific and technological progress, we have come to appreciate that plants are far more complex than we previously imagined. Our growing intelligence has led us to the realization that the depth of plant life's intricacies far surpasses what we once thought possible. In the current era, we are far from understanding the totality of plant life. Our understanding of plant functionalities is only as good as the instruments we have developed thus far. We can confidently assert that as we develop more advanced instruments, we will discover even more complex aspects of plant life.

This trend of discovery is boundless, stretching indefinitely into the future. As mentioned earlier, the trajectory of intelligence inherently leads toward greater complexity without an endpoint. Therefore, it is unlikely and nearly impossible that there will ever be a point in time where we fully comprehend the entirety of plant life, devoid of further discoveries about their complex role in the natural world. This means that even if we study plant life for another trillion years, each new scientific advancement will reveal yet more functions and capabilities of plants that were previously unimaginable.

Another groundbreaking discovery occurred in the mid-twentieth century when scientists noticed something peculiar about photosynthesis and enzyme reactions in plants. These processes displayed remarkable efficiency that classical physics could not fully explain. They seemed to involve quantum features, where particles behave as both waves and particles simultaneously. This discovery led to the development of a new field of science called quantum biology.

The emergence of quantum biology feels like hitting the reset button on our understanding of plant life at the molecular and subatomic levels. Despite all of our understanding of plant life, the advent of quantum biology has opened a gateway to an entirely new realm of plant functionality—one that stretches far beyond our current comprehension. Only a few decades old, quantum biology is still in its infancy, reminding us how much there is yet to uncover about the mysterious quantum world.

Quantum biology has also discovered that quantum-like behavior is not limited to plants only or a select few organisms but appears to be a fundamental aspect of life itself, woven into the fabric of the entire biological realm. It's as if every living being carries subtle quantum features, mysteries we are only beginning to unravel. For example, scientists have long wondered how birds navigate vast distances over seas and oceans. While still being debated, studies in quantum biology suggest that birds use quantum entanglement and quantum tunneling to sense the Earth's magnetic field for navigation. This method of using quantum entanglement for navigation by birds is far more advanced than the GPS and other methods we currently use for navigation.

Now, let's look at scientific discoveries from a different angle. Science, for all its precision and accuracy, does not represent the absolute truth—at least not entirely. Despite its remarkable achievements, science is not immune to error. Its methodologies, while designed to minimize mistakes, cannot completely eliminate them. Misinterpretations, incomplete data, or unforeseen complexities can lead to flawed conclusions that persist until new evidence compels us to revise or abandon our previous scientific understandings.

Most recently, at the time of writing this book, the James Webb Telescope was launched into the sky to explore the depths of the cosmos. The telescope's initial observations have left scientists perplexed, as it has captured images and data that defy explanation. It has revealed galaxies so distant and ancient that they do not fit any of our current models of the cosmos. These galaxies were completely mature during the infancy of the universe. Until recently, we believed that there were no mature galaxies in the early universe. However, recent discoveries are telling us otherwise, casting doubt upon our established science.

At this point, some scientists even doubt the accuracy of the Big Bang theory. We might have been wrong all along about our model of the universe, its age, and how it has evolved over time. In the course of time, we will undoubtedly uncover answers to these enigmatic questions, only to face even more astonishing and mind-boggling questions and wonders.

The point being made here is that science progresses indefinitely toward greater complexity through rigorous examination and evaluation. Even then, despite science's remarkable accuracy and advancements, it is not infallible. Throughout history, science has sometimes veered off course, developing models of reality that were later revealed to be flawed. These missteps can persist for centuries before we uncover the errors, retrace our steps, and refine our understanding. This is all pointing to how complex the world truly is.

In each of the instances mentioned above, we have achieved a solid understanding of the respective topics, only to witness the expansion of our knowledge to a level where an entirely new realm of complexity unfolds before us. It is as if each answer to scientific pursuits opens the door to a whole new set of scientific wonders. This recurring pattern has persisted throughout the history of science, and the examples provided here, while significant, are not isolated or exceptional in any way. The world is infinitely complex, and we can only grasp the level of complexity that matches our current level of intelligence. As our intellect grows, so does our realization of the complexity of the world around us.

This brings us to the central idea of this chapter: the quaternity concept. This is a relatively obscure and lesser-known concept. The quaternity concept posits the idea that understanding of the world involves a four-step journey, progressing from extreme simplicity to infinite complexity. Quaternity also indicates that this trend applies universally to any subject, anywhere, at any time.

Thus far, we have explored the idea that human understanding tends to evolve toward greater complexity indefinitely when considering any subject at any time, like the example we explored about plant life and how they are infinitely complex. This idea is embedded in the framework of the quaternity. Yet, what remains to be elucidated about the quaternity is the exact essence of the four-step progression in understanding.

There are various ways to construct the four-step journey within the quaternity concept. The simplest version of the four-step journey can be structured using two self-explanatory variables: "known" and "unknown." By pairing these variables with each other and with themselves, we construct the four steps as follows: known of the known, known of the unknown, unknown of the known, and unknown of the unknown. Let's define each step.

The first step, *the known of the known*: this step involves aspects of a subject that are already known and well understood. It represents the familiar territory of our understanding. This stage embodies truths and established facts. It represents the bedrock of knowledge, firmly supported by concrete evidence. In the case of plants, we know they are composed of roots, branches, leaves, flowers, and fruits. These are *the known of the known* of plant life—the most basic and visible aspects.

The second step, *the known of the unknown*: here, we explore and understand parts of the subject that are known, but within the context of something unknown. It's a bridge between the familiar and the unfamiliar, where we apply what we know to better understand what we do not know. In this step, we enter the domain of assumptions and theories, building upon the known but not yet proven. In the example of plants, we know that plants use the mycorrhizal fungal network, the wood wide web, to communicate and share resources. However, we still do not fully understand the extent of their functionalities. The interactions between mycorrhizal fungal networks and plants, which are currently being studied, are an example of *the known of the unknown* of plant life.

The third step, *the unknown of the known*: this step involves delving into aspects of the subject that are still unknown despite our existing knowledge. It highlights the limitations of our understanding and prompts further exploration beyond our current knowledge. Here, we explore hypotheses that expand upon what is known but largely unknown. While rooted in existing knowledge, these ideas push beyond the boundaries of our understanding of the world. In the example of plants, their functionality in the quantum world surpasses our current understanding. While quantum biology acknowledges that plants exhibit quantum-like features, the extent of their quantum capabilities is completely beyond our reach at this point in time. This would be an example of *the unknown of the known* of plant life.

The fourth step, *the unknown of the unknown*: this is the most challenging and mysterious stage, where we encounter aspects of the subject that are entirely unknown. It represents uncharted territory, pushing far beyond the boundaries of our comprehension and curiosity. This stage delves into beliefs or imaginations unsupported by any evidence. It encompasses ideas and concepts that lie beyond the scope of our knowledge, relying on faith rather than proof. At the farthest edges of this step there exist aspects of reality so elusive that we don't even know that we don't know. In the example of plants, there are undoubtedly features that we have not yet even considered, or perhaps we have only explored them in science fiction stories or in our imaginations. Whatever plant functionalities remain beyond our current understanding fall into the category of *the unknown of the unknown* of plant life.

You can use the quaternity to create a four-step framework for any topic of your choosing. Let's explore the quaternity's four-step journey through the cosmos:

The first step, the known of the known of the cosmos: this represents our home, planet Earth. It is known to us as we live on it, understand it, and are fundamentally connected to it. Earth is a familiar territory in our cosmic understanding.

The second step, the known of the unknown of the cosmos: the Moon, Mars, and our solar system fall into this category. While we are familiar with these celestial bodies and have sent spaceships to explore them, they are still cloaked in mystery, waiting to be unraveled. We have knowledge about them, but there are aspects we have yet to fully understand.

The third step, the unknown of the known of the cosmos: this step encompasses objects like other galaxies and black holes. While we acknowledge their existence, their fundamental nature remain beyond our full grasp. They stand as cosmic enigmas, challenging our understanding.

The fourth step, the unknown of the unknown of the cosmos: this final category delves into profound mysteries, including what lies beyond black holes, what existed before the Big Bang, the nature of parallel universes, and the possible existence of other dimensions. These are the deepest unknowns of the cosmos.

We can see that the quaternity four-step journey, regardless of the subject we pick, always follows the trend of ranging from the familiar and comprehensible to the mysterious and uncharted. This progression helps us navigate our understanding in any field, moving from what we know and understand well, to what we are aware we do not fully grasp, to areas where our knowledge is still developing, and finally to realms that are entirely unknown and beyond our current understanding.

As time progresses and our knowledge expands, the boundaries of these four steps will shift. For example, a thousand years from now, we may have successfully established populations on the Moon and Mars and ventured to explore other galaxies. In this scenario, the concept of the known of the known, which only includes Earth at this point, would eventually extend to encompass the Moon and Mars as well. The dynamic nature of human exploration continually reshapes the boundaries of the four-step journey of quaternity. As our knowledge expands, concepts once considered advanced shift to the earlier steps, while new ideas emerge to occupy the final stages.

Let me explain this in another way to make it more clear. The boundaries of the four steps in the quaternity framework are not fixed but shift and adapt based on our understanding—both individually and collectively. For example, if we draw these boundaries using humanity's collective knowledge, they would reflect the cutting-edge discoveries and limitations of our species as a whole. However, if we were to draw them based on our personal understanding, the framework would vary greatly from one individual to another.

Imagine a subject where you and I have different levels of expertise. For a topic I am less knowledgeable about, my first and second steps—*the known of the known* and *the known of the unknown*—would consist of the few things I understand about the subject. Meanwhile, the third or fourth steps—*the unknown of the known* and *the unknown of the unknown*—would remain almost entirely unfamiliar to me.

Conversely, if it is a subject you are highly skilled in, your first and second steps would be far more extensive, reflecting your familiarity and mastery. Your third and fourth steps would then encompass concepts that lie on the fringes of human understanding, ideas that I might not even know about.

This fluidity allows the quaternity to serve as a tool for self-assessment. By mapping your understanding of any topic using these four steps, you gain clarity about the boundaries of your own knowledge. The importance of this will soon become apparent. As we explore further, you'll see how this framework not only helps you understand your relationship with knowledge but also guides you in how to apply your knowledge while communicating with others, fostering mutual respect.

Now, let's imagine yourself as an example. Your journey through life can be divided into four distinct steps:

The first step, the known of the known of your life: this step represents the most familiar and unequivocal aspects of your life. It includes facts that you readily know about yourself, such as your name, place of birth, general personality traits, and routine hobbies. These are familiar and unambiguous details about you.

The second step, the known of the unknown of your life: in this phase, you encounter things that you can anticipate or expect to happen, but you cannot be entirely certain about the outcomes. For instance, you might anticipate the possibility of receiving a promotion at work by the end of the year or plan to buy a house within a few years. These are events within the realm of possibility based on known facts, but their final results remain uncertain.

The third step, the unknown of the known of your life: This category includes parts of life you recognize but over which you have limited or no control. You may not know the precise moment of your passing, the cause of your eventual demise, or whether your grandchildren will attain certain achievements in life. These variables lie beyond your knowledge.

The fourth step, the unknown of the unknown of your life: finally, the most unanswerable questions about your life fall into this category. These are the contemplations you cannot help but ponder, such as whether you have been reincarnated, if you will be resurrected after this life, what awaits you after death, and whether there is a divine entity waiting for you on the other side. These are questions that can only be answered by faith and not by logic or evidence.

You can frame every detail of your entire life journey into four steps, with each step including (1) the concrete, (2) the uncertain, (3) the uncontrollable, and (4) the deeply philosophical and unknowable aspects of your existence.

Understanding the quaternity concept is invaluable because it helps you set clear boundaries in your thoughts, beliefs, and interactions with others. For example, no matter how deeply you believe in your faith or religion, quaternity reminds you that such matters belong to the fourth step—representing the realm that is ultimately unknown and unknowable.

If you honor the principles of quaternity, you approach your faith with humility, recognizing it as your personal belief rather than asserting it as the absolute truth about reality. This perspective fosters respect, open-mindedness, and meaningful dialogue, allowing you to share your beliefs without imposing them on others and creating conflict. It's a way to communicate about deeply held beliefs while staying grounded in mutual respect.

Imagine you are talking to your friend about the mysteries of death and what might come afterward. Quaternity immediately places such a topic in the realm of *the unknown of the unknown,* reminding you not to speak with certainty about what you think might be the true reality after death. Quaternity encourages you to respect different viewpoints, as the nature of life after death is inherently unknown. It tells you to respect your friend's opinion even if it vastly differs from your own. Whether someone believes in reincarnation, heaven and hell, or nothing at all, it's all a matter of faith without absolute certainty.

If you and your friend accept and respect the boundaries of the quaternity concept, your discussion about the afterlife will be held with mutual respect, never ending in arguments. You both would acknowledge that you are exploring beliefs in the realm of *the unknown of the unknown,* without bias or prejudice toward each other. You will gain insight from each other's reasoning and viewpoints, using them to deepen and enhance your overall understanding of the topic. This approach fosters peace and respect in your discussions, maintaining the health of your friendship and keeping your mind open.

However, if you or your friend assert your different beliefs about the afterlife as fact and absolute truth, it will lead to arguments and tension. These arguments will deteriorate your friendship, promote resentment and dislike toward each other, and ultimately cause separation and distance between you and your friend. Embracing the quaternity concept offers a way to avoid these pitfalls by encouraging humility, openness, and respect for differing perspectives, fostering discussions without the need to "win" or assert superiority.

A quote attributed to Keanu Reeves captures this beautifully: "I have reached a point in my life where arguments have lost their charm. I am in pursuit of the true essence of peace, choosing to value my serenity over the urge to win at all costs. I have learned that calmness is a greater triumph than any dispute." If you seek peace, then the path lies in letting go of arguments and conflicts. True serenity comes from understanding, rather than the need to dominate or prove others wrong. Always aim to hold open dialogues, enhance your current understanding, and remain receptive to exploring new ideas.

The heart of many disputes throughout human history can be traced back to disregarding the teachings of the quaternity framework. Wars and conflicts, especially religious ones, often stem from individuals asserting their beliefs as absolute truths and attempting to impose their beliefs on others. These conflicts arise because people refuse to recognize the limits of their knowledge and the complexity of the unknown.

To ensure peaceful coexistence and cooperation on a global scale, it is essential for individuals and societies to honor the quaternity concept in all discussions. Our understanding is limited, and certainty is often an illusion, especially when dealing with speculative topics like the afterlife, the nature of divinity, or the ultimate meaning of existence.

The quaternity concept is the best tool for promoting effective and harmonious communication among people. It helps bridge gaps in understanding and promotes unity. It nurtures a culture of humility and mutual respect; it encourages open-mindedness and reduces the potential for conflict. Embracing the quaternity concept preserves friendships and social bonds and also paves the way for a more peaceful and enlightened global community.

Do not approach *the unknown of the unknown* with certainty; embrace humility in the face of mysteries that lie beyond your understanding. Arrogance has no place in confronting the vast, uncharted realms of existence. Similarly, when it comes to *the unknown of the known*, resist the temptation to believe you have it all figured out. Recognize the inherent limitations of your current understanding and accept that your knowledge remains incomplete, no matter how advanced it may seem.

Remember, even within *the known of the unknown*, there is always more to uncover. Each discovery opens the door to new questions and deeper layers of understanding. Knowledge is an endless journey, not a finite destination. And finally, within the realm of *the known of the known*—the seemingly solid foundation of what you believe you fully grasp—realize that true understanding is far more nuanced and intricate than it appears on the surface; acknowledge the inherent complexity and depth of all knowledge.

Up to this point, we have applied the quaternity concept with two variables. However, there are more complex variants of the quaternity concept that involve four variables. The initial two variables remain the same: "known" and "unknown." The two additional variables are referred to as "visible" and "invisible." This four-variable model of quaternity is used to represent more comprehensive concepts. It enables us to include both the moral and physical realms within a single quaternity model.

The two new variables, the visible and invisible, bring forth two attributes: logic and morality. Within the visible realm, everything can be investigated and understood using logic as the most effective tool. In contrast, the invisible realm is associated with the non-material world, and morality is the most suitable instrument for understanding the invisible realm.

By cross matching the four variables with each other, we establish the four steps as follows: known visible realm, known invisible realm, unknown visible realm, and unknown invisible realm.

Let's delineate the quaternity four-step journey of your life again, but this time, using four variables instead of two.

The first step, *the known visible realm* of your life: this realm is the most familiar and unambiguous aspect of your existence. It encompasses the material world you live in, where logic and evidence are sufficient to satisfy your curiosity about the world around you. This realm includes your daily activities, such as the work you engage in, the art you create, and the interactions you have with others. It also involves the practical aspects of life, such as managing your finances, maintaining your health, and fulfilling your responsibilities. In this visible realm, the cause-and-effect relationships are clear, and the knowledge you acquire is grounded in logic and observable reality.

The second step, *the known invisible realm* of your life: in this realm, logic takes a backseat, and morality becomes the main tool for understanding the world. It's a space where feelings serve as the framework for your understanding. When you experience love, empathy, fear, sadness, or any other positive or negative feelings, you are immersed in the known invisible realm. Additionally, in this realm, your internal moral compass continuously evaluates your thoughts and actions in terms of positive or negative, good or bad. Morality serves as the tool that aids you in understanding the world in terms of its quality and value. This realm encompasses the intangible aspects of life that shape your ethical and emotional landscape, guiding your interactions and decisions based on your sense of right and wrong. Here, the unseen forces of morality play the main role in defining your personal and social experiences.

The third step, *the unknown visible realm* of your life: this realm is unfamiliar but visible, representing the unknown aspects of your physical reality. It encompasses scientific and artistic knowledge that you have not acquired. This includes the unexplored potential of your talents, future career opportunities, and the cause of your eventual demise. While these elements are observable, their full implications and outcomes remain uncertain and unknown.

The fourth step, *the unknown invisible realm* of your life: this is the realm of morality that lies beyond your immediate grasp. It's where you contemplate the nature of good and evil. Here, you grapple with understanding complex concepts such as karma and luck, where the outcomes are uncertain and undefined. In this mysterious realm, you ponder the long-term moral consequences of your actions and judgments, wondering how they might ripple through the fabric of reality. This invisible realm of morality remains a mystery and unknowable in your quest for understanding the world.

As you can see, defining the four-step journey in quaternity is quite different when we use two variables versus when we use four variables.

By using four variables, human experience breaks down into two realms: the visible, which represents the logical realm, and the invisible, which represents the moral realm. Within each realm, there is a portion that is known to us and a portion that is unknown.

Everything you have ever experienced in your life can be categorized as either a logical or a moral experience. Logic and morality together form a duality that serves as the foundation of how you interpret and understand reality. Logic governs your reasoning and understanding of facts, while morality guides your sense of right and wrong.

When you understand how you wield your logic and morality, you gain deep insight into your own perception of reality and the reasoning behind every decision you make. Your logical and moral understanding creates an elegant dance between your rational thoughts and ethical considerations, forming a lens through which you view and interpret the world.

Gauge whether your perception leans more toward logic or morality by asking yourself a few basic questions. Is your mind oriented toward facts and figures, or does it gravitate toward emotions and ethics? Do you tend to resolve conflicts by analyzing the facts objectively, or do you focus on emotional concerns and fairness? Are you more comfortable presenting a rational argument supported by evidence, or do you focus on connecting with others emotionally and empathetically to make your point? When faced with uncertainty, do you seek clarity through logic and analysis, or do you lean on your moral compass to guide your choices? Some people navigate the world predominantly through reasoning, while others are guided more by emotions and ethics. Many fall somewhere in between, balancing both approaches to varying degrees.

Recognizing this balance—or imbalance—in yourself and others is invaluable. Logical individuals tend to rely only on reason, structure, and evidence to make sense of the world, whereas moral individuals prioritize emotional reasoning, ethical principles, and shared values. Understanding these differences not only allows you to better comprehend your own mental framework but also equips you to better understand those whose perspectives differ from yours.

When you grasp the underlying principles of how someone approaches the world—whether through logic, morality, or a blend of both—you foster deeper understanding and compassion. This awareness enables you to bridge gaps in communication and build meaningful connections, even when someone's mental functionality contrasts sharply with your own.

Consider this. You're having a discussion with someone who relies heavily on logic. Approaching the conversation through emotional reasoning will likely create a disconnect, causing you both to talk past each other and leading to frustration on both sides. However, as a wise person, you can choose to adapt your approach and rely on logic to make your point. By doing so, the logically-oriented person will better understand your perspective and the reasoning behind your stance. This will improve communication and also foster a meaningful exchange of ideas.

Similarly, if you're speaking with someone who is morally and emotionally oriented, dominating the discussion with cold, hard logic will likely create resentment. This approach can push the person further away and cause them to shut down emotionally, making it difficult to connect. Instead, it's far more effective to engage them using moral and emotional reasoning—connecting with their values and empathizing with their feelings.

Before engaging in any meaningful discussion, take a moment to gauge your audience. Are they logical or morally oriented? Tailor your communication to match their "language." Otherwise, you might both be speaking English, yet fail to understand a single word exchanged between you. True connection requires understanding how others think and feel and communicating in a way that resonates with their unique perspective.

Let's take a closer look at logic and morality. Strong logic consistently produces reliable results. When we use concrete logic, the outcomes are precise, exact, and replicable. For instance, solving a mathematical equation involves rigorous reasoning that leads to a precise solution. If two different mathematicians work on the same problem, they will arrive at the same answer regardless of the time or place. In short, robust logic remains universally valid, precise, and reliable. When employed correctly, logic yields concrete and dependable results.

However, there are aspects of life where logic is not the proper tool, and we must rely on morality to achieve understanding. Morality guides our ethical and emotional understanding. Unlike logic, which offers clear and definitive outcomes, morality deals with ambiguity and subjective interpretation. For example, consider a mother's love for her child. The depth of this love cannot be quantified by a mathematical formula; there is no exact method that can measure how much a mother loves her child. It is an experience grounded in morality and emotions.

Moreover, the morality of human experiences varies over time and among different people. Even a mother's love for her child changes over time, and it also differs from one child to another. Additionally, different mothers experience love for their children differently. Morality, by its very nature, is inexact, imprecise, and dependent on the individual undergoing the experience. It is impossible to measure morality with the same level of precision as logic because morality is qualitative, while logic is quantitative.

If you perceive the world solely through logic, you only see one side of the coin of reality. Conversely, if you perceive the world solely through morality, you only see the other side of the coin. To grasp the totality of the world, you must utilize both logic and morality simultaneously, understanding which aspects of life can be comprehended with the certainty of logic and which parts can only be understood through the lens of morality.

Logic and morality form a duality much like the yin and yang symbol. Logic is represented by yang, the white portion of the duality, symbolizing clarity, precision, and reliability. However, logic is short-sighted and only effective when exploring the visible, measurable, and quantifiable aspects of reality. The short-sightedness of logic and its inability to understand abstract and invisible aspects of reality are denoted by the black dot within the white portion of the yang.

On the other hand, morality is represented by yin, the black side of the symbol, reflecting the inexact and imprecise nature of moral understanding. Morality often leaves us in the dark with its lack of exact measures. However, morality has the profound ability to pierce into the depths where logic has no value. It can unveil the most complex, elusive, and invisible aspects of existence. When things become too abstract to be quantified, they are measured in quality, and morality is the tool to understand this qualitative aspect, represented by the white dot within the dark side of the yin.

Do you recall when in the first chapter, we mentioned that the entirety of life and the way we perceive and experience the world is through duality? Life is inherently dualistic: death is the counterpart to life, day turns into night, good opposes bad, and hardness contrasts with softness. Everything we encounter is based on duality.

Any duality in the visible realm is logic-based. Examples include hard and soft, warm and cold, long and short. These pairs are quantifiable and can be measured and analyzed using logic. They belong to the tangible, material world where empirical evidence and rational thinking provide clarity and understanding.

On the flip side, every aspect of duality that is invisible is based on morality. Examples include hope and despair, good and bad, just and unjust. These pairs are qualitative and rooted in moral and emotional understanding. They belong to the intangible, invisible realm where subjective interpretation and moral reasoning guide our judgments.

Logic governs the visible aspects of your life, offering precise and reliable outcomes. Morality, on the other hand, guides your moral and emotional understanding, dealing with the qualities and values in your life. Together, the duality of logic and morality, along with every subsequent duality that arises from them, shapes the entirety of your life experience. Embracing both logic and morality allows you to see the full spectrum of human experience, the tangible and abstract dimensions of existence.

Now, let's apply the four-variable quaternity concept to describe the entirety of existence, or more precisely, to articulate the totality of consciousness.

The first step, the known visible realm of consciousness: This realm encompasses everything within the material world that can be observed and measured. This domain covers all areas of art, science, and technology. It includes everything in three-dimensional space. All stars, galaxies, and everything within them belong to this realm. This realm is defined by the tangible and observable aspects of reality.

The second step, the known invisible realm of consciousness: this realm is where morality is imbued with meaning. Here, concepts such as good and bad are established. In this realm, values and qualities are shaped, and ethical principles like honesty and integrity find their roots. All human feelings are rooted in this domain, including sentiments like love, hate, hope, and despair. This domain is where the intangible aspects of our virtues, feelings, and moral judgments are formed and nurtured.

The third step, the unknown visible realm of consciousness: this realm encompasses phenomena that extend beyond our familiar world. It includes the hypothetical domains of parallel universes and other dimensions. In this realm, we also encounter entities such as ghosts, angels, spirits, and demons—labels we've assigned to beings that might exist in other universes or dimensions or are purely products of imagination. These entities cannot be confirmed or refuted through the known realm; thus, they are classified within the unknown realm. Also, these creatures are not visible within our three-dimensional space, but they may exist in the visible realms of other dimensions and universes. Therefore, entities like demons and angels, as well as the dimensions and worlds they inhabit, belong to the unknown visible realm of consciousness.

The fourth step, the unknown invisible realm of consciousness: this step delineates the moral behavior of entities from the unknown realm, such as the treacheries of the devil and the righteousness of the angels. This realm can only be perceived through faith and imagination. It is the domain where our beliefs about the afterlife, divine justice, and eternal moral principles reside. In this realm, concepts such as divine purpose and cosmic morality are shaped. This is the realm that imbues the journey toward enlightenment with meaning.

If you integrate all these four domains mentioned above into one big picture, you gain a comprehensive view of consciousness as a whole. This holistic perspective allows you to see the entirety of the world you inhabit. Everything exists within consciousness, and by understanding consciousness, you grasp the essence of everything.

We used the quaternity concept to segment and classify consciousness into four distinct realms: the known visible, the known invisible, the unknown visible, and the unknown invisible. This segmentation is a tool designed to simplify our understanding of the overarching concept of consciousness. By breaking down the vast and complex nature of consciousness into more manageable parts, we can gain a better grasp of its multifaceted nature and the interplay between logic and morality, as well as visibility and invisibility.

When looking at the rainbow, human eyes can see a continuous spectrum of colors ranging from red to violet that reach over a million different colors. Yet, to simplify our understanding, we break down this array of rainbow colors into seven basic colors of red, orange, yellow, green, blue, indigo, and violet. Thus, what we've achieved with the categorization of consciousness is similar to what we have done with categorizing rainbow colors–breaking down a complex phenomenon into more digestible parts for easier understanding.

This is another application of the quaternity concept. Previously, we mentioned that quaternity encourages respectful communication. Now, we see that it also allows us to simplify extremely complex ideas, such as the boundaries of consciousness. The real value of quaternity lies in its ability to promote understanding, whether it's improving communication among people or explaining complex concepts. Quaternity is a powerful tool for making sense of the world and enhancing our ability to grasp and articulate complex ideas.

Now, let's go back to the four-step breakdown of consciousness. Did you notice that we grasp only a fraction of the true nature of consciousness? On the grand scale of the visible realm, our knowledge is mostly limited to our own planet, Earth. Given the vastness of the universe, humanity's collective knowledge is extremely limited, making up only a tiny fraction of the known visible realm of consciousness.

Moreover, our understanding of moral values of the known invisible realm is also extremely limited. This limitation is evident in how we treat each other across different races, countries, and religions. We often fail to show respect and true understanding of morality. The disparities, conflicts, and wars among us are due to this lack of moral understanding. On a societal level, this shortfall is clear in the way we handle issues of equality, justice, and compassion. We struggle to demonstrate respect and empathy toward one another, leading to mental isolation. The widespread prevalence of depression and various mental health illnesses is a testament to the fact that many of us are morally malnourished.

Given the state of the world today, it is safe to say that our understanding of morality and known invisible realm is extremely limited, just as our understanding of the known visible realm is infinitely limited.

If the first two steps of the quaternity, which are ostensibly the easiest to grasp, remain shrouded in mystery, how much further are we from grasping the depths of the third and fourth steps? Our understanding of the unknown visible realm, such as the nature of demons and angels and the world they inhabit, and the unknown invisible realm, including the ethical values of these entities and cosmic morality—is close to nothing.

That is why the meaning of consciousness is so difficult to grasp: we know very little about it. Defining something we do not understand is nearly impossible. However, the quaternity concept helps us form an idea of consciousness despite our limited knowledge. By breaking down the complex and elusive aspects of consciousness into more manageable parts, quaternity provides a framework that aids our understanding of this phenomenon, even if we cannot fully grasp its entirety.

Let's reiterate the premise of the quaternity concept. It posits that understanding the world involves a four-step journey, progressing from extreme simplicity to vast complexity. Quaternity conveys that this trend of understanding applies universally to any subject, anywhere, at any time.

The quaternity concept insists that despite our intelligence, we will never fully understand any subject due to the infinite complexity of the world. Let's examine this idea more closely by considering the simplest form of life on Earth: the virus. Scientists still debate whether viruses should be classified as living creatures or not due to their super simple structure. Yet, despite their simplicity, our knowledge of viruses is surprisingly limited. Even with centuries of research and medical advances, we remain vulnerable to viral infections, because we still don't know much about these tiny organisms.

HIV, for instance, is a virus that we currently cannot completely eradicate. Even the medications we develop to manage it can lose their effectiveness as the virus evolves to resist our treatments. Similarly, the COVID-19 virus is another example of how a seemingly simple entity can shake humanity to its core.

If we cannot comprehend the inner workings of the simplest form of life on our own planet, how can we ever claim to possess substantial knowledge of anything at all? The quaternity concept embodies the value of humility, reminding us that, despite being the most intelligent creatures on Earth, we are but a minuscule part of this vast existence. Embracing and respecting this concept helps temper our ego, arrogance, vanity, and pride.

When you engage in a conversation, regardless of the topic, maintain an awareness of your limited understanding of the mysteries of life. This will eliminate your desire for disputes over who is correct or mistaken. The truth is that your understanding, my understanding, or that of anyone else is far too limited to definitively determine what is absolutely right or wrong.

After all, what is the purpose of winning an argument, vanquishing another human being, hurting their feelings, and diminishing their confidence? We are all fragments of consciousness, fundamentally the same essence. In truth, prevailing in arguments represents a missed opportunity to connect with another facet of consciousness, another facet of yourself. When you strive to defeat others, you become less, not more.

The point of communication is not to win an argument but to forge deeper connections, embracing and understanding each other's differing perspectives. In reality, when two human beings connect, two distinct facets of consciousness blend, elevating both of their awareness to the broader and deeper layers of consciousness.

The quaternity concept equips us with the ability to distinguish between fact, theory, assumption, hypothesis, faith, and imagination.

This understanding allows us to approach discussions with a reasonable level of respect for differing perspectives, recognizing that not everything we call knowledge is a proven fact.

Let's revisit the two-variable quaternity framework and explore an example. Consider the theory of evolution—it falls within the second step of quaternity concept, the known of the unknown. It is a theory, and not a fact. This indicates that we do not definitively know whether humans evolved from monkeys, were created in the Garden of Eden, or were engineered by extraterrestrial beings in a neighboring galaxy. We simply do not have a definitive answer.

The theory of evolution persists as a theory because no one has managed to disprove it, but it also remains unproven. It stands as the scientifically sound explanation we have developed up to this point in time, which is why it is referred to as "evolution theory" and not "evolution fact." There is still so much we do not know about the nature of evolution. This inherent uncertainty about this theory necessitates ongoing evaluation through continued examination and scrutiny of our science and our belief systems.

If someone firmly believes that the theory of evolution is an undeniable fact or, conversely, that it is entirely false, they are not adhering to the principles of quaternity. According to quaternity, anything beyond the first step—the known of the known—cannot be determined with absolute certainty. Since theories inherently fall into the second step—the known of the unknown—they are, by definition, subject to refinement, reinterpretation, or even replacement as new knowledge emerges.

Our debates about any theory should be based on evaluation of the concept rather than arguing about who is right and who is wrong. The quaternity concept represents the best path forward to enhance our intelligence—through humble communication and the exchange of information as opposed to argumentation and disregard for alternative perspectives.

Another example is the Big Bang theory. Similar to the theory of evolution, we cannot be certain whether the Big Bang occurred as we currently understand it. Some scientists, while analyzing data from the

James Webb telescope, are starting to question the accuracy of our current model of the universe. In light of our latest discoveries, some scientists are openly considering that our understanding of the Big Bang Theory might have been fundamentally misconstrued.

The Big Bang Theory is just that—a theory. While many scientific understandings revolve around it, this does not make the theory an absolute fact. Science has been wrong before, and we might be wrong this time as well. Therefore, it is best not to approach even scientific theories with absolute certainty. In writing this book, I place significant emphasis on science, but I also acknowledge that many concepts I explain here, even with scientific backing, might be far from the true reality.

The quaternity concept has taught me that I can only articulate my understanding of the world based on the limited knowledge humanity has gained up to this point. I recognize that I might be wrong. The best any of us can do is to remain skeptical, even of our own beliefs. This mindset encourages continuous questioning and openness to new information, preventing us from becoming overly attached to potentially flawed or incomplete understandings. By maintaining a healthy skepticism, we allow ourselves the flexibility to adapt and grow as our knowledge and insights evolve. This is the core teaching of the quaternity concept.

If we wish to bring an end to wars and conflicts among us one day, if we hope to cease violence and live in a world of peace, safety, and harmony, we must embrace the quaternity concept. We must acknowledge that each of us may hold different viewpoints, and that's perfectly acceptable because we are all in the dark together when it comes to unraveling the mysteries of the universe.

By humbling us, the quaternity concept teaches us to appreciate different perspectives and see the world through various lenses. The best way to enrich our life experience is through engaging in meaningful communication and connection with one another. The world is incredibly complex. Each of us possesses, and will continue to hold unique outlooks, and this diversity is inherent. In actual reality, our collective array of differing viewpoints contributes to a more comprehensive and holistic worldview overall.

Those among us who gain the ability to understand other people's perspectives and simultaneously hold various viewpoints are the wisest among us. As we foster deeper connections with each other, free from prejudice and judgment, we become increasingly more interconnected as a human species and more connected to consciousness.

Even in the simplest aspects of life, where you feel absolutely confident in your understanding, do not harbor judgement as you might still be wrong. A single overlooked detail, no matter how small, can blind you to the truth, no matter how intelligent you may be. There's a parable that illustrates this idea beautifully.

At an airport, a woman buys a coffee and a package of cookies to enjoy while waiting for her flight. She sits on a bench next to a man, placing her coffee beside her. She opens the package of cookies lying on the bench between her and the man, takes one, and begins to eat. To her surprise, the man reaches over, takes a cookie, and eats it too. Shocked and annoyed by his audacity, she says nothing, choosing instead to silently endure the situation.

With each cookie she takes, the man also takes one. Her irritation grows with every bite. When only one cookie remains, she decides to see how far his boldness will go. To her disbelief, the man reaches for the last cookie, breaks it in half, and offers one piece to her. Outraged but still silent, she grabs her belongings and storms off to her gate.

After boarding the plane, she sits down, adjusts her belongings, and places her bag under the seat. As she does, she notices an unopened package of cookies in her bag. In that instant, she realizes the truth: the cookies she had been eating were the man's, not hers. He had been sharing them generously, while she had judged him harshly for his supposed rudeness.

This parable reminds us of how easily we can misjudge situations when we miss simple details. Our assumptions and judgments are often flawed, shaped by incomplete information or misplaced certainty. Quaternity teaches us the importance of observing reality without prejudice, humbling ourselves in the face of the unknown. Instead of clinging to judgments, we should embrace patience, understanding, and humility to recognize that we may not see the full picture.

If we can be completely wrong about something as simple as who bought the cookie—an event that belongs to the *known of the known*, the first step of quaternity—then we must acknowledge the possibility of being mistaken about much more complex ideas. And theories that have been developed over centuries with extensive research, like the Big Bang and evolution, belong to the *known of the unknown*, the second step. These theories are carefully constructed through observation and reasoning, yet they may be entirely incorrect and subject to revision or complete replacement.

Now, consider the third and fourth steps of quaternity—the *unknown of the known* and the *unknown of the unknown*. These steps encompass the vast mysteries of existence: the meaning of life, the nature of divinity, and the faiths we hold so deeply. If we accept that we could be wrong even about well-researched theories, then we must also recognize the immense potential for error in our understanding of these greater unknowns.

All quaternity asks of you is humility. It does not demand that you abandon your beliefs, nor does it ask you to reject science, faith, or philosophy. Instead, it urges you to hold your belief with openness rather than arrogance—to acknowledge that your understanding is always incomplete. The willingness to question, to explore, and to accept the limitations of your knowledge is what keeps you moving toward deeper truths. Arrogance leads to stagnation, but humility keeps the door open for new discoveries and growth.

In the first chapter, we introduced the concept of duality, highlighting how our experience of life is shaped by contrasts and differences. Duality enables us to perceive and understand life as we do. Duality has been skillfully woven into the fabric of the world and human experience. There is no escape from this inherent duality; instead, we must adapt to a life of abstractions and cultivate the ability to see its contradictory beauty. The duality concept encourages us not to overly glorify its goodness nor excessively demonize its darker aspects.

In the second chapter, we delved into the concept of trinity, exploring how individuals who pursue trinity—whether through science, art, religion, philosophy, psychology, or spirituality—share a common goal: striving to become the best versions of themselves. The pursuit of trinity represents a pathway to unification with oneself, a higher existence, or the divine. The only path to divinity, knowledge, love, peace, and a higher quality of existence is through unification and not separation. Also, at our core, we are all composed of the same fundamental elements, each representing fragments of a greater whole. The realization of our interconnectedness and the universal nature of our journey toward self-improvement and spiritual unity is the core purpose of humanity as a whole, as delineated in the trinity concept.

Now, in this chapter, quaternity reminds us that it is equally important to evolve collectively as well as individually, fostering collective coherence and cooperation. It is in our best interest to unite as fragments of a greater essence, coming together as a whole, as one consciousness. Quaternity also provides the tool to break down exceedingly complex concepts to be able to better understand the world we live in. Together, these three concepts—duality, trinity, and quaternity—offer valuable insights into the importance of optimizing our life experiences, discovering our true selves, developing genuine connections, walking the path of unification, and enhancing our collective intelligence as a species. In the final chapters, we will explore the practicality of these concepts.

Chapter 4: Types of Awareness

The idea that the universe tends to grow more complex over time is a well-stablished concept in philosophy, referred to as "the law of increasing complexity" or "the complexity trend." This principle implies that the universe, and everything within it, has always evolved toward greater complexity and will continue to do so indefinitely. To understand this, let's journey back to the dawn of time and explore how the universe has evolved and grown more complex over the ages.

According to the Big Bang theory, the universe was born from an extremely small, hot, and dense core, commonly known as Singularity. During this primordial epoch, the universe was devoid of elements and materials we see today.

In a fraction of a second, the universe underwent a rapid expansion known as Cosmic Inflation. As the universe expanded, it also began to cool down, starting the formation of the material world. During this early period, the universe was primarily composed of energy, quantum fluctuations, and fundamental particles such as quarks and electrons. There were also unified forces, which eventually split into gravity, electromagnetic forces, nuclear forces, and other natural forces.

Within a few minutes after the Big Bang, the universe had cooled enough for a process called nucleosynthesis to occur. This process marked the birth of the first atomic nuclei—primarily hydrogen, helium, and lithium. However, these nuclei were still ionized, not yet combined with electrons to form neutral atoms we see in the world today. They were the precursors to the elements in the periodic table.

The universe continued to expand and, over the course of another 380,000 years, underwent a process known as recombination. During this time, electrons combined with nuclei to form atoms, creating the first elements of the periodic table as we know them today.

At this point, gravity, along with dark energy and dark matter, began to draw these elements together. Over the next several million years, stars and other cosmic structures started to form. As stars shone and progressed through their long-life cycles, they eventually exhausted their internal fuel.

In the final stages of their lives, medium-sized stars run out of their main fuels of hydrogen and helium. As a result, their cores shrink and heat up under intense pressure. This extreme heat allows carbon to be forged in their core. However, carbon marks the beginning of the end.

As carbon begins to form, stars continue to heat up, causing their outer layers to swell dramatically into a Red Giant. Eventually, these layers are cast off into space, creating a beautiful glow known as planetary nebula. What remains is star's dense and hot core—called a white dwarf, destined to cool slowly over eons. Medium-sized stars, like our own sun, will one day meet a similar fate, dying as they forge carbon.

Herein lies a fascinating paradox: carbon is the element of life. It is the foundation of everything you are and everything you eat. It is the backbone and skeleton of your body at the molecular level. All living creatures on Earth are carbon-based and owe their existence to this essential element. Without carbon, life as we know it would not exist. Yet, paradoxically, carbon is also the silent killer of medium-sized stars. The element that breathes life into the universe also ensures the death of the stars that create it.

On the other hand, massive stars undergo a different process at the end of their lives. Unlike smaller stars, which stop at carbon, these giants go on to forge heavier elements, ultimately producing iron. Iron, however, becomes their elemental killer. As their cores accumulate iron, they reach a point where no further fusion can occur to produce energy. Star, then, collapses into itself under its own gravity, triggering a catastrophic chain reaction that leads to a spectacular explosion known as a supernova.

In this violent finale, the extreme conditions forge the universe's heaviest elements, such as gold, platinum, and uranium, which are scattered into space. These supernovae enrich the cosmos with the raw materials needed to form everything you see in the universe including planets and even life. The remnants of these massive stars collapse further, forming either neutron stars or black holes, depending on their mass.

Supermassive stars that evolve into black holes play an important role in shaping the universe. These black holes become gravitational anchors around which galaxies form, pulling stars, gas, and dust into their orbits and sculpting the galaxies we see today.

Everything discussed so far occurred within one to two billion years after the Big Bang. Initially, the universe began as an unimaginably hot and dense state of pure energy. Over time, this energy cooled and condensed, giving rise to fundamental particles like electrons, neutrons, protons, and bosons. Simultaneously, forces such as gravity, electromagnetism, and nuclear forces emerged.

From these building blocks, the cosmos created black holes, stars, planets, moons, and countless other celestial objects—all within just a few billion years of its birth. With mind-boggling speed, the universe marched forward toward greater complexity, transforming chaos into order with extraordinary precision.

Over the next several billion years, these celestial bodies created the conditions necessary for life to emerge. On Earth, the arrival of life became part of the universe's ongoing journey toward increasing complexity, further amplifying the beauty of existence.

Around 3.5 to 3.8 billion years ago, viruses and single-cell microorganisms like bacteria appeared on Earth, marking the earliest life forms. Viruses were the silent architects and choreographers of life's elegant dance. Tiny viruses weaved the threads of genetic exchange and adaptation of living creatures on Earth.

Viruses caused genetic mixing among bacteria and other living organisms. They inserted their genetic material into the genomes of single-celled organisms. Through this integration, they orchestrated a delicate symphony of genetic exchange, promoting diversity among species and blurring the boundaries between them.

Viral infections also forced other creatures to adapt to changes. Those who resisted viral onslaughts survived to pass on their resilient traits, gradually shaping the evolutionary landscape with each successive generation.

During this period, single-cell microorganisms developed the ability to perform photosynthesis. Over a span of approximately 1 to 1.5 billion years, some organisms began forming cooperative groups, with different members taking on specialized roles. This gradual specialization led to the emergence of more complex multicellular organisms, including the early ancestors of sponges, which still inhabit the ocean floor today.

Approximately 541 million years ago, during the Cambrian period, there was a remarkable diversification of animal life, referred to as the Cambrian Explosion. This period saw the emergence of various major animal groups, including arthropods (the early insects), mollusks (such as snails and clams), and chordates (the early fish-like creatures).

Approximately 40 million years later, the first vertebrates emerged in the form of early fish. While relatively simple compared to the diverse vertebrates we see today, these fish ushered in a new era in which animals developed a backbone and an internal skeleton, setting the stage for the incredible diversity of vertebrate life we witness today.

Shortly after, during the Ordovician Period, a significant ecological shift occurred. A transition took place as certain aquatic algae species ventured onto the uncharted territory of dry land, marking the advent of early terrestrial plants. This transition from water to land laid the foundation for the diversity of plant life that would eventually cover Earth's landscapes.

Fish also made a similar journey approximately 360 million years ago, leaving the water to become terrestrial animals known as tetrapods. This marked the very first step in the emergence of land-dwelling vertebrates. Over the course of the next 40 million years or so, roughly 320 million years ago, reptiles evolved from these early tetrapods. Then, around 230 million years ago, dinosaurs emerged from reptilian ancestors, becoming some of the most iconic creatures to ever roam the Earth.

Mammals stepped into the evolutionary drama around 200 million years ago. Following their appearance, approximately 50 million years later, birds emerged as descendants of theropod dinosaurs. About 60 million years ago, primates entered the scene, a diverse group that includes monkeys and apes. Over time, this lineage led to the emergence of hominids, a family that includes our early human relatives, and eventually culminated in *Homo sapiens*, the species to which we belong.

This elegant web of evolutionary events has shaped the diversity of life on our planet and our own place within it.

The question of whether earthly creatures evolved from one form to another or were each created separately by a divine entity remains unanswered. However, what is clear is the gradual evolution of DNA sequences across various life forms. We can clearly observe that DNA sequences were upgraded over time through the creation of different species on Earth, reaching their culmination with the arrival of humanity. For instance, you share less than 1% of your DNA codes with viruses, 10% with certain bacteria, 23% with yeasts, 25% with grass, 33% with ants, 40% with earthworms, 44% with bees, 50% with apple trees, 60% with chickens, 70% with frogs, 80% with cows, 84% with dogs, 85% with mice, 90% with cats, 98% with pigs, and nearly 99% with chimpanzees. You share DNA with every creature on Earth. There is not a single biological creature on Earth that does not share some level of DNA with you or with other creatures. We are all intermingled, whether through evolution, creation, or both. We are all part of a big genetic family.

Regardless of whether creatures on Earth progressed through evolution or creation, their DNA underwent changes step by step over time, increasing in complexity and ultimately leading to the emergence of humans.

Commencing with the singularity of the Big Bang and extending to the present day, the universe has undergone an unceasing progression toward greater complexity, evident in every moment, element, cosmic entity, and form of life.

As humans, we have been continuing this trend. Consider our own history. Humanity has always been inexorably drawn toward complexity. From our earliest days, we marveled at the allure of metals. They started as rudimentary tools. Over time, these tools evolved into intricate instruments for hunting, cultivating, and advanced weaponry.

As the Industrial Age dawned, metals became the backbone of our technological progress, driving the machinery that transformed society. Then came the Digital Age, where metals were harnessed to create computers, machines more sophisticated than us in certain aspects.

Now, we find ourselves on the cusp of merging with these machines. With prosthetic limbs and artificial enhancements, we have begun integrating metals with our bodies, pushing the boundaries of human potential. The next frontier, driven by nanotechnology, promises micro-robots that can be injected into our brains, bloodstreams, and other body parts. We are on the path to fusing human flesh with metallic robots and evolving into even more complex beings. Our history with metals is a testament to our unceasing drive toward greater complexity. This drive is a reflection of the universe itself. The same force that forged stars and scattered elements across the cosmos lives within us, propelling us forward on a shared journey of growth and complexity.

The universe, despite its 13.8 billion years of existence, is but an infant, with an immense stretch of time ahead before any potential annihilation. Throughout this vast expanse of time and space, the pursuit of greater complexity will endure.

Consider yourself for a moment. The elements comprising your body have a history as ancient as the universe itself. They began as pure energy, transformed into fundamental elements, coalesced into stars, and metamorphosed into other elements. These materials later took shape as asteroids and cosmic dust. Eventually, they became an integral part of Earth's composition, existing as rocks, rivers, plants, insects, animals, and all the diverse elements and life on our planet.

Now, these very elements converge to create you. Yet, in the grand scheme of the cosmos, they are transient residents within your body. Their journey continues as they depart your body to become something else, perhaps something even more complex than you, each step contributing to the universe's relentless drive toward greater complexity.

The point being made here is that every aspect of existence serves a purpose. Nothing comes into being without reason or intent. Just as you believe in the purpose of your life, so too the particles composing your very being have a purpose. These particles have embarked on an extraordinary journey, taking on various forms like water, rocks, stars, and a myriad of other objects since the inception of time.

This purposeful progression of the universe toward complexity at the level of particles and nonliving entities encapsulates what I refer to as *ground zero awareness*. It displays the profound interconnectedness and purpose woven into the very fabric of reality, from the smallest particle to the grand tapestry of the universe.

You, and I, and everything surrounding us embody ground zero awareness. It is this awareness that propels us toward a relentless pursuit of greater complexity—a level of awareness we share with the rocks and rugs beneath our feet. This is the awareness at the particle and quantum level shared by all that exist in the world.

However, awareness itself needed to evolve as part of its journey toward greater complexity. With the emergence of life, a higher level of awareness began to surface. To delve into this heightened state of awareness, let's examine the simplest form of life again: the virus. Viruses are structurally so basic that some scientists do not classify them as living entities. They consist of genetic material, either DNA or RNA, enclosed within a protective protein coat called a *capsid*, along with enzymes for various functions. Some viruses also possess outer fatty tissues. This simple structure, apart from minor variations, is common among all viruses.

Viruses are extremely tiny, much smaller than the cells in your body. Think of yourself. You are roughly made up of 30 to 60 trillion cells. Cells are already pretty small, but compared to viruses, they are gigantic. A single cell can be thousands, or millions, or even billions of times larger than a virus. A virus can theoretically be up to 130 billion times smaller in volume than a human cell. To put this into perspective, if a single cell were the size of a car, a virus would be like a tiny pebble or a grain of sand in comparison. That's how incredibly small viruses are.

Now, let's take a closer look at just how astonishingly intelligent these tiny creatures are. Viruses remain dormant in the environment until they enter a host through various means, such as inhalation, ingestion, direct contact, or other modes of transmission. Due to their extremely small size, they usually go undetected by the host's immune system.

Once inside the host's body, viruses cannot simply infect any cell at random. They often have specific structures, like antenna-shaped proteins or spikes, that allow them to bind to certain types of cells.

Viruses travel through the host's body, examining various cells until they find one that is suitable for them.

Once a virus identifies a potential host cell, it clings to the outer surface of that cell. At this point, the virus uses various methods to enter the cell. These methods can involve endocytosis, where the virus deceives the cell into engulfing it, as if it were a harmless entity or food. Alternatively, some viruses fuse their fatty outer layer with the host cell's outer surface. This allows them to inject their genetic material into the cell's cytoplasm (the gel-like substance inside the cell). Additionally, some other viruses can create holes, pores, or channels in the host cell outer layer to create a pathway for their entry. The precise mechanism used by a virus can vary depending on its structure and the host cell it is targeting.

Once a virus infiltrates a cell, it sets in motion a series of actions to hijack the cell's machinery, effectively taking control and turning the cell into a replication factory for the virus itself. First, it releases its genetic material into the cell. Then, it deftly manipulates the cell's enzymes and ribosomes to duplicate its genetic code and manufacture the necessary proteins for creating new viruses. These freshly replicated viral genetic components and proteins are skillfully assembled to give rise to a new generation of virus particles, commonly referred to as virions. These virions are essentially the virus's offspring. Subsequently, these newly generated viruses are released from the host cell with one mission in mind: to infect other cells elsewhere in the host's body.

Just imagine how incredibly smart these viruses are. They target cells that are billions of times larger and more complex than themselves, yet they navigate this vast world with precision and purpose. Like skilled spies, they bypass the intricate security checkpoints of the cell, slipping past its defenses unnoticed. Once inside, they move with a high level of mastery, heading straight for the "government" of the cell, where they seize control. With astonishing efficiency, they reprogram the cell's entire system, turning it into a virus-producing factory, forcing it to create copies of the invader instead of carrying out its normal functions.

When a virus invasion occurs, the human body deploys its skilled assassins known as Natural Killer Cells. These vigilant cells traverse the body, assessing cell health by examining molecules produced by the cell called the histocompatibility complex. These molecules provide insights into the cell's well-being, signaling whether it has been infiltrated by foreign entities. If Natural Killer Cells detect any irregularity in histocompatibility complex, they swiftly launch an attack and destroy the compromised cell.

Within the body, another defense mechanism operates involving T-Cells. They are born in the bone marrow from stem cells and then migrate to the thymus, a small gland nestled in the chest. Here, T-Cells undergo rigorous education and testing to assess their ability to correctly recognize antigens presented by histocompatibility complex molecules, similar to the evaluation carried out by Natural Killer Cells. During their training in the thymus, if T-Cells respond with excessive aggression or excessive passivity, they face immediate elimination. The training process is incredibly meticulous, with fewer than 1% of T-Cells successfully completing the training and surviving the journey out of the thymus; more than 99% of T-Cells are executed on the spot for failing the training process.

The surviving T-Cells are akin to special forces in the military, nothing short of elite warriors, highly trained and equipped with specialized skills and formidable immune capabilities. Those that successfully complete their bootcamp training in the thymus gland are permitted to circulate throughout the body. These T-Cells selectively bind with cells that have viral antigens on their histocompatibility complex. There are many different types of T-Cells in your body; some collaborate with other immune cells in the battle against invaders, while others directly target and destroy infected cells.

Viruses under attack by Natural Killer Cells, T-Cells, and other immune cells begin to develop strategies to counterattack. Viruses employ various methods for their survival. Some alter their surface proteins, which means changing their appearance, to avoid detection by immune cells. Certain viruses prevent viral antigens from showing up on histocompatibility complex molecules, making it harder for Natural Killer Cells and T-Cells to recognize infected cells. Furthermore, viruses can interrupt the signaling pathways that trigger immune responses, hindering the activation of T-Cells and Natural Killer Cells.

When all direct combat methods fail, viruses turn to indirect strategies. Some establish a latent infection where they stop actively replicating, making themselves invisible to the immune system. With the passage of time, latent viruses, hidden safely somewhere in the body of the host, capitalize on the opportunity to evolve, altering their appearance and tactics to enhance their resilience against the immune system.

Patiently biding their time, these viruses wait for the right conditions. When the host's immune system becomes weakened or compromised, they re-emerge, launching an aggressive attack on the host's cells with renewed vigor and adaptive tactics, increasing their chance of survival and replication.

We can confidently assert that viruses, despite being the tiniest of all creatures on Earth, exhibit a remarkable level of intelligence and awareness of their surroundings. Yet, they are just one of infinite many microscopic creatures. Other single-celled and multicellular organisms demonstrate even greater intelligence and complexity. When we delve into life at the microscopic scale, it becomes strikingly clear that these tiny creatures possess a profound level of awareness. They exhibit exceptional sophistication and intelligence as they diligently, structurally, and purposefully fulfill their tasks and duties for the survival of their kind.

While microscopic organisms possess what I call ground zero awareness, their perception and understanding of reality extend further. They are aware of their surroundings and interact with the environment to contribute to a broader complexity. This level of awareness is what I call *autonomous survival awareness*. Within this level of awareness, almost all actions are autonomous, driven by environmental cues and responses. These living entities are extremely intelligent, but their intelligence comes mostly from the programming that nature has designed and embedded within them, nearly devoid of deliberate critical thinking, thoughtful evaluation, or complex calculation.

Up to this point, we have explored the idea that everything in existence, living or non-living, possesses ground zero awareness, which represents an inherent drive toward greater complexity. Additionally, we have established the concept that all living creatures, regardless of their simplicity or complexity, exhibit ground zero awareness along with autonomous survival awareness. This implies that they not only seek complexity but also engage in complex interactions with their surrounding environment.

As creatures evolved into even more complex life forms, yet another higher level of awareness emerged. When sets of cells and organs collaborate to form a unified entity, the awareness of that entity surpasses that of the individual cells and organs within it. Insects, plants, and animals fall within this category. Even the tiniest insects are composed of millions of highly specialized and remarkably intelligent cells, each performing its role with precision. Yet, the insect as a whole possesses an intelligence far greater than that of any individual cell within its body. The distinction in awareness here is that these species have various roles, functions, and unique personalities among themselves.

Let's delve into the captivating world of ants. At the heart of every ant colony lies the queen, the reproductive powerhouse responsible for ensuring the colony's survival by laying eggs.

Next, we have the male ants. Their function is extremely limited—they mate with the queen and die shortly after.

The rest of ants in the colony are known as worker ants, which are sterile females tasked with a wide array of responsibilities. These tasks encompass foraging for food, scouting, tending to the young, defending the colony, and maintaining the nest. Worker ants are the backbone of the colony.

The worker ants known as queen attendants have the responsibility of caring for the queen. They are responsible for feeding, grooming, and protecting the queen. Additionally, they assist the queen in her egg-laying responsibilities and ensure that eggs are appropriately positioned within the nest for optimal development. Queen attendants also play a role in transmitting pheromones that contribute to regulating the queen's reproductive behavior. These pheromones signal the queen when to increase or decrease her egg-laying activity based on factors such as colony size, food availability, and environmental conditions.

Another category of worker ants is called nurse ants. They have a distinctive role in the colony. They take on the responsibilities of feeding, grooming, and protecting the developing larvae as they progress into adulthood. These nurse ants secrete a liquid from their salivary glands, which serves as nourishment for the larvae. Nurse ants wield considerable influence over the fate of the larvae, as their specialized care directly shapes the type of ants the larvae will eventually become as they mature.

Moving on, another group of worker ants takes on the role of sanitary workers, focusing on the cleanliness and structural integrity of the nest. These ants diligently work to remove debris, eliminate deceased ants, and clear away waste materials, ensuring a clean and healthy nest. They also engage in the essential task of grooming other ants to eliminate dirt, pathogens, and parasites. These cleansing processes prevent the spread of diseases within the colony. Moreover, when the nest structure is damaged or compromised, these ants take action to repair and reinforce it, preserving the nest's integrity.

In addition, another group of worker ants is responsible for feeding the entire colony and are referred to as forager ants. Forager ants are tasked with searching for, locating, and collecting food resources to sustain the entire colony.

Apart from foragers, there are other specialized ants known as scouts. These ants have more expansive roles and responsibilities. They explore the environment not solely in search of food but also to evaluate potential new nest sites, discover valuable resources, and assess potential threats or opportunities.

Ants employ chemical signals as a means of communication. These chemical signals, known as pheromones, play a critical role in various forms of interaction. Notably, foragers, and scouts utilize pheromones to convey essential information, including the presence of food sources, the location of the nest, and the recognition of nestmates. Moreover, pheromones serve as a means to transmit alarm signals, alerting the colony to potential threats or disturbances in their environment.

In addition to general pheromones, ants utilize a specific type of pheromone known as chemical trails for long-range communication. These chemical trails are employed to mark the path between the nest and a food source. Foragers, in particular, play a key role in laying down these chemical trails as they travel back and forth between the nest and the food source. These marked pathways enable other ants to locate the same food source by following the trail left behind.

Certain ant species have specialized soldier ants, distinguishable by their larger mandibles or stingers. Some ant colonies also produce unique broods that mature into larger and heavily armored ants. These soldiers are the guardians of the colony, providing protection against potential threats and predators.

Ants are also remarkably intelligent engineers. Deep underground, their nests are designed with complex ventilation systems that ensure proper airflow, keeping the colony well-ventilated even in tight spaces. In addition to managing air circulation, ants build specialized channels and pathways within their nests to control the flow of water. These clever designs help prevent flooding during heavy rain, ensuring their home remains safe and dry underground.

These roles and responsibilities among ants represent only a few of the common ones found across various ant species. Each ant species possesses a multitude of highly specialized and specific roles that vary significantly from those of other ant species.

From afar, it may appear that ants within the same colony share a similar appearance and behavior. However, upon closer inspection, it becomes evident that their tasks and responsibilities are highly specialized and tailored to the needs of the colony. This level of specialization in roles and duties is a common characteristic of all socially structured insects living in organized colonies.

From the example of ants, we can observe clear distinctions in roles and functions within a colony. However, in solitary species that live alone, the differentiation is not typically in roles and responsibilities as seen in social insects. Instead, distinctions among creatures who live in solitude are related to their personalities, living tactics, and preferences.

To explore this further, let's take a close look at spiders as an example. Even within the same species of spiders—and even among siblings from the same mother—we can observe distinctive individual personalities. These subtle differences are shaped by developmental conditions and environmental influences.

For example, a spider's web-weaving can vary in size, placement, or structural complexity. Some spiders construct large, symmetrical webs in open spaces, while their siblings build smaller or more asymmetrical ones in sheltered areas. In terms of web maintenance, some spiders are meticulous, repairing even minor damage, while others are more indifferent, abandoning damaged webs and rebuilding elsewhere.

Behavioral variation also appears in hunting. Within a single species, some spiders display bolder, more aggressive foraging behavior, venturing out frequently and attacking prey swiftly, while others are more cautious, preferring to wait patiently in concealment. These differences reflect how individual temperament and local environment shape behavior.

Alongside these traits, some spiders consistently display a more defensive or assertive temperament, while others remain noticeably docile, affecting how they respond to threats or interact with other spiders.

Even in reproduction, variations can be observed. Some males are more persistent or expressive during their courtship rituals, while others take quicker, more direct approaches. Likewise, in certain species where maternal care is flexible, females may differ in how attentively they guard their eggs—with some remaining close to their egg sacs for extended periods, while others depart sooner after laying.

Each and every spider has a distinct personality and character, shaped by a combination of genetics, environmental influences, and personal life experiences.

From the examples of spiders and ants, it becomes clear that their level of awareness surpasses that of viruses, bacteria, and microorganisms. Viruses of the same species behave in remarkably similar ways, with negligible differences in their roles or behaviors. In contrast, ants and spiders display notable individuality and varying responsibilities within their colonies and ecosystems. This difference places ants and spiders in a higher category of awareness compared to viruses, bacteria, and other microorganisms.

For ants and spiders, much like microorganisms, their autonomous survival awareness allows them to respond to their environment in an automated manner. However, unlike microorganisms, ants and spiders also engage in decision-making based on instincts. This decision-making process contributes to the development of distinct individual characteristics not observed in cells or viruses.

I refer to this enhanced level of awareness, where survival instincts contribute to individuality and unique personality, as *instinctive survival awareness*. It marks a significant step up in the spectrum of awareness, building upon complex automated responses to develop even more sophisticated cognitive processes observed in more advanced creatures.

Plants also have personalities. When we explore their lives and interactions with the environment, we can discern their uniqueness. Even within a single species, individual plants or trees vary in growth patterns, including differences in height, branching structure, and overall shape. Leaves on plants of the same species can differ in size, shape, and coloration. Some may flower earlier or later than others. In fruit-bearing species, individual plants may produce fruits of varying sizes, shapes, and flavors. They also show varying levels of resistance to environmental challenges like pests, diseases, droughts, or extreme temperatures. Root systems can also vary among individual plants. Some have deeper or more extensive root systems than others.

Just like insects, plants also demonstrate distinct personalities and behaviors shaped by their instincts and life experiences. Within the animal kingdom, it is well known that each and every animal possesses unique personality and character. It can be inferred that instinctive survival awareness is inherent in all animals, plants, and insects. They all have personalities and instincts.

In this way, insects, animals, and plants share an innate drive to survive and evolve toward greater complexity with every particle and atom in the universe—an awareness I refer to as ground zero awareness. They also exhibit automated responses to their environment, much like viruses and other microorganisms—a category I call autonomous survival awareness. However, what sets insects, animals, and plants apart is their instincts, which elevate them to a higher level of awareness—one that I call instinctive survival awareness. These instincts shape unique personalities and define specific roles within their ecosystems.

Now, let's examine awareness from a physical perspective. Across the spectrum of life, there is a noticeable correlation between a creature's physical complexity and its level of awareness. More advanced physical forms are often associated with higher levels of awareness and cognitive abilities. For example, it is evident that an elephant is more aware than an earthworm, or that a tree is more aware than grass. As creatures evolve to possess more sophisticated structures and functions, their potential for awareness also tends to increase. In contrast, simpler life forms exhibit less apparent levels of awareness, reflecting their more basic physiological structures and functions.

Arguably, humanity possesses the most complex physical structure among all creatures on Earth, which contributes to our unmatched level of awareness. While some individual traits may be less remarkable compared to other species, our overall physical attributes are superior. Some of our features are exceptional within the animal kingdom, while many others are among the most advanced, collectively giving us a distinctive advantage. Let's delve into some of these extraordinary human attributes.

One of our most prominent features is our relatively large brain in relation to our body size, giving us a complex neural structure that grants us superior cognitive capabilities. Large brain size places us among the most intelligent beings on the planet, a distinction we share with certain dolphins, great apes, whales, and elephants. Within our brain, the neocortex, responsible for higher-order thinking and complex cognitive functions, is exceptionally developed, surpassing that of any other species on Earth. Our neocortex is both large and intricately folded, contributing significantly to our exceptional cognitive prowess.

Moreover, the opposable thumbs in our hands enable us to skillfully handle tools and objects with precision. Also, the ability to walk upright on two legs not only liberated our hands for tool use but also allowed us to conserve energy by balancing efficiently on two legs. While most animals can run faster in short bursts, humans are among the most advanced creatures for long-distance walking, enabling us to travel great distances and migrate to new places.

Our complex vocal apparatus, including the larynx and vocal tract, empowers us to produce sophisticated sounds and develop language, enabling the transmission of complex ideas. Depth perception, a product of our binocular vision—where our eyes are slightly separated—enables us to accurately judge distances in our environment. Our naked skin, distinct from most creatures, enables efficient cooling through sweating, affording our ancestors adaptability across diverse environments. Finally, our omnivorous diet—the ability to eat both vegetables and meat—allows us to digest a wide range of foods, contributing to our adaptability and overall success as a species.

These extraordinary physical attributes, among many others, collectively shaped our unique position in the natural world, bestowing upon us the capacity to far surpass the awareness of any other creature.

Because of this higher awareness, humanity has mastered the art of harnessing, controlling, and utilizing natural elements like fire and water. In ancient times, our ability to generate and control fire elevated us to the pinnacle of the animal kingdom, making us the ultimate apex predator. With the advent of fire, our ancestors gained the power to repel any predator, as every living creature on Earth fears fire. Fire also enabled us to craft superior tools and cook food.

Additionally, our ability to collect and control the flow of water revolutionized agriculture, enabling us to cultivate crops in diverse environments and ensure a steady supply of water and edible vegetation. This mastery over water management supported the growth of civilizations and also laid the foundation for technological and social advancements.

Over time, as we were freed from the relentless pursuit of safety and food, we honed our skills in crafting even more fascinating tools, marking the dawn of technology. Simultaneously, we evolved our capacity for communication through the ingenious use of sounds, writing, and body language. This innovation gave rise to the birth of language, art, and ultimately culture. These milestones bestowed upon us adaptability, creativity, and a relentless quest for mastery over the world around us.

Furthermore, unlike any other animal, we possess the ability to pass down the knowledge and skills we acquire over our lifetimes to our offspring and successive generations in a meaningful manner. We construct our languages, cultures, societies, and all aspects of our existence upon the foundations laid by our ancestors, who, in turn, built upon the wisdom of their forebears.

This continuous passing down of knowledge and values across generations has been a driving force behind our development and the evolution of our collective wisdom. This unyielding pursuit of progress sets us apart from all other creatures on Earth, elevating our awareness to an even higher level, which I refer to as *intuitive progressive awareness*.

In summary, the various forms of awareness discussed in this chapter find their culmination in humanity. Every element and molecule within your body, which are as ancient as the universe itself, possesses the innate drive for complexity, which I termed *ground zero awareness*. Additionally, each cell in your body engages with its surroundings with an unwavering commitment to survival, referred to as *autonomous survival awareness*. At the next level, your survival instincts, that shape the most basic aspects of your personality, align with those of animals, insects, and plants—a concept I call *instinctive survival awareness*. Beyond these instincts, your ability to advance in fields like art, science, technology, culture, and language spring from the next tier of awareness, which I have named *intuitive progressive awareness*. These are the four levels of awareness evident on planet Earth.

Pause for a moment to take a marvelous look at yourself. You are not just a mere mortal; you are the epitome of the entire existence itself, a cosmic masterpiece. You are as ancient as the universe itself, made from particles that have journeyed since the dawn of time and the birth of space. At the deepest level, you are a staggering 13.8 billion years old, with ground zero awareness rooted in every essence of your existence. Your DNA carries the echoes of eons' past, stretching back to the emergence of the tiniest microorganisms and bacteria, nearly 4 billion years ago, carrying within you the autonomous survival awareness. You are intricately connected to every living being on this planet, sharing a considerable genetic bond with every insect, every plant, and every animal alike, all endowed with an instinctive survival awareness over millions of years. In the blink of an eye, in the grand tapestry of time, your *Homo Sapiens* ancestors have propelled your genetic code forward, passing down their life experiences through an evolutionary journey of many millennia. With each passing generation, your awareness has expanded, evolving into a beacon of intuitive survival awareness, forging a path of progress through the ages. Embrace the marvel of your existence, for you are not just a product of the past, but a pathway into the future, like a beacon shining with the brilliance of billions of years of cosmic evolution.

As humanity, we are on the cusp of merging our biological bodies with the robots we have created. The potential for a future in which robots and humanity unite into a singular entity raises the possibility of achieving an even higher level of awareness. Alternatively, we may not merge with robots, but picture a scenario in which every human being attains such a pinnacle of intelligence that we seamlessly coalesce into a unified whole without conflicts, wars, and separations, with everyone contributing to a greater entity as humanity, much like our individual cells and organs function as integral parts of our being. This could represent one possibility for the next level of awareness we might attain.

Another intriguing prospect could be that we become coherent enough to form a unified entity as one humanity while simultaneously merging with robots, resulting in an even more intelligent, unified entity composed of metallic robots and biological humans. The future remains uncertain, and the possibilities are indeed infinite. These scenarios offer glimpses into the realm where higher levels of awareness await discovery. As we navigate these potential pathways into the future, the right direction for the evolution of our awareness remains uncertain. With one misstep in our evolutionary journey, we could annihilate ourselves, but with the right step, we could grow increasingly more intelligent. One can only hope for a time when our collective intelligence enables us to make the right decisions and access the right path to the next elevated tier of awareness, deepening our connection to our essence and to the broader consciousness.

However, what the future holds—and what heights of awareness humanity may one day ascend to—is not the focus of this book. What we're here to explore is how you can expand your awareness in this lifetime, within the category of intuitive progressive awareness.

Your awareness shapes your entire experience of reality. When it drops, life becomes reactive, stressful, and survival-driven—dominated by fear, impulses, and unfulfilled desires. This state breeds inner conflict, dissatisfaction, and a sense of lack that darkens the path ahead.

But when you elevate your awareness, everything begins to change. You rise above fear and scarcity. You begin to see life through a lens of abundance. Compassion naturally grows. Clarity emerges. You become more conscious, more connected, and more at peace with the world and yourself.

The goal is to awaken the highest version of who you already are. Within you lies extraordinary potential—infinite strength, untapped wisdom, and a deep well of love and creativity, all lying dormant in the recesses of your being, waiting to be brought to life. Elevating your awareness is the key that unlocks this greatness.

In the chapters ahead, we'll explore how to awaken that infinite potential and weave it into your reality—making your life more peaceful, more purposeful, and deeply fulfilling.

Chapter 5: Laws of Consciousness

Do you recall the definition of consciousness as defined earlier? Consciousness is the repository of the meaning embedded within all the data in the world, encompassing the entirety of the existence within itself. To better understand this concept, we applied the quaternity framework, deconstructing consciousness into four realms: the known visible realm, the known invisible realm, the unknown visible realm, and the unknown invisible realm.

As humans, we are fragments of this broader consciousness, and our interactions with it, as well as our ability to access its depths, are regulated by several laws. These laws of consciousness are like the laws of physics, universal and impartial. Just as gravity applies to all of us equally, preventing anyone from floating away, the laws of consciousness apply to everyone without exception.

In this chapter, we will explore some of the basic laws of consciousness. These laws govern our experiences and interactions with the broader consciousness, defining the pathway toward greater knowledge, wisdom, and enlightenment.

The first law of consciousness lays the foundation for enlightenment and self-discovery. It posits that "the level of abstraction increases as one transitions from the known realm to the unknown realm and from the visible realm to the invisible realm. Concurrently, the path to self-discovery and enlightenment lies at the farthest reaches of the unknown and invisible realms."

Let's take a more detailed look at this law: the known realm, characterized by familiarity and comfort, encompasses the aspects of life you have explored and experienced. It represents your personal comfort zone, where you navigate with ease and confidence. Transitioning into the unknown realm, on the other hand, leads you into uncharted territories—spaces filled with novelty, mystery, and unfamiliarity. In these unfamiliar territories, you will constantly sense fear and discomfort, requiring you to stay vigilant and alert. This constant sense of unease in the unknown realm sharpens your mind and is essential for developing your potential to achieve greatness.

Anyone who has achieved success in any endeavor, whether as a businessman, political figure, spiritual guru, or in any other field, has at some point in their career pushed the boundaries of the unknown and ventured into uncharted territories before reaching success. They did not confine themselves to the safety of familiar ground; instead, they embraced uncertainty, took risks, and faced their fears. This willingness to explore the unknown and face challenges head-on is a common trait among successful people.

No one is born brave and courageous; these are skills that can only be developed by facing and overcoming fears. If you choose the easy path in life, remain in your comfort zone, and avoid challenges, you will never conquer your fears. In such a scenario, unaddressed fears will follow you like shadows, hindering your self-confidence, personal growth, and journey toward self-discovery. The best version of you is hidden behind every fear you harbor. Only by confronting and conquering these fears can you uncover the bravest version of yourself and, ultimately, discover your true self.

Similarly, the law distinguishes between the visible realm and the invisible realm. The visible realm encompasses elements of reality that are logical, empirical, and measurable, representing the tangible and rational aspects of your existence. In contrast, the invisible realm extends into the moral and ethical dimensions, defining the quality and value of human life. Transitioning from the visible to the invisible realm involves shifting from an objective, fact-based domain to a subjective realm where values, qualities, and moral considerations become the primary forces guiding your actions.

If you attempt to understand the world solely through facts and certainties, you fall short of grasping true reality. While mathematics and physics can explain the mechanics of the universe, they cannot end wars and conflicts or bring about peace and harmony. These deeper aspects of human experience lie beyond the reach of science. Attaining peace and harmony at both the individual and societal levels require more than just scientific knowledge; it involves an understanding of moral, ethical, and emotional dimensions.

For instance, earning a PhD in psychology does not guarantee enlightenment or inner peace. No degree from any university can ease mental agony and ensure peace of mind and tranquility. These states of being are not products of the visible world of facts and figures but of the invisible realm of values, principles, and self-awareness.

The only path that can truly promise inner peace and tranquility is the path of spirituality and morality, the journey into the invisible realm. This invisible realm bestows upon you a deeper sense of morality, and as your moral understanding grows, so do your values and qualities. The best version of you is the one that embodies your highest values and finest qualities. Therefore, by enhancing your moral understanding, you unlock the doors to these elevated aspects of your character.

By sharpening your moral compass and enhancing your ability to recognize your greatest qualities and values within, you embark on a journey of discovering your life purpose. When you identify a purpose that aligns with your core values, you begin to experience a profound sense of fulfillment and satisfaction that surpasses anything the material world can offer. Deep moral understanding fills the void you sense within, providing a sense of wholeness and completeness.

The main idea here is that different aspects of life vary in terms of their familiarity, comfort, abstraction, and complexity. If you desire to become the best version of yourself, if you desire to end your mental suffering, if you desire to enrich your life with a sense of serenity, peace, and happiness, you must diligently work on enhancing your understanding of the unknown and invisible realms. You have to face your fears and overcome them in the unknown realm and discover your values and true potential in the invisible realm.

Think of it this way: enlightenment means discovering and embodying the best version of yourself. Now, imagine you want to achieve enlightenment. This is never going to happen if you spend every night sitting on the couch, watching movies, and eating popcorn. It won't happen if you're always at a bar, watching sports, and drinking with friends. In these scenarios, you might be having fun and enjoying yourself, and you might even learn a lot from the movies you watch and the friends you interact with. However, learning and gaining knowledge without the wisdom to implement that knowledge meaningfully into your life is essentially useless.

If you do not confront your fears and deepen your moral understanding, your knowledge will never transform into wisdom. Think of it this way: you could read a hundred books on how to play the guitar, but unless you pick up the guitar and practice daily, you will never truly learn to play. Reading books or watching videos on how to play the guitar represents knowledge; wisdom is the ability to actually play.

If you wish to become enlightened, improve your mood, and end your mental suffering, you must change your life and the way you live. If you continue to do what you have always done, you will continue to feel the way you have always felt. To experience different and better feelings, you must take different actions.

Stop wasting hours glued to movies or endlessly scrolling through your phone. Stop filling your weekends with drinks and parties, chasing temporary highs with friends. Instead, start dedicating your time to the things you've always dreamed of doing. Pursue what truly matters to you—whether it's learning a new skill, building something meaningful, or exploring a passion that's been calling out to you for years.

The path to greatness is always uncomfortable, frightening, and uncertain. It requires you to step out of your comfort zone and embrace challenges that will test your resilience and determination. You must venture into the unknown and confront your fears. You have to elevate your moral understanding to attain higher qualities and values. Only by doing so can you unlock your full potential and achieve true enlightenment.

The second law of consciousness states that "Individuals who have gained access to deeper layers of consciousness naturally harbor more power than those who have less access to consciousness."

The notion of power here differs significantly from the common perception of power associated with material wealth, physical strength, or control over others. True power cannot be inherited from parents, purchased with money, or bartered for material possessions. It is not an external force exerted over others for personal gain but an internal force that emerges from within, empowering one to tame and control the mind. True power does not belong to the visible realm; it exclusively exists within the invisible realm. True power is the embodiment of self-control, encompassing the ability to tame, maintain, control, and direct one's impulses, thoughts, feelings, and actions.

When you begin to understand your own true nature, you also begin to gain control over your wild inner beast. This requires mastery of introspection and self-reflection. If you ever notice that your thoughts and feelings run wild on their own course, it is only because you are not fully aware of your internal state, turmoil, and fluctuations. Only by fully understanding yourself can you gain control over your own wild thoughts and feelings. Think of your internal state as a dog under training. If the dog is not trained at all or trained improperly, then its behavior will be aggressive or unpredictable. However, if the same dog is trained properly, it can be easily controlled even without a leash. Your mind is a wild beast—it needs to be trained to behave in a predictable manner. The fluctuations of feelings and thoughts of the trained mind are predictable and controllable.

To train your mind like a skilled trainer, you must first learn the appropriate techniques. Attempting to tame the mind without proper knowledge, wisdom, and strategies is like facing a lion in the wilderness, trying to tame and control it with bare hands. The human mind is like a wild beast, one that resists control and refuses to be tamed. However, once you understand the right methods, you can begin to tame and train this inner beast.

In the chapters that follow, I will deconstruct the mind, exploring its various components and mechanisms, and provide detailed guidance on how it can be controlled. We will delve into practical methods and strategies for achieving self-mastery, offering you the tools needed to harness the full potential of your mind.

There is another aspect to true power. The one we have discussed thus far is individual power. However, there is also collective power; we become even more powerful as we unite. One person is never as strong as a community. The more people who coherently unite, the more collective power they will attain. Therefore, the best way to gain maximum spiritual power is to first gain self-mastery and control over oneself, and then unite with others who have also achieved self-mastery. A community built upon interlinked individuals who have gained mastery over themselves is the strongest and most reliable power that humanity can hope to achieve. This is the essence of the second law of consciousness: the power arising from self-reflection and genuine connection.

True power is often not noticeable by external observers, especially by those who have not attained similar power themselves. This kind of power does not manifest through external symbols or displays of authority. Instead, it resides deep within the recesses of the mind, influencing one's decision-making, relationships, and overall outlook on life. The quality of true power radiates through one's actions and interactions. True power is marked by authenticity, not authority; it harbors compassion, not oppression; and it requires wisdom, not conformity. Those who have attained this level of empowerment have explored the depths of their own consciousness, discovering a clear and profound understanding of their purpose, values, and the interconnectedness to all life and the totality of existence.

The third law of consciousness posits that "physical and mental well-being is intricately tied to the accuracy of one's understanding of truth." In other words, your well-being, both in terms of your physical health and mental health, is influenced by your capacity to understand, acknowledge, and accept the truth.

Let's imagine for a minute that you lack self-confidence and do not believe in yourself. In this scenario, you would not recognize your own powerful qualities, you would not believe you are worthy of love, and you would not see your own beauty. With such a limiting belief system, you would constantly feel a sense of lack, as if something vital is missing in your life. This pervasive sense of emptiness would negatively impact your physical, mental, and emotional health, leading to depression, devastation, and demotivation.

However, none of these negative beliefs are true. You may have experienced harsh realities and faced tough life circumstances, but these do not define who you truly are or what potential lies within you. Your life circumstances are merely external conditions and do not determine your intrinsic worth, values, and capabilities.

The truth is that you are worthy of love, you are beautiful, and you possess great qualities within you. Every human being does, and you are no exception. Even if you have not yet reached the point where these qualities are fully manifested, it does not mean they do not exist within you. The first step toward becoming the best version of yourself is to believe in yourself. You must recognize and embrace your inherent worth, your unique qualities, and your inner beauty.

Knowing the truth means recognizing that your belief system and current actions may be holding you back from becoming the best version of yourself. It requires an honest assessment of your behaviors and an understanding of the changes you need to make to grow and mature. When you believe in your potential for greatness and understand the truth about the bad habits and misguided beliefs that are preventing you from achieving your goals, you will begin to see the path from where you are to where you need to be. You will know who you are and who you need to become.

This realization allows you to identify the gap between your current state and your desired state. It is at this point that you will find your life's purpose and the motivation to wake up with resilience every morning, ready to face the challenges of the day. It is only then that you will recognize the beauty within you that will drive you to manifest that beauty in your actions and interactions. It is only then that the qualities that have been dormant within you will start to flourish and become active components of your life.

Understanding the truth about yourself will transform your perspective and ignite a desire for self-improvement. If you truly grasped how much better your life could become by knowing and embracing the truth about yourself, you would stop doing everything that causes you self-harm and embark on a journey of self-discovery. You would start uncovering your true potential, shedding limiting beliefs, and adopting behaviors that align with your highest values.

Truth is like an unfiltered mirror, reflecting reality with stark clarity. Truth neither glorifies nor demonizes but simply reveals things as they are. Confronting this mirror of truth highlights your shortcomings and unachieved goals, and it exposes the challenges you must overcome to find your true selves. The raw honesty of truth forces you to stand at a crossroads: to embark on a tough and challenging journey toward fulfillment or to settle for an easy, comfortable, but ultimately hollow existence.

Do not choose to have an easy life, for it leads only to emptiness. Life without challenges is life without meaning. Avoid indulging in self-destructive behaviors—such as excessive sex, drugs, and alcohol—as they serve to numb your mind, making you forget who you truly are and what you are destined to become. Do not sacrifice your integrity, and do not trade your soul for wealth, fame, and earthly power, mistaking these to be the ultimate markers of a good life. Without a deep understanding of truth and morality, even the most precious material possessions cannot ease the torment of a restless mind. Earthly pleasures may bring fleeting joy, putting a smile on your face, but behind the facade of your laughter will remain a void that no riches or accolades can fill. Without truth, genuine happiness and inner peace will remain forever out of reach.

Living in denial of the truth prevents spiritual growth and leads to a superficial existence. The pleasures gained from denial offer temporary comfort, but it cannot fill the emptiness that comes from neglecting your potential and purpose. True fulfillment comes from facing the truth head-on, embracing responsibility, and overcoming challenges. It is through this process that you achieve true happiness and lasting peace.

No matter how harsh it may be, truth is a call to action. It urges you to take responsibility, own your past mistakes, and commit to improvement, physically, mentally, and emotionally. Truth is the foundation for motivation, inspiration, and hope. When you seek and embrace the truth, it provides clarity and direction, guiding you toward meaningful change and personal growth.

Truth will set you free from the burdens of denial, deception, and self-doubt, empowering you to live authentically and purposefully. Truth challenges you to confront your fears, step out of your comfort zones, and address the areas of your life that need attention. This process, though uncomfortable, is a powerful catalyst for transformation.

The fourth law of consciousness asserts that "the sole gateway to access consciousness is through the lens of awareness, and the extent of one's awareness is directly contingent on the effort exerted to elevate one's access to consciousness." Put simply, the more you make an effort to be aware, the more aware and connected you become to consciousness.

In life, you have two paths to choose from in any situation: denial or awareness. Denial might feel easier at first—it lets you avoid facing difficult truths and provides a temporary escape. But in the long run, it keeps you stuck, preventing your growth and leaving you with a sense of unfulfilled potential.

Awareness, on the other hand, is about truly seeing things as they are. It takes courage to confront uncomfortable truths, but it opens the door to understanding—both about yourself and the world around you. Awareness invites you to look deeper, to recognize what is happening within you and around you, why it's happening, and how it affects you and others.

At its heart, awareness is tied to truth. Clinging to illusions or falsehoods keeps you in denial. However, gaining awareness through the lens of truth—no matter how hard it might be—leads you toward clarity and understanding.

This is not going to be easy, but it's worth it. The path demands that you commit to honesty and integrity and to be real with yourself and others. It calls for letting go of lies and stepping into reality with clarity and integrity. When you do this, you reach a heightened state of awareness where you can face life's challenges with the strength of your integrity and navigate them with the wisdom of your honesty.

Like anything else in life, if you focus on and practice elevating your awareness, it will naturally increase. Your awareness is not controlled by anyone or anything but yourself. No external force can take away or bestow awareness upon you. The only factor determining your level of awareness is the effort, time, and energy you dedicate to cultivating it. It is a deeply personal and internal attribute that you harbor and nurture within.

When you learn the truth and attain higher levels of awareness, you gain access to deeper layers of consciousness. This deeper access allows you to tap into your true power—the power to control your own mind. As a result, self-control leads to a profound sense of fulfillment and satisfaction, contributing to your overall well-being.

Also, as you gain mastery over your impulses, thoughts, feelings, and actions, you become more attuned to your true self. This alignment fosters a journey toward enlightenment, where you achieve greater clarity, inner peace, and self-realization. In this way, the various laws of consciousness interconnect and support each other.

This interconnectedness of the laws of consciousness means that as you progress in one area, you naturally improve in other areas as well. For example, the truth fosters awareness, awareness deepens consciousness, deeper consciousness strengthens your self-control, and self-control results in a higher sense of satisfaction and well-being.

These laws about venturing into the unknown invisible realms, gaining true power, improving overall well-being, and increasing awareness come into focus in a few chapters where we delve into the realm of the soul. There is no need to memorize any of these laws or the concepts mentioned thus far in this book. Instead, these pieces of information will gradually come together to draw a bigger picture. When combined with the background we've discussed so far, this picture will begin to make sense.

For now, all you need to remember is this: you are capable of becoming the best version of yourself. It is not only possible but also absolutely achievable. The first step is to prioritize the discovery of your true self. The fact that you are reading this book means you are already interested in self-discovery, as that is the core purpose of this book. As you read on, the bigger picture will gradually take form. By the end, you will have all the essential tools and techniques needed to unleash your greatest talents, find your life purpose, achieve success, and live as the best version of yourself.

Once you begin this process toward self-discovery and enlightenment, improvement will happen gradually over time. Continuous, incremental improvements will eventually lead to a profound transformation. The old, less optimal aspects of yourself will gradually die out, making way for new, more refined qualities to emerge and flourish within you.

Just as a caterpillar transforms into a butterfly, you too can undergo a profound change, shedding outdated behaviors, thoughts, and beliefs to emerge as a new you, empowered by the wings of awareness and ready to soar into the depths of consciousness. If the caterpillar only thinks of itself as a worm, it will never metamorphose into a beautiful butterfly. It will never experience the freedom of flight or recognize its beauty and the power of transformation. You were born with the potential for greatness, much like caterpillars with the potential to become butterflies.

To achieve this, you must undergo your own human metamorphosis and transform yourself into your new you. By doing so, you can attain the most beautiful version of yourself.

Through this transformation, you begin to experience a sense of inner harmony and equilibrium as you align yourself with the fundamental truths of your existence. This newfound equilibrium empowers you to navigate life's challenges with greater composure and a sense of ease. The inner landscape of your feelings and thoughts becomes more serene, allowing you to face life's ups and downs with resilience.

In parallel, your interactions with the external world take on a new dimension. Life itself starts to flow more naturally and effortlessly. You find yourself releasing the need for excessive control over the uncertainties of the future and instead begin to embrace and enjoy the serendipity and unpredictability of existence. This shift in perspective empowers you to experience life's events with a sense of ease and acceptance. You come to understand that there is a greater plan at play, and by relinquishing the need for excessive control, you begin to trust the unfolding of your destiny.

A heightened awareness of connectivity and synchronicity dawns upon you. Seemingly random consequences in life begin to hold deeper meaning. You start to recognize that your actions and choices have weight. You begin to notice patterns and connections between different occurrences in your life. The dots start to connect, revealing the interesting web of synchronicity and interconnectedness. You begin to see the meaning of everything around you. All the good and bad that exist within you and the world around you begin to make sense. This heightened awareness enables you to see how events and experiences are interwoven, each playing a role in your personal development and growth.

You transition from a state of resistance and control to one of acceptance and flow. This shift allows you to navigate life with greater wisdom and grace, experiencing the profound beauty in existence. Your interactions with the external world become richer and more meaningful, and you begin to perceive the subtle threads that link the events and circumstances of your life. This journey of self-discovery and alignment ultimately leads to a deeper sense of purpose, connection, and fulfillment.

Chapter 6: Logical and Moral Balance

In the beautiful tapestry of existence, picture life as a delicate balancing act; tilt too far in one direction, and the consequences can be dire, making living harsher and less forgiving. Yet, when balance is struck just right, life flows smoothly.

This delicate balance of life rests on two pillars of logic and morality. Imagine the pillars of logic and morality as your own legs, keeping you upright, balanced, and in control. To navigate life's twists and turns, you must constantly strive to keep yourself balanced by correctly using logic and morality, ensuring you stay on your feet and move forward with ease. When both are in harmony, you walk through life with grace and ease. But when one falters, you limp along, and when both collapse, you find yourself crawling through the journey of life.

Now, let's discuss logic first, then we will get into morality a bit later. What is logic?

Logic enables you to perceive reality through the power of reasoning. It illuminates your path through the maze of choices in your daily life. When used properly, logic enables you to make optimal decisions while minimizing risks and maximizing outcomes.

Now let's discuss what it means to have balanced logic or imbalanced logic? Achieving logical balance means being able to make sound decisions in all aspects of life. Yet, many times, as we navigate through our daily choices, inconsistencies arise in how we use logic. We may excel in one area, wielding reason skillfully, while stumbling in another, giving in to irrationality and inconsistency. This is when someone is logical but off-balance.

Imagine a brilliant scientist, admired for his intellect and discoveries. He's a genius whose logical acumen is beyond question. Yet, when it comes to his own well-being, he neglects simple things like exercise and healthy eating. Instead, he immerses himself in science, ignoring the importance of taking care of his body. Then, this neglect catches up with him, his health declines rapidly, and he becomes extremely ill. Despite his logical mind in science, he meets an early death due to his illogical choices regarding diet and exercise. This is what I would refer to as unbalanced logic or logical imbalance.

The tale of the scientist is a poignant reminder that being logical in one aspect of life doesn't protect you from the consequences of ignoring logic in other areas. The key lies in finding a balance and applying logic holistically to all areas of life.

Imagine you're a mathematician, exceptionally skilled with numbers, and you earn your living through this talent. However, let's say you lack an understanding of the logic behind finance, investments, or how money flows within society. Despite your mathematical expertise, you could still struggle with managing your finances. This disconnect diminishes the potential of your talent because, while you excel at generating income through your skill, you lack the logical framework necessary to ensure your money is managed and invested wisely. Math and finance, while seemingly connected, operate under entirely different frameworks of logic.

Now consider diet and exercise. If you follow a well-balanced diet without exercising, you won't fully enjoy the benefits of a healthy body. To achieve true health, both proper nutrition and regular exercise are essential. Neglecting one will prevent you from fully reaping the rewards of the other and an overall healthy lifestyle. Similarly, to thrive in life, you must apply logic thoughtfully and consistently across each and every domain of your life.

Balanced logic serves as the thread linking the different aspects of your life, creating a harmonious flow between them. For instance, the logic you use to build your career and generate income connects with the logic required to manage your finances. With better financial stability, you gain the freedom to invest in quality food, improving your diet. A healthy diet, in turn, nourishes your body and mind, providing the energy and motivation needed to exercise and further nurture both your physical and mental well-being. Having a healthy body and mind can significantly enhance your ability to excel in your career, which, in turn, can lead to generating greater income. This interconnectedness creates a positive feedback loop that enhances every area of your life.

Now imagine this link is broken. Let's say you never took the time to become educated in financial literacy, leaving you struggling to manage your finances and constantly finding yourself short on money. Even though you earn a good income, it never feels like enough. This financial instability affects your choices when buying food, pushing you toward cheaper, processed options to save money. A poor diet leaves you without the proper energy to motivate yourself to work out. Without exercise and a good diet, your physical and mental health begins to decline. With poor health, your ability to perform well at work diminishes significantly, reducing your productivity and hindering your ability to advance in your career and generate higher income. This will keep you in a cycle of financial instability, which, in turn, affects your ability to maintain a healthy diet, engage in regular exercise, and ultimately negatively impacts your overall well-being. Thus, the cycle continues in a downward spiral of negative feedback.

Logic is like a chain. Picture it in your mind—a series of interlocking loops, each one essential to the strength of the whole. Each loop of this logical chain represents a specific aspect of your reasoning. This is what I call balanced logic—a system where every link works in harmony to hold things together. But like a chain, the strength of this system is only as good as its weakest link.

When the links in the chain are strong, they work together seamlessly. Imagine a chain suspending a weight. As long as each link holds firm, the entire structure remains solid, capable of withstanding tension, strain, and pressure. Balanced logic works in the same way. For example, if your logic for maintaining a healthy diet is strong, it supports the next link: exercise. Exercise then reinforces your health, which, in turn, strengthens your performance in daily life. This steady progression ensures that the chain of logic keeps your life aligned and moving forward.

Now, visualize what happens when one link in the chain is weak. Let's say you neglect your diet. That link begins to bend and crack under pressure. The next link—exercise—loses its support, making it harder to maintain physical activity. As this weakness spreads, your health begins to falter, your performance drops, and the entire chain begins to unravel.

Eventually, the strain becomes too much to bear, and the chain snaps under the weight of life. When this happens, the heavy pull of life drags you down, causing you to stumble and lose your logical balance.

On the other hand, when each link is strong, the chain becomes almost unbreakable. Even under the greatest stress, it holds together because the force is distributed evenly across the links. Balanced logic works in much the same way. When your reasonings align with a healthy lifestyle and your choices support your goals, every aspect of your life reinforces the others. The chain of your logic doesn't just endure—it thrives under the weight of challenges, pulling you toward greater aspirations.

If you find yourself limping along your life journey, unable to find stability or direction, take a moment to look for a broken link in your logic. There is something you do that you shouldn't, or something you don't do that you should, which holds you back and keeps you stuck, preventing you from moving forward with ease. Sometimes, one small inconsistency or overlooked issue can disrupt the balance of your entire life. Identify the root cause of that imbalance and work to fix it. Once you address the core issue, you'll notice how many other aspects of your life begin to improve naturally, as if a chain reaction of positive change is set into motion.

As for myself, I wasn't a particularly bright kid growing up, and I had many bad habits that kept me stuck in a cycle of frustration and dissatisfaction. Over the years, however, I learned to identify the broken links in my logical understanding and began to fix them. One of the biggest broken links in my life was my addiction to cigarettes.

I grew up as a smoker from a very young age. By my late teens, I was already a heavy chain smoker, consuming at least a pack a day. During that time, I always felt unsatisfied with life. I was constantly angry, disappointed, and overwhelmed, unable to figure out what was wrong with me. No matter what I tried, nothing seemed to go my way, and happiness felt out of reach. It wasn't until I started noticing patterns in my own behavior that I began to understand the root of the problem.

I realized that every time I felt stressed, I would smoke. When I was disappointed or faced failure, I smoked more. Cigarettes had become my primary coping mechanism. I also used smoking to suppress my negative feelings and amplify the positive ones. When I was angry, I would smoke to calm down; when I was sad, I smoked to feel better. Yet, when I was happy, I smoked to celebrate, and when I was excited, I smoked to stay elated. Worse yet, smoking wasn't just about coping and modifying my feelings; it had also become a reward system. This is true for many smokers. Let's say I had been working hard on a task and finally completed it—my first instinct was to reward myself with a smoke. Here's where the logic completely breaks down: I would push my body and mind to complete a difficult task, stressing myself out, and instead of nourishing myself with something healthy, I would reward myself with a cigarette—something my body absolutely didn't want or need but that my addiction craved.

When I recognized that I was using cigarettes as a reward system, a coping mechanism, and modifying my feelings—neither of which actually helped me—I became more motivated to quit. I started developing strategies to replace smoking with healthier alternatives. For example, when I felt down, instead of lighting up another cigarette, I'd call a good friend to talk about my feelings. When I felt the need for a break, I started drinking a glass of water instead of reaching for a cigarette. Water became my replacement for smoke breaks.

Quitting wasn't easy. I spent years in a cycle of quitting and relapsing, only to quit and relapse again. But every time I smoked less, I began to feel a little better. When I finally succeeded in quitting for good, my life changed drastically. I realized how much time, money, and energy I had wasted on smoking for so many years. My health improved significantly. I could exercise more, my body felt better, my focus sharpened, and my mental clarity increased. Most importantly, I began to discover who I truly was—I began to understand the fluctuations in my thoughts and feelings and how they impact my mood and personality.

Logical imbalances—such as rewarding oneself with something harmful or using something destructive to cope with life's challenges—are incredibly common practices. When the mind is not trained to face challenges properly, we will fall into self-destructive patterns to numb ourselves—patterns that only make things worse.

Think about alcoholics, for example. When life gets tough, they drink more, even though sobriety is what they actually need most. Or, when stumbling around drunk, they reach for another beer, instead of water. It's the same with people who are struggling financially. As soon as they make a little extra money—money that could genuinely solve some of their problems—they spend it on gadgets or things they don't need.

Today, the most widespread coping mechanism is mindlessly scrolling through a phone screen. When someone feels bad, instead of addressing their problems, they turn to social media, endlessly scrolling for a distraction. This behavior is illogical. And it's not just limited to uneducated or struggling individuals—successful people, including doctors, lawyers, and entrepreneurs, fall into these traps as well.

The truth is that logical imbalance doesn't discriminate. Even intelligent, accomplished people can engage in self-sabotaging behaviors when they fail to identify and repair the broken links in their logic. As a result, they will suffer despite their success and accolades.

Similarly, if you find yourself struggling with life and unable to make meaningful progress, take a closer look at your vices. Ask yourself: what habits or behaviors are holding you back the most? These vices often serve as coping mechanisms for deeper issues, masking the root of your struggles. Yet, they are the very things hindering your growth and well-being.

Your most persistent problems are deeply tied to your habits, which may seem like small comforts in the moment but cause significant harm over time. These vices could range from substance abuse to excessive screen time, porn addiction, procrastination, overeating, unhealthy relationships, or even negative thought patterns. They feed into a cycle that keeps you stuck, creating temporary relief but worsening your situation in the long run.

To truly transform your life, you must confront and resolve the root causes of your struggles. Simply trimming the weeds in your backyard won't prevent them from growing back; you must pull them out by the roots. Trying to change surface-level behaviors without addressing their deeper causes will not lead to real or lasting improvement. The roots will keep feeding the same destructive patterns, and the cycle will continue.

The root of your problems lies in the weakest link in the chain of your behaviors, habits, impulses, and thoughts. Identify that weakest link, strengthen it, and you'll find that your entire life transforms along with it.

If your struggles are tied to a logical imbalance, the path to resolution lies in identifying and confronting these behaviors. This requires honesty with yourself and the courage to change what isn't serving you. By fixing the roots, you set the stage for real and sustainable growth, allowing yourself to finally move forward and enjoy the improvements you've been seeking.

The point here is simple: as long as there are broken links in your logic—whether in your actions, thoughts, or feelings—you cannot make meaningful and lasting changes in your life. Every small inconsistency, every overlooked misstep in your reasoning, holds you back more than you might realize. It's tempting to focus on chasing after big goals or solving grand problems while dismissing the smaller, seemingly insignificant issues. But this approach is flawed.

True transformation begins when you address the little things—the overlooked habits, the minor inconsistencies, the small cracks in your foundation. When you take the time to fix these, larger, positive changes follow naturally.

Imbalanced logic is like trying to run a marathon while limping. No matter how much effort you put in, the imbalance keeps slowing you down. You cannot expect to get ahead, no matter how much you push, if you're dragging the weight of broken logic along with you. To truly move forward, you must first learn to walk steadily by addressing the small cracks in your reasoning, enabling you to take purposeful and effective strides toward your goals.

In later chapters, we will delve deep into the techniques for addressing logical imbalances, overcoming bad habits, and cultivating productive ones. For now, focus on identifying the elements in your life that need to change—whether they are habits, routines, behaviors, or even relationships. Take note of the things that need to be added to your life to propel you forward, as well as the things that must be removed to stop holding you back.

For now, take a moment to identify and write down the logical imbalances in your personality. Create two columns: one for missing links—things you need to add to your life—and another for weak links, your vices and bad habits that need improvement. As the days go by, whenever you realize another weak or missing link in your personality, add it to the list.

Once your list begins to take shape, prioritize these links based on their importance, the intensity of their negative impact on your life, and your current level of strength to overcome them. Use a numbering system to assign weight to each link. Some changes will require more effort, while others may be easier to tackle first. Organize them in a way that makes sense to you.

Next, take it a step further—write down how each weak or missing link negatively affects your life. Be specific. Perhaps your bad diet has led to weight gain, and that extra weight demotivates you from exercising. Maybe your poor sleep habits make you sluggish and unproductive throughout the day. If you struggle with procrastination, note how it has delayed your progress in different areas of life.

Make your list elaborate—detailed enough that, when you look at it, it reflects an honest portrait of your weaknesses. Let it be a map of your logical imbalances, showing both your missing and weak links. To improve yourself, you must first know your own weaknesses. Recognize what's keeping you stuck, and in later chapters, we will discuss how you can address them—one link at a time.

Awareness is the key point here. You cannot fix what you do not acknowledge. Once you have clarity about what needs to change, you'll be better prepared to implement the strategies that will be discussed later.

Now, let's examine the broken links of logic within humanity as a whole and the imbalances that manifest on a global scale.

In our modern world, we are surrounded by technological marvels and mass-produced goods—testaments to human ingenuity and sharp logic. Yet, amidst this progress, there's a glaring issue and that is our inability to manage the waste generated by these production lines. As we chase after progress and new technologies, we find ourselves hurtling toward disaster, drowning in the waste of our own creation.

If this lopsided pattern persists, our planet will drown in a sea of waste, making it uninhabitable. Yet, despite this glaring illogicality, we seem unwilling to fix this destructive cycle of production and waste mismanagement.

When we, as individuals, fail to apply logic holistically, we negatively impact the quality of our own lives and those around us. On a larger scale, when humanity collectively neglects the proper use of logic, the consequences become alarmingly dangerous, threatening the well-being of not just individuals but the entire planet.

Globally, we've become addicted to production and consumption, all while neglecting the crucial need for proper waste management. It's like an alcoholic who becomes increasingly dehydrated with each drink but, instead of reaching for water, keeps pouring more alcohol. The consequences of this unchecked cycle of accumulating waste—quite literally piling up in landfills and oceans—are dire, posing a severe threat to our planet's future.

You and I cannot single-handedly resolve these global issues, but that doesn't mean we should simply throw our hands up in defeat. Even small, conscious efforts can make a difference. Start by minimizing your participation in this destructive cycle of waste generation. Resist the lure of consumer culture, which constantly pressures you to buy new gadgets, toys, and things you don't truly need. Corporations produce products based on demand—they only manufacture as much as they can sell. If people stop buying excessively, these production lines will be forced to scale back. It's simple: less demand means less production, which in turn means less waste.

Be mindful of your consumption. Buy only what you need, and don't overindulge. When you do make purchases, consider their environmental impact. Choose products with minimal packaging, biodegradable materials, or those designed to produce less waste. Buy your products from companies that actively strive to reduce their ecological footprint and manage their waste responsibly. Every dollar you spend, you're casting a vote for the kind of world you want to live in—so use your purchasing power wisely.

You're a creator of the future. With every choice you make and every dollar you spend, you contribute to shaping the world. Think carefully about who you're supporting and what kind of impact your actions have on the planet. Be mindful, and let your choices reflect the change you wish to see.

Now let's look at one more example of humanity's illogical thinking. Consider the atomic bomb—a testament to humanity's capability for destruction. With atomic bombs, we pose a significant threat to our own survival. While it is logically sound that higher power weapons can protect us from our enemies today, it becomes equally illogical when we consider that the enemies we aim to eradicate are fellow humans on our own planet. It is further illogical to anticipate that tomorrow, those very adversaries we strive to eliminate might retaliate with even more potent weapons if given the chance. The continuous cycle of mutual destruction with increasingly formidable weapons can only lead to one inevitable outcome: the annihilation of all.

For millennia, our history has been marred by tales of conquest, violence, and exploitation. Despite our advancements, the cycle of wars and self-inflicted disasters persists. If the ultimate aim is to ensure the survival of humanity, then much of what we've done throughout history doesn't align with this goal.

Don't fuel this violence. Disagreements over political views, religious beliefs, or cultural differences should never justify conflict or hatred. The world already bears enough pain and suffering caused by those in power. Don't walk in their footsteps. Instead, strive to build bridges where divisions exist. Use the concept of quaternity—balancing understanding, empathy, and logic—to approach others with compassion, even when their views differ from yours.

Once again, you and I cannot single-handedly resolve the world's problems, but we can choose not to be part of the problem. Instead, we can strive to be part of the solution. By promoting understanding, refusing to participate in cycles of violence and division, and extending kindness to others, we take small yet meaningful steps toward a better world. Every individual choice matters, and even a ripple can contribute to the larger wave of change.

The key takeaway here is that addressing illogical thinking is crucial. When left unchecked, it can severely degrade the quality of life. On a larger scale, logical imbalances negatively affect our collective welfare, steering humanity toward catastrophic consequences—even the risk of the extinction of our species.

If humanity is to survive these precarious times, it comes down to the choices we make today. Collectively, we possess the intelligence, power, and resources to shape Earth into either a heaven or a hell of our own making. The future isn't some distant, intangible thing—it's built moment by moment through the actions we take now. Every decision matters. Every small act of goodness, every step in the right direction, contributes to the larger picture.

If you strive to become a better person than you were yesterday, no matter how small the improvement, you're making a positive impact. Change begins within. When you commit to doing what is right—choosing integrity, compassion, and kindness—you will inspire others around you. And if enough of us make this commitment, the ripple effect can shift the direction of humanity as a whole.

Positive change is possible when we act collectively. Let us each do our part, and together, let us show the world that the light of hope and progress can shine brighter than the darkness of despair and stagnation. A better world begins with us.

Thus far, we've explored the importance of balance in logical reasoning. Now, let's turn our attention to the significance of moral balance. Just as logic weaves its threads through the fabric of our decisions and actions, morality forms the moral compass that guides our behavior. Having moral balance means holding and embracing an unwavering commitment to truth across all aspects of life.

Navigating the realm of morality is a challenging journey. The difficulty lies in the fact that distinguishing right from wrong is rarely straightforward, as it's easy to rationalize wrongdoings. Let's begin with a simple example where distinguishing between right and wrong is relatively clear. Take, for instance, someone who refrains from stealing from friends but sees no issue in stealing from large corporations, convinced they're striking back against perceived injustices and that these corporations are the true culprits.

Theft, an inherently immoral act, defies justification given the far-reaching consequences it brings. Let's discuss why stealing from corporations remains immoral regardless of their perceived evil nature. When corporations endure losses, they refuse to let their profit margins shrink. Instead, they stabilize their profit margin by reducing employee wages and bonuses, placing a heavier burden on everyday workers. Furthermore, corporations may opt to increase the prices of their products, affecting all consumers. While some may justify stealing from corporations as a blow against big business, they're actually harming the most vulnerable people who rely on these corporations for jobs and resources.

Sometimes we not only justify moral wrongdoings but even glorify them. This is when we utterly fail to distinguish right from wrong. One legendary figure in our culture is Robin Hood, a symbol of supposedly righteous defiance who takes from the wealthy to provide for the less fortunate. In Robin Hood's tale, the wealthy are humbled, brought to their knees, and yield to the needs of the less privileged. However, this narrative, while captivating, seldom actualizes. In truth, such a happy ending is an empty dream, and the likelihood of it ever becoming a reality remains slim.

Stealing from the rich doesn't address the root causes of wealth inequality. Instead, it deepens resentment and animosity between the wealthy and the less fortunate. Stealing from the wealthy might seem like a way to balance the scale, but it often backfires. Those in control of the economy, who are typically the wealthy, will retaliate against such actions by increasing prices, healthcare costs, and interest rates, while reducing benefits, retirement plans, and wages for the less fortunate. This Robin Hood mentality only leads to a more hostile environment for the poor, exacerbating their struggles and hardships, and making their already difficult lives even tougher.

In the real world, as wealth starts to accumulate in the hands of a privileged few within a country, one group of people align themselves with the interests of the wealthy, creating an oppressive and rigid system for the rest. Concurrently, another group of people rise to prominence, demanding liberation and wealth redistribution.

The core moral issue with wealth redistribution through force lies in the fact that it isn't a willingly bestowed act. Moreover, it fails to address the root causes of wealth concentration, leaving the system vulnerable to recurring wealth inequality. Taking wealth by force from one group and redistributing it to another will breed animosity and resentment, exacerbating the existing divisions. This sets the stage for a polarized society that erodes the system from both ends, akin to a building collapsing from opposing sides.

If this trend persists, the middle class will continue to shrink. Some individuals will ascend toward greater wealth, while many others will plummet into financial turmoil and scarcity. Consequently, cities will become increasingly unstable, with crime rates soaring in both frequency and severity. The impoverished will incite chaos and destruction, while the affluent will further indulge their greed, mercilessly exploiting the poor without remorse. The wealthy show no compassion for the less fortunate, while the poor are depicted as unruly and crude.

In this dire scenario, the opposing governing bodies find themselves locked in a relentless struggle to dominate one another, with their followers mirroring the divisive actions of their respective factions. The result is a society marred by a toxic cocktail of anger, hatred, despair, and misery.

As turbulence intensifies, society will find itself in freefall, spiraling into an abyss of darkness. The divisive forces tearing at the societal fabric leave a void, as loneliness and a yearning for meaningful connections increasingly take hold within the hearts of people living in these troubled societies. In these societies, suffering knows no distinctions. It befalls every individual, whether rich or poor, powerful or weak, as darkness, in its indiscriminate nature, envelops all.

One underlying reason for such a dire situation is our tendency to romanticize figures like Robin Hood and glorify the immoral act of stealing. In today's world, many advocate for taking wealth by force from the rich, which in essence is no different than stealing. This stems from a moral imbalance, where we perceive actions that are morally wrong as virtuous and admirable. We have to give up the Robin Hood mentality and find real solutions to the problems of our current era that are rooted in high morality.

The moral dilemma lies in the realization that we cannot rectify a situation by worsening it. Simply, we can't fix anything by breaking it. Responding to resentment with more resentment only perpetuates the cycle. Anger, hatred, and similar divisive forces cannot unite us or solve the challenges our world faces today. The abundance of hate, anger, and revenge in the world is already fracturing our societies. Adding more anger and hatred will not remedy anything; history has shown us that it never has and never will. Morality, like the laws of gravity, entails steadfast principles. We cannot eradicate impurity by embracing further impurity.

Another instance of imbalanced morality emerges in the dynamics surrounding revenge, where truth becomes obscured and rationalized. Revenge is often portrayed as justice, but this could not be further from the truth. Revenge is often glorified in movies, where mistreated protagonists seek vengeance, presenting a seemingly satisfying conclusion where villains are vanquished. Unfortunately, reality rarely mirrors this cinematic narrative.

Retaliation, instead of extinguishing animosity, typically fuels greater resentment, setting in motion a destructive cycle of retaliatory actions from both sides. This perpetual cycle of hate and anger only deepens the chasm of separation and isolation. Mahatma Gandhi summed up the problem with revenge in one simple sentence: "An eye for an eye leaves the whole world blind."

As individuals drift farther from the truth, the line between revenge and justice becomes blurred. While justice is intended to halt negative and malevolent acts, revenge responds to malevolence with further malevolence, representing a morally flawed structure. In truth, revenge does not serve justice, and justice does not advocate revenge. Revenge aligns with darkness and evokes evil, while justice embodies light and glory.

Unfortunately, this view of revenge as a virtuous act is widespread in our societies today, largely promoted by Hollywood movies. Promoting revenge as a virtue deepens the anger and hatred within the hearts of those who embrace this immoral act, causing them to drift further away from the truth.

Do not fall for Hollywood's portrayal of virtue, nor accept the broader moral standards imposed by society. If you allow revenge to fill you with anger and hatred, you will unknowingly choose actions you perceive as virtuous but are, in reality, tainted by malevolence. True understanding of morality lies in your ability to discern truth, and when negative emotions take root within you, they cloud your perception, blinding you to that truth.

The concept of trying to cleanse one impurity with another is fundamentally flawed. Consider examples we've discussed, such as justifying theft from the rich because they've exploited the poor, or seeking revenge against someone who wronged us in the name of justice. These actions, while seemingly well-intentioned, stem from a misguided belief that one can counteract malevolence with malevolence, which only perpetuates a cycle of moral deterioration. Such solutions are at times embraced as benevolent and justified actions, constituting the core of moral imbalance within society.

Distinguishing the virtuous from the malevolence is a considerably complex endeavor. This creates a space within the domain of morality where deceit and falsehood can flourish. It's essential to recognize that most people do not inherently desire to commit evil acts; rather, they grapple with confusion between what is truly good and what is perceived as evil. The problem deepens when a majority within any society misconstrues darkness as light, creating an environment where advocating for truth becomes exceedingly challenging. Imbalance in morality degrades both the individuals and the system. It takes away the glory bit by bit until nothing is left.

Across the wisdom of many faiths and ancient texts, this message has been clearly announced: beware of confusing good with evil, truth with falsehood, light with darkness.

The Bible warns directly: "Woe to those who call evil good, and good evil; who put darkness for light, and light for darkness; who put bitter for sweet, and sweet for bitter!".

The Qur'an echoes this caution, saying: "And do not mix the truth with falsehood or conceal the truth while you know [it]."

In Buddhism, the Anguttara Nikaya states: "There is a way in which someone thinks wrong is right and right is wrong. The fool, overwhelmed and corrupted by wrong thoughts, sees things upside down." Similarly, the Dhammapada warns: "If one sees what is not as what is, and what is as what is not, then they follow falsehood and seek the fruit of deceit."

In the Bhagavad Gita, it is written: "That understanding which considers irreligion to be religion and religion to be irreligion, and which operates under a distorted perception, O Partha, is of the nature of ignorance."

The Sikh Guru Granth Sahib teaches: "They are mistaken, misguided; deluded by doubt, they dwell in the darkness of falsehood. Without the Guru's light, they wander, perceiving wrong as right and right as wrong."

In Taoism, Zhuangzi speaks of this confusion: "Right is not always right, and wrong is not always wrong; what seems beautiful may be ugly, and what seems ugly may be beautiful. Only when one aligns with the Way is the true nature of things revealed."

In all these teachings, the message is clear: it's easy to mistake darkness for light and light for darkness, especially in today's world where truth and deception often mix. Only through an earnest desire to seek truth can one see the world as it truly is.

Across the ages, we have borne witness to the rise of leaders who wield their influence through hatred, anger, racism, and other divisive attributes. Leaders characterized by imbalanced morality draw followers who share their moral misalignment. At the same time, as societal morality wavers and tilts toward imbalance, it inadvertently creates fertile ground for next leaders and followers to share similar traits. In such societies where morality is lacking, individuals with vanity, narcissism, and sociopathic traits are attracted to power and rise to the top promoting the worst of human traits. Such leaders are present among all branches of power such as religious leaders, political leaders, business leaders and such.

If the societal system does not have enough checks and balances in place to limit the concentration of power and wealth, then narcissists naturally rise to the top because they feed off the greed and pleasure they receive from accumulating more power and wealth. This is what is wrong with our societies today. Narcissists are attracted to wealth and power, and ordinary people admire both power and wealth, as well as the individuals possessing them, thus glorifying and reinforcing narcissistic traits.

Moreover, in societies facing moral decline, dogmas, cults, religions, and ideologies become exceptionally dangerous as they can be misused. Remember the first law of consciousness: as we move from the known to the unknown, and from the visible to the invisible, the level of abstraction increases. This increase in abstraction within unknown and invisible realms leads to heightened complexity, confusion, and creates fertile ground for darkness and deceit to flourish.

Since religions claim to have comprehensive knowledge of God and the afterlife, they belong to the far end of the unknown and invisible realms. Religions can become deadly weapons in the hands of corrupt leaders. We've witnessed the havoc wreaked by religion throughout history and even in modern times. Such potent tools as religion attract psychopaths and narcissists in morally depleted societies. They thrive on dominating and controlling other people's minds and bodies. Religion empowers them, allowing them to claim divine authority and manipulate people into action by promising salvation.

Consider the unsettling cases of certain Catholic priests who have faced accusations of child molestation. These individuals, ordained as men of God and entrusted with the sacred responsibility of spreading love and peace, have instead become the very source of suffering for vulnerable children. Their actions represent a deep betrayal of the very faith they claim to serve.

When morality declines within a society, the worst of humanity inevitably rises to positions of power. And this corruption is not limited to Christianity alone. Throughout history, various religious groups, at different points in time, have been involved in acts of mass murder, genocide, rape, and abuse, all under the banner of righteousness. These horrors stem from misunderstanding of truth in morality.

The inability to accurately measure morality creates fertile ground for deceit, allowing lies to be cloaked in the guise of truth and wielded as tools for power and personal gain. When there is no clear and collective understanding of what is truly moral, morality becomes a weapon in the hands of those who seek control. They exploit the faith and trust of others, turning sacred principles into instruments of oppression rather than liberation.

In these examples, we have discussed how imbalances in morality can lead to theft and revenge being glorified, and how narcissistic and psychopathic traits can become admired. When it comes to religion, even mass genocides in the name of God can be exalted.

In a nutshell, our mental well-being depends on our understanding of morality. Morality is elusive, subtle, and invisible. Its boundaries vary from person to person and from time to time. It cannot be seen, touched, smelled, heard, or tasted. It cannot be written and described by science. It cannot be drawn or crafted by art. Morality can only be sensed through a relentless hunt for the truth.

The central theme of this chapter emphasizes the imperative need to constantly maintain a check and balance on both our logical and moral understanding, ensuring that we steadfastly tread the path of righteousness. The allure of greed, vanity, and self-importance poses a constant threat, making it remarkably easy to deviate from the path of light.

The gravity of the situation intensifies when these logical and moral imbalances proliferate among many individuals in a society, causing the entire societal fabric to unravel and descend into imbalance and destruction. Whether it's a lapse in logical understanding or a breakdown in moral comprehension, the consequences are severe and far-reaching, ushering in a cascade of agony, pain, misery, despair, and destruction. Here, the emphasis is the fragility of the delicate balance we must maintain within ourselves and in our societies to safeguard against the perils of misdirection and chaos.

Departure from truth plunges us into darkness, where unease, distress, and anxiety prevail. In the broader context of society, moral and logical imbalances manifest as detrimental forces, sparking a chain reaction of negative consequences. These imbalances become a catalyst for increased illnesses, a rise in suicide rates, the exacerbation of dogmatic polarization, and a surge in societal separation and isolation.

The core message of this chapter revolves around the importance of balance and alignment with truth. In today's world, you may find yourself crushed under the weight of life's demands, beaten down into submission, and forced to crawl through life. The initial step toward reclaiming your strength is to establish balance. This metaphorical balance can only be attained by refining, honing, and improving your faculties of logic and morality. Just as you rely on your legs to lift you upright and maintain physical balance when rising from the ground, you must rely on proper logic and morality to uplift your mental state and stand tall when feeling mentally down.

Without proper logic and morality, you are destined to endure endless suffering. However, with your moral and logical balance finely tuned, you can stand tall, regardless of the pressure of society on your back. In the final chapters, we will delve into strategies for achieving this moral and logical balance.

So, the idea here is simple: you've got to make sure your head and your heart are in tune with what is true. It's about standing tall and walking confidently through life's ups and downs, instead of staying stuck in a crawl.

Chapter 7: Thoughts and Emotions

Have you ever wondered why you think so much? Why is it that you are unable to stop the ceaseless chatter of your mind? Let's break down the structure of the thoughts so we can better understand what is happening in the mind.

First, let's categorize thoughts into two types: passive and active. Picture passive thoughts as the constant murmurs that persist in your mind. You can't stop these passive thoughts from crossing your mind. As soon as you stop thinking about a subject, another thought replaces it. They persist, unbidden, like chatter in a crowded room. You can practice meditation and slow down your thoughts, but you can never fully stop them. As soon as the meditation is over, passive thoughts come right back.

Conversely, active thoughts arise when you purposefully engage your mind, pondering, problem-solving, and seeking solutions to your daily problems. Sometimes, you use your active thinking to find answers to the puzzles that passive thoughts pose in your mind. It's as if your active thoughts try to untangle the problems presented by your passive mental chatter.

But where do these passive thoughts originate from? While many believe we create our own thoughts, I propose an alternative perspective. I believe some of our thoughts are planted in our minds through a concept called "collective consciousness." Imagine a vast web of interconnected human minds, with each thought acting as the thread that weaves our minds together, forming a network known as the collective consciousness. Let's explore some examples of collective consciousness and its relation to our passive thoughts.

In the 1970s, there was an experiment known as the Hundredth Monkey Effect. Basically, on an island in Japan called Koshima, monkeys started washing sweet potatoes, and once enough of them picked up the habit, monkeys on other islands started washing their sweet potatoes as well, without any direct contact with the monkey's in Koshima island. Basically, monkeys on different islands learned behaviors from one another without any physical interactions, as if they could read each other's thoughts across vast distances.

As humans, we also have a profound impact on each other in ways that are subtle yet powerful. One example of this interconnectedness is a concept introduced in the 1970s by Maharishi Mahesh yogi, an Indian spiritual leader, which has come to be known as the Maharishi Effect. He noticed that when a certain percentage of a population practices group meditation, it leads to positive societal outcomes, such as reduced crime rates, decreased violence, and increased social harmony. The underlying principle is that the coherent, peaceful energy generated by group meditation influences and uplifts the collective consciousness, fostering a more harmonious and balanced society.

Furthermore, an organization named Institute of Noetic Science is working on a project called the Global Consciousness Grid, also known as the Global Consciousness Project. This project is an international, multidisciplinary collaboration of scientists and engineers which seeks to understand the interactions between human consciousness and the environment.

In one specific experiment, two people were brought into a room to meditate together in a synchronized manner. After establishing this connection, one of the participants was moved to a separate, isolated room. Researchers then monitored both participants' brain activity using EEG (electroencephalogram) and fMRI (functional magnetic resonance imaging).

During the test, one participant was exposed to flashes of light, which would naturally stimulate specific areas of their brain. Remarkably, researchers observed that the brain of the other participant—who was not exposed to the light—showed activity as if they, too, were perceiving the flashes of light. This phenomenon, referred to as "entangled minds" or "non-local consciousness," suggests that our minds are interconnected in ways that science has yet to fully understand.

In another experiment, the Institute of Noetic Science placed several dozen computers in various locations around the world. These computers are programmed to generate random numbers continuously.

Scientists then analyze these numbers to look for patterns. Over time, they noticed something intriguing: during significant global events—such as natural disasters, major terrorist attacks, or large-scale celebrations—the random numbers showed unusual patterns and deviations from their typical randomness.

A similar study was done at Princeton University, as a collaboration on the Global Consciousness Project. The university website features a quote noting that "coherent consciousness creates order in the world. Subtle interactions link us with each other and the Earth." Princeton University researchers calculated the odds of one in a trillion that the impact of our thoughts and emotions on our surroundings, including computers, is purely random. Essentially, they believe that every thought and emotion influences the world in ways that go far beyond our current scientific understanding.

Yet, another organization, the HeartMath Institute, is working on an international project called the Global Coherence Initiative to explore the link between human consciousness and the Earth's magnetic fields. Utilizing advanced technology, they are determined to discover how collective human emotions, thoughts, and intentions influence the Earth's energetic systems. They aim to uncover how our collective thoughts and emotions impact the Earth's magnetic fields and, in turn, how these fields influence human behavior and well-being.

Scientists, all around the world, are exploring many similar groundbreaking research projects that delves into the mysteries of collective consciousness and its far-reaching implications. Their findings imply that our thoughts and emotions are not isolated experiences; they extend outward, subtly affecting the behavior of other people as well as computers and everything else in existence. In essence, every thought and emotion you experience has a ripple effect on the entire planet, all its inhabitants, and every entity within it.

There are moments in life that hint at this interconnectedness, suggesting that our minds are intertwined in a vast network of collective consciousness. Have you ever noticed how you might think about a friend, only to receive a message from them shortly after? These events are not meaningless coincidences; they are the result of our deeper interconnectedness. When your thoughts align with another person, it creates a shared string of thought, an invisible thread that ties your minds together within the fabric of collective consciousness.

When you think of a friend and then receive a message from them, it's clear they must have been thinking of you too. These similar strings of thought—between you and your friend—are the threads that weave the fabric of the collective consciousness, linking minds together in subtle yet profound ways.

In essence, your passive thoughts emerge from the collective consciousness and manifest as voices in your head. Your active thoughts are the critical thinking of the rational mind responding to the passive thoughts that emerge before it.

Your passive thoughts spontaneously make you think of a friend, as if the idea floated into your mind out of nowhere. Then, your active thoughts take over, analyzing and deciding, propelling you to pick up the phone and give them a call. This interplay between passive and active thought is how your mind functions—a delicate balance of the automatic and the controlled, the passive and the active.

Researchers propose that each person generates at least 10,000 thoughts daily, equating to a new thought emerging in the mind every 5 to 10 seconds. Your passive thoughts resemble the rhythm of breathing—they occur automatically, coming and going until you deliberately focus on them. By directing your attention to your thoughts, much like monitoring your breath, you attain a degree of control over them. Just as you can slow down and hold your breath for a while but can never completely stop breathing, you can slow down your thoughts and stop thinking for a short period but can never completely stop thinking. In short, this interplay between passive and active thought mirrors the relationship between automatic and controlled breathing: passive thoughts arise naturally, while active thoughts require deliberate focus.

So, this is how your mind process thoughts: approximately every 5 seconds, a new thought arises in your mind, presenting you with the choice to pursue and follow the thought or let it go. If you allow the thought to pass, another will surface within a few seconds, continuing the cycle.

Thoughts keep coming, and they have the power to greatly impact your overall well-being. Every time you think of something, it triggers an emotion within you that literally alters your physiology and impacts your physical health. For example, thinking about past grievances can make you feel angry, leading to an increased heart rate, dilated veins, higher body temperature, and the release of hormones like cortisol. On the flip side, reflecting on love can bring about a sense of joy, energy, and motivation, releasing hormones such as oxytocin, dopamine, or serotonin. Moreover, pondering sex may spark feelings of lust, causing sexual arousal. Dwelling in sadness can cause fatigue, changes in appetite, or bodily discomfort. Overthinking and worrying excessively about the future results in anxiety, characterized by fast breathing, tense muscles, and potential digestive disturbances. On the other hand, cultivating hopeful thoughts encourages optimism, which lowers stress levels, relaxes muscles, and potentially slows down the heartbeat. Focusing on gratitude brings about a sense of satisfaction, linked to reduced stress and improved immune function. Furthermore, thinking about potential dangers can trigger fear, leading to the release of adrenaline, an increased heart rate, and sweating. Essentially, whenever you experience a thought, you also experience an emotion that impacts your physical and mental state. Your overall well-being, thoughts, and emotions are all chained together.

In a nutshell, you encounter a new thought roughly every 5 seconds, often without conscious effort. From there, you decide whether to engage with the thought actively or let it pass. If you opt to let it go, another thought swiftly takes its place, presenting a similar decision. However, if you choose to explore a thought, an emotion also arises, triggering physical and mental responses in your body, which ultimately influence your behaviors and actions. But this is just part of the story. To fully understand the mechanism, we must differentiate and redefine emotions and feelings. Although often used interchangeably, emotions and feelings are two entirely distinct aspects of human experience.

Emotions are similar to passive thoughts, both stem from collective consciousness. Feelings, on the other hand, are much like active thinking. You create your feelings but not your emotions. Every time a passive thought crosses your mind, it is accompanied by an emotion. When you choose to delve into a thought and keep thinking about it, you are inevitably bound to deal with the attached emotion. Furthermore, your response to any emotion is to generate a feeling. Just as active thinking follows passive thoughts, feelings follow emotions.

Active thoughts and feelings are how you respond to passive thoughts and the emotions tied to them. Emotions hold a more fundamental role in reality compared to feelings. Emotions exist in the collective consciousness much like passive thoughts. Feelings, in turn, represent your subjective interpretations of these emotions much like your active thinking interprets your passive thoughts.

Imagine you're hiking through a mountain trail when suddenly, a snake appears before you. Regardless of who you are, for a fraction of a second, an emotion of danger grips you along with the passive thought of having to deal with the snake. These instinctive responses of thoughts and emotions are common among all of us. However, what comes next is entirely within your control.

You may choose different ways to deal with the emotion of danger and the thought of how to deal with the snake. If you're experienced with snakes, you might acknowledge the danger but remain composed, lacking the feeling of fear or the thought of fleeting. You might even get excited and chase after the snake to grab and play with it. In this case, your initial emotion of danger transforms into the feeling of excitement, and the thought of how to deal with the snake turns into a thought of chasing after it and playing with it. Conversely, if you've never encountered a snake up close, fear may flood your senses along with the thought of distancing yourself from the snake. In this scenario, the emotion of danger is followed by the feeling of fear, and the initial thought of how to deal with the snake is followed by thought of running away.

The alertness sparked by the presence of the snake is a primal response, an emotion that surges within you involuntarily, accompanied by a thought of having to deal with the snake. Passive thoughts and emotions act as your immediate, instinctual reaction to a situation. In contrast, feelings and active thinking emerge from a more nuanced contemplation of those initial responses.

Let's redraw the web of the human mental landscape in a new light. At the core lies the collective consciousness that injects passive thoughts into your mind roughly every 5 seconds. Each thought arrives with its own emotional charge, awaiting your attention.

When you opt not to entertain a thought, a new one swiftly takes its place, presenting you with a recurring choice. Yet, once you choose to engage with a thought and pull at its thread, your active thinking springs into action. Concurrently, you analyze and interpret the emotion tethered to the original thought, generating feelings within yourself. The way you choose to actively think and feel directly influences the state of your physical and mental well-being, with every cell in your body corresponding to the situation you are in.

Furthermore, the state of your being, prior experiences, and the interplay of active thinking and feeling prompt you to behave in certain ways, thus shaping your actions. These active thoughts, feelings, and actions ripple out into the world, leaving their mark on the fabric of collective consciousness. In response, collective consciousness absorbs your thoughts, feelings, and actions, weaving them into its vast tapestry, while simultaneously sowing the seeds of new thoughts and emotions within your mind. And so, the cycle perpetuates itself forever, an endless dance between individual consciousness and collective consciousness, shaping your life experiences with each passing moment.

Now, think back to the earlier chapters where we explored the idea that every particle comprising your body has traversed the universe for billions of years and that you share your genetic material, your DNA, with all life forms on Earth. Furthermore, we touched upon the notion that all things stem from a shared essence, fragments of consciousness.

Now, let's layer this understanding with the concept of your perpetual connection to the collective consciousness. At every moment, you receive a stream of thoughts and emotions from a higher, more intelligent source—the collective consciousness. Consider that your thoughts and emotions are not solitary experiences but rather threads woven into the fabric of the entire world. You are, in essence, a conduit

131

through which the collective consciousness flows, sharing your innermost experiences with the universe.

In short, the particles comprising your body are what you share with the entire universe. The molecules in your body are what you share with Earth. Your DNA is shared with all living creatures on Earth. And your thoughts and emotions are shared with all of humanity. You are a fragment of consciousness, sharing your essence with all living and non-living entities in the entirety of existence.

We will come back to the concept of the interconnectedness of our existence in the next chapter to draw a more comprehensive picture. But for now, let's switch our focus to the concept of morality to better understand emotions and feelings as well as the distinctions between them.

What exactly is morality? According to the dictionary, morality is "conformity to the rules of right conduct." But what determines what is truly right and wrong? At the surface level, right and wrong seem to be determined by the ethics of society. Yet, the true essence of morality transcends mere societal standards. It is not society that defines morality; rather, it is a universal law rooted in the invisible realm of consciousness.

In its purest form, morality aligns with the harmony of existence. All that supports and sustains this harmony is inherently good, while all that disrupts or resists it is bad. However, as humans, our understanding is limited. We cannot fully grasp what aligns with or disturbs the grand harmony of existence. This limitation means that we do not and cannot know the essence of true morality. However, the essence of morality has been absorbed, reshaped, and modified by our collective consciousness through eons past.

Collective consciousness is a dynamic intelligent entity that encompasses all thoughts, emotions, and experiences of humanity since the dawn of time. This understanding of morality through the lens of collective consciousness has been instilled within you as an inner moral compass. This compass, shared by all humanity, provides you with a foundation for understanding right and wrong.

However, this moral compass also evolves and adapts based on your personal experiences, making morality a unique and ever-changing aspect of your spiritual journey. While the totality of morality is universal and unchanging, your personal moral understanding is fluid, shaped continuously by the experiences you encounter. It is through the lens of this inner moral compass that you discern what is good or bad, navigating your life in the context of an ever-evolving moral landscape.

Your emotions originate from the raw essence of morality that resides deep within the invisible realm. Feelings, on the other hand, are shaped by how you interpret these emotions through the lens of your unique inner moral compass. The closer your inner moral compass aligns with the morality of the collective consciousness—and ultimately the raw essence of morality in the totality of consciousness—the more accurately you interpret emotions and translate them into feelings within your physical body. Conversely, the further your inner moral compass deviates from the totality of morality, the less accurately you interpret emotions, leading to distorted and harmful feelings in your physical body.

Throughout the day, collective consciousness presents you with a series of emotions. You have the power to choose which emotion to focus on and harness its energy. Once a choice is made, you inevitably generate feelings. These feelings interpret the emotion you choose to harness. Your feelings influence how you act and interact with the world around you. These interactions create a ripple effect on the collective consciousness, which in turn recalibrates your inner moral compass and then injects you with a new set of emotions to contemplate.

In essence, your behavior in any given situation determines the refinement of your inner moral compass. The more aligned your actions are with truth and reality, the better calibrated your inner moral compass becomes. This, in turn, allows you to experience more refined emotions, enabling you to better interpret these emotions and cultivate more positive feelings within yourself. Consequently, your actions improve, leading to further refinement of your inner moral compass in a perpetuating cycle of growth.

Conversely, when your behavior deviates from truth and reality, the calibration of your moral compass weakens. You experience conflicting and unsettling feelings, resulting in less optimal actions. The negative impact of these actions reverberates through collective consciousness, further destabilizing your inner moral compass.

This cycle continues indefinitely, either toward improvement or deterioration, depending on the choices you make. The key lies in maintaining a well-calibrated inner moral compass, which allows you to clearly discern between right and wrong. If you misinterpret emotions, you generate incorrect feelings, leading to a distorted perception where wrong may feel right and right may feel wrong.

Consider this scenario: Jealousy, inherently a detrimental emotion, is sometimes viewed as a positive motivator. You may have heard someone say, "I use my jealousy to motivate myself and achieve success in life." This person interprets the negative emotion of jealousy in a positive light, generating a sense of motivation. However, embracing jealousy as a source of motivation will lead down a dangerous path of self-destruction and de-calibration of their inner moral compass.

The reality is that prolonged jealousy ultimately leads to mental erosion. The emotion of jealousy generates a gnawing void, an aching sensation of something missing, which gradually eats away at the mental landscape of the individual, deteriorating them from the inside out.

Rather than finding comfort and motivation in jealousy, one should evoke feelings of fear, alerting themselves to the danger posed by the internal gnawing void of jealousy. The feeling generated by jealousy should serve as a warning, not a source of comfort.

When someone claims to use jealousy as motivation for success, they're essentially admitting that their inner moral compass is malfunctioning. They're finding solace in something inherently negative, mistaking it for a positive emotion. The fundamental issue with harnessing motivation from jealousy is that it is rooted in a sense of lack. A jealous person perpetually feels the absence of something they desire, always feeling unfulfilled.

This persistent feeling of inadequacy ensures that there will always be something to be jealous about, resulting in a continuous cycle of dissatisfaction and a sense of void within their heart. Such a mindset prevents a person from ever feeling a true sense of fulfillment. Without experiencing wholeness and fulfillment, higher orders of peace and happiness remain unattainable. The pursuit of success driven by jealousy leads to an unending void, as the satisfaction derived from negative emotions is fleeting and ultimately hollow.

Understanding the distinction between emotions and feelings enables you to recognize when you've veered off course. It allows you to acknowledge your mistakes and prevent them from happening again. For example, by accepting jealousy as an emotion that inherently erodes and destroys, you can avoid confusing it with any sense of positive feeling or genuine motivation.

Do you recall our discussion on moral balance in the last chapter? We explored how revenge is sometimes mistaken as a benevolent act and the detrimental effects this perception has on individuals and societies. Similarly, considering jealousy as a positive motivator is just as flawed as viewing revenge as a form of justice.

Let's further differentiate between emotions and feelings. The most apparent distinction between emotions and feelings lies in their consistency and variability. Emotions remain remarkably consistent among all people at any time, while feelings are highly dynamic and subject to constant change. Emotions are universal, experienced in the same way by every individual throughout history. In contrast, feelings are personal creations, unique to each individual's interpretation and experience.

For instance, every person who senses jealousy experiences the gnawing void sensation within, experiencing the universal nature of this emotion. However, when it comes to feelings, individuals may respond differently. One person might feel a surge of anger, while another might find themselves sad and desperate.

Consider two jealous individuals vandalizing a car out of jealousy. Despite sharing the same underlying emotion, their feelings may diverge significantly. One may find a sense of happiness in the act, finding satisfaction in seeing someone else's prized possession harmed. Meanwhile, the other person may feel anger and frustration, driven by resentment and a longing for what is lacking in their lives.

Now, let's examine how emotions stay consistent while feelings change and evolve over time. Imagine someone acting on their jealousy by damaging a car and initially feeling a sense of anger. However, as time passes, a transformation occurs. They begin to feel ashamed of their actions, leading to sadness and ultimately remorse. As they reflect on the consequences and ethical implications of their behavior, their feelings shift further. Remorse deepens, and the gnawing void of jealousy in their heart starts to dwindle. Eventually, genuine happiness emerges as jealousy fades away and disappears, liberating the person from its sensation of hollowness.

In this example, jealousy serves as a constant backdrop, while feelings change based on whether jealousy is present and how intense it is. When a person senses strong jealousy, their moral compass becomes misaligned, leaving them with a deep, hollow sensation. Damaging the car, in this scenario, provides temporary relief and a feeling of anger and does nothing to heal the deeper pain. As long as the person remains prone to jealousy, the gnawing void inevitably returns.

However, as the person reflects on their actions and becomes more self-aware, the intensity of jealousy decreases, and their moral compass gradually realigns. The feeling of anger derived from acting on jealousy transitions to sadness and remorse. Over time, as the person repents and consciously avoids harnessing and feeding the emotion of jealousy, the gnawing void starts to diminish and eventually disappears entirely. This marks the arrival of true happiness—a genuine joy that comes from being free of the hollow sensation of jealousy.

In short, the emotion of jealousy is always accompanied by a gnawing sensation of emptiness—a void that eats away at the person experiencing it. The intensity of this hollowness directly correlates with the intensity of the jealousy being harbored. However, feelings are fluid, constantly shifting and evolving based on personal experiences, external influences, and time.

In this example, what begins as a fleeting surge of anger fueled by emotion of jealousy gradually transforms. The fire of envy cools into sadness, then melts into remorse, and, finally, blossoms into genuine happiness. This progression illustrates the dynamic nature of feelings in correlation with the constant nature of emotions.

In summary, there exists a collective consciousness, which is the amalgamation of all human experiences throughout history and the totality of existence in a broader sense. This collective consciousness injects a new thought along with its corresponding emotion into your mind approximately every 5 seconds. If you let go of the thought, the associated emotion also dissipates, and shortly afterward, a new thought with its accompanying emotion takes its place.

However, when you choose to hold onto a thought, the rational part of your mind engages, actively contemplating, thinking, and pursuing the thought. Simultaneously, you generate feelings to interpret the emotion attached to the thought. This active engagement in thinking and feeling directly influences every cell in your body, altering blood flow, hormone levels, heart rate, muscle tension, and stress levels, among other physiological and psychological factors, thereby impacting your overall physical and mental well-being. Consequently, this new physical and mental state shapes your subsequent actions.

These active thoughts, feelings, and actions become part of the vast collective consciousness, slightly altering its form. Depending on the quality of your thoughts, feelings, and actions, the collective consciousness recalibrates your inner compass of morality. Sound and soothing thoughts, feelings, and actions properly calibrate your inner moral compass, while wrongful thoughts, feelings, and actions that do not reflect reality, cause your moral compass to become de-calibrated.

The precision and accuracy of your inner moral compass—shaped by your previous thoughts, feelings, and actions—determine the subsequent thoughts and emotions that the collective consciousness instills within you. And so, the cycle repeats itself, again and again. Life is a constant back-and-forth exchange, a dance between fragments of consciousness and the whole of consciousness, between you and your essence. Within the next few seconds, the collective consciousness imbues your mind with a new thought and its corresponding emotion, initiating this cyclical process once again. This endless rhythm will persist indefinitely throughout your life.

Chapter 8: Soul

In this chapter, we'll weave together the ideas and concepts we've covered in earlier chapters to form a more comprehensive picture of reality. In the first chapter, we explored the idea that the universe follows specific laws and regulations. Later, we introduced the concept of "ground zero awareness," where every particle and entity in existence naturally evolves toward greater complexity. Such harmony in the universe, with a definite purpose to evolve toward greater complexity, was not formed by mere chance but was intentionally designed and crafted.

If the world were formed by random events, it would be impossible to see this consistent progression toward greater complexity. Randomness lacks purpose and structure, making it impossible for random occurrences to result in such precise and structured development of the universe.

Consider this: the human body is an incredibly complex machine, composed of trillions of cells that work together in perfect harmony. Even if we accept that we evolved from single-celled organisms to this highly developed human body, it reveals something profound about the nature of evolution itself. Even if evolution theory is true, it has been following a definite and consistent trajectory toward greater complexity for more than two billion years. This long, uninterrupted path toward increasing complexity cannot be explained by randomness alone.

This purposeful trajectory toward greater complexity is evident not only in the evolution of life on Earth but also in the evolution of the entire universe and each particle within it since the dawn of time. This world cannot be the result of aimless random events. Randomness, by its very nature, is chaotic and lacks direction. It cannot produce precise, deterministic, and goal-oriented processes.

People who believe that randomness created the world often cite the "infinite monkey theorem." as their reasoning for how the world could have been formed through random events. This idea was originally introduced by French mathematician Émile Borel in 1913. He claims that if a monkey were randomly pressing keys on a keyboard for an infinite amount of time, it could eventually produce the works of Shakespeare by sheer chance. Now let's analyze to see if that's possible.

Consider the number of particles in just one person. The average human body is made up of about 35 trillion cells, but particles are infinitely smaller than a cell. To put this into perspective, the average human body contains around 70 octillion particles. That's 70 thousand trillion trillion particles, or 70,000,000,000,000,000,000,000,000,000, or 7×10^{28} particles. But how does this compare to the probability of a monkey typing out Shakespeare's work by random chance?

The probability of a monkey producing the complete works of Shakespeare by randomly pressing keys is estimated to be around 1 in $10^{229,000}$. To put this in context, the entire observable universe is estimated to contain about 10^{83} particles. This number is extremely big. It includes all the particles in 8 billion people, all animals, insects, planets, moons, galaxies, stars, and everything else within the observable universe.

To understand these numbers, let's look at the powers involved. A single person, like you, has particles represented by the power of 28. When we include all the particles in the entire universe, that power only increases from 28 to 83. But the probability of a monkey typing out Shakespeare's works randomly: That number is raised to the power of 229,000. Think of it this way: 28 represents the particles in one person (70 octillion particles), 83 represents all the particles in the entire universe, and 229,000 is an unimaginably large jump beyond that. The difference is astronomical.

These numbers grow exponentially, which means numbers get way bigger, really fast. If 28 represents the particles in one person, then 29 would represent around 10 people, and 30 would cover about 100 people. By the time we get to 38, we're talking about more particles than the entire human population of Earth!

When we reach 51, that's enough particles to cover everything on our entire planet. Then at 68, we have the total number of particles in the Milky Way galaxy, which has 400 billion stars plus all the planets, moons, clouds of dust, and everything else in it. Moving from 68 to 83? That covers 10 trillion galaxies, each with one trillion stars and all their planets, moons, and other stuff. Adding just one more—moving from 83 to 84—would represent a universe 10 times larger than our entire observable universe.

Do you see how just adding one number here makes things grow huge? Now imagine going from 83 all the way to 229,000. That's a number so massive, it's almost beyond our imagination!

Now imagine you are given an impossible task: to find one special particle hidden somewhere in the entire universe. This particle could be one of the 70 octillion particles within your own body, or it might be nestled in a single grain of sand in the vast Sahara Desert—a sea of sand stretching over 9 million square kilometers. This particle could be drifting on the moon, lodging in the soil of Mars, or floating somewhere within the Milky Way galaxy. Perhaps it resides in a distant galaxy we've yet to discover, in a corner of the cosmos no human has ever seen.

Your task is to pick this one particle out of the incomprehensible vastness of the entire existence. You must pick a particle at random, without any intelligence guiding your choice—placing blind faith in the hope that you will pick the right one. The odds of choosing correctly? Astronomically slim. And yet, even with such an impossible task, your chances of success are vastly greater than the probability of a monkey typing out Shakespeare's complete works by random chance.

It's not even a fair comparison—your task would be infinitely easier than the poor monkey's attempt at typing a Shakespearean work. Do you think you could randomly pick a single particle in the entire universe, without any guidance, and be lucky enough to choose the right one? If you don't have much confidence in your ability to do so, then you shouldn't have much confidence in a monkey being able to type out a Shakespearean masterpiece—even if given an infinite amount of time.

Furthermore, infinite monkey theorem assumes that a functional typewriter, ink, paper, and everything else have been magically provided for the monkey. This means the probability does not account for the monkey somehow engineering the typewriter and all necessary materials by pure chance to reproduce Shakespeare's work. If these conditions were included, the probability would be so vast that even supercomputers and quantum computers couldn't calculate the odds.

Even if the monkey somehow produced the Shakespearean work, imagine the probability of it typing every book ever written, all human inventions, or creating the entire universe at random. Not even infinite time would be long enough to achieve this.

Can you see how impossible it is to believe that the universe, with all its vastness and harmony, came together purely by random chance? Think about it: even a written work, crafted by a single person, couldn't just come together by chance. The idea that something as immense and beautifully balanced as the universe could randomly assemble itself is beyond the limits of probability and reason. How could all the galaxies, stars, and life itself simply appear out of nowhere, perfectly ordered, without any guiding force?

So, if random occurrences did not create the world, then what did? This question brings us to the concept of a creator, or God. Such complexity and order in the universe can only be explained by the presence of an intelligent design, a mastermind who endowed the universe with purpose and direction.

Every individual who believes in a creator or God holds two fundamental beliefs about God: firstly, that God is the source of all things, and secondly, that they came from the kingdom of God and will return to God. Interestingly enough, atheists also share this concept of God, albeit with a minor distinction.

If one were to ask an atheist about the origins of existence or what preceded the Big Bang, they might respond, "There was nothing before the Big Bang, and everything emerged from nothing." Similarly, when questioned about what occurs after death, they might say, "There is nothing after death; I will cease to exist." Thus, an atheist essentially perceives the essence of everything as nothing: they believe they were created from nothing and will return to nothing. The God of an atheist is nothing—nothing created everything, and everything returns to nothing. This distinction is the primary difference between an atheist and a believer; one believes in the God of everything, while the other believes in the God of nothing. Nevertheless, both ideologies entail that we were created from a singular source and will ultimately return to that same source.

Therefore, I argue that indeed, God exists, even if perceived as the God of nothing, should one choose to see it that way. God exists at the apex of existence, possessing three core attributes: it is the essence of all things, the origin and destination of all, and the ultimate creator. Essentially, God's primary function is creation. But what did God create, and where did it all begin?

God, itself, exists as a singularity, the ultimate source from which all things emanate. Within the realm where God resides, there is only God—pure and all-encompassing. It embodies everything simultaneously. In the purest form of singularity, nothing can exist because everything is one thing, and every one thing is everything. Within singularity, there is no space, time, object, energy, or matter. There is only God, ineffable and beyond description by human limited intelligence.

In essence, God is both everything and nothing at once. When something exists everywhere, it becomes undetectable, blending so seamlessly into all that it eludes perception. Picture an unfurnished room; we call it empty. Or a cup without liquid—we say it is an empty cup. Yet, neither the room nor the cup is truly empty; both are filled to the brim with air. We overlook the air because it exists all around us. When something exists everywhere, it appears as nothing. We know air exists because it can change—when the wind blows, we feel it moving around us. And while air molecules are invisible to the naked eye, they become visible under a microscope.

God, however, is far subtler and more elusive than air. It is omnipresent and unchanging, existing beyond the bounds of time, space, matter, energy, or anything that human minds can grasp. This boundless nature makes God appear as absolutely nothing to our senses while it is absolutely everywhere. For this reason, humanity will never be able to prove the existence of God.

In this way, atheists touch on the truth when they argue that the origin of all things is nothing. Indeed, everything did emerge from the singularity of this "nothingness." But this nothingness is, paradoxically, everything that lies beyond human perception. Thus, God is both everything and nothing at the same time. Even nothingness cannot exist outside of God.

From this state of nothingness and everythingness, God first created the concept of information. Then, God endowed all created information with a key attribute: the innate drive to persist, to exist, and to evolve toward greater complexity. This is what we named "ground zero awareness." In other words, God imbued information with ground zero awareness to create consciousness. Consciousness literally means being with knowledge. Therefore, information that possesses knowledge of ground zero awareness represents the most basic form of consciousness.

However, consciousness could not yet be created on its own, as it needed distinct features to differentiate it from the state of singularity. Therefore, for consciousness to exist, the concept of separation must exist—separation from singularity into duality. God employed the method of separation to stretch its singularity into two opposing forces interlocked together indefinitely. This act of separation led to the emergence of consciousness, with two complementary realms of visible and invisible, representing the everythingness and nothingness of singularity itself. These are the same two realms we introduced when we used the quaternity concept to deconstruct consciousness. The other two realms of known and unknown, introduced by quaternity, hold significance only from the human perspective. From God's omniscient viewpoint, everything is known. Thus, when God first created consciousness, it employed duality to split consciousness into the realms of visible and invisible.

Furthermore, in order for existence to permeate both the visible and invisible realms, consciousness required a vessel to traverse within each realm. God created light to traverse the visible realm and truth to permeate the invisible realm. Everything in the totality of existence exists either as a form of light or truth. There is really nothing else in the world except light and truth. Everything within the visible realm is constructed from light, while everything within the invisible realm is built upon truth.

Let's explore how the visible realm is constructed from light. Consider yourself for a moment. Your physical body is fundamentally composed of light. Let's dissect this layer by layer. At the surface, your body is composed of skin, flesh, bones, organs, and other body parts, primarily made up of oxygen, nitrogen, carbon, and hydrogen—the very same elements that form the soil beneath your feet. Basically, the dirt you walk on is largely made of the same exact primary particles that comprise your body. Now, if you were to add water to soil, the resulting mud would contain approximately 60% water and 40% soil. Similarly, you are composed of approximately 60% water, with the remaining 40% formed from the very same elements of soil.

Your body also contains small amounts of various other elements—such as iron, silicon, magnesium, potassium, and calcium—all found in Earth's soil. There is not a single element in your body that does not exist on Earth. Your physical body is made from the soil of the Earth. The universe constructed your physical body out of the Earth's soil and the Earth's soil itself was predominantly forged in the cores of stars.

Stars are the light factories that brighten up our day and night sky, but they are also the factories that produce natural elements. Almost everything in the universe is made of stardust. The Earth itself was formed from the remnants of ancient stars that exploded long ago. Since the Earth is composed of stardust, it follows that you are also made of stardust. Most elements within your body were forged in the hearts of stars billions of years ago. In fact, the particles of nearly everything you encounter are also crafted within the hearts of stars—from precious metals like gold and silver to everyday items like cars, computers, and houses.

It's no coincidence that stars are both factories of light and creators of elements. This is because all elements are forged through processes driven by light. Another fascinating aspect is that stars are also factories of energy. We use solar panels to capture the Sun's light energy, and the heat it provides serves as a direct source of energy for us. In this way, stars function as light factories, energy factories, and element factories. This reveals an undeniable interconnectedness of matter, energy, and light.

Consider the famous equation $E = MC^2$ developed by Albert Einstein. This formula represents the fundamental relationship between matter, energy, and light. In this equation, E represents energy, M signifies mass (matter), and C symbolizes the speed of light. What this equation essentially means is that matter can be converted into energy, and energy into matter, with light acting as a crucial link between the two. In other words, everything existing in the universe, whether in the form of energy or matter, exists within the framework of light.

Light itself embodies both matter and energy. Light is made up of photons, which are quantum particles that exhibit both matter-like and energy-like properties. Furthermore, the pure energy of light is also associated with its electromagnetic wave properties. To understand this better, you can search for the "double-slit experiment" online. This experiment shows that light has a dual nature, exhibiting properties of both matter and energy simultaneously. Light possesses the remarkable ability to alter its form at will, acting as a matter sometimes and as energy at other times.

In a nutshell, everything in the visible universe exists either in the form of matter or energy. Whether matter is converted into energy or energy materializes into matter, both processes are governed by the principles of light. Moreover, light itself embodies the ultimate form of both energy and matter, seamlessly transitioning between the two states as needed. Light is the only entity that bridges matter and energy in this way. Therefore, it is the most fundamental building block of the entire observable universe.

God created light and employed the concept of duality, splitting light into matter and energy, thereby establishing light as the ultimate source of matter and energy in the universe. God then used matter and energy to construct the entire observable universe.

This is how your physical body fundamentally originated from light. Your physical body is composed of soil and water from the Earth. The Earth itself was formed from the remnants of ancient stars. Stars act as factories that create elements, and all elements are forms of matter and energy that originated from light.

Let's take this one step further. Science claims that particles are made from quarks, one of the most basic forms of energy we have ever discovered. However, even quarks are interlinked with light. Particle physics shows that when high-energy light beams interact with particles, they create quark-antiquark pairs. In this way, every quark also has a direct relationship with light. Light is the primary link among all building blocks of the visible world. Even all boson and lepton particles, as well as the forces they carry, interact with light either directly or indirectly. Nothing in the visible realm is independent of light and its properties. Light is the most primal entity in the entire universe. Thus, the visible realm is fundamentally made of light.

Also, you have never truly seen matter itself. All you've ever seen is light reflecting off it. Even sound, in its essence, is born of light. Sound waves are mechanical vibrations that your ears can detect, but at a fundamental level, they are shaped by electromagnetic forces—the very nature of light. Touch, too, is the sensation of electromagnetic interactions, a subtle dance of forces that allows your fingers to feel surfaces and textures. Everything you smell and taste is made of particles that are composed of light. The friction that holds your feet to the ground and allows you to walk is also an electromagnetic force, rooted in the nature of light. Without light, you could not see, hear, taste, smell, touch, or even walk. Without light properties, nothing physical would exist. All you are, all your basic senses, and everything around you are ultimately woven from light.

Ultimately, every exchange of energy in the universe is bound to light. Whenever energy is expended or absorbed, photons play a part. There's a concept called "black body radiation," which tells us that any object with a temperature above absolute zero emits photons. This means that the entire physical reality, simply by existing, radiates light. You, quite literally, are made of light and have been radiating light at every moment of your existence. Every sensation you perceive and every experience you have is intricately tied to the properties of light. No matter how you look at it, all aspects of physical reality are traced back to light and its fundamental properties.

This is all one side of creation within the duality of consciousness. Everything that was created from light belongs to the visible realm. On the other hand, God imparted truth to the invisible realm, initiating a different set of creations that exist in parallel to that of the visible realm.

147

The method of separation that God applied to light to create matter and energy was similarly employed on truth, giving rise to two vital forces of love and peace. As truth is complementary to light, peace and love are complementary to matter and energy. Peace brings harmony to the world, while love fosters coexistence.

Consider a newborn baby. We often think of newborns as naked. However, that's not entirely accurate. As a mother prepares to give birth, bacteria become aware of the situation and flock to the birth canal, covering the child from head to toe. Bacteria create an invisible protective jacket, shielding the baby from external threats. Without this bacterial armor, a newborn's chances of survival would be impossible. Bacteria teach the immune system of a newborn how to distinguish between harmful invaders and harmless entities. Additionally, bacteria colonize the gut, helping with nutrient absorption and overall health of the digestive tract of the baby. This is the natural love of the universe bestowed upon you at the moment of your birth.

Right now, as you read this, your body hosts about as many bacteria as cells. If you have around 35 trillion cells, you are also hosting roughly 35 trillion bacteria. These bacteria are crucial for your health; without them, your survival would be at risk. From birth until death, you live in harmony with these bacteria. This is an example of the peace and harmony of the universe that has been bestowed upon you.

35 trillion cells and 35 trillion bacteria, along with countless other molecules, all function around the clock in unison just so you can live. That's just you, only one person. Now, multiply that by nearly 8 billion people on Earth today, not to mention all the animals and other life forms. This harmony isn't merely a result of the laws of physics or random occurrences; it's a meticulously orchestrated phenomenon.

One might argue that the harmony observed in the world is entirely governed by the laws of physics. However, physics itself suggests a more complex picture. When physicists and astronomers attempt to calculate the harmony of the entire universe, they find that mathematical models can only explain less than 5% of the harmony observed in the world. To address this significant discrepancy—often referred to as the "missing 95%"—scientists have introduced the concepts of dark energy and dark matter. These are crucial forces that help sustain cosmic balance. These forces keep the entire universe in harmony and are essential in maintaining the structure and expansion of the universe.

Dark energy and dark matter are completely invisible, as they do not interact with light in any way. They cannot be measured or understood through scientific methods, nor can they be quantified like the rest of the observable universe. They form the quality of existence and are the essence of harmony and coexistence in the entire universe. Dark energy and dark matter belong to the invisible realm, aligning more with the concepts of morality rather than physicality. I believe that these mysterious forces are the powers of love and peace, which, invisibly, hold all existence together and enable the peaceful coexistence of all things.

Love is fundamentally about spreading goodness, which is essentially what the universe continuously does. Everything in existence contributes something back to the universe, evolving and enhancing its complexity. Every particle plays a role in this trend of increasing complexity, driven by the love ingrained in its core. The power of love ensures that everything in existence carries value and purpose. Science confirms the inherent purpose of all things. It has not discovered a single particle that lacks purpose or is disconnected from the rest of reality.

Consider how creation showers you with the love of trillions upon trillions of cells and bacteria, all working together just so you can exist and enjoy the day. Your body works tremendously hard so you can live. You are blessed with love at every moment, though it may not always be apparent. No matter how challenging your life may seem, it is fundamentally a gift of love.

The true essence of love, by its very nature, is invisible; you won't find it materialized in the world through money, bigger houses, ideal partners, obedient children, good friends, or delicious food. The love you experience in physical reality is merely an extremely limited expression of love, not its true essence. Love isn't something you find externally; it's what you embody. Love is a state of being in complete surrender and flow with the harmony of the universe. When you recognize the part of yourself that is made from love, you will naturally be drawn to honor and nurture it. Love is one of the most venerable aspects of your being.

On the other hand, there is an undeniable force of peace permeating the entire universe. Look up at the night sky—trillions upon trillions of galaxies, all coexisting in harmony, perfectly balanced, each spinning at mind-boggling speeds around themselves and around each other, creating life on a tiny blue dot we call Earth. This peaceful harmony and loving coexistence are the touch of invisible hands.

In the grand scheme of things, galaxies, stars, planets, and all celestial bodies coexist in balance. Galaxies exist so stars can find stability; stars exist to give rise to planets; planets exist to foster life; life exists so you and I can be here. Similarly, all fundamental particles—electrons, protons, neutrons, positrons, bosons, quarks, and other building blocks of the universe—also coexist peacefully. This harmony is a hallmark of existence and serves as evidence of the power of peace.

Wherever there is harmonious coexistence, love and peace are present. When love and peace are fully understood, truth becomes clear, and truth has the power to uncover the deepest and most mysterious aspects of existence. Without love and peace, the entire existence would falter. Think about it this way: as long as humanity upholds some measure of love and peace, our species can survive. However, the moment we abandon these values and fully succumb to hatred, greed, and chaos, we will annihilate ourselves, leading to the extinction of our species. Similarly, as long as dark energy and dark matter exert their forces on the universe, existence persists. If these forces were to stop, the entire universe would collapse. Only love and peace possess the power to ensure the harmonious coexistence of all things. Therefore, the forces of dark energy and dark matter are synonymous with the power of love and peace.

Let's reiterate what we have discussed so far. At the highest level, there exists an ultimate creator. At the beginning, God created the concept of information, then infused information with ground zero awareness to transform it into consciousness. Next, God employed the method of duality to forge separation from singularity, thus creating the two opposing realms of consciousness: the visible and invisible realms. God then endowed each realm with an attribute. Light was given to the visible realm and truth to the invisible realm. In the next step of creation,

God once again applied duality to both light and truth. The duality of light resulted in the creation of matter and energy, while the duality of truth led to the emergence of love and peace.

Everything you see and experience is shaped by the principle of duality. In the universe, nothing exists without its counterpart. Similarly, you embody this duality: you possess a physical body in the visible realm, made of matter and energy, and another form in the invisible realm, crafted from love and peace. This part of you, purely made from love and peace in the invisible realm, is known as the human soul.

The visible portion of your existence was made from light, which transformed into matter and energy, and eventually became your physical body. In parallel, your invisible body, emerging from truth, transformed into love and peace and eventually became your soul. You are as much a creation of matter and energy as you are of love and peace. You embody both light and truth, existing simultaneously as a physical body and a soul.

The physical body is like a vehicle for the soul, designed to support the soul on its journey toward its ultimate destination. Just as a car's primary purpose is to transport you to where you need to go, the body exists to help the soul achieve its purpose. In this analogy, if the physical body is the car and you are the driver, then the soul is your passenger. As the driver, it is your responsibility to care for your car and your passenger, ensuring the soul arrives at its destination. You must care for your physical body, just as you care for your car by maintaining it, refueling it, and driving it carefully. But beyond the physical aspects of your existence, you must ensure that the journey you undertake serves the soul's higher purpose.

However, a more accurate description of the soul is that it resides deep within you, at the very core of your being. If you were to examine your existence layer by layer, you will first see the skin, the outermost surface of your appearance. Delve deeper, and you will find the organs and body parts that constitute your physical form. Beneath that, you will see the cells that make up these organs, and deeper still, the molecules that form the cells. As you continue inward, you will reach the particles that compose the molecules, and further down, the quarks that form the particles.

But when you look beyond the quarks and the quantum level, you encounter the mysterious realms of dark energy and dark matter, concepts even deeper than quarks and the quantum realm. At this threshold, the rules of reality as we know—where everything interacts with light—suddenly change. Here, light is no longer able to describe what is happening, and science begins to lose its ability to explain this hidden aspect of your existence. This is why scientists refer to these phenomena as dark energy and dark matter—they are "dark" because they do not interact with light in any way that we can understand.

Dark energy and dark matter are gateways to the invisible realm of consciousness. Beyond this point lies a reality where the physical realm bridges to the spiritual realm. In this deepest, most unseen layer of your existence, your soul resides. It is a realm where scientific methods fall short, and where understanding emerges not through logical observation of the external world, but through inner awareness, moral understanding, and spiritual insight.

In this way, the soul is not just a part of you; it is the innermost core of your existence, hidden beneath layers of physical reality and connected to a vast, invisible realm of consciousness.

The space you occupy with your body consists of about 5% of matter and energy, while the remaining 95% is composed of dark energy and dark matter. In other words, you are 5% physical body and 95% soul. This 95% represents the deepest, most profound part of your being. Everything you experience in the physical world—daily routines, delicious foods, interactions with family, time spent with friends, creating art, work, finance, travel—all these aspects of your physical life contribute to less than 5% of your sense of fulfillment.

The remaining 95% of your life experiences and sense of satisfaction reside deep within you, within your soul. This means that even if you possessed all the money, fame, and power in the world, you would only be fulfilling 5% of your true needs. The other 95% is rooted in your inner world—your moral values, your spiritual growth, and your connection to deeper truths. The essence of who you are and what truly fulfills you extends far beyond the material world and is found in the realm of the soul, where morality, love, peace, and wisdom reside.

That is why you often hear that the path to enlightenment is an inner journey of self-discovery and introspection. To truly understand your soul, you must delve deeply within yourself, exploring the inner depths where your soul resides. This journey requires you to move beyond the surface, beyond the physical aspects of your existence, to grasp the essence of love and peace. Only by digging deep within can you uncover the true nature of your soul and the vast, mysterious realms that exist within you.

Within the invisible realm of the soul, where light cannot penetrate, truth takes over where light leaves off. While we comprehend light through logic, we grasp truth through morality. The more you refine your moral understanding, the better you can navigate and comprehend the realm of the soul. Morality acts as your invisible eye, enabling you to perceive the unseeable. It is through this moral vision that you gain insights into the deeper truths that logic alone cannot reveal.

Now, let's review and weave together some of the concepts from previous chapters to gain a better understanding of the soul. Let's begin with the idea of human collective consciousness. We discussed how we are connected at a level that goes far beyond our five basic senses, forming a vast network of interconnectedness that binds us all together. In essence, collective consciousness is the communication network of the soul. In other words, interactions among souls weave the fabric of our collective consciousness. This is how souls interact and influence one another.

For instance, imagine you're thinking about a friend, and shortly afterward, you receive a call from them. This seemingly coincidental event is actually an example of how our souls communicate with one another. In this scenario, your soul and your friend's soul interacted with one another within the collective consciousness, injecting thoughts of each other into your minds that eventually led to the phone call.

Furthermore, within the collective consciousness, there is a flow of energies that manifest as emotions. Different regions of the collective consciousness contain different types of emotions. In areas rich with love and peace, the emotions tend to be soothing and nurturing for the soul. Conversely, in areas where love and peace are scarce, emotions can be harsh and unsettling.

When people stray from truth, love, and peace, they find themselves in a barren landscape of collective unconsciousness. When people disregard their inner connectedness to others, nature, and the world itself—when they elevate individualism above all else, amplifying competition, and ignoring the importance of collaboration—they willingly turn away from the richness of collective consciousness, pushing their soul into the desolation of collective unconsciousness.

Imagine collective consciousness as a lush, abundant forest, overflowing with resources and offering a soothing life. In contrast, the collective unconsciousness is like an arid desert, where nothing thrives, and survival is harsh. Though love and peace permeate all existence, some spaces within consciousness make it easier to harness this positive energy than others.

Collective unconsciousness is a region within the totality of consciousness where connections to other areas are sparse and distant. In consciousness, the more pathways that connect different regions, the more abundantly love and peace can flow. But where connections are few, the flow of love and peace diminishes. When people mentally isolate themselves from the world, they invite suffering—not to be confused with physical isolation. In an ironic twist, many spiritual individuals seek solitude in the physical realm to deepen their spiritual connection to the world.

The isolation here is mental: it happens when people nurture hatred toward others, feed vanity to gratify their physical desires for material success and glamor, or harbor anger against those with different beliefs. These choices draw the soul away from interconnected regions of collective consciousness, pushing it toward unconsciousness, where genuine connections are rare and far in between. Collective unconsciousness is the realm where interactions are veiled in hidden agendas, and motivations are driven solely by self-interest and material success.

Each soul possesses a receptor finely tuned to sense emotions from its surroundings. The soul continuously receives emotional signals from its interactions with the collective consciousness or collective unconsciousness. When your soul is in an environment rich in love and peace, it absorbs positive emotions. Conversely, when there is a scarcity of love and peace, your soul experiences negative emotions.

Depending on the emotions your soul experiences, corresponding feelings are generated within the physical body to interpret and understand these emotions. Positive emotions often transform into feelings of hope, happiness, satisfaction, and fulfillment. Conversely, negative emotions tend to manifest as feelings of scarcity, despair, fear, anger, and greed.

When the soul receives an emotion, it also communicates that emotion to the physical body through passive thoughts in your mind, which is essentially the voice of the soul. The voice of the soul consistently nudges you toward self-improvement and growth. It does this by cultivating positive and empowering thoughts, helping to build your confidence when you are on the right path. Conversely, the soul can also evoke fearful or discomforting thoughts in your mind, when you are heading in a harmful direction.

On the other hand, active thoughts and critical thinking are functions of the physical body, used to interpret and make sense of the messages received from the soul. While the soul communicates through subtle, passive thoughts, it is through rational thinking that you analyze and understand these messages.

Therefore, the region within consciousness where your soul resides, profoundly influences how you feel and think. This is because your emotions are the sensation of the soul and your passive thoughts are the voice of the soul. Your soul is always in communication with you, subtly guiding and influencing your thoughts and feelings. If you turn your attention inward and listen closely to the voice of the soul, and truly tune into your emotions, you can begin to notice what it is that the soul is trying to communicate with you. Your soul always has your best interests at heart; no one can offer better guidance on how to live your life than your own soul. You carry within you the ultimate teacher, constantly present to help you become the best version of yourself.

Remember when I said that the collective consciousness instills a thought with an emotional charge in your mind every five seconds? And that if you choose to engage with that thought, your active thinking analyzes the passive thought, and that you create feelings to interpret the emotion attached to the thought? This process is the fundamental communication between your individual consciousness and the collective consciousness—the bridge between the physical and spiritual realms, the dialogue between you and your soul.

And do you recall when I explained that your actions influence the collective consciousness, which in turn determines the nature of the next thought and emotion that will be instilled in your mind? That alteration of the collective consciousness I mentioned in the last chapter is the movement of your soul within consciousness—whether it moves closer to the collective consciousness or drifts toward the collective unconsciousness.

The closer your soul aligns with the collective consciousness, the more attuned you become to truth, wisdom, and enlightenment. Conversely, the further it leans toward the collective unconsciousness, the deeper it sinks into ignorance, illusion, and detachment from reality. In this way, your thoughts, emotions, and actions are all part of an ongoing dialogue that determines whether your soul moves toward higher awareness or gets lost in the fog of collective unconsciousness.

Now, let's integrate another topic we've previously discussed: moral balance. Moral balance is determined by the accuracy of your understanding of the truth. The more your beliefs align with truth and reality, the more balanced your moral understanding becomes. Conversely, when your beliefs are rooted in falsehood, you become morally imbalanced. This balance significantly affects how freely your soul can navigate the invisible realm of consciousness.

Consider this analogy: having a healthy physical body allows you to move with ease and attend to your daily responsibilities. However, an injury can limit your mobility, making it harder to complete your tasks. Similarly, the state of your moral understanding influences how easily your soul can move through the invisible realm of consciousness. When your actions and moral understanding align with truth and reality, your soul can access regions rich in love and peace. Conversely, if your beliefs are based on falsehoods, your soul struggles to find love and peace, leading to an unsatisfying and unfulfilling life.

Take, for example, the concept of revenge. Some people think revenge is the same as justice, but in truth, justice does not promote revenge. Revenge fuels resentment and further conflict, whereas true justice seeks to resolve and eliminate conflict. Justice is rooted in truth, and truth is grounded in love and peace; therefore, anything that opposes these principles—such as revenge—cannot align with the truth. When someone views revenge as a benevolent act, they are experiencing a moral imbalance.

There's a story that warns of the dangers of revenge and resentment. One cold night, a snake curled into a tool shed, seeking warmth and comfort. As it moved inside, it brushed against a saw on the ground, cutting itself on the sharp edge.

Thinking it was under attack, the snake grew angry. It snapped back, biting the saw, only to severely injure its mouth. Blinded by anger, it wrapped around the saw, determined to crush it in revenge, squeezing tighter and tighter.

But in its desperate grip, the snake only hurt itself further. Though the saw bent and broke slightly, the snake's own body was cut too deeply, and it bled to death. Had it only ignored the initial cut and moved on, it would have stayed alive.

The moral of the story is that when you enact viscerally with anger and condemn those who have wronged you, you often create more pain—much of which reflects back onto yourself. When hatred, anger and resentment drive your actions, they lead only to destruction and misery, harming you as much, if not more, than those you seek to harm.

If you succumb to the hatred and anger that comes with seeking revenge, your soul suffers from a lack of love and peace. In this state, the soul absorbs negative emotions from the collective unconsciousness and transmits them to the physical body. These negative emotions act as a reminder for you to reevaluate your beliefs and values.

The soul's ongoing effort to consistently realign your beliefs with the truth shapes your inner moral compass. This compass equips you with the ability to determine what is right or wrong, and what is good or bad.

Suppose you continue to believe that revenge is equivalent to justice. In this scenario, your inner moral compass becomes misaligned, meaning that you have suppressed and disregard the emotional signal and the voice of the soul. Thus, you suffer mentally, emotionally, and psychologically. You will struggle to tell the difference between what is genuinely good and what is harmful. Revenge is always harmful to everyone. But with a misaligned inner moral compass, you might view revenge as a justified action, further deepening your own suffering.

The inner moral compass is a reflection of your soul's needs and desires, a tool designed to help you align your actions with the principles of love and peace. The more you pay attention to your soul, the better you understand its true needs. This understanding enables you to accurately interpret the signals it sends, guiding you toward actions that are genuinely good and away from those that are harmful.

When your inner moral compass is correctly calibrated, it means you have developed a deep understanding of your soul's desires. You are in tune with truth and your inner self, allowing you to make decisions that align with your highest values that lead to true fulfillment. A calibrated inner moral compass enables you to live in a state of love, harmony, and peace. As a result, your attitude and actions reflect the love and peace at the core of your being. As you draw closer to your soul, your life experiences become morally sound and deeply satisfying, enabling you to live in a state of bliss. Your soul is an integral part of your being. You belong to your soul, and your soul belongs to you.

Now, let's incorporate the concept of true power. In the chapter where we discussed the laws of consciousness, we noted that individuals with greater access to consciousness possess more power. The soul is the most conscious part of your being and the only gateway to truth and morality. It represents your truest self, embodying the most loving, peaceful, wise, and knowledgeable version of who you are. In essence, your soul is the best version of you.

When you come to understand and form a deep connection with your soul, you unlock a profound inner power that brings forth and manifests your greatest talents, guiding you toward achieving all forms of greatness in life. This intimate connection with your soul allows you to tap into an infinite reservoir of hope, wisdom, motivation, and strength, leading you toward your true purpose and potential.

As you align yourself more closely with your soul, you begin to access higher levels of consciousness and gain insights into the mysteries of the invisible realm of reality. The soul's inherent qualities of love, peace, wisdom, and knowledge start to shine more prominently in your daily life. You begin to radiate these qualities outward, positively influencing those around you and creating a ripple effect of harmony and understanding.

This is the true power that dwells within you, waiting to be discovered, unleashed, and fully expressed in your life. Your soul lives within you, expresses itself through you, and it is the best part of who you are. By embracing and nurturing this connection, you allow the highest aspects of your being to flourish, transforming not only your life but also the lives of those around you.

This brings us to the central dilemma presented in this book: all of human mental sufferings stem from our failure to acknowledge the existence of the soul and our neglect in nurturing it.

Just as you need to care for your physical body to function properly, you must also nurture your soul to maintain your mental, emotional, and psychological health. The soul does not age or struggle with physical ailments like back pains or headaches. However, the soul can still be harmed, not by external forces, but through your own actions and choices. The good news is that you have the ability to provide the soul with everything it needs, regardless of who you are or where you are. The challenge lies in knowing how to nourish the soul.

Your soul is composed of peace and love, which are themselves derived from truth. Therefore, whenever your beliefs stray from the truth, your soul suffers. Likewise, when there is a deficiency of love and peace, you experience suffering. Suffering arises when chaos replaces peace and fear supplants love.

Just as your physical body suffers when deprived of water and food, your soul deteriorates when starved of love and peace. Today, many souls are starving. In our current era, there's a growing emphasis on physical desires over spiritual health—money has become more important than love, and earthly power more valued than peace. You're given this one life to explore both the light and the truth, to appreciate both the physical and spiritual dimensions of existence. Sacrificing love for money or peace for fleeting power is the wrong way to go. Wealth, power, fame, and worldly glamours cannot alleviate mental suffering if you lack love and peace.

The one who balances oneself delicately between light and truth, between the physical and mental state of being, between the flesh and the soul, finds that suffering ends instantly. When the soul and the body are in harmony, all suffering ceases, and mental health is fully restored. Nothing is more valuable than the end of suffering and a complete sense of serenity. When one is filled with love and fueled by peace, nothing in the world can surpass that sense of completeness.

Let's summarize the process of creation once again. There exists a point of singularity, often referred to as God, which is the essence of all things. God is the ultimate creator, and everything created by God ultimately returns to God. The primary function of God is creation, and the fundamental building block of this creation is information.

God endowed all created information with a key attribute: the innate drive to persist, exist, and evolve toward greater complexity. This foundational impulse is what we refer to as ground zero awareness, a basic level of consciousness shared across all existence.

For creation to take form, God employed the method of separation, dividing its singularity into duality. This led to the creation of the visible and invisible realms of consciousness.

Just as information was endowed with ground zero awareness to become consciousness, the visible realm was granted the attribute of light to turn into physical existence, and the invisible realm received the attribute of truth to create spiritual existence. Once again, duality was employed to create matter and energy out of light, and to draw love and peace from truth. We, as humans, were created in both the visible and invisible realms—made of light and truth, composed of matter and energy as well as love and peace, existing as both flesh and soul.

Each aspect of God's creation was given specific attributes: Information received ground zero awareness to transform into consciousness. The visible realm was endowed with light, creating physical existence, then light was further imbued with the attribute of logic to create the concept of correct and incorrect. On the other hand, the invisible realm was given the attribute of truth to create spiritual existence, with truth itself being imbued with morality to create good and bad. Thus, logic and morality gave rise to yet another duality.

For humans, the soul was endowed with the attribute of emotions to perceive morality, while the heart of our flesh received the attribute of feeling, enabling us to use morality to discern right from wrong. Similarly, the soul was given a voice manifesting as passive thoughts in our mind to grasp logic, and the brain of our flesh was given the attribute of critical thinking, allowing us to use logic to differentiate correct from incorrect.

Within the invisible realm, God created the collective consciousness—a vast network that connects all souls, forming the spiritual space where they reside. At the farthest edge of the collective consciousness, a region was formed where connections are scarce, giving rise to the collective unconsciousness. Furthermore, the more your beliefs align with the truth, the deeper your understanding of morality becomes. A clearer grasp of morality enables your soul greater access to collective consciousness, allowing it to move freely toward regions rich with love and peace. When your soul experiences an abundance of love and peace, your inner moral compass becomes more aligned, and you begin to sense more positive thoughts and emotions. This greater access to collective consciousness also grants you higher access to your true inner power.

When this inner power is fully realized, you are able to unleash and manifest your greatest talents, and you gain clarity about your true purpose in life. This spiritual journey allows you to connect with your highest self, where the alignment of your inner moral compass with the truth helps you tap into the limitless potential that resides within you.

God designed all this beautifully through the concept of duality so that you might seek out and uncover the mysteries of existence that have been coded into creation. Through seeing God's creations and exploring the attributes of duality, you are invited by God to discover the underlying singularity beneath it all.

Since creation unfolded through the method of separation and duality, it moved further from singularity, unity, and God. Each subsequent creation through duality caused further distance from God. As humans, we stand as the pinnacle of creation, the furthest from God. To reconcile this separation and return to our true essence, we were gifted with the tool of the trinity. The purpose of the trinity is to unite the opposing forces of duality, restoring singularity. When two opposing forces of duality are fully understood, they merge to manifest the unity that was the origin of the duality. For example, when the duality of energy and matter unites, light manifests, forming the trinity of light, matter, and energy. When peace and love merge, truth becomes evident, completing the trinity of truth, love, and peace. And when truth and light unite, the presence of God can be sensed.

From a human perspective, the path back to God is through moving from duality to singularity, achieved via the concept of the trinity. Duality represents separation, whereas trinity symbolizes unification. Across every culture, the concept of trinity promotes unification.

Historical and spiritual figures across different traditions illustrated this: Jesus united with the Holy Spirit to become one with the Father, Muhammad became intimate with Gabriel to hear God's voice, followers of Mithraism sought intimacy with Mithra for access to Sol Invictus and immortality, Zoroastrians seek communion with the holy immortals to reach Ahura Mazda, and Buddhists aim for alignment of sangha with dharma to achieve the state of Buddha. In Taoism, the unity of Wu Wai with the flow of Qi leads to oneness with the Tao. Kabbalists employ the methods of trinity within a trinity to ascend the steps of Sefirot to Keter. Freud noted that when the id and ego harmonize, the superego emerges. Modern spirituality teaches unification of the inner child with the intellectual self to reach the higher self.

The concept of the trinity can also be applied to the visible and invisible aspects of ourselves, unifying soul and flesh to reveal the true essence of our spirit. In this higher state of being, suffering is transformed into bliss. When passive and active thoughts harmonize, mental coherence manifests. When emotions and feelings align, a sensation free from conflict arises. Furthermore, when humanity unites as one entity and one society, wars cease, conflicts dissolve, and true human intelligence begins to emerge. This unity is the path that leads us to the kingdom of God—a point of singularity and ultimate bliss—and the concept of the trinity is a key factor in this endeavor.

This journey from duality to singularity through the concept of trinity involves tremendous effort to move against the natural gradient of creation which is based on separation. This ascent against the gravity of creation of duality and separation, is the central theme of the remainder of this book. Essentially, we must understand the soul and become one with it.

In this harmonious state, the conflicting clamor of inner voices gives way to tranquil inner conversation. A sense of serenity takes precedence over the turmoil of conflicting feelings. Order prevails over chaos. Happiness takes over madness. Peace replaces conflict. Suffering ends and a true sense of joy takes its place.

Now, the question arises: how do we apply the concept of the trinity to achieve unification with the soul? This journey toward becoming one with the soul is referred to as the path of spirituality. Just as we grow and mature physically, we must also strive for spiritual growth and maturity. For our physical body to develop, we nourish it with food and water, then it grows naturally over time. Similarly, the soul requires nourishment to flourish and evolve. But what exactly does it mean to "feed" the soul, and how do we go about doing this?

To understand how to nurture the soul, let's revisit the analogy of the apple tree discussed in the first chapter. An apple seed inherently possesses all the knowledge needed to grow into a full-fledged tree, provided it receives essential elements like light, water, and fertile soil. Similarly, the soul can be seen as the seed of humanity, containing all the knowledge necessary for you to evolve into the best version of yourself.

When the soul's needs are met, your spiritual growth unfolds automatically.

Like the apple seed, your soul yearns to undergo its automatic growth process, ready to unfurl its potential to the fullest. Your role in this metaphorical journey is akin to that of a caretaker, tasked with providing the necessary nourishment for the soul, with the ultimate aim of liberating it from the shackles of suffering.

For the tree, light is an absolute necessity. Deprived of light, the seed lacks the warmth needed to break open its shell, and it cannot engage in photosynthesis to grow. In the realm of the invisible, light has a counterpart—the truth. Just as light provides warmth and essential nutrients to help an apple seed flourish into a majestic tree, truth offers the warmth and vital knowledge needed to illuminate the path of enlightenment for you to find your soul and grow into the best version of yourself. Just as the apple seed requires light to thrive, your soul needs truth to reach its full potential.

Truth, unlike fleeting falsehoods, is omnipresent, unchanging, everlasting, and indestructible. It pervades every aspect of your being, casting its unwavering influence on the landscape of your mind. Lies may momentarily cast a shadow over truth, but they cannot alter its essence. Truth may fade from memory, but forgetting does not erase the truth. Even in the face of denial or deception, truth remains steadfast, unyielding to the whims of human actions.

Truth is always within reach for those who genuinely seek it. If you are earnest in your search and open to exploring beyond surface appearances, you will eventually uncover the deeper truths that lie beneath. The path to truth demands patience, self-reflection, and a willingness to question and challenge your own beliefs. However, with sincere effort and intention, it is always possible for everyone to find truth. A tree reaches toward the sky in pursuit of light, while the human soul naturally gravitates toward the infinite consciousness through the beacon of truth.

In essence, truth is the light that unravels the mysteries of your internal landscape and paves the way for liberation from the shackles of suffering. By nourishing the soul with the sustenance of truth, you cultivate a harmonious state where the pursuit of genuine happiness prevails over the chase for momentary satisfaction. Light is truth, and truth is light.

In the elegant dance of nature, where a tree relies not only on light but also on the life-giving sustenance of water, a parallel can be drawn in the invisible realm—the realm where love takes on the role similar to water, nourishing the soul and facilitating its growth toward truth.

Water, the essence of life for a tree, defies the relentless force of gravity, rising from the roots deep underground to the highest branches, providing nourishment for the tree's growth toward the sky. Similarly, love emerges as a force that transcends the challenges posed by darkness. Like water, love has the remarkable ability to move against the currents of adversity, empowering the soul to reach for truth.

Love becomes the lifeblood of the soul, infusing it with comfort and rejuvenation. Just as a tree continually needs water to sustain its vitality, the soul requires an ongoing supply of love to flourish in its quest for truth and self-realization. Love acts as the sustaining force that defies the darkness, just as water defies gravity to uplift the tree. Love also provides the soul with the resilience needed to weather the storms of life, just as water enables a tree to endure changing seasons.

Furthermore, good soil is the bedrock that provides a tree with essential nutrients and a stable foundation for growth. Good fertile soil offers both support and sustenance. Similarly, in the invisible realm of your existence, the responsibility you take for your actions and the quality of your intentions serve as the metaphorical soil for the soul.

Just as good soil provides nutrients for a tree, taking responsibility for your own life becomes the nourishment that feeds the soul. Your choices, actions, and decisions shape the landscape of your inner world. Your willingness to take charge of your own life is the foundation upon which the soul can nourish and flourish.

Taking responsibility for your downfalls is an essential part of this analogy. Just as the soil is responsible when a tree falls, taking responsibility for your downfalls and learning from your mistakes is vital for the growth of the soul. It's a call to be in charge of your own life, recognizing that the power to make positive changes lies within you.

Moreover, the quality of your intentions is crucial for the stability of the soul. Just as good soil supports the tree, having positive and well-intentioned thoughts and feelings provides the soul with a supportive environment. The intentions you cultivate become the groundwork in which the soul can grow its roots.

In essence, taking responsibility and fostering good intentions are the food and support system for the soul, much like fertile soil for a tree. It is extremely important to tend to the invisible dimensions of your being with the same care and mindfulness that you would provide for a growing tree. Your mental and psychological health is intricately connected to the choices you make and the intentions you hold.

In the choreography of life, the soul, like a delicate yet resilient entity, yearns for simple yet profound nourishment—truth, love, responsibility, and good intentions. These elements form the essence of the soul's sustenance, guiding it through an automatic growth process toward the infinite depths of consciousness. The soul's satisfaction lies in its inherent yearning to unfurl its infinite potential locked within. It's a journey of self-discovery and self-realization.

Truth serves as the guiding light, illuminating the path for the soul's journey. Love, the lifeblood, provides comfort and rejuvenation, fostering an environment where the soul can thrive. Responsibility, like the nutrient-rich substance, influences the quality of the soul's development. Good intentions ground the soul, providing stability and a foundation for growth.

The soul finds satisfaction not in material accumulation or external validations but in the nurturing embrace of these fundamental elements. By cultivating truth, love, responsibility, and good intentions, you become the gardener of your own soul. A soul, satisfied in its growth, becomes a beacon of authenticity, radiating harmony and fulfillment throughout your life.

Lastly, beneath the beautiful tapestry of truth, love, responsibility, and good intentions that nurture the soul lies a powerful force essential for growth of the soul—the power of imagination. Imagination is the catalyst that guides the soul toward its greatest potential, enabling it to break free from the confines of self-limiting beliefs.

Just as an apple seed, armed with the elements of light, water, and good soil, needs the power of imagination to envision itself as a majestic tree, your soul requires similar imaginative prowess. The seed of the soul, if confined to a limited perception of its capabilities, will remain stagnant. It is through the power of imagination that the soul dares to dream beyond its current state, envisioning a reality in which it reaches its full potential.

Imagination is the bridge between the present and the limitless potential of the soul's future. It is the force that drives you to imagine the best version of yourself and believe in the possibility of its actualization. Much like the apple seed cracking open its hard shell to become a towering tree, the soul, fueled by imagination, breaks through the barriers of life. You need to be able to envision breaking through the constraints of self-doubt, soaring above the mundane, and reaching for excellence.

The soul needs the power of imagination as its ally. Imagination allows the soul to transcend perceived boundaries, encouraging it to envision a reality where the seed of the soul cracks open the shell of limitations, touches the air of possibilities, rises above challenges, defies the gravity of adversity, and reaches for the sky of enlightenment. Imagination becomes the key that unlocks the dormant potential within, transforming the seed of the soul into a flourishing, vibrant entity.

The growth of the soul enriches your moral understanding, significantly influencing your emotional and mental well-being. As your sense of morality strengthens and matures, the health of the soul improves in tandem, promoting positive emotions and bolstering your mental state. Resilience becomes a natural response, enabling you to weather the storms of life with strength and fortitude. Independence and determination follow suit, as a healthy soul is not easily swayed by external pressures but remains grounded in its values and convictions. Clarity of purpose emerges, shining light through life's complexities. Generosity flows effortlessly, and serenity becomes a constant companion. Sincerity in actions and interactions becomes a natural flow.

A rich soul, cultivated in the soil of high morality, has the capacity to enjoy the luxury of happiness and peace. External influences have less impact over its internal state, enabling it to maintain a sense of joy even in challenging circumstances. The richness of the soul creates a sacred space within the mind—a sanctuary of peace where pure love-energy flows effortlessly. This space is alive, vibrant, and abundant, holding the essence of life's greatest treasures. It transcends feelings; it's a mental space where calm and joy coexist, where love isn't sought but simply exists, radiating brighter than stars.

In stark contrast, a stagnant or declining morality impedes the soul's growth, leading to negative emotions and a decline in mental health. Negative emotions pervade, creating an atmosphere of scarcity and insecurity. Dependency and confusion take root, inhibiting the sense of satisfaction. Indecisiveness becomes a stumbling block, and greediness replaces generosity. Jealousy, anxiety, and unrest become unwelcome companions, and hypocrisy becomes a shadow that dims the soul's radiance.

A poor soul, deprived of the nourishment of moral growth, suffers from a lack of enjoyment in life. Every experience adds to its suffering, making life seem consistently dark and gloomy. The soul becomes vulnerable to negative external influences, amplifying its struggles and diminishing its capacity for resilience.

Consider the example of a wealthy and powerful individual who possesses an impoverished soul. Despite owning a mansion with twenty bedrooms, this person grapples with mental unrest, unable to find solace in any of the luxurious rooms. The mental anguish this person endures cannot be alleviated by wealth. They exist in a state of being comfortably uncomfortable, lounging on a plush couch physically, yet suffering mentally.

In contrast, consider individuals with modest financial means but exhibiting a resilient and powerful soul. While their external circumstances might appear bleak, they do not endure mental suffering. These individuals are uncomfortably comfortable; they may sit on a hard rock, but they derive joy from the sunlight and the melodic chirping of birds.

In the best-case scenario, having both earthly wealth and power alongside a healthy, vibrant, and nourished soul is an absolute blessing. However, one is infinitely more important than the other.

In today's world, the pursuit of wealth and material prosperity is a common societal goal. However, the essence of true richness lies not in external possessions but in the depth and well-being of the soul. Consider this scenario: Would you prefer to be a wealthy individual, driving the most luxurious car through the darkness of night, only to arrive home with the heavy burden of mental anguish and thoughts of suicide? Or would you rather be an ordinary person walking through the dead of night, passing the most luxurious car on the road, yet finding solace in contemplating the forthcoming sunrise from the summit of a hill?

This juxtaposition highlights a critical truth: the richness of the soul far surpasses any material wealth. No earthly possessions, regardless of their opulence, can compare to the value of a thriving and fulfilled soul. The state of your soul, as the arbiter of your internal well-being, plays a pivotal role in determining your level of misery or contentment.

Nothing is more precious than a mind free from suffering. A healthy, calm, and quiet soul is the catalyst for a happy and peaceful mind. In this state, external circumstances lose their power to dictate your sense of fulfillment. Regardless of where you are or who you are in the world, living in bliss becomes a tangible reality when the soul is nourished.

Soul searching, the path to true richness, involves a journey within, cultivating a state of internal harmony that transcends the external trappings of wealth. The best outcome in life, the ultimate goal, is to attain a mind free from suffering, live in perpetual bliss, and find contentment in small things in life.

Let's quickly recap the key points from this chapter. We discussed how our world is not the product of random occurrences; everything has a purpose and moves toward greater complexity, indicating the existence of a creator, whom we refer to as God. God exists in singularity, embodying the essence of all things, with everything ultimately returning to God. As the ultimate creator, God's creations started with information, which allowed for differentiation between separate creations. The creation of information imbued with ground zero awareness aimed at evolving toward greater complexity is what we call consciousness.

To enable creation, consciousness had to emerge from singularity, where everything is unified. To facilitate this, God introduced the concept of duality, creating the separate realms of the visible and invisible. The visible realm was endowed with the attribute of light, while the invisible realm was granted the attribute of truth. Consequently, everything in the visible realm is made of light, encompassing both energy and matter, while everything in the invisible realm is derived from truth, manifesting as love and peace.

Our physical bodies are constructed from light (matter and energy), while our spiritual bodies are formed from truth (love and peace). God gifted us with logic to navigate the world of matter and energy in terms of correct and incorrect, and with morality to understand love and peace in terms of good and bad. Our physical health and our mental health depend on our logical and moral understanding.

We also explored how duality led to separation from God, singularity, and bliss, and how the concept of trinity can reverse this effect. When the two ends of duality come together, unity at the apex of the trinity becomes apparent. When light and truth are aligned, when logic and morality harmonize, when our intuition syncs with our desires, when our emotions and feelings are in concert, and when our soul and physical body unite as one, we are then able to sense the presence of God and attain a state of bliss.

Drawing an analogy with an apple seed, which contains all the information needed to grow into a tree, the soul possesses all the knowledge required for you to become the best version of yourself. Just as a seed requires light, water, and fertile soil to flourish, your soul needs truth, love, responsibility, and good intentions to thrive. Furthermore, the power of imagination is absolutely necessary for overcoming self-limiting beliefs and unlocking your greatest potential. Imagination allows you to envision possibilities beyond your current reality, helping you break free from the constraints of your fears, doubts, and perceived limitations. A nourished and empowered soul is free from suffering and mental anguish, enabling you to live with vitality, serenity, resilience, and purpose, consistently in a state of peace and love, regardless of external circumstances.

Now, a new question arises: How can you consistently embody truth, love, responsibility, and good intentions throughout your life to elevate your happiness and live in a state of bliss?

Chapter 9: Truth in the Darkness

Duality permeates all creation, beginning at the highest levels as pure and perfect, where each end of duality represents the ultimate goodness. These are the divine dualities of the visible and invisible, light and truth, energy and matter, love and peace. Yet, as creation evolved, new sets of undivine dualities began to emerge. These lesser dualities rather than complementing each other, they opposed one another.

In the visible realm, light found its counterpart in darkness. In the invisible realm, truth met its opposite in falsehood. The divine partner of light is truth, while its undivine counterpart is darkness. Similarly, the undivine counterpart to truth is falsehood. Thus, light and darkness formed one undivine duality, while truth and falsehood formed another undivine duality.

Furthermore, all divine dualities coexist within the same space. Where there is light, there is truth. Where love is found, peace follows; similarly, matter cannot exist without energy. However, as dualities were created beyond the divine realm, they began to oppose each other, occupying separate spaces where one could not exist within the other. Where there is light, darkness cannot dwell, for darkness is merely the absence of light. The same holds true for truth and falsehood: if something is true, it cannot be false, and falsehood can never be truth. These are the subsequent dualities formed outside of the divine realm.

These undivine dualities introduced the concept of absence—the absence of the divine. Darkness and falsehood came into being as the absence of light and truth. Through this interplay of opposing forces, everything else in existence was created.

God employed countless dualities within the framework of light and darkness, truth and falsehood, giving rise to all subsequent undivine dualities that govern the universe. These include black and white, day and night, good and bad, just and unjust, hope and despair. However, an infinite gap existed between these opposing forces. To bridge this void, God created a spectrum—a seamless transition between extremes, allowing for the manifestation of all possibilities in between.

Consider the spectrum of colors: at one end lies black, at the other, white. But between them exists an infinite range of colors, each blending into the next, forming a continuous, harmonious spectrum of colors. Furthermore, when all colors combine, they produce white, while the absence of all color results in black. Through this, the very concept of color was born.

Similarly, other opposing forces gave rise to entire dimensions of understanding. Between long and short, the concept of length emerged. Between hot and cold, temperature was defined. Between positive and negative, potential was delineated. Between right and wrong, the foundation of ethics was established. Between just and unjust, the framework of justice was formed. Between hope and despair, the essence of motivation took shape.

Duality, therefore, became the source of diversity—introducing contrasts that define the world as we know it. Size, shape, color, ethic, and motives all emerged as part of this elegant balance of undivine dualities, forming the foundation of existence itself.

Furthermore, darkness, unable to penetrate light directly, intwined with light's divine partner—the truth—casting a shadow over it. Where there is truth, there is light; yet, truth itself became veiled by darkness, keeping the light of truth hidden. In a parallel twist, falsehood, unable to overwrite truth, intertwined with truth's divine partner—the light—shrouding it in deception.

In this way, the undivine gap began to take form—a chasm between humanity and the divine, between the physical body and the soul. On the surface lies darkness and falsehood, creating the matrix and veiling the deeper reality that exists beyond. But beyond and through the darkness and falsehood, the light of truth remains, untouched and eternal. Therefore, to reach the soul—and ultimately God—you must traverse this folded reality. You must pass through the layers of darkness and falsehood to reach the light of truth.

At one extreme of all undivine dualities lies the complete absence of the divine. Darkness and falsehood exist as the pinnacle of this absence, forming a void where the divine light seems unreachable. From this nothingness, from this absence of all that is divine, a being was created—one that embodies and amplifies this separation from divinity, widening the rift between humanity and its soul. From the depths of darkness and falsehood, this entity emerged, known across time and traditions as the devil.

The devil represents the great barrier that stands between you and the light of truth, between you and your soul. It is the force that thrives in illusion, deception, and fear, weaving its influence into the fabric of reality to keep you bound within the limitations of undivine dualities. To move beyond this barrier, you must first confront the devil within yourself. You must face your fears, your insecurities, your illusions, and the false beliefs that cloud your vision.

Only by confronting, understanding, and ultimately overcoming the devil can you break through its darkness. Only then can you pierce the veil of deception, uncover the hidden truth, and be illuminated by the light of truth. And when you do, you will unite with your soul, no longer fragmented but whole, standing in the presence of God—the source of all light, love, and reality.

The devil represents the darkness within you, the internal shadow that obstructs your path to self-awareness and connection with your soul. Yet, the devil does not act alone. The devil is a powerful ruler of an entire realm of reality, commanding and ruling over what are known as demons. These demons serve as the legion and army of the devil, embodying its attributes and extending its influence. Within you, they take the form of fears, insecurities, and destructive impulses—forces that strengthen the devil's grip on your mind. Together, they create barriers that separate you from your soul, shrouding the light of truth in layers of deception and chaos.

However, the devil's reach does not end with your inner world. The devil also manifests in external reality, giving rise to acts of conflict, betrayal, and injustice that pervade the world around us. These manifestations are what we perceive as evil.

When we say, "That's an evil act," we are witnessing the devil's dark morality taking form in physical reality. When we say, "That person is evil," it means the devil has overtaken that person's soul, using them as a vessel to project its darkness into reality.

In this way, the devil and its demons represent the inner darkness dwelling in the recesses of your mind, while evil signifies the outward expressions of this darkness in the external world. The battle against darkness is both an internal and external journey. To overcome darkness, you must face the devil and its army of demons within, while striving to bring the light of truth into the external world as you face evil.

When I speak of the devil or demons, I am referring to the darkness in the recesses of your mind. When I speak of evil, I am pointing to the dark forces that manifest in our external reality. Both must be confronted and understood to uncover the light of truth that lies hidden, guarded by these dark forces, waiting to be reclaimed by you.

Each time in life you fail to see the truth, resist it, or refuse to accept it fully, the fog of darkness grows thicker, surrounding you and obscuring your path. To move forward, you must be willing to accept the truth fully no matter how unsettling it may be. You must pierce through the deceptions of darkness and confront your inner demons. Only by facing these challenges can you uncover the wisdom and peace that lie within. Paradoxically, the devil's most potent weapon against you is the harsh reality of truth itself.

The devil manifests its evil morality into the external reality, shrouding the beauty of truth with its dark nature. Then, the devil works tirelessly to make you resist the harsh reality of truth by questioning its seemingly unkind nature. Devil stirs anger, resentment, and defiance within you, driving you to fight against what is real. This resistance against truth blinds you, keeping you trapped in confusion and turmoil. However, if you recognize and understand the devil's deception, you begin to see the wisdom hidden within the truth. Through this wisdom and clarity, the very thing that once felt harsh becomes your pathway to light and freedom.

In this way, the truth holds a dual role: it can be wielded as a weapon of darkness, pushing you into struggle and despair, or it can become the key to your liberation, guiding you toward wisdom and inner peace. The choice lies in how you confront and embrace truth.

Imagine you're in a monogamous relationship, deeply in love with your partner, believing he or she is the one you want to spend the rest of your life with. Then, soon after, you discover that your partner has been cheating on you all along. This revelation shatters your reality, plunging you into darkness as you struggle with the conflicting feelings you sense toward someone you once loved deeply. This turmoil arises because you failed to see the truth earlier—the truth that your partner was unfaithful.

In this scenario, as you retreat into the dark corners of your mind, you come face to face with your inner demons. Now, the question becomes: What will you do with your darkness? Will you allow it to consume you, choosing to cheat on your partner in retaliation, mirroring the very betrayal you despise? Will you become bitter because of the experience and lose trust in others, shutting yourself off from meaningful connections? Will you let the betrayal erode your sense of self-worth, making you question whether you were ever enough? Will you carry this pain into future relationships, sabotaging them with fears of being hurt again? Will you lash out at the world, projecting your anger and disappointment onto those who had nothing to do with the betrayal?

But now, consider a different path. Will you take this experience as an opportunity to grow, to learn, and to gain wisdom? Will you use it to better understand yourself and the type of love and respect you deserve? Will you reflect on the red flags you may have overlooked and sharpen your intuition for the future? Will you use this pain to strengthen your boundaries, ensuring you are treated with honesty and care in the relationships to come?

Will you find a way to forgive—not necessarily for the sake of your partner, but for your own peace, freeing yourself from the burden of resentment? Will you embrace the understanding that betrayal is not a reflection of your worth, but of your partner's choices? Most importantly, can you allow this hardship to teach you resilience and compassion, empowering you to face the future with an open heart, wiser and stronger than before?

The choice is yours. You can resist the truth and remain in the darkness, consumed by rage, hatred, and thoughts of revenge; Or, you can choose to accept the truth and learn from the darkness, using it as a catalyst to move toward the light, creating a brighter and better future for yourself.

Consider an even more extreme case: imagine your teenage daughter is kidnapped on her way home from school, brutally assaulted, and murdered. This unimaginable tragedy forces you into the darkest recesses of your mind, forcing you to confront the harsh truth of reality and bringing you face to face with the devil itself. In such a moment, you are left with a heart-wrenching question: What will you do now? Will you hunt down the perpetrator and take their life, becoming a killer yourself, mirroring the very evil you abhor? Will you allow darkness to consume you, pulling you into the depths of hatred and despair, where you find yourself wishing for the killer's agony and death?

Or will you confront and accept the harsh truth—that such horrific events, as unthinkable as they are, happen in the world? This time, it happened to your daughter. Will you use this tragedy as an opportunity to become more resilient? Will you rise above this unimaginable pain by choosing forgiveness and compassion? Not because you feel bad for the perpetrator, but because you deserve peace. Compassion, even in such an extreme situation, is not about condoning the evil act or absolving its consequences; it is about breaking the cycle of hatred and refusing to let the darkness of another's actions dictate the rest of your life.

The truth is that no matter how painful, her fate was beyond your control. Fighting reality, questioning why it happened, or fueling yourself with anger, hatred, and despair will only deepen your suffering. That is precisely what the devil desires—to keep you lost in his den, trapped in darkness. The only way out is to face the truth and accept it with grace, no matter how unbearable it seems. Acceptance like compassion doesn't mean condoning the event; it means acknowledging that life, in its unfathomable complexity, has plans beyond what you can comprehend or control.

The truth is that death comes for everyone—some sooner, some later. Some leave this world peacefully, while others endure unimaginable pain. This is the reality you must grapple with. Your choice is simple yet profound: resist the truth and spend the rest of your life consumed by sorrow, anger, and hatred; or accept the truth, become stronger, and move forward. Beneath every tragic event lies a hidden wisdom, waiting for you to uncover. Only by accepting the truth can you transform your suffering into strength and your pain into a deeper understanding of life.

The devil's role is to reveal the harsh truths of life to you, often in the most unexpected and uncomfortable ways. Each time you accept a truth, the devil moves on to present the next one—another truth you might be resisting or denying. The devil is relentless and does not stop. Its sole purpose is to force you to see the truth and tempt you to fight it, deny it, or look the other way.

When you're confronted with a truth, it places a profound responsibility upon you. You must choose what to do with it. If you accept it, dissect it, and unlock the wisdom it holds, you are rewarded with clarity, peace, and a deeper understanding of yourself and the world. But if you resist or fail to extract its meaning, truth itself becomes your suffering, trapping you in a cycle of confusion and turmoil.

In this way, the devil becomes both a challenger and a teacher. It forces you to confront what you may not want to see, driving you to either grow through wisdom or endure the endless pain of ignorance. The choice to rise or fall depends entirely on you.

Consider the story of Adam and Eve: the devil told them that if they wanted to know the truth, they should eat from the Tree of Knowledge. They ate the fruit, and humanity has been in the process of digesting the truth ever since. The devil didn't lie about the consequences—eating the fruit brought knowledge, but with it came immense responsibility and suffering as humanity began grappling with truth.

Now, imagine you've made your way to heaven after this lifetime. Upon arriving, the devil appears again, offering you another fruit from the Tree of Knowledge. This time, you might respond, "No, thank you, devil. I've tried that before and suffered greatly for it. I appreciate the offer, but I'm not eating that fruit again. I've learned my lesson, I have gained wisdom, I know the truth now, and I don't wish to return to Earth. The kingdom of Earth is all yours, Devil. I am content here in heaven."

When you truly know the truth, you will never make the same mistake twice. Mistakes are repeated only as long as the wisdom of truth eludes you. This is the game of the matrix you are here to play—a journey of discovering the truth. The quest for truth is embedded deep within the core of your psyche. There is no escape from it, for it is an inseparable part of who you are.

Look at humanity on Earth—our thirst for truth is insatiable. We have developed sciences to peer into the depths of the cosmos and the intricacies of atoms. We've created countless forms of art to explore music, language, painting, and dance, all in an effort to understand existence. And we're only just beginning. With AI powered-computers by our side, our quest for truth and knowledge is accelerating at an unprecedented pace. This hunger for understanding is the lingering effect of the fruit of knowledge that Adam and Eve consumed—the fruit we are still in the process of digesting to this day.

To know the real truth, you must understand and accept the darkness. Become knowledgeable about the darker aspects of reality. The darkness of the devil is extremely important in your journey—it serves as both the path to your salvation and the source of your misery, depending on how you confront and navigate your inner darkness. Therefore, we begin this chapter by uncovering the truth within the darkness.

To reiterate, truth and light coexisted harmoniously during the initial phase of creation, enhancing one another. But with the introduction of darkness and falsehood, light became intertwined with falsehood, and truth became enshrouded in darkness. This twist in creation introduced opposing and contradictory dualities, layered upon the original divine and complementary ones. And the devil became the possessor of the truth, standing between you and the divine.

In this way, your soul stands as your divine partner, a creation of love and peace, firmly rooted in truth. On the other hand, the devil acts as your undivine counterpart, veiling your path with layers of darkness and falsehood. The devil positions itself between you and the truth, trapping your soul in a fog of deception. This weakens and obscures your connection to your soul.

To rediscover your soul, you must confront the devil, peeling back the layers of darkness to reveal the light within. This requires embracing the truth, no matter how harsh it may seem, as well as understanding and utilizing the boundless power of love and peace. This journey—facing the darkness to embrace truth, love, and peace—is the very process of salvation.

In short, with the emergence of the devil, truth—once clear and visible in the light—now lies shrouded beneath a veil of darkness. Light, which originally resided in truth, has become cloaked in falsehood. The human soul, once filled with love and peace, is now touched by chaos and fear. While we retain our divine partner within the soul, we are also interwoven with our undivine counterpart through the devil. This twist in creation has sown paradoxes, contradictions, and confusions throughout all creation.

For humanity, understanding and navigating these layers of reality has become a formidable task. Self-discovery and soul-searching require you to confront the layers of darkness that pervade both the external world and your inner being. To truly know yourself, you must pierce through the veil of evil manifesting in your physical reality and dismantle the devil's deceptions that cloud your minds. The path to enlightenment is, paradoxically, the darkest and most falsehood-laden path you can embark on. Thus, the journey to enlightenment begins in darkness which is the central theme of this chapter.

Truth in the darkness is all about understanding, accepting, and embracing the fact that the entirety of truth can never be fully known; a portion of it will forever remain veiled in darkness, beyond our grasp.

Accepting the certainty of death is a starting point for understanding truth in the darkness. Death will come to all. The inevitability of death confronts us with the realization that we truly know very little about life and what may come after death. Even the greatest minds in human history passed away with mysteries still unsolved, never fully unlocking the secrets of the universe. No one will ever completely solve the puzzle of life before facing death.

This realization should humble you. Your lifetime is too brief to acquire anything more than a fragment of the vast knowledge that exists. Approach life and its mysteries with humility; recognize that the journey toward enlightenment begins with acknowledging how much remains unknown and unseen.

As I write this book to share what I've explored about the deep mysteries of the world, I must confess that nothing I say here represents the absolute truth. I do not possess the absolute truth, nor will I ever fully know it. My understanding is limited to what I can conjure up in my imagination. The model of reality I'm presenting here is based on what I believe might be true, designed to ease my mental distress. This model has worked for me, making my days much brighter, and I share it in the hope that you might find elements within these pages that help alleviate your mental suffering as well.

I urge you not to take my words at face value. Instead, approach them with skepticism. Question and critique every concept that resonates with you, then mold and reshape it to align with your worldview, creating your own personal model of reality. What doesn't make sense within these pages, discard freely, as it may not be the truth.

I constantly question my own beliefs, searching for flaws in my understanding. There have been many times when I encountered truths that contradicted my model of reality, forcing me to rethink and redesign my framework. As a result, my beliefs today are different from what they were years ago. They may change again if I encounter higher truths that I do not yet comprehend.

I approach my beliefs with skepticism, and I caution you to do the same. The complexity of this world makes it impossible for me to claim absolute certainty about the ultimate reality.

I am aware that at the moment of my death, I will depart with as many questions as anyone else regarding life's purpose and what comes after. The complete truth will always remain elusive. I am in search of my own truth, and you are responsible for finding your own truth; I can only offer guidance to help you navigate your own path. And remember, the only truth you can grasp is relative—mere crumbs and fragments of truth during your brief existence on this tiny planet.

The first step on the path to enlightenment, and a crucial element for the growth of the soul, is the acknowledgment of your own ignorance, realizing that you do not and cannot know the whole truth. Humility is the first lesson in the path of enlightenment.

Recognizing the complexity of the world you inhabit naturally diminishes your arrogance and fosters a more humble attitude. Throughout history, true spiritual leaders have openly confessed their lack of complete knowledge of the truth. It is often the arrogant people who mistakenly project their own pride and ego onto these figures.

Consider these profound admissions from revered figures across different faiths and philosophies:

Mahatma Gandhi remarked, "I claim to be a simple individual liable to err like any other fellow mortal. I own, however, that I have humility enough to confess my errors and to retrace my steps."

Mother Teresa expressed, "I am a little pencil in the hand of a writing God who is sending a love letter to the world."

Jesus stated, "By myself I can do nothing; I judge only as I hear, and my judgment is just, for I seek not to please myself but him who sent me."

Mohammad declared, "I am only a man like you. My duty is to convey the message."

In the Book of Numbers, Moses is described: "Now Moses was a very humble man, more humble than anyone else on the face of the earth."

Abraham confessed, "I am nothing but dust and ashes."

Lao Tzu observed, "The more that you know, the less you understand."

Rumi noted, "Sell your cleverness and buy bewilderment."

Buddha advised, "Do not believe in anything simply because you have heard it. Do not believe in anything simply because it is spoken and rumored by many. Do not believe in anything simply because it is found written in your religious books. Do not believe in anything merely on the authority of your teachers and elders. Do not believe in traditions because they have been handed down for many generations. But after observation and analysis, when you find that anything agrees with reason and is conducive to the good and benefit of one and all, then accept it and live up to it."

The first step and every following step in the path of enlightenment must be filled with humility. But why is this so? Why have such bright and legendary figures in the history of humankind expressed humility with such great importance? Let's explore why those who seek the truth come to the realization that they indeed do not know the truth.

One of the most powerful tools we have to make sense of the world is through our imagination. Albert Einstein once said, "Imagination is more important than knowledge. For knowledge is limited, whereas imagination embraces the entire world, stimulating progress, giving birth to evolution." Imagination is the building block of our discoveries and technologies. We first imagined flying before we made airplanes. We wrote many books about traveling to the moon and even made the movie *A Trip to the Moon* in 1902—decades before we actually landed there in 1969. Many sci-fi movies we make today might become reality in the future because we have conjured them in our imagination. However, our imagination, with all its power, has its limitations.

There are concepts in existence that surpass our capacity for imagination. For instance, the essence of God is beyond description: a realm where there is neither time, space, matter, light, truth, existence, nor any recognizable concepts. We cannot fathom what existed before time; attempts by scientists to decode the Big Bang at time zero result in mathematical breakdowns and inconclusive answers. Imagining a place devoid of space and devoid of distance is beyond our grasp. Yet, the nature of God transcends the concept of time and space and what we normally consider as existence.

This limitation of human imagination is acknowledged across various spiritual traditions. Lao Tzu, in his renowned work Tao Te Ching, articulates this, stating, "The Tao that can be told is not the eternal Tao; the name that can be named is not the eternal name." Here, Tao is analogous to the concept of God in the Chinese tradition of Taoism, highlighting the ineffable quality of the divine. Similarly, Saint Augustine from Christianity remarked, "If you understand it, it is not God,". In Sufism, Rumi expressed that "Silence is the language of God, all else is poor translation." The Upanishads of Hinduism reflect a similar sentiment: "Words turn back along with the mind, not reaching the Brahman," where Brahman refers to the ultimate reality, analogous to the infinite nature of God in Western contexts. The Quran also supports this view: "Vision comprehends Him not, but He comprehends [all] vision," asserting that divine understanding lies beyond human perception.

This acknowledgment that we cannot fully understand God leads to another question: If we cannot understand the creator, is it possible to understand its creation? Let us examine what God has created to gauge how much of it we truly understand.

Earlier we discussed that science can only account for less than 5% of true reality which we call observable universe. This 5% of reality encompasses everything we know about the universe from both the macro and micro scales. Let's start with the macro scale: the cosmic level. Within the universe there exist infinitely many galaxies, stars and celestial objects that remain enshrouded in mystery and are largely unknown from a human perspective. It's not just that we have limited understanding of distant galaxies; we do not even fully understand our own planet, Earth. Our knowledge of the Earth, quite literally, only scratches the surface.

For instance, the details of what lies beneath the surface of the Earth remain largely unmapped. The deepest hole ever drilled into the Earth reaches just over 12 kilometers, while the Earth's crust—which you can think of as the skin of the planet—is about 70 kilometers deep. This means we haven't even pierced through the Earth's skin, the outermost layer. While we have some understanding of the Earth's layers from the surface down to the core, we have not thoroughly explored or examined them. Additionally, even our planet's oceans, which cover more than 70% of the Earth's surface, have only been explored to about 10% at the time of writing this book.

We know very little about our own planet, and we know almost nothing about other planets and celestial objects. There are countless objects in the sky that remain largely shrouded in mystery. This is just on the macro scale of existence.

Now, turning to the micro scale, the universe likely contains an infinite variety of particles, of which we have only begun to understand a small fraction. Even the most accomplished scientists in the field of particle physics have acknowledged the possibility that there could be an infinite number of particles yet to be discovered, making it unlikely that we will ever fully map out all the fundamental building blocks of the universe.

At the quantum level, the mysteries only deepen. The quantum world is so abstract, so unlike the tangible reality, that our understanding of its nature and its complexities remains in its infancy. Despite decades of research and groundbreaking discoveries, we've barely scratched the surface of quantum functionalities.

From the micro scale to the macro scale, our understanding of the world we inhabit is minimal, nothing more than a fragment of truth about our physical reality. Now consider everything we discussed, from the smallest particles to the vast expanse of galaxies, all of this comprises less than 5% of reality. Then there is the other 95%—often referred to as dark energy and dark matter—that is completely unknown to science. The remaining 95% is filled with concepts even more complex than those within the observable 5%, not to mention the potential existence of parallel universes and other dimensions that are entirely out of our reach.

These mysteries—at the cosmic level, the microscopic level, and other dimensional levels—are all parts of the truth hidden in darkness. You and I will perish in a few short decades, without ever having a chance to fully understand these mysteries of reality.

Considering future generations, you might wonder whether humanity will ever uncover all the mysteries of existence in some far-distant future. However, the concept of quaternity firmly stands against such a fantasy. Quaternity posits that every subject, regardless of its apparent simplicity, embodies infinite complexity, and a portion of its truth will forever remain unknown—this is referred to as *the unknown of the unknown*. Science itself corroborates the quaternity claim, as every scientific discovery, rather than simplifying our understanding of the universe, tends to raise new questions and reveal deeper layers of complexity. This has been the enduring trend of scientific journey, never really finding answers, just more questions.

Science has never reached a definitive end to any field of study; we have not and will never publish the final book on mathematics, physics, chemistry, or any other discipline. Even if humanity's knowledge continues to expand exponentially for an indefinite period of time, we will still not grasp the full truth about the world we inhabit. Much like the concept of God, the ultimate reality will always be shrouded in mystery from the human perspective, veiled by an impenetrable darkness that our finite understanding cannot illuminate.

We cannot fully understand God, nor can we fully comprehend God's creation. This is precisely why the greatest minds in human history approached truth with profound humility, fully aware of the vastness of their own ignorance.

This realization is deeply humbling, acting as a reminder to keep your vanity in check and not mistake your perception of reality for absolute truth. Always remain open-minded, your beliefs flexible, and your outlook susceptible to change. Avoid rigid beliefs, and refrain from claiming certainty about the absolute truth.

Truth in the darkness reveals the infinite complexity of the world, planting the seeds of doubt in your mind about what you believe to be true. This encourages a perpetual process of examination, reevaluation, and the ongoing refinement of your belief system. It becomes a catalyst for change, growth, and transformation. This is the path that sages and legendary figures throughout human history have followed to achieve enlightenment. Their greatness emerged not from their arrogance and assurance but from a foundation of doubt and relentless refinement of their beliefs, allowing them to evolve and shape themselves into the best versions of who they could be.

Socrates elucidated this concept when he declared, "the one who knows, never learns," highlighting the fact that certainty is the barrier to further understanding. When you become certain about what you know, you inadvertently close the door to new information and insights that might be more accurate than the knowledge that has shaped your current beliefs.

Certainty is the work of the devil, a clever means to feed your vanity with a false sense of assurance. Beliefs rooted in certainty foster a sense of superiority and self-glorification. Superiority creates distance, a chasm where unity once stood. This is evident in religious doctrines veiled by darkness: the Jewish people see themselves as chosen ones, Christians claim a direct link to God, Muslims believe all faiths were perfected through Muhammad, Buddhists hold their connection to the natural world as their crowning belief, and Taoists pride themselves on never waging war. Each considers themselves superior to others. While speaking of unity, they all create separation by viewing those who think differently as inferior or flawed.

When certainty seeps into your belief system, it becomes a catalyst for division, isolation, and strife. It pushes your soul toward the realm of the collective unconsciousness, a domain where genuine connections are scarce. When you view yourself as superior and your beliefs as better than others, you naturally sever the genuine bonds with those you perceive as inferior.

As a consequence, your soul retreats further into the collective unconsciousness, where meaningful connections are few and far between. You become superficially connected only to those who think like you, while distancing yourself from everyone else. This is where the devil thrives—a domain of separation, where isolation and conflict flourish, pulling you further from the light of unity and harmony.

There is an ancient story, passed down through generations and often attributed to Moses, that reveals a profound lesson. One day, God called Moses to the mountain and gave him a peculiar task. "Go down to the city," God said, "and find any person or creature that you are certain you are better than. Bring that being to me, and if you are correct, I will grant you one of the deepest secrets of the universe."

Moses descended from the mountain and entered the city. As dusk fell, he saw a man stealing bread from a market stall. He thought, "Surely, I must be better than this thief. I have never stolen." He followed the man and watched as he went to the poorest corner of the city and shared the stolen bread with starving orphans. Moses' heart stirred with shame. "I have never sacrificed my dignity to steal so that others might eat," he thought. "I may not be better than this man, who dares to risk his name to save others from hunger."

Determined, Moses pressed on. Word reached him that a man had committed murder, and he felt certain that this must be the one he sought. Killing with intent, after all, was the greatest of sins. He pursued the trail of the murderer, only to learn that the victim was a rich man known for his corruption, cruelty, and abuse—crimes for which he had evaded justice through wealth and power. Moses thought to himself, "I have never willingly sacrificed my future or risked imprisonment to stop a wicked man and end his reign of suffering. I am not braver than this man."

Disheartened, Moses turned back toward the mountain, feeling the weight of his failure. As he made his way, he came upon a lifeless dog lying by the roadside. "At last," he thought, "I am a human being; surely, I am better than a dead dog." He lifted the animal onto his shoulders and continued his ascent.

Before he reached the summit, he noticed the dog bore bite marks. A thought pierced his heart: "Perhaps this creature died defending its master from a wild beast. I have never given my life, or even considered doing so, to protect another." Reverently, he buried the dog and continued up the mountain, empty-handed.

When Moses stood before God, he said, "I have traveled the earth searching for someone or something inferior to me, but I found none."

God replied, "And that, Moses, is the lesson I wanted you to learn."

The moral of this tale is clear: the sense of superiority over others—whether in occupation, social standing, beliefs, or any aspect of life—is an illusion rooted in falsehood. The moment you cling to certainty and see yourself superior to others, pride takes hold, and darkness creeps into your soul. The truth is that while you may hold beliefs and values, they do not make you superior, nor do they represent the absolute truth over those of others.

Certainty and humility cannot coexist harmoniously, as certainty stands in direct opposition to humility. To claim to know the absolute truth is, to elevate oneself above others, implying a sense of superiority and vanity. Certainty implies that your perspective is the definitive one, leaving no room for the possibility that you may be mistaken.

True humility requires an open mind and a flexible belief system. You can believe in what you like and hold on to values that resonate deeply with you, but humility demands that you do not elevate your beliefs above others simply because they feel right and logical to you.

Belief should not be a tool for self-exaltation or a pedestal from which to look down on others.

The only certainty in life is uncertainty itself—the understanding that the absolute truth is beyond human grasp. The vastness of existence, the mysteries of consciousness, and the intricacies of the world far exceed your capacity for comprehension. This realization should inspire humility, not arrogance. Your knowledge is always incomplete, your perspective limited, and your beliefs subject to error. Free yourself from the chains of vanity and superiority. Humility in the face of uncertainty is not a weakness but a profound strength. Cultivate a mindset that values learning and growth over being "right."

Now look at the complexity of truth in this way: unraveling the mysteries of truth is a time-consuming endeavor. You need to observe, listen, learn, read, and explore life to grasp the truth, and all these activities require time. Unfortunately, your time on this planet is typically less than a century. Simply put, you do not have enough time to learn everything you might want to learn.

For instance, I would like to be able to speak every language in the world fluently—an impossible task. Additionally, I am drawn to diverse fields such as science, medicine, religion, law, art, music, history, and philosophy, but my limited lifespan will prevent me from mastering any of these disciplines. I would like to read every book ever written. Yet, even if I begin now and read until my death, I would only manage to read a small fraction of humanity's written works. Even if I could read every book, my grasp of the full truth would still remain completely out of reach.

Let's look at our limited knowledge from a different angle. In early years of your life, your primary focus was on learning basic survival skills. As you mature into adulthood, when the pursuit of truth could become more feasible, you find yourself entangled in the daily grind. Many of these daily struggles involve mundane, repetitive tasks that do little to enlighten you about the deeper truths and purpose of your life. You consistently have to work and perform the same routines. Your days are a constant juggling act—satisfying hunger, quenching thirst, and tending to the necessities of your bodily needs. This relentless cycle of sustenance, rest, and hygiene is compounded by a ceaseless stream of life's problems and diversions.

Additionally, your family and friends demand your attention. Some may be too old or too young, requiring you to attend to their needs, which often takes time away from pursuing your own path and personal development. Life, by its very nature, is short, and your precious time is disproportionately consumed by the demands of your daily existence. Before you know it, the effects of aging will set in—your hair will turn gray, your skin begin to sag, your muscles decay, and the pains of old age reduce your mobility and diminish your drive to pursue the deeper truths and purpose of your life.

With all that said, you face an even more profound challenge in your pursuit of truth—you are inherently a forgetful being. Your recollection of your own life experiences tends to fade as the years pass, rendering anything older than a decade or two a blurred haze in your memory. Despite your effort to accumulate information from numerous sources, the details often slip through the fragile hold of your memory. Consider all the books you might have read; the majority of the details within those books gradually fade away, leaving behind only a faint trace of the concepts elucidated in those pages.

Tasks as seemingly simple as remembering the content of an old exam or recalling the meals you had in the past week elude you. Names of individuals you've just met slip from your memory, prompting you to ask for their names once again. Your capacity for forgetfulness extends beyond what you might be comfortable acknowledging. The nuances of your daily experiences, the details of conversations, and the depth of the knowledge you acquire slip from your grasp more frequently than you might care to admit. Accepting your nature as a forgetful creature is paramount. The knowledge and insights gained today will fade away tomorrow, creating an additional barrier in your quest for truth.

Continuing with the concept of your innate forgetfulness, psychology posits that the bulk of your mental development occurred during the first seven to ten years of your life. However, the cruel twist lies in your limited memory of this crucial period, during which decisions were often made for you by parents and other adults. This means that you did not consciously construct your own personality, nor are you fully aware of your true identity. Much of who you are today was shaped during your early childhood that you can scarcely remember, leaving gaps in your understanding of the very foundation of your own personality.

Taking a darker turn, some experts propose that extreme traumas, especially in early childhood, may induce memory blockage, rendering some individuals unable to access the root memories of their suffering. The inability to recall traumatic events raises questions about healing and self-discovery—how can one heal from past traumas when the memories are not even accessible?

The final and perhaps most challenging aspect of truth in the darkness is the undivine counterpart of truth itself: falsehood. In today's world, seeking the truth through news outlets leads to misinformation, while choosing to ignore the news leaves you uninformed. In this way, you are either misinformed or uninformed. The quest for truth is like searching for a needle in a haystack, but with the added complexity that falsehood and lies masquerade as truth. In a literal haystack, the distinction between hay and a needle is clear, making the needle identifiable once found. Unfortunately, the same clarity does not apply to the truth.

Lies skillfully camouflage themselves, obscuring, replacing, and substituting the truth. Lies' resemblance to truth further compounds the challenge, making it difficult to discern one from the other. Unlike a tangible needle, truth lacks a distinct marker, making it susceptible to manipulation and disguise. This blurring of the lines between truth and falsehood complicates your understanding of reality and challenges your ability to make informed decisions.

Another old story, passed down through generations in oral tradition, beautifully illustrates this concept. One day, Truth and Lie were walking together. As they strolled, Lie said to Truth, "Today is a beautiful day, isn't it?" Truth looked around and, seeing that it was indeed a beautiful day, agreed. Lie then suggested, "The weather is perfect, why don't we go for a swim in the lake?" Truth, trusting Lie, agreed, and they both went to the water and swam.

But suddenly, Lie stepped out of the water, took Truth's clothes, dressed in them, and ran away. When Truth emerged from the lake, it found its clothes gone and realized what had happened. Unwilling to wear the garments of a lie, Truth walked through the streets naked.

Since that day, Lie has walked around in Truth's clothing, pretending to be Truth, and people, comfortable with the dressed-up Lie, accept it without question. Meanwhile, the world turns away from the naked Truth, for few are brave enough to face it as it truly is.

The devil always disguises itself as the truth, wearing a mask so convincing that without discerning eyes, you risk mistaking lies for reality. If you lack the insight to perceive the true nature of deception, you are destined to accept falsehoods as truths, leading you astray from understanding and wisdom.

To effectively distinguish truth from falsehood, there is only one viable approach: you must be willing to confront uncomfortable questions and face uncomfortable realities. Are you prepared to consider the possibility that some of your long-held beliefs—whether they are religious, political, cultural, or deeply ingrained social convictions—might be based on falsehoods? Is it possible that your political leaders could deceive you in their quest for power and glory? Could your religious leaders be promising you salvation in the name of God for their personal benefit? Might it be that those you admire have motives that do not align with your best interests? Could you yourself be the creator and architect of the most significant lies ever told to you, hiding your true self from your own awareness?

These are daunting questions that require courage and openness to address. Are you ready to challenge yourself and potentially overturn your existing belief systems? Can you humble yourself to accept truths that may radically alter your understanding of the world and your place within it? Are you prepared to dismantle your old beliefs and construct a new framework based on a deeper, perhaps more accurate, understanding of reality? Facing the truth, especially when it contradicts what you have always believed, demands a profound level of honesty and bravery.

In legal systems that use courts, judges, and juries aimed to uncover the truth, unfortunately falsehoods can still prevail within these structures. When a judge makes an error, an innocent person might unjustly face imprisonment, bearing the brunt of this flawed judgment.

On the path to enlightenment, you are the judge and jury responsible for finding the truth in your life, and the courtroom is your own mental landscape. If you falter in your judgment in the pursuit of truth, if you fail to identify falsehoods, the repercussions are deeply personal and devastating. Failure to see the truth will stunt your spiritual growth, distort your understanding of reality, and negatively influence the trajectory of your life. Thus, to discover the truth, you must probe even deeper than a judge in a courtroom, recognizing that the consequences of your judgments directly impact the very essence of your life. You must become more vigilant, more critical, and more reflective to ensure that you live based on truth to enhance, rather than hinder, your personal and spiritual growth.

In a nutshell, traversing the path of enlightenment is fraught with multifaceted challenges rooted in the following concepts: the vastness of the universe, time constraints, daily distractions and responsibilities, inherent forgetfulness, the elusive nature of self-knowledge, and the falsehood that permeates everywhere. These intertwined elements create formidable barriers in your quest for truth.

Don't be disheartened by these seemingly dark and gloomy facts; remember, stars shine the brightest on the darkest nights. To heal your suffering, you must first understand its depths by venturing into the unknown aspects of your being and embracing the darkest parts of your existence. Within the depths of your struggles lies the key to understanding and healing. Accepting the darkness that dwells within you and around you is akin to finding yourself in a dark room—your initial instinct might be to panic and flee, but as you give yourself time to adjust, your eyes gradually acclimate to the darkness, unveiling mysteries previously hidden from you.

Similarly, confronting the devil within you and embracing the darkness in your life allows you to become accustomed to its chilling and foreboding nature. This acceptance is transformative; it instills in you a readiness to change for the better and grow stronger. It also helps you find comfort in the unknown and develop resilience against your deepest fears. Through this process, courage blossoms, and bravery takes root.

The darkness that surrounds you serves to teach you valuable lessons. Be humble, test your bravery, and strive to change your life for the better. It is okay not to know everything. No one possesses the complete truth, yet some sages have reached enlightenment despite the pervasive unknown and darkness around them. Thus, you too can find enlightenment amidst the darkness in the world. You don't need to understand everything to find your path; you just need to be flexible enough to accept and embrace the truth when you encounter it, even if it means that this truth shatters your current beliefs.

To reach heaven, you must go through hell, as heaven lies beyond the boundaries of hell. Truth in the darkness highlights the limitations, distractions, and challenges that persist in your life. It exposes the temporal constraints that shape your existence, the inherent forgetfulness that clouds your perception, the elusive nature of self-knowledge, and the lies that complicate your daily experiences. Once you become brave enough to accept life with its evil nature, you then possess the necessary prerequisites to traverse through your personal hell and reach your personal heaven. This journey of acceptance and understanding not only challenges you but also transforms you, allowing you to emerge enlightened and at peace, having confronted and overcome the darkest aspects of your reality.

It is said that after his agonizing death on the cross, Jesus left behind his mortal form and descended into the depths of hell before his resurrection. In hell, he was tasked with bearing witness to the suffering of all humankind. He endured the weight of that immense suffering before resurrecting and eventually reuniting with the Father. This path, marked by sacrifice and redemption, is one that every soul on a spiritual journey must traverse.

You may not need to face the torment of physical crucifixion or descend into a literal hell, carrying the weight of humanity's anguish. But you must be willing to die upon the cross of your old, worn-out beliefs, to descend into your personal hell. Only then can you be reborn in spirit, with beliefs more closely aligned with truth.

Truth in the darkness operates as a purely informative entity, demanding no immediate action. Much like being in a darkened space where your actions are limited to understanding your surroundings, the darkness that engulfs your soul doesn't necessarily prompt immediate action. Instead, darkness beckons you to keenly and patiently perceive and acknowledge the elements that dwell within the recesses of your being.

The pursuit of truth prompts you to question the authenticity of your identity. Contemplate whether you are ready for substantial changes in your life. Scrutinize the intention of your convictions and question how much of your cherished beliefs are, in fact, untrue. Evaluate whether the activities you enjoy and the relationships you maintain contribute positively or detrimentally to your well-being.

Now, the ultimate query emerges: Can you accept the unsettling notion that enlightenment might necessitate sacrificing your current way of life, which may include beliefs, families, friends, jobs, and the familiar comforts that define your daily habits? Are you prepared to pay the considerable price for the enlightenment and peace of mind that truth will bring?

In short, your current task is to humble yourself to the extent that you will be prepared to stand before the naked truth of your reality, a prerequisite for any meaningful steps toward healing and enlightenment.

Let us now turn our gaze towards a more uplifting chapter in this narrative. The forthcoming section may not be devoid of challenges, but it certainly does not seep itself entirely into darkness. Instead, it navigates the nuanced space between light and darkness—the realm of shadows. Within the shadow, there exists a delicate equilibrium, a fusion of light and darkness in measured proportions. Shadow is the only realm where these contrasting forces of light and darkness coexist harmoniously.

The beauty of the shadow lies in its subtle contrasts, for it can help you discern between light and darkness. To uncover the truth, you must traverse the depths of darkness, locating the edge where darkness and light converge within the shadow. It is from this vantage point that you can gradually shift toward the light of truth, guided by the wisdom acquired along the journey.

Chapter 10: Truth in the Shadow

Before we delve into this chapter, let's first understand some terms that will appear throughout the book. I will often speak of a "lost soul" or say that "your soul has been trapped in the tunnel of darkness or devil's den." This is when you feel an inner void, an aching emptiness, as if something is missing from your life; this is when others' behavior tends to trigger you, when you are unsure about your life's purpose, when thinking of the past causes regrets, resentments, and sorrow, when thinking of the future causes stress and worries, or when you feel a sense of unease for any reason. It's the heaviness pressing on your shoulders or the repeated surge of negative emotions. These are all signs that a gap has formed between you and your soul.

This gap is the realm where the devil thrives, casting its shadow and weaving darkness between you and your soul. The emptiness you feel within becomes a void filled by the devil, distorting the voice of your soul and twisting its emotions. Basically, the devil intercepts the signals sent by the soul, corrupts and alters the message with its deceptive tactics, and then delivers them to you disguised as your soul and your true desires. If your soul craves love, the devil tempts you toward despair and hatred. If your soul longs for peace, the devil drives you toward rage and conflict. If your soul yearns for fulfillment, the devil lures you toward wealth and material possessions.

This is how people wage wars, spark conflicts, and cause immense suffering in the name of God, justice, or other noble ideals. History has shown how often wars are fought with the promise of peace and how hatred toward others is justified in the name of love for one's own kind. In doing so, people generate thoughts and feelings that stray far from their soul's desires, de-calibrating their inner moral compass and blinding themselves to the light of reality.

Here, the devil masquerades as truth, tricking you into fighting for its causes of darkness while convincing you that you are serving righteousness. When the devil claims the space meant for the soul, it weakens the connection of the soul to collective consciousness and pushes it into the dark abyss of collective unconsciousness, a realm short on resources of love and peace, starving the soul. As a result, the soul's growth is stunted, leaving people desperate to fill the void they sense within. Some turn to fear, anger, and hatred; some turn into drugs, gambling, and addictions, while others seek to fill the emptiness with money, fame, or earthly power. This is how the devil plays its part in the grand design of creation.

To find your soul, you must embark on a mental journey through this dark gap, confronting the devil head-on. You must overpower it, push through its web of deception, and reclaim your soul from the depths of the collective unconsciousness. This journey is like crawling through a labyrinthine tunnel, where dark narrow pathways twist and tangle in an endless and intricate manner, crafted by the devil to keep you lost and wandering. When you finally reunite with your soul, you are only halfway there. You are still in the devil's den; you must then guide your soul back to the realm of collective consciousness. This is the moment of the highest enlightenment, where love and peace become integral parts of your being.

So, if at any time—whether awake or dreaming—you feel uneasy, believe that tomorrow holds something you don't yet possess within, experience repeating and extreme emotional shifts, or sense an emptiness or yearning for something missing in your life at this very moment, these are all signs that part of your soul is lost in the devil's den: a dark void within you, lying between you and your soul, where your inner demons dwell.

Now, let's get started with this chapter. In the invisible realm of consciousness, the devil fills the spaces where love and peace are scarce, called collective unconsciousness. When your soul resides within the collective unconsciousness, the soul becomes engulfed by darkness and you encounter negative feelings such as anger, hate, jealousy, fear, and despair. These feelings serve as signals to alert you that a part of your soul is trapped in darkness, deprived of the light of truth, love, and peace. In these moments, you subconsciously begin to look for your soul. You deeply yearn to improve your life situation. Yet, the devil resists fiercely and clings tightly to your soul, using its powerful weapons—distraction, confusion, and deception—to prevent you from reclaiming your lost soul and returning it to light.

Frank Herbert once said, "No man chooses evil because it's evil; he only mistakes it for happiness." Devil always promises happiness and success, but then, it takes your soul in exchange. If you try to resist the devil and reclaim your soul, the devil will attempt to distract you, offering fleeting moments of happiness to temporarily ease your pain in exchange for abandoning your quest to rediscover your soul.

For example, when people feel down, they might turn to alcohol, drugs, gambling, or other negative activities in an attempt to lift their spirits. Indeed, they will feel better temporarily as the effects of intoxication and excitement mask their pain. This is the devil's weapon of confusion—offering false joy and comfort that ultimately deepens the suffering. Once these fleeting and deceptive effects wear off, it becomes clear that the joy they felt wasn't genuine but a trap, pulling them further into darkness. They sink deeper into depression and sadness, often feeling worse than before, much like the regret and misery of a morning after a night of heavy drinking.

Then, the devil plays its next trick: it makes people forget. When people forget the terrible feelings they experienced after making a mistake, they are more likely to repeat that same mistake. By the time the next weekend comes around, they have forgotten the misery they felt after the last bout of drinking, and so they find themselves in the same situation, intoxicated again, burdened with the aftermath once again. Forgetting the painful consequences of their choices, they retrace the same path of misery over and over, unable to break free from the grip of their own repeated missteps. This is how people get caught in the vicious cycle of addiction. The devil numbs their minds and lures them into a cycle of depression, sadness, and despair, wielding confusion as a weapon to keep them lost in its den.

Some of us are not so easily confused or deceived by the devil. However, devil has other tricks up its sleeve to mislead us. When feeling down, you may engage in healthy habits like exercising, working, creating art, or a myriad of other positive activities. However, even these can represent another guise of darkness. This is when darkness cleverly masquerades itself as light, suggesting that overworking or over-exercising is a healthy habit and convincing you that acquiring more money, power, spending time with friends, or engaging in sports and adventures can alleviate your suffering.

This strategy represents one of the devil's greatest tricks: distractions. If part of your soul is indeed trapped in a cold and dark tunnel of deception, if you sense uneasiness deep inside you, no amount of health, wealth, power, or friends can rescue your soul from its misery. Sometimes, being distracted is even more detrimental than being confused. At least the confused person, like a drug addict, recognizes their state of confusion. In contrast, someone who distracts themselves with seemingly healthy habits might truly believe they are in the light, all the while unknowingly walking further into darkness. This illusion of well-being is a more insidious form of darkness because it hides the need for real change and deeper introspection under the guise of success.

Whenever you are feeling down, it means that there exists an underlying issue that needs to be addressed. Distracting yourself by exercising or immersing yourself in work may temporarily lift your spirit, but these activities only offer short-term relief. They don't resolve the root cause of your emotional distress; they merely mask it, allowing the unresolved issues to persist and resurface later. This cycle will continue to persist because your trauma has not been resolved and a part of your soul remains trapped in darkness, and as long as your soul resides in that darkness, deprived of love and peace, you will inevitably plunge back into those negative feelings time and again.

So, if it's unwise to confuse yourself with drugs or to distract yourself with seemingly healthy habits, then what is the solution? When you feel low, engaging in healthy activities is beneficial, but not as a means to distract yourself or to falsely believe you have overcome the moment of distress. Instead, these activities should serve as a way to buy enough time to willingly revisit the mental space where you initially felt down and low.

This means willingly delving deep into the darkness within you, facing your fears, facing the ugliest version of yourself, and exploring uncomfortable feelings until you find a resolution. Rather than avoiding or suppressing your emotions, you need to confront them head-on, understanding their origins and meanings. The next few chapters are dedicated to exploring how to face your inner demons, what you can do, and how to go about doing it to rescue your soul and discover true bliss and peace.

For now, all you need to understand is that addictions—whether gambling, drugs, TV binges, shopping sprees, endless video gaming, or any other compulsive behavior—are mechanisms to numb your internal pain. They offer temporary relief while masking the deeper wounds you carry within. The euphoria of the high, the engrossing escape of gaming, or the fleeting excitement of having a new gadget is not the solution; it's a detour. While it may feel good in the moment, these patterns ultimately plunge you deeper into the very pain you're trying so desperately to avoid.

Similarly, the excess pursuit of external achievements—wealth, success, power, or even physical health—stems from the same desire to fill an internal void. You may think that accumulating riches will ease your worries, but more money often brings more responsibilities and anxieties, not happiness. Power gives you influence but cannot provide a sense of inner completeness. Even a healthier and more attractive physical appearance, while beneficial, won't necessarily improve your mental health.

These pursuits, when motivated by a desire to escape inner turmoil, can actually exacerbate your suffering. Wealth brings more options but not happiness. Power extends your reach but doesn't heal the soul. Physical health improves your body but doesn't automatically mend your mind.

The truth is, these external accomplishments can be tools for good if pursued with the right mindset, but they are not the ultimate answer to your suffering. True relief and fulfillment come from addressing the root of your pain from deep within.

Now, imagine you are sober-minded, undistracted, and not misled by the deceptive tricks of the devil. You're focused and determined to embark on a quest to find your lost soul and improve your mental health. You are determined to seek out the darkness that resides within you, unearthing the buried traumas and personal struggles that have been the root causes of your mental suffering. At this moment of determination, you are standing at the entrance of the devil's den, face-to-face with the darkness that has hidden your soul. This is the critical point where your journey of enlightenment begins—the point of confronting the pain, fear, and unresolved wounds that form the foundation of your mental suffering.

The entrance of the devil's den is a place where light and darkness coexist. The light from the outside and the darkness from within the tunnel merge at the entry point, allowing you to discern the difference between light and darkness, and between truth and falsehood. This juncture, which I refer to as *truth in the shadow*, offers you the wisdom of balance between light and darkness.

Truth in the shadow is the point of equilibrium, the perfect balance between light and darkness. This willingness to face your fears and voluntarily relive your darkest moments to heal your past traumas is akin to standing in the light but walking toward the darkness, entering the realm of the devil. In the last chapter, we explored the realm of truth in the darkness. Now, you understand what it is to walk the tunnel, to be swallowed by darkness. You've come to see the limits of your understanding, to know that knowledge alone won't guide you through darkness. The only way through the devil's den is with humility, letting go of rigid beliefs and holding nothing too tightly. You have become flexible and adaptable enough to navigate and pass through the dark, narrow, and intricate pathways of the devil's den. You have become brave enough to face your own fears, break down your old beliefs, and confront your own darkness.

Now, in this chapter, as you stand in the shadow at the entrance of the tunnel, you will gain the prerequisites and skills needed to willingly walk into the tunnel of darkness in the quest to find your lost soul.

First, let's establish a fundamental rule required for your journey into the devil's den. When you stand before the devil, you must possess the quality I am about to share. Without it, you will never conquer your inner demons. This crucial rule for eradicating suffering and reaching enlightenment is this: You are entitled to nothing at all, not even life itself. One of the devil's most potent strategies is to show you what you lack and whisper in your mind that you deserve better—that you deserve to have what is missing in your life—planting the seeds of arrogance within you.

More than 30 trillion cells are working nonstop for you to be alive. Every moment of your life is a blessing, a gift of love; you are not entitled to a single breath you take. If your heart decides to stop beating, you will surely die. If your brain ceases to function, you will perish. If your lungs collapse, you will suffocate. You are neither in control nor entitled to the inner workings of your brain, the beating of your heart, or the contractions of your lungs. Every second of your existence rests at their mercy.

Every cell in your body does its work diligently. They simply sacrifice every moment of their existence through their hard work so you can live. Therefore, if you believe you are entitled to a better life than the one you have and think the world owes you something more without you earning it through sweat and hard work, then there is no hope for you to find your salvation. If you feel entitled to a better life, you are refusing to accept the gift of life as it has been given to you. If you do not realize that at this very moment you live exactly as you deserve, then you have been tricked by the devil.

Be grateful for your life at this very moment, which is the pure gift of love. Remember that the first lesson of enlightenment is to be humble. Being ungrateful is not humble; it is arrogant and vain. Humble individuals are always exceedingly grateful for everything they have and do not complain about what they lack. Thus, the second lesson in the path of enlightenment is to be grateful for all that you already have. It is only then that you can successfully strive for a better life and the end of your suffering.

There are people today lying in hospital beds in excruciating pain, awaiting death, yet they are grateful for the lives they had and the few remaining days they have to live. Nelson Mandela spent 28 of the best years of his life in prison, facing racism and discrimination, and remained grateful for his life throughout. Sean Stephenson, a 3-foot-tall midget born with brittle bone disease who endured unimaginable pain of broken bones constantly throughout his life, could never walk on his feet or even lift a book with his arms, yet he was exceedingly grateful for his life until the day he died. If these individuals can be grateful for their lives, there is no reason you can justify your ungratefulness. You can be grateful for the gift of life; however it has been given to you. Gratefulness is a choice, not a circumstance.

Remember when we talked about trillions of galaxies all working for us to be alive? If these galaxies stop spinning and doing what they do, life on our planet will come to an end. The world is intricately intertwined, and all of it has to work for any of it to function. Now consider all the cosmos, all the cells, and particles working for you to live and experience life. If you can't be grateful for this, there is nothing else in the universe that will help reduce your suffering. Life even gives you the option to end it anytime if you so desire. If you think life is too cruel, you can end yours right now in a million different ways. However, if you decide to take another breath and live another day, then you are simply taking advantage of the gift of life that has been given to you. And if you decide to live, then why suffer? If you follow the path of enlightenment, your suffering will eventually end, and you will reach a state of bliss. It is not an easy path, but it is not an impossible path either.

As I mentioned in the previous chapter, you have to be ready to destroy all you have ever learned and rebuild yourself anew. You have to die and be reborn in spirit again. Letting go of your old belief system is not going to be easy, but it is mandatory to reach enlightenment. If, up to this point, you believed you were entitled to a better life, you can shatter that symbol of darkness within you and begin to embrace gratitude instead of arrogance. Embrace what you are and where you are in life at this very moment. Be humble and be grateful.

Take a moment right now. Pause for a second. Let yourself settle into stillness. Close your eyes if you'd like and turn your attention inward. Sense humility, that gentle reminder of how small yet significant you are in the vastness of existence. Let it flow through you; soften your heart and quiet your mind. Now, invite gratitude to join. Picture it as a warm light, filling every corner of your being. Let it illuminate every good thing you have in your life, however small they may seem—your breath, the space you occupy, the simple fact that you exist in this moment.

Embrace it all. Embrace the beauty, the challenges, and the mystery of being here, exactly as you are, in this infinite tapestry of existence. Let humility and gratitude permeate every cell in your body and anchor you to the present moment, filling you with a sense of peace. Smile at yourself, hug yourself, and embrace yourself. Now, you are ready to embark on the path of enlightenment with every step filled with humility and gratitude.

Before you venture into the tunnel of darkness in search of your soul, let's pause in the shadow where light and darkness converge at the tunnel's entrance. This realm is the point of balance, where every teaching revolves around the equilibrium between light and darkness of your mental landscape.

Within the devil's den, darkness, in its cunning nature, disguises itself as light, weaving a deceptive web of lies and falsehoods. Darkness will illuminate every path of the devil's den that leads you away from your soul. It lures you with false light, leading you to stray further from your soul. If you mistake darkness for light, your soul will be forever lost in the devil's den, leaving you searching in all the wrong places. That is why it is important to understand this equilibrium point of truth, knowing the difference between light and darkness.

Do not associate fleeting happiness with light. People frequently make the mistake of believing they see light and true happiness when it is merely a fleeting, empty shell of joy. Some find their happiness in shopping, others in making excess money, seeking fame, or craving social validation. Some see it in pleasing others, watching movies, or engaging in sports. Others find it by belonging to a community, cult, or religious group. Many find happiness in the power that comes from controlling others. Devil always promises power, success, joy, and happiness; otherwise, no one would choose it over the light.

The key to happiness does not lie in pursuing possessions you do not currently have. Instead, it is found in appreciating everything you already possess. The darkness of your thoughts and feelings persistently emphasizes what is missing in your life, luring you to chase a mirage of happiness across the desolate landscape of future aspirations. Once you attain your desires and achieve success, the water of happiness disappears, only to reappear at a greater distance, luring you to chase happiness in your next endeavor. This cycle compels you to strive even harder to reach the mirage of happiness once again, only to find yourself facing the same elusive dilemma. The relentless pursuit of future achievements never leads to mental satisfaction, relaxation, or peace. If you cannot find happiness today, the promise of happy-tomorrow will always remain an unreachable future.

Everything essential for your happiness is already within your grasp. True contentment is not a destination to be reached in the future; it is a state of mind fostered by appreciating the present moment and recognizing the beauty in the world that surrounds you at this very moment.

Do not perceive the world as too dark, nor believe that your suffering will never end in such a cruel world. Your true happiness is achievable, and it is linked to understanding the depth of your suffering. If your soul is lost in darkness, it has reached that state through past traumas and life choices. Since your experiences have created your suffering, you already possess the knowledge needed to eradicate your suffering. The wisdom locked and ingrained in these past experiences is the light you harbor within that can eradicate your suffering.

In other words, the path to happiness is not about your future rather it lies in understanding your past—your life story, traumas, experiences, and the unique traits that shape your personality and character. Every trauma and challenge in life carries a lesson waiting to be learned. When you fully understand and learn the lesson embedded in your past traumas, you gain the wisdom needed to overcome the trauma itself.

Think of it this way: every venomous creature carries within it either an antidote or a mechanism to protect itself from its own venom. Similarly, your traumas contain within them an antidote that can neutralize their psychological and emotional impact. Therefore, your inner darkness and inner light are always equal in measure, as they both stem from your life experiences.

This means that as an individual, you already know everything you need to know to end your suffering. You do not need to learn something new tomorrow, buy a house, find your soulmate, or seek a new spiritual teacher for your suffering to end. Your suffering has nothing to do with your tomorrow or with anyone else or anything else in the world. Your suffering is rooted in your past, and since you have already lived through it, you have everything within you to overcome it.

You can begin to walk the path of enlightenment at any moment if you choose to do so. It does not matter where you are or who you are; there is no discrimination when it comes to becoming enlightened. If you are willing to walk the path of enlightenment, success is guaranteed. Once the price is paid, sacrifices made, transformation occurred, wisdom gained, and the path walked, enlightenment follows naturally and automatically. This is the first promise of the truth in the shadow: your suffering is not greater than you. You have all the knowledge needed within you to end your sufferings.

While external teachings and the experiences of others can offer new insights into navigating the path of enlightenment, the ultimate key to salvation rests within your own mind, heart, and soul. You possess all the necessary elements for your salvation and the responsibility of walking that path is uniquely yours. Only you know what causes your suffering, and only you have the power to articulate a solution to eradicate your suffering. No one else can traverse the path of enlightenment on your behalf; you must undertake the journey yourself.

The main point to takeaway here is that, regardless of circumstances, anyone, in any place, at any time, can choose to embark on the journey toward light and enlightenment. Each individual's path is distinct, influenced by their varying levels of knowledge and suffering. Although we might share similar experiences, each of us is on a unique path, even when walking together.

Not only do you possess all the knowledge needed to end your suffering, but you also have the ability to do so. There is tremendous power within you to bring an end to all your suffering. Everything in creation is perfectly balanced. Consequently, your suffering is balanced with your ability to overcome it. This means that those who experience greater suffering also possess a greater ability to end their suffering, while those with less suffering have a lesser ability to do so. However, the amount of suffering and the ability to overcome it is exactly equal for each individual. In this way, life is perfectly fair and balanced for everyone.

No one holds an advantage over another on the path of enlightenment. The difficulty of this journey is the same for everyone. Life's suffering spares no one, and no one is born privileged against it. Those with societal privileges—whether wealth, fame, or power—still experience suffering, calibrated precisely to the full extent of their strength, no more, no less. Your suffering, too, is matched to the maximum of your strength.

You must, first, find your truth before you can end your suffering. You must summon every ounce of your strength to confront your reality and inner demons, no matter how harsh, ugly, or unsettling they may be. The journey of discovering your true self is a demanding one, pushing you to the very edge of insanity before granting you access to your soul.

The devil subjects you to distress and grief before finally lifting the darkness it casts over the truth. The cost of uncovering the truth is steep, demanding a toll on your emotional and mental well-being. However, the reward for enduring this arduous process is equally substantial, as it opens the gateway to your soul and ultimate tranquility.

Now, consider yourself standing at the entrance of a dark tunnel, ready to enter and find your soul. While this is a commendable journey, everyone standing outside may call you insane for willingly facing your demons, darkness, sadness, madness, despair, rage, and all the negative feelings dwelling within you. They will warn you against plunging into darkness in search of your soul. They will tell you that true happiness does not exist and that only fools believe in such fairy tales. They will label you as depressed, sad, mad, or insane, urging you to see a doctor and take medication. Some might even tell you that you have serious mental illness.

The saddest part of it all is that some of these people will be your closest friends, your loved ones, and your family members. It would be extremely unusual to find anyone who supports you on the path to enlightenment. This path is the loneliest journey one can undertake because the price to pay is so tremendously high that only a mad person might consider it. On the other hand, the reward is so great and perfect that few believe such a state of permanent bliss can exist in our lives on this planet. People are scared of the price that needs to be paid, and they do not believe in the reward that the path offers. In this way, most people simply do not believe in the path to enlightenment in its true sense and will surely try to stop you from treading this path.

What is truly heartbreaking is that they try to hold you back out of love. Because they don't believe in it, they don't want you to believe in it either. This is one of the costs of enlightenment: knowing that those you love may actively try to keep you from finding your peace and happiness—and yet, you can't be angry with them, for they do it out of love.

People around you will urge you to never be sad, to avoid darkness, and to stay in the sunshine and enjoy the day. Society tells you to seek happiness in TV shows, social media, shopping, consumption, fame, power, money, vacations, watching the sunset, bathing in the ocean, and fun adventures. However, if you wish to walk the path of enlightenment, you must understand that these temporary enjoyments will never become permanent.

In the previous chapter, we discussed how confronting truth in the darkness prompts you to question your faith and belief system, compelling you to reevaluate and refine your understanding of what you once considered to be true. Now, as you explore the truth in the shadow, I urge you to break away from societal standards and seek authenticity beyond societal teachings. Challenge yourself to stop conforming to external norms and delve deep within yourself for truth, regardless of how unconventional it may appear to be.

Throughout your life, you've been conditioned by society to suppress the truths you sense within. You have been thought to disregard your inner intuition while accepting societal prescriptions of truth as your own. This behavior has cloaked numerous veils over your inner truths, concealing the truth even from your own awareness.

True, permanent happiness has nothing to do with a luxurious vacation by the beach, staying in a penthouse at a five-star resort with a piña colada in hand. Permanent happiness is not in owning a nice car or a nice house. It is not found in adventures, friends, or even genuine connections. Permanent happiness is not in finding your soulmate, building a nuclear family, or raising perfect children.

Permanent happiness simply does not exist in the outside world. It stems from within. That is why it is permanent. Once attained, no one can take it away, as it is not a material possession that can erode or be taken.

However, truth in the shadow is all about balance. Without balance, you are doomed to fall. This means that you should still find joy in the outside world. You should cherish your good relationships and friendships, enjoy sunny days at the beach and snowy afternoons in the mountains, and take pleasure in finding a soulmate and having children. You should derive temporary happiness from the world around you, but you must not mistake these fleeting joys for true, lasting happiness.

To attain permanent happiness, you must realize that while you can derive joy from external influences, you must be mindful not to form attachments to them, as they are susceptible to being taken away. Savoring joyful, fleeting moments and letting them go with grace is essential because holding onto external sources for happiness is at the core of your struggles. Even your partners and children are not the source of your happiness. They, too, can leave you or die before you do. You should love them and enjoy spending quality time with them, but you should not tie your happiness to their existence. You should be consistently happy on your own and share that happiness with those you love. When your loved ones are gone, whether through leaving or dying, your happiness should not diminish. You must accept the truth, learn to let go, and remain grateful for the joyful moments you were able to share with them.

This is precisely when the practice of true gratefulness becomes exceedingly difficult but essential in preserving your peace and happiness. Imagine the unimaginable—your child dies in a tragic accident. Could you still find the strength to be grateful for all the loving years you were privileged to share with them? Could you accept the difficult truth that death is an inevitable part of life, often arriving sooner than expected or wished for? Could you unconditionally embrace the hand of destiny that has been dealt to you, and accept the unpredictable twists of fate that shape your journey? Could you smile, even through your tears, as you stand above your child's grave, knowing you fulfilled your duty as a parent, loving them as deeply as you could during their time with you?

And even if you feel that you failed as a parent to appreciate them fully while they were alive, could you take this tragedy as a profound lesson—to cherish those who still surround you, to love them openly and deeply while you can? Would you rise from this heartbreak, stronger and wiser, allowing it to shape you into a better person?

This is not about denying reality or suppressing emotions—it's about accepting life's harsh truths and preserving your own mental and emotional well-being. To achieve lasting happiness, you must understand that life will inevitably bring sorrow, loss, and tragedy. These moments are unavoidable. But what defines you is your ability to rise above them, unbroken by the weight of grief and pain. True strength lies in finding meaning amid the sorrow and emerging from it with greater resilience, wisdom, and love.

Ultimately, even your own body and mind cannot be the vehicle that takes you to the place of permanent tranquility as they too decay and lose their strength. This means that you should not even rely on your physical and mental health as the vehicle to your happiness. To attain lasting happiness, you must delve beyond the physical realm and discover your soul, nestled deep within. The soul is the exclusive means by which lasting permanence can be assured.

The crucial takeaway here is to savor fleeting moments of joy without forming attachments and learn to let go gracefully when time demands it. Untangle and free yourself from the web of earthly attachments. Be of the world but not in the world. This practice reduces your level of suffering.

The outside world is neither the source of your happiness nor the root of your suffering. You may have heard expressions like "you make me sad" or "you make me mad" or "I suffer because I didn't have good parents" or "the corrupt government makes it impossible for me to build a good life here." Just as your true happiness is not dependent on the outside world, neither is the root of your suffering.

Blaming the outside world for your own shortcomings is a sign of weakness. When you link your suffering to external factors, you relinquish the life-given power to be the master of your own life. When someone says, "you make me sad", they are actually stating that someone else has control over their feelings. They have given that person the power to control their mood. They become puppets, and the one who controls them becomes their puppet master.

You may also have heard people say things like, "I want a partner that makes me happy," or "I'm so happy when you're around." On the surface, these statements seem positive and harmless, even sweet. But they reveal a deeper issue: the person is experiencing a lack of happiness within themselves and is seeking to fill that void through someone else. The problem with this approach is that it creates dependency. If the other person fails to provide that happiness, then suffering is inevitable.

This mindset is a trap because the external world is inherently subject to change. People evolve, relationships shift, and situations transform. Relying on someone else as the source of your happiness makes your emotional state vulnerable to forces outside your control.

A better way of expressing this sentiment would be in this way: "I enjoy sharing my happiness with you when you're around." This statement reflects self-sufficiency and an internal source of joy, while also acknowledging the added value of another person's presence. It shifts the dynamic from dependency to mutual sharing, creating a healthier, more balanced foundation for relationships. True happiness begins within, and only then can it be shared authentically with others.

Be cautious with the words you choose and the way you articulate your sentences. Every word you speak makes you the first audience to hear your own words and your own thoughts. The way you speak has a profound effect on your mind, shaping your beliefs and influencing your emotional state. Choose your words carefully, ensuring they reflect a mindset of internal abundance rather than internal lack. Speak from a place of fulfillment and joy, sharing your happiness rather than seeking it from others.

Whenever your words hint at an inner void or dependency on the external world, you reinforce the belief that you need something outside yourself to feel whole. This dependency binds you, making you vulnerable to external circumstances and turning you into a puppet, easily manipulated by the world's ever-changing forces. Such a mindset inevitably invites suffering into your life.

To achieve permanent happiness, you must create a secure and impenetrable sanctuary within your mind—a peaceful space where external forces cannot intrude. This inner fortress safeguards your permanent attributes, allowing you to weather life's storms without being swept away. Without this internal sanctuary of peace, lasting happiness will remain elusive. Happiness that depends on external conditions is fleeting; it rises just as easily as it falls.

Permanent happiness doesn't mean that life will no longer have its ups and downs. Instead, it means you learn how to maintain a stable mental state regardless of life's fluctuations. It's about becoming anchored in your inner state of being, rather than being swayed by external circumstances.

The more you cultivate comfort, companionship, happiness, and peace within yourself, the less reliant you become on external influences, thereby diminishing the impact of life's challenges on your emotional and mental state. In essence, there exists a delicate equilibrium between your suffering and your dependencies. Conversely, there exists a balance between your bliss and your independence from the external world.

When you seize control of your life, disentangle yourself from external influences, and truly embrace internal independence, you discover stability and equilibrium. This is when you create an impenetrable peaceful space within your mental landscape, ready to host and nourish your permanent state of bliss and happiness.

To build this indestructible state of being, you must first remove the darkness that has already penetrated the depths of your essence. You need to cleanse and purify yourself. This cleansing process starts with learning to let go of the resentments and regrets you hold from your past experiences.

Mandela once said, "Resentment is like drinking poison and then hoping it will kill your enemies."

You may have been mistreated or abused as a child by your parents or other adults, or perhaps you've faced abuse as an adult, whether in the workplace or through betrayal by friends and partners. Such experiences often lead to deep-seated resentment toward those who caused you harm. However, holding onto resentment keeps these traumas alive in your mind, capable of resurfacing and causing pain whenever you think about them. Resentment doesn't help you heal; it only perpetuates negative emotions and prolongs suffering. It keeps your emotional and mental wounds open and bleeding, preventing them from healing.

To truly heal from past traumas, you must grow stronger than the pain itself. No matter what has happened to you in the past, however horrific, it cannot strip you of your ability to heal. The path to enlightenment is about understanding suffering. The deeper your suffering, the greater your potential to attain the highest levels of purity and enlightenment. Your past traumas can only break you if you allow yourself to believe they have that power. Instead, you can choose to change your beliefs, affirming that you are stronger than your suffering.

Let go of the resentments you hold toward those who have wronged you because the suffering they caused is, paradoxically, your gateway to enlightenment. Wisdom can only be gained when you understand your sufferings. In this ironic twist, you should be grateful for all who caused you suffering, for they are the very catalyst for you to become wiser. And wisdom is your key to freedom and liberation. With this perspective, letting go of resentments becomes not only possible but mandatory, as it enables you to gain wisdom and completely transcend your sufferings.

By letting go of resentment, you transform your pain into a powerful catalyst for growth and self-discovery. Suffering becomes a valuable lesson and a stepping-stone on your journey toward a higher state of consciousness, guiding you toward inner peace and a deeper understanding of yourself.

Consider it this way: when you exercise, you subject your muscles to immense stress, causing them to break down and endure pain. The soreness you feel afterward is a result of this process—your muscles are nearly destroyed under strain. Yet, it is precisely through this stress and the subsequent healing that your muscles grow stronger.

The same principle applies to mental suffering. When you endure hardship and allow yourself to heal from it, you emerge stronger and more resilient. Growth, whether physical or mental, requires pain and suffering—it is through this process that strength is built.

Another form of resentment is the kind you direct inwardly, toward yourself, for past mistakes. These internal resentments manifest as regrets. Regrets over past decisions can be just as harmful as resentments toward others. When you hold onto regrets, you weaken your mental resilience and undermine your happiness, fostering self-dislike and dissatisfaction. Like resentment, regret inflicts deep suffering without offering any constructive resolution, as the past cannot be changed or undone.

Instead of allowing regrets to dominate your mind, use them as lessons. Let your past mistakes guide you in growing and transforming you into a better version of yourself. When you learn from your past mistakes and learn not to repeat them, you emerge stronger. It is then that regrets lose their grip on you, having fulfilled their purpose of helping you evolve and improve.

Regrets and resentments create a fertile ground for negative feelings and thoughts to invade and dominate your mind. In later chapters, we will delve into strategies on how to gain wisdom and let go of regrets and resentments. For now, the takeaway is that one necessary step on the journey toward enlightenment is learning to let go of your regrets and resentments. Letting go of these burdens unshackles you from the chains of the past and allows you to move freely toward the future.

Earlier we discussed the importance of letting go of joyful moments when their time has come to an end. Now, in this lesson, we mentioned the art of letting go of pain when the lesson has been learned. Just as clinging to fleeting joy can hinder your journey toward tranquility, holding on to past pain can weigh you down, impeding your growth and well-being. Learning the skill of timely release, whether it be of joy or pain, is a necessary step on the path of enlightenment.

Pain is unsettling physical, mental, emotional, and psychological sensations. Suffering, however, is the act of holding onto these painful experiences. Life is inherently painful, and you cannot eliminate pain entirely. Yet, suffering is optional. You can choose to fully experience the pain the moment it occurs, extract the lesson it holds to deepen your wisdom, let go of the trauma caused by the pain, and continue on your path toward enlightenment, unbroken and unshaken. By releasing pain completely when it has served its purpose, you prevent it from turning into suffering. Pain is inevitable, but suffering is a choice.

The path of enlightenment is not about accumulating knowledge, possessions, or achievements. It's not about gaining anything at all. Enlightenment is, in fact, the opposite—it is about becoming less, needing less, doing less. It is a process of shedding, releasing, and letting go. To walk this path is to free yourself from the weight of old beliefs, to detach from earthly attachments, and to sever the emotional dependencies that cause suffering. It is about relinquishing resentments and regrets, letting go of even the joyful moments of the past, and putting less emphasis on material possessions and worldly success.

Enlightenment is about knowing yourself, finding comfort in your own presence, and discovering that everything you once sought from the outside world already exists within you. Paradoxically, abundance comes not from having more but from desiring less. The more desires you harbor, the more lack you feel. By contrast, the fewer desires you have, the more you experience a sense of abundance and wholeness. To become whole, you must become less. When you reach the point where you seek nothing, you will realize you are already complete.

The wisdom of letting go is as ancient as human existence, beautifully encapsulated in Egyptian mythology—particularly in one of the oldest writings in human history, the *Book of the Dead*, which dates back 4,500 years. This amazing book describes the soul's journey after death and the transformative trials it must endure to achieve enlightenment and transcendence.

When a person dies, their Ba (the soul) departs from the physical body, referred to as the Ka. The soul begins its passage into the Duat, the treacherous Egyptian underworld, a realm analogous to the concept of hell. This journey through the Duat represents the soul's confrontation with challenges, both external and internal.

The first trial involves crossing an impossible river, a feat made possible only through the assistance and protection of divine beings. This test symbolizes the soul's reliance on faith, belief in destiny, trust in God, and harmony with the universal flow of existence. Next, the soul must pass through numerous gates guarded by divine entities, each requiring specific passwords, incantations, and spells. These gates symbolize the wisdom gained from life experiences, as only those who have unlocked the hidden truths of existence can proceed.

As the journey continues, the soul faces terrifying monsters lurking in the Duat, ready to devour it. Overcoming these creatures signifies the individual's mastery over their inner darkness and demons, a triumph over the deceptive forces of the devil. These challenges in the Duat represent one's spiritual preparedness and self-awareness during life.

Should the soul falter at any stage, it becomes trapped in the Duat, unable to transcend to higher realms of existence, condemned to hell for eternity. However, if the soul overcomes these trials, it emerges purified and united with its body, forming the Kha—the highest spiritual form of the individual.

Kha is the harmonious unification of Ba and Ka—the spirit that emerges from the sacred union of body and soul. In ancient Egyptian belief, this union was the key to reaching the next stage of existence. This is how they understood the concept of resurrection. That is also why the Egyptians mummified their dead, preserving the body as a vessel in case the soul became lost in Duat (hell). If the soul could somehow find its way out of hell, it could reunite with the mummified body, allowing the individual to metamorphose into spirit—prepared for the continuation of the journey.

After this union, the spirit encounters Ra, a divine being of sixth-density being representing immense wisdom and light. Ra travels with the spirit, guiding it through the final journey over the Duat, battling lingering darkness, demons, and the serpent Apophis, the embodiment of chaos. This confrontation cleanses the spirit entirely, purging all traces of darkness and preparing it for the ultimate judgment. Ra is analogous to Archangel Michael as the defender of heaven and the one who triumphs over dark forces.

Finally, the spirit enters the Hall of Ma'at, or the Hall of Two Truths, where the Weighing of the Heart Ceremony takes place. This ceremony, overseen by Osiris, the angel of resurrection and the afterlife, represents the culmination of the spirit's journey. Here, Ma'at, the angel of ultimate truth and cosmic balance, provides a feather from her wings, which is placed on one side of a scale. The deceased is then asked to place their heart on the other side.

If the heart outweighs the feather, it signifies a heavy heart—a life burdened with attachments, desires, regrets, and resentments. Such a heart is unworthy of transcendence and is devoured by Ammit, a monstrous creature combining the features of a crocodile, lion, and hippo. This outcome represents complete annihilation of the spirit, a fate considered worse than eternal damnation in hell. It reflects the tragedy of knowing the truth, yet resisting and fighting it, ultimately failing to live by moral principles.

However, if the feather outweighs the heart, it indicates a light-hearted individual—someone unburdened by earthly attachments who was able to let go of resentments, regrets, and desires. This purity of heart grants them entry into Aaru, the Field of Reeds, a paradise analogous to heaven. In Aaru, the spirit finds eternal harmony, united with divine beings, and existing in a state of infinite peace.

Is your heart lighter than a feather? Or is it heavy with burdens?

To become enlightened, you too must cultivate a light heart. This means carrying fewer burdens, fewer regrets, fewer resentments, fewer desires, and fewer rigid beliefs. It means consuming less, resisting less, and flowing harmoniously with life's rhythm. Let go of emotional dependencies, reduce your attachment to material possessions, and release the importance placed on external success.

Becoming enlightened is about becoming one with the flow of existence. It is about moving smoothly and gracefully through life's inevitable ups and downs, without resistance or disturbance. To live lightly is to live in harmony with the universe, embracing life with grace and ease. Only then can you achieve enlightenment.

Another principle of balance is that emotions and thoughts tend to move toward equilibrium. This concept is similar to the second law of thermodynamics, which states that "every system naturally evolves towards a state of equilibrium, where forces are balanced..."

Imagine two rooms separated by a wall and a closed door between them. We cool one room while heating the other. One room becomes very hot, while the other becomes very cold. Then we open the door between the two rooms. Suddenly, heat begins to flow from the hot room to the cold room until both rooms reach the same temperature. This process of heat transfer and stabilization between the two rooms exemplifies the second law of thermodynamics.

Emotions and thoughts also follow this universal law. People's thoughts and emotions affect others, meaning you are indeed influenced by the external world. While your inner state of being can be impenetrable and unaffected by external circumstances, the outer and more surface layers of your being are significantly impacted by the outside world.

Imagine you come home to find your partner extremely angry, radiating intense rage like a heater. Meanwhile, you are feeling calm and peaceful, emanating cool, tranquil energy. The anger your partner projects onto you disrupts your peace. To maintain your inner tranquility, you must exert extra effort to generate even more peace within yourself to counterbalance the rage you are receiving. If you successfully maintain your cool calmness and counterbalance your partner's fiery rage, your internal state remains undisturbed, allowing you to preserve your inner peace. In turn, this steady inner peace can eventually calm your partner as well.

However, if you are unable to generate enough inner peace, your partner's rage will overpower your calmness, causing you to absorb their anger. This dynamic causes you to become overwhelmed by your partner's rage, or you both reach a middle ground where neither of you is as peaceful nor as enraged as before. Regardless, both of you will be affected by each other's emotional state.

In such scenarios, it's not only emotions that are exchanged; your thoughts are also affected by the exchange of energy. For instance, if you are unable to generate enough peace within you to counteract your partner's rage, you will lose your composure and engage in a verbal argument. As a result, you will notice that your once quiet and peaceful inner voice becomes louder and harsher. Your partner's rage infiltrates your mind, causing your thoughts to become agitated and enraged.

This is how external factors influence your thoughts and emotions when you lack the internal strength to generate enough positive energy to counterbalance them. Emotions and thoughts constantly strive for equilibrium, allowing outside circumstances to exert their influence upon you.

Now, consider having a lovely and calm partner. When you come home, you are greeted with a warm hug and a gentle, soothing attitude. In this scenario, maintaining your inner peace becomes much easier and even effortless. Both you and your partner are experiencing peaceful emotions, resulting in minimal exchange of contradicting emotions. Consequently, you can both easily hold, harbor, and maintain your peace.

Similarly, your thoughts remain undisturbed by your partner. The voices in your mind stay calm and quiet. In such an environment, you do not need to exert any extra energy to maintain your peace. In fact, you may even be able to relax further, expending less energy to sustain your tranquility. You are in a safe environment where the outside influence provides you with positive energy, reinforcing your inner peace.

While you should strive to remain unaffected by the negative energies of the outside world at the deepest core of your being, it is also important to interact more often with those who do not hinder your pursuit of inner peace and happiness. Consider it this way: you are swimming in a river. It is much easier to reach your destination if you swim with the current, rather than against it.

The state of your soul naturally tends to move toward equilibrium with your surroundings, which you cannot control, much like the current of a river. Therefore, it is wise to choose environments and people whose energy aligns with yours. In life, there will be times when you must swim against the current of adversity. However, through your choices, you can also surround yourself with people and activities that move with the same current propelling you forward toward your goal and purpose in life.

Choose your close friends wisely. Just because you've known someone for a long time, or even if they're family, doesn't mean you must stay in close contact with them if their energy disrupts your peace. Sometimes, creating distance to stabilize your emotions and build an unbreakable mental barrier allows you to support them from afar more effectively than if you remain close while feeling unsettled. The people closest to you have a profound impact on your life. Surround yourself with those who share your values and are willing to swim in the same direction as the current of your life.

It is also worth noting that external influences have a lingering effect. For instance, if you had a fight with your partner and their rage has affected your soul, leaving the house won't instantly restore your peace. Your mind, now infused with anger, requires time to regain tranquility. You must draw on your inner reserves of peace, gradually dispel the rage, and quiet your mind to fully regain emotional and mental control. The duration of this lingering effect varies, depending on how long you hold onto the negative emotions transmitted to you. Therefore, learning to let go of negative emotions is crucial, as their lingering effects can weigh heavily on you.

Consider the extreme cases of a child enduring severe trauma or a soldier scarred by the brutalities of war on the frontlines. Such deeply emotionally impactful experiences can leave a mark that lingers for a lifetime if the person cannot confront, process, and ultimately overcome the trauma. Sadly, it's all too common to see people carrying the weight of these painful experiences throughout their lives, unable to release the burden.

Whether the trauma is immense or seemingly small, its lingering effects persist as long as the person holds onto it. Without addressing and letting go of these emotional wounds, they continue to shape thoughts, behaviors, and relationships, in ways that perpetuate suffering. Healing begins with the willingness to face the trauma, to acknowledge its impact, gained the wisdom locked within the experience, and to gradually release its hold, allowing you to reclaim your life and find peace. Letting go does not mean forgetting—it means no longer allowing the pain to define you.

Conversely, positive emotions also have a lasting impact. You can retain and nurture the positive energy you receive from your surroundings. As long as you don't form attachments to them, these positive emotions can have a lasting beneficial effect on your life. Consider having a pet. Your pet lives with you for several years and then passes away. If you love your pet unconditionally, without attachment, you can forever cherish the memory of the beautiful years spent together without being overwhelmed by grief after they are gone. This ability to harness powerful positive emotions and thoughts allows you to endure the storms of life's daily struggles. Good memories, cherished purely and without attachment, can serve as your anchors during difficult times.

An old tale speaks to this very concept. Once, a deeply spiritual man, revered for his wisdom and devotion, fell gravely ill in his later years. Bedridden and in constant pain, he remained serene and peaceful, a state that puzzled those around him.

One day, a group of his followers, unable to contain their confusion, approached him with a question. "Master," they began, "you've lived a life of devotion and love for God. Yet now, in your old age, you suffer so greatly. If God truly loves you, why would God allow this pain to befall you?"

The man smiled gently, his face radiating peace despite his frailty. "My friends," he replied, "for more than seventy years, God has blessed me with health, joy, and countless blessings. And now, for these few years of illness, should I suddenly question God's love? How can I, after all the good that God has given me, find room to complain? Life is a gift, both in joy and in suffering. In each, there is a lesson, and in all, there is God's presence."

In this story, the man drew upon his good memories to weather the storm of pain that consumed him in the later years of his life. The ability to recall joyful moments without attachment or longing for their return is a profound mental tool. It can empower you to face your darkest days with grace, strength, and inner peace.

To reiterate, it's best to process and release negative emotions as soon as possible to minimize their lingering effects. Holding onto these emotions can weigh you down, limit your growth, and hold you back from living fully. By addressing them promptly, you free yourself from their burden and create space for healing and clarity.

At the same time, it's equally important to learn how to harness and cherish positive emotions. Embrace the joy, love, and gratitude that life offers, allowing them to uplift you and provide strength. However, avoid forming attachments to these emotions, as clinging to them can lead to disappointment when circumstances change. Instead, let these positive emotions linger naturally and indefinitely, serving as anchors to guide you through life's inevitable storms.

By releasing negativity and nurturing positivity without attachment, you strike a balance that helps you navigate life with resilience and grace. This balance allows you to move forward through the toughest terrains of life, while remaining grounded in the strength and wisdom gained from your experiences. In short, bad experiences grant you wisdom, while good experiences provide you with strength. You can always draw something positive from any life event if you choose to do so.

Now let's delve into the subtle yet profound impact of emotional exchange during interactions with others. When engaging with others, there exists a subtle exchange of emotions and thoughts—a give-and-take that strives for balance. When both parties contribute positively, they each find joy in the interaction. Conversely, if one person is laden with negative emotions, it has the potential to bring down the emotional state of the other, and vice versa. Worse yet, when both parties contribute negatively, the aftermath leaves both individuals feeling emotionally drenched and depleted after the encounter.

This process of natural emotional equilibrium is influenced by three primary factors: the nature of relationship between the two individuals, the emotional state of each person, and the time spent together.

Let's dissect these three steps. Firstly, those closest to you exert a greater impact on your emotional and mental state. For instance, if your partner is upset with you, it affects you more profoundly than if an acquaintance, whom you barely know, expresses anger. Secondly, the intensity of your partner's anger is directly proportional to the fluctuation in your emotional and mental state. If your partner is only mildly irritated, the impact is minimal; however, if their rage is intense, the effect is significantly more pronounced. Lastly, the duration of the interaction matters. The more time you spend discussing an issue while angry, the more the emotion of anger is harnessed and fueled within you.

This dynamic doesn't just apply to negative emotions—it works the same way with positive energies. Someone who carries a profound sense of peace and joy within them naturally radiates those emotions outward, lifting the emotional state of everyone around them. The closer your bond is with such a person, and the more time you spend in their presence, the more you absorb their positive energy.

Now, if you also bring your own peace and positivity to the table, the interaction transforms into something extraordinary. Together, you and the other person create a powerful synergy, where your energies intertwine and amplify each other, spiraling both of you into higher emotional and mental states. This kind of connection is the pinnacle of human interaction—an exchange that uplifts your emotional state, expands your awareness, and deepens your sense of harmony with the world around you.

Be mindful of the company you keep and be cautious about who you allow into your inner world. Those you let close to your heart will inevitably have a greater impact on your emotions, energy, and sense of peace. When you sense that the emotions or energy surrounding you are detrimental to your well-being, it's essential to create distance. Protecting your inner peace should always be a priority. Seek out environments and connections that radiate soothing, uplifting energy—spaces and people that nurture your spirit and bring you calmness.

Be especially cautious around intense individuals with strong energy. While their presence can be exhilarating and inspiring when it's positive, it can also be overwhelming and draining when it's negative. Their intensity amplifies everything, both good and bad. Before engaging deeply with such people, ensure you have the emotional resilience and clarity to handle the extremes they may bring.

Let's review what we have discussed thus far in this chapter. First and foremost, practice gratitude. Be grateful not only when life is smooth but also when it is challenging. Gratitude is the engine that propels you forward toward growth and resilience. Without it, you will forever remain stuck, unable to create meaningful and positive changes in your life.

Moreover, your level of suffering is exactly equal to the knowledge you gain from your life experiences. Therefore, you already have all the knowledge needed to heal yourself mentally, psychologically, and emotionally. The key lies in your ability to extract the wisdom embedded in your past experiences.

Healing begins when you take the time to reflect, understand, and internalize the lessons life has taught you. By transforming the raw knowledge of your experiences into wisdom, you gain the ability to heal your past wounds. Everything you need to heal yourself is already within you—waiting to be recognized and embraced.

Additionally, your ability to combat your demons, traumas, darkness, and adversity is exactly equal to the maximum of your inner strength. This means that if you perceive the world as overwhelmingly dark and cruel, and believe that happiness is unattainable in this lifetime, you are mistaking some of the light that exists in this world as darkness. Conversely, if you believe that life is all good and beautiful and think that you can live happily ever after without much struggle, you are mistaking darkness for light. Life is challenging, and true happiness is not easily attainable.

When you enter the dark corners of your mental landscape, you must depart from the light and embrace the darkness. This is akin to learning to let go of joyful aspects of life. For example, when someone you love passes away, your mind naturally sinks into a dark place, consumed by the overwhelming tides of sadness, sorrow, and grief. But instead of being stuck in that pain, try to accept this loss as a natural part of life. Stop holding onto the sadness and begin to cherish the good memories you shared with them. This is the only way to find solace and peace in darkness. Finally, look within yourself, let go of your attachment to them. Set them free in your heart, and in doing so, set yourself free.

Furthermore, to be able to exit out of darkness, you must let go of your traumas and past suffering. Let go of resentments and regrets, as they are the darkness that resides within you. Instead of dwelling on the pain you've endured, focus on healing and the wisdom that comes from the journey.

Sometimes in life, you have to enter the tunnel of darkness and let go of light and good things in life, swimming against the current of adversity. At other times, you need to exit the tunnel of darkness, letting go of past suffering and traumatic experiences, and swim with the current of life toward light and tranquility. When you master knowing when to do each, you find comfort in both darkness and light. Whether you swim with the current of life or against the current of adversity, practice to hold, harbor, and generate peace and tranquility within yourself to stabilize your emotional and mental state of bliss at all times.

By identifying when you are in the dark and when you are in the light, you can adapt and act accordingly to eradicate your suffering. In this way, the eradication of your suffering can occur in both the darkest and the brightest moments of your life. This is when you build and maintain an impenetrable fortress of peace within that retains your joy and happiness.

When you learn to maintain your inner peace through life's inevitable ups and downs, the peace you cultivate naturally gives rise to happiness. True happiness isn't something you can directly obtain—it is a byproduct of a stable and peaceful mind. When the mind is at peace, happiness flows effortlessly from within.

Most importantly, learn to become whole by becoming less. Let go of the weight that binds you to suffering—lessen your desires, your attachments, your regrets, your resentments. Consume less, worry less, stress less. Loosen your grip on rigid beliefs, release the importance you place on material wealth, power, and possessions. Quiet your mind and learn to remain calm and collected, even amidst chaos.

There is nothing you truly need to accomplish in this life except knowing yourself. All the achievements, accolades, and ambitions of the external world pale in comparison to the profound inner journey of self-discovery. Nothing else truly matters except cultivating a mind that exists in a state of absolute peace and bliss. The path to enlightenment isn't found in acquiring more, but in shedding what weighs you down. If you want to fly, you have to be light. In simplicity, you will find your true self; in stillness, you will uncover your eternal essence.

Now, let's delve into the most marvelous fruit that flourishes in the pursuit of truth in the shadow: true intelligence. This is not the type of intelligence you acquire in school, through reading books, gaining scientific knowledge, gaining intellect, developing artistic talent, or honing physical skills. True intelligence is the ability to understand the world as it is, without prejudice or comparison. True intelligence observes everything without biases. Here's how it works:

Take wealth as an example. Those who bask in the warmth of financial freedom and those ensnared in the abyss of financial struggles both may fail to grasp the full reality of what the financial world truly offers and what it does not, as each misses the perspective offered by the other.

Consider those born into prosperity, dwelling in lavish mansions, and never engaging with the poor in any intimate or genuine way. They are unable to comprehend the life of the poor. They do not understand the bliss that comes with a lack of financial success. Conversely, those grappling with the challenges of street life who have not been exposed to the reality of financial freedom are equally unaware of the struggles that the wealthy face in their everyday lives.

The mistake often made by the wealthy is the assumption that poverty equates to complete misery—a condition so unbearable they cannot imagine life without their material comforts. Meanwhile, the poor often fall into the opposite trap, believing that money is the golden key to happiness, that wealth alone will dissolve their struggles and usher in fulfillment. Both of these beliefs are cunning tricks of the devil, perpetuating illusions about the power of money.

Happiness and misery are not inherently tied to wealth or the lack thereof; they are separate from the material realm and are not influenced by the presence or absence of riches. True happiness arises from inner peace, love, and a connection to the soul, while misery is rooted in internal discord, discontent, and desires. Wealth and poverty merely serve as settings and backdrops in the human story—they shape the challenges faced or the resources available, but they are not the authors of joy or sorrow.

In India, if you were to visit the slums, you would see that the entire slum cities are built from garbage, with many people living within these wastelands. The smell that arises from these slums is unbearable to the average person. The inhabitants live alongside wild dogs, rats, and insects. They mix mud with cow dung and apply it to the interior and exterior walls of their homes to keep insects out. By "walls," I mean garbage pieced together, and by "homes," I mean a space often smaller than a camping tent, just big enough for a family to lay down and sleep.

These individuals take on the hardest and least desirable jobs, working long hours to feed their families. They own only a few torn clothes, a worn-out blanket, a plate to eat, a mug to drink, a pan to cook, and an unframed family picture. Their homes are often overrun by rats, diseases, fires, and even government demolition to make room for further city development. No one comes to their aid; they are on their own in their misery. For most of us, living in such conditions is beyond imagination.

Yet, if you get to know the slum dwellers, if you become intimate with them, you will notice that some of these people, despite their horrible living conditions, are genuinely happy. They cherish their lives and wake up every day with a smile on their face. Their community is often filled with love and cooperation. They drink tea made with dirty water, yet they drink it with joy. They dance at night and cherish their lives. A few of them are grateful for their lives, and their overall mental health can be estimated to be better than that of an average person living in first-world countries.

Some slum dwellers find happiness easier than others because they have nothing to lose. They are simple people with simple lives, and they do not have much to stress about. This is the unique bliss that comes from a lack of financial success—a perspective that is often unacknowledged and not understood by those who are wealthy and living complex lives.

In stark contrast, there are those born into immense wealth. Their financial freedom is assured from birth, with wealth so vast it could not be exhausted in a lifetime. They reside in the most expensive neighborhoods around the world, in mansions that others can only dream of. They consume healthy food and drink clean water. They travel wherever they wish in private jets and can hire the best experts to make their lives even more comfortable. Despite these advantages, some rich people truly struggle with life. They suffer from sadness and anger, unable to find happiness amidst their lavish possessions. They live in despair and misery.

An interesting fact to consider is that suicide rates tend to be high among both the wealthiest and the poorest. Those who are miserable tend to remain miserable regardless of their financial status, while those who are genuinely happy retain their happiness irrespective of their wealth. If one believes that money brings happiness, they either misunderstand the nature of happiness or overestimate the power of money and its offerings.

Miserable poor people believe that money will solve all their problems and that without it, they can never be happy. This belief drives them to despair and misery. On the other hand, miserable wealthy people try to fill the emptiness they feel inside with money, new toys, and gadgets, not realizing that true happiness cannot be found in external possessions. This lack of understanding leads to a deep sense of unfulfillment, despite a life overflowing with material wealth.

In short, miserable people will find misery in any circumstance, while grateful people will discover joy no matter the situation. True intelligence is about understanding the reasons behind the happiness and misery of both the slum dwellers and the wealthy. True intelligence understands that money provides options and privileges, but it does not correlate with happiness nor misery.

Another hallmark of true intelligence is its impartiality—it does not discriminate or harbor biases based on appearances, wealth, or status. True intelligence does not look down on the poor, nor does it envy the rich. It evaluates people solely based on their character and moral understanding, free of premature judgments or assumptions.

True intelligence does not admire someone merely for their riches or fame, nor does it rush to condemn them as greedy or assume their success was built on the exploitation of others. Conversely, it does not pity the poor, viewing them as helpless victims, nor does it fear them with the unfounded assumption that poverty equates to criminality.

True intelligence understands that wealth and poverty are circumstances, not identities, and it approaches every person with fairness, curiosity, and a willingness to see beyond the surface. True intelligence mainly focuses on understanding, compassion, and a deeper connection to the essence of humanity.

True intelligence doesn't even hate the darkness or fall in love with the light. It recognizes that life has a balance: sometimes it is dark, and sometimes it is bright. True intelligence embraces both light and darkness simultaneously.

When you gain true intelligence, you will not look up to those more fortunate than you nor look down upon those less fortunate. You will refrain from judgment and comparison. The problem with judgment and comparison is that it inherently positions you either above or below others. When you put yourself below someone else, you immediately feel a sense of lack, and when you put yourself above others, you succumb to vanity and self-delusion. In both cases, you would fail to harbor bliss and tranquility. Because serenity and bliss cannot be experienced through vanity or self-pity.

Some people are quick to be impressed and show respect to the wealthy and powerful, often without knowing whether the person truly deserves it. It's common in society, where wealthy and powerful individuals receive admiration despite not necessarily embodying goodness. Conversely, society often exhibits a tendency to shun those who are poor. There's a collective reluctance to associate with the homeless, fueled by fear, ignorance, and prejudice.

In the path of enlightenment, there is no difference between the wealthy and the poor; between the smart and the mentally challenged; between the educated and the uneducated; between the strong and the weak; between the powerful and the powerless. In fact, those who are considered less fortunate, less intelligent, poor, uneducated, weak, and powerless can sometimes harbor more bliss and joy than those who are fortunate, wealthy, smart, educated, strong, and powerful. None of these praised attributes are signs of true intelligence, nor are they necessities on the path to enlightenment.

True intelligence allows you to look beyond the surface and glitter of material possessions or the lack thereof. It enables you to recognize the true character of any individual, without being deceived by external factors. Offer your respect where it is genuinely earned, not where it is merely demanded. Protect yourself by keeping distance from those whose hearts are tainted by darkness and whose minds are corrupt, even if society admires them. Conversely, extend your respect to those with pure hearts and clear minds, even if society frowns upon them. Perceive the intrinsic value in every person, regardless of external circumstances.

Additionally, true intelligence allows you to observe reality without bias or prejudice because it recognizes that change is possible. The poor man you see today may become rich tomorrow, just as the rich man may fall into poverty. People change, and circumstances change. Someone who dwells in darkness today may step into the light tomorrow. This is why harsh judgments are not aligned with the path of enlightenment.

Consider the example of addicts who, in their relentless pursuit of the euphoria that drugs provide, sacrifice their dignity, resort to theft and lie, jeopardize relationships, and even risk their own lives through overdose. As an intelligent person, avoid judging addicts harshly. Recognize that some of us endure greater suffering than others and sometimes, we must journey into the darkest parts of our being before finding the light.

Some of the most admirable individuals are those who, out of ignorance or arrogance, sold their souls to the devil but later realized their mistakes and transformed their lives. Many who now dedicate themselves to saving addicts and helping them achieve health, success, and happiness were once deeply lost in addiction themselves. From struggling addicts, they rise to become heroes and saviors for others facing similar battles.

The person you see today high on drugs, stealing, and selling their dignity might be the very same person who, in the near future, becomes the best among us. In the same light, never judge yourself too harshly. If you find yourself lost in darkness, do not lose hope and do not be disheartened. You, too, could one day become someone else's hero, offering hope and guidance to those who share your dark past. Learn from your darkness and use it to transform you into a brighter version of yourself. Then, let that light illuminate your life and the lives of those around you.

A legendary example is the character of Paul in Christianity. Initially, Paul was a fierce persecutor of early Christians, actively seeking them out to imprison and punish them, driven by intense hatred. He plunged deeply into darkness, committing acts of violence against the very vulnerable. After a profound realization of his mistakes, Paul transformed into someone who dedicated his entire life to promoting love and became a legendary figure in Christian history.

Now, imagine living in that era as a Christian. If Paul had hunted you down, punished you, or imprisoned you, and you judged him solely based on his actions, you would have misunderstood his true potential and character. In our daily lives, it can be challenging to see how light can emerge from the depths of darkness, but history has repeatedly shown that profound transformations are possible, even from the darkest places. This is why judging and comparing others based solely on their actions or their past is not aligned with true intelligence. Recognize the potential for growth, redemption, and enlightenment in every individual.

Do not see darkness as inherently bad and light as inherently good. Instead, embrace both light and darkness as necessary threads woven into the fabric of existence, designed to teach us how to walk the path of enlightenment.

Think about it in this way: a single tree can produce millions of matchsticks, but one matchstick can burn down millions of trees. A bird may consume millions of ants while alive; when it dies, millions of ants will eat the bird. See the beauty in these ebbs and flows—the natural cycles that shape existence.

There's no need to pity the ants when they are eaten by the bird, nor the bird when it becomes food for the ants. These ebbs and flows are part of the natural order, neither cruel nor kind—simply life in motion.

Similarly, consider the ambition that fuels success. It's like a fire that drives you forward, perhaps to great heights. But that same ambition can one day become the source of your failure, burning down the very foundation it helped to build. Yet, this doesn't make ambition inherently good or bad—it's just part of the same cycle. Your life may oscillate between triumph and hardship. One day you might be on top of the world, only to fall beneath it all the next day. But this is not a cause for despair; it is a gentle reminder of life's balance.

Look at your own life and the lives of others—notice how they flow through cycles of rise and fall, joy and sorrow, gain and loss. Learn to appreciate the ever-changing rhythm of life. Do not let yourself be consumed by sadness when you find yourself at the bottom, and do not lose yourself in excitement when you are at the top. Life is fleeting and constantly oscillating, like waves on an infinite ocean.

Once, I knew a brilliant doctor. His expertise helped countless people, and he built a remarkable life for himself through his dedication and skill. But in the later years of his life, fate took a turn—he fell ill with cancer. The man who had once brought healing and hope to so many found himself lying in a hospital bed, bedridden until the end of his days. The same hospital space, the same beds that had been the foundation of his life's work and success, became the place that held him captive in his final chapter.

There's no need to envy the man for his achievements when he was alive, nor to feel sorrow when he passed. His life, like all lives, was part of the elegant rhythm of existence. It oscillated, shifted, evolved, and eventually ended, moving to the unseen pulse of time. This is not a tragedy; it is the profound beauty of life itself—a cycle of growth and decline, woven together seamlessly. It reminds us that nothing stays the same forever, and there is grace in both the rise and the fall, the creation and the eventual return to stillness.

Once you fully accept this truth deep within your heart, you begin to appreciate it all—the rise and the fall; you begin to see the beauty in both growth and decay. This acceptance is the essence of true intelligence. It grants you a profound sense of emotional stability, easing the turbulence within. With this understanding, you stop resisting life's natural rhythms and start flowing with its waves, moving gracefully through its ebbs and flows.

This perspective doesn't eliminate life's challenges, but it changes how you navigate them. Instead of fighting against the currents, you float with them, finding peace in their motion. Acceptance reduces your suffering, freeing you from the futile desire to control what is beyond your grasp. It allows you to embrace life for what it truly is—a beautiful, ever-changing dance that needs no resistance, only harmony.

Try not to cling too tightly to anything. Learn to flow with life, enjoying what surrounds you in the present moment and gracefully letting go when life's waves carry those things away. Be in a state of full acceptance with what life offers and takes. Have trust in life's greater plan and the perfection in creation. If you lack the riches you desire or have lost the ones you once possessed, don't allow worry to dominate your mind. The ups and downs of life are natural and transient, and fretting over them only disrupts your inner peace.

Recognize that external reality can change in an instant. Understand the impermanence of all things. The waves of life may lift some and drop others, but these fluctuations do not define a person's worth. Care for every human soul as you would for your own. True balance lies in seeing yourself and others as part of the same great unity, riding the same waves of life together.

Practice humility and cultivate gratitude. Let these qualities guide you in integrating true intelligence into your character to gain a genuine sense of equality with everyone. Do not suppress or look down upon those below you, and do not envy or idolize those above you. There will be times when you fall and times when you rise, times when you succeed and times when you fail. None of these outcomes indicate the true essence of your soul that resides deep within your visible appearance. Every soul is made of truth, love, and peace, and deserves due respect on its journey through life. No one is to judge, no one is to blame, no one is to be envied, and no one is to be placed on the pedestal.

It is important to recognize the shared essence of humanity beneath daily struggles, to understand the reasons behind difficult choices, and to refrain from judging and adopting a stance of moral superiority. Instead, cultivate empathy, and acknowledge that under different circumstances, you too might face judgement and fall low in the eyes of society. Struggles and mistakes are inevitable parts of life.

Let's recap what we've covered so far. In the previous chapter about truth in the darkness we discussed the following concepts: Be comfortable amidst challenges, do not panic, and do not flee from your struggles. Be brave and face your fears. Learn to navigate through the narrow passages of the devil's den with flexibility and malleability in your belief system. Break down your old beliefs, consistently question your logic and morality, refine and reexamine what you know to be true, and never stop learning, as the world is infinite, and knowledge has no end. Believing that you know the truth hinders your ability to learn new ways. Most of the world's wonders are hidden from you, and humility is essential for understanding. When you explore the darkness of your mind long enough, your sense of panic will dissipate, your inner eye will adjust, your moral sight becomes stronger, and you regain a sense of calm, collectedness, peace, and happiness even in the depths of the darkest moments in your life.

Now let's add what was discussed in this chapter about truth in the shadow. Darkness is not inherently bad. People suffer equally in both light and darkness. Darkness is as essential as light, representing the two sides of the coin of duality. Sometimes you must willingly walk into darkness to find your soul and at other times move toward the light to save your soul. Challenge societal norms and beliefs. Refrain from judging those in the dark, as they might be close to finding their lost soul, and do not idolize those in the light, as their soul might still be lost in the dark.

Live in the present moment and let go of both joyful and painful past experiences, as clinging to the past hinders your ability to move into the future with ease. Be grateful in all aspects of life and know that your suffering is never greater than your capacity to overcome it.

Unload your mental burdens. Become lighter than a feather. Remove your desires to achieve wholeness. Be more but have less. Be complete with nothing as with having anything else you become incomplete.

Everything you need to know is within you, and you already possess the skills needed to achieve enlightenment. Within the landscape of your mind, create a safe haven made of peace where you can maintain everlasting happiness. While the external world influences your state of mind, mindfulness allows you to counterbalance the fluctuations caused by outside circumstances.

Make better decisions and improve your surroundings whenever possible, enable yourself to swim more often with the current of life. Know that it is okay and necessary to swim against the current of adversity at times to navigate through hard times in life. You possess the inner strength to maintain your joy even in your darkest days.

Do not judge others and see everyone as equal. Do not compare yourself to others. You are not better than anybody else and no one is better than you. The level of difficulty on the path to enlightenment is the same for everyone. Achieving enlightenment requires you to push to the maximum of your ability—no more and no less.

Now that we have explored the truths found in darkness and shadow, let's turn to the light for answers. It's crucial to recognize that understanding the truth in the light holds significance only if you fully accept the truths in darkness and shadow. Without a grasp of the nature of darkness and a willingness to deconstruct and reconstruct your belief system in the light of truth, you risk perpetually descending back into darkness.

Mistaking darkness for light is a significant danger at every step on the path to enlightenment. You are never entirely safe or knowledgeable enough to disregard the deceptions that devil employs, as it often disguises lies as truth, creating potential pitfalls for those unfamiliar with the terrain. The risk of being lost in the darkness is very high when you willingly enter the devil's den and face your inner demons in order to find your lost soul. The next chapter is about the journey of walking deep into the devil's den, seeking answers, searching for the soul amidst the darkness. Devil, desperate to keep your soul hidden, employs various tricks to prevent you from finding your way. If you fall for these tricks and mistake darkness for light at any point, you risk being lost in darkness forever.

You must wash your eyes, cleanse your heart, clear your mind, and purge yourself of darkness before searching for the light. You shall humble yourself and gaze low as you walk the earth, for the intensity of the light blinds those who hold their heads high with pride and arrogance. Trees that bear the most fruits hang low and close to the ground. If you respect the light, it will provide you with answers that will lessen or even eradicate your suffering. Embracing the light of truth requires real-world practice. Integrating the light of truth into your life is no easy task. This is the path of fearless warriors who accept nothing but truth—warriors who are willing to sacrifice everything in the pursuit of truth.

Understanding and embracing the light of truth is one of the most challenging endeavors in life, yet the rewards are equally profound. The possessor of truth is rewarded with clear sight. Truth removes the fog that clouds your vision, providing you with courage to navigate through the storms of life. It clears the mind, allowing you to perceive the depth of consciousness and comprehend the meaning of life.

Chapter 11: Truth in the Light

Up to this point, you have grown accustomed to dwelling in the shadows and accepting the darkness. Now it is time to willingly step into the devil's den and find your lost soul. If you have ever ventured deep into a cave, you realize that it is pitch-black coldness. No matter how bright and warm the outside world is, inside the cave remains dark and cold. The darkness that exists in the recesses of your mind is much like a deep cave; despite the light and warmth outside, its interior is perpetually dark and cold.

Consider the light outside the cave as a metaphor for earthly possessions. This means that no matter how much wealth you accumulate, knowledge you acquire, the quality of your relationships, the power you wield, or the diverse artistic and athletic skills you possess, none will aid you in shining light on the darkness, coldness, and emptiness that dwells within you. These external resources are much like the light and warmth of the outside world, unable to penetrate the darkness within the cave.

When you struggle with mental torment or emotional instability, nothing from the outside world can eradicate your internal agony and break the shackles of suffering. The only way to navigate through the dark and cold void you sense within and reclaim your lost soul is by kindling a light within your heart. This inner light has the power to illuminate your path into your inner darkness and provide the warmth needed for your journey toward enlightenment.

This inner light begins to shine when you act according to the deepest truths you can embrace with each breath you take and every action you perform. This light radiates from your heart when you uphold honesty and integrity, enabling you to illuminate the darkness that resides within. Therefore, truth in the light is a long path through the dark passages of the devil's den that is paved by the virtue of honesty and walked with strides of integrity. This means that to ease and ultimately eradicate your suffering, you must uphold honesty and integrity.

Without these two attributes, perpetual suffering is inevitable. Let's delve into what it means to be honest and to possess integrity.

Being honest has two components. The first component of honesty is expressing exactly how you feel. Honesty is the truthful outward expression of your internal state. This occurs when your words align with your thoughts and feelings. For example, if you're not feeling well and a coworker asks, "How is your day?" you might respond, "I'm good", and smile before walking away. Many people use phrases like "I'm good" to avoid further inquiry or because they see no importance in telling the truth. However, no matter how insignificant it may seem, this is still a form of dishonesty. A person who practices honesty never lies or modifies how they feel internally.

If you're not feeling well and don't want to talk about it but still want to be honest, you could say something like, "I've had better days" or "I'm not feeling particularly well today, but don't worry about me. I'll be okay." While this might feel heavy, it is the truth. If you are further asked, "Why? What happened? What's wrong?" you can simply respond by saying, "I don't really want to talk about it" or "It's a personal matter." At this point, you might be labeled as rude or cold, but that's the price of honesty.

Honesty stands against avoidance. Honest people never shy away from difficult and uncomfortable situations. Additionally, if you respond in such a direct and honest manner, there will be no uncomfortable follow-up questions next time. People will acclimate to your attitude and begin to accept you for who you are. Over time, those who know you well will come to respect you for your honesty.

Practicing honesty requires facing awkward situations and engaging in uncomfortable conversations. Honesty is brutally confrontational. On the other hand, dishonesty provides an easy escape from difficult situations and avoids confronting the truth. When you say, "I'm good", while you are not, you not only deceive the other person but also yourself.

Though it may seem harmless and insignificant to be dishonest in small talk, it will become a habit and become ingrained in your personality. Then comes the time when honesty becomes crucial, yet you are most likely to revert to dishonesty because it has become your habitual response. It is impossible for a dishonest person to suddenly become honest, just as someone who has never run a mile cannot run a marathon overnight. Being honest requires daily practice; you must build your honesty one day at a time so that, over the years, you can fully embody it.

Honesty shines a light on what lies hidden in darkness. Practicing honesty allows you to see the darkness within yourself. But honesty doesn't stop there—it also casts its light on others, revealing their hidden truths and unmasking what they prefer to keep in the dark.

This revelation comes with a cost, one you must be willing to pay if you choose to live honestly and truthfully. Honesty constantly tests your resolve. Both you and the people around you carry unspoken truths, buried fears, and hidden flaws—skeletons in the closet that are easier left undiscovered. Yet, honesty does not avert its gaze. It seeks, it questions, and it reveals.

When honesty becomes part of who you are, it transforms you into a confrontational person. You will put people in uncomfortable situations to reveal the truth, and this will cost you the image of being a "nice" person. You will gather more enemies, because you expose their darker side. Your presence will make people uncomfortable, as many shy away from honesty and confrontation. You will be disliked by many. Your honesty will often be mistaken for cruelty, and you will be called harsh, bitter, mean, or other names.

Living honestly is not for the faint-hearted, but it is the only way to align yourself with truth. Be honest but also be kind and compassionate. Embracing honesty does not mean condemning others harshly for the darkness they carry within. Instead, it calls for understanding and empathy, allowing you to see people for who they truly are without judgment. In the same light, when you confront your own darkness through honesty, refrain from judging yourself too harshly. Have compassion and understanding for yourself.

Honesty also involves another key aspect: being transparent about what you did or what you plan to do. It is the truthful outward expression of your actions. For example, if you have done something

243

and are questioned about it, honesty requires you to state exactly what you have done without modification, omission, or intentional misrepresentation. Any distorted expression of your actions is dishonest.

Imagine you are particularly tired at work one day. During your lunch break, you fall asleep for longer than allowed, causing you to not complete your assigned project by the end of the day. When your boss asks, "Why the project isn't finished?", the easy response might be, "My computer was malfunctioning, and I couldn't log in on time." This response deflects the responsibility and provides an easy way out of a difficult situation.

A more difficult, but honest, response would be, "I failed to finish my task today because I was tired and overslept during my lunch break." Many would avoid such honesty due to potential negative consequences like being reprimanded or even fired. However, when you embrace honesty, you will not yield to fear or shift blame. You will report events as they occurred and accept the consequences of your actions. An honest person would rather face losing their job while being truthful than retain their job through deceit.

Although being honest can seem risky in many situations, good-hearted people inherently value honesty. If your boss is understanding and kind-hearted, they may not be pleased about the incomplete task, but they will appreciate your honesty and recognize your truthfulness and trustworthiness. A good boss will understand that everyone has off days and may falter at times. A good boss would not punish you for not finishing your project and might even trust you more for being truthful.

Conversely, if your boss is not kind-hearted and punishes you for your honesty, it might be better for you to find a new job in a less hostile environment. In this case, honesty helps you or even forces you to leave your current job and find a new one where you are surrounded by those who value honesty and trust rather than merely progress and profit. Losing your job for being honest might initially seem like a setback, but finding a new job with a supportive boss will lead to a better outcome.

Being dishonest keeps you stuck in a hostile environment because you avoid difficult situations. This is how people end up in jobs they hate.

They wake up every day, go to work they dislike, interact with people they don't get along with, and spend their time at work in misery.

Use honesty as a tool to guide you away from hostile environments and toxic people. If your workplace is toxic and harmful to your mental well-being, voice your concerns and discomforts. Speak with kindness and clarity, but don't stay silent.

Being honest about your struggles at work will result in one of three outcomes: you might actually inspire change and improve the situation, or you might be pushed out, or you may willingly choose to leave. Either way, honesty will set you free from an environment that stifles your growth and peace of mind. If you need to find a new job, have the courage to choose one that might pay less or require more work, but ensure the environment is healthy and upholds virtues like honesty. Never trade your peace of mind for a few extra dollars.

In actual reality, honesty ultimately helps you find opportunities that align with your true value and character. By being genuine and upfront about your values, you naturally gravitate toward workplaces where your honesty is appreciated, and your contributions are truly valued.

This alignment fosters a sense of purpose and passion in your work, enabling you to give your best without the burden of compromise. As a result, your talents will flourish, your efforts recognized, and your work becomes more fulfilling. Over time, this authenticity and dedication will lead to greater success and higher income.

Honesty brings light to every situation. It severs superficial connections and strengthens genuine relationships. When you are true to yourself, you simply do not tolerate toxicity, whether in romance, friendship, or business partnership. You understand that staying authentic may sometimes lead to uncomfortable changes, but you trust the journey. Over time, through honesty, you find yourself surrounded by better jobs, genuine partners, and quality friendships. Through your openness and honesty, you reshape your world, attracting connections that reflect your own sincerity.

However, honesty will only benefit you if it is wielded with the right foundation. If humility and gratitude are not deeply rooted within you, your honesty will merely manifest as nothing more than complaining and nagging when things don't go your way. In such cases, honesty becomes a tool of toxicity rather than a force for growth. An inflated ego or an exaggerated sense of self-importance transforms honesty into a weapon that erodes relationships.

Without compassion, kindness, and empathy, your honesty will manifest harshly and cruelly. If you lash out at the world under the guise of being truthful, people will naturally distance themselves from you, leaving you isolated. In such a state, honesty becomes your own solitary confinement—a prison within your mind, fostering bitterness and loneliness.

Furthermore, if you have not developed true intelligence—the ability to see everyone as your equal and to discern their true character beyond physical appearances—your honesty will likely be riddled with misjudgments and false accusations. Rather than revealing the truth, it will project your own misunderstandings and insecurities onto others, causing more harm than good.

The path of enlightenment requires that you take each step in the proper order. You must first cultivate foundational qualities like humility, gratitude, compassion, and intelligence. Without these virtues, honesty, like many tools on this journey, becomes a double-edged sword. If you do not know how to wield it wisely, you risk cutting yourself rather than using it to illuminate your path.

Everything in the pursuit of enlightenment carries the potential to either elevate or harm you, depending on how you approach it. When nurtured within a heart filled with compassion, gratitude, intelligence, and humility, honesty becomes a guiding light that leads you toward growth. Misused, it can plunge you further into darkness. The key is to first strengthen your foundation, ensuring that honesty is wielded with precision and care.

Honesty also has a mirror effect, reflecting your internal state to the outside world and, in turn, showing your own image back to you. Think of it this way: imagine you're feeling particularly angry one day. If you suppress your anger and hide it behind a smile, you are not being honest with yourself and those around you. This is particularly harmful because your outward smile conceals the anger you sense within, preventing you from receiving genuine feedback from the outside world. Your fake smiles elicit fake responses from others, feeding back a false image to yourself. This kind of dishonesty stunts your personal growth, as you would live with an illusory image of yourself instead of confronting your true self.

Additionally, by not expressing and channeling your anger outwardly, the rage only intensifies within you, slowly consuming you from the inside. As this anger becomes entrenched in your heart and mind, it amplifies with every negative encounter, consistently increasing the rage you harbor within. This would lead you to develop passive-aggressive behavior, smiling on the surface while raging within.

Imagine you are angry with your colleague one day because they are not completing their assigned tasks. As a result, you cannot finish your own work. You are stressed and angry. If you pretend everything is okay and ignore the situation, nothing will change, and your anger will compound with each interaction. As an alternative, if you vent your rage by shouting at your colleague, you only fuel your anger, and your colleague is unlikely to respond positively, leaving the problem unresolved.

Instead, you can effectively communicate the cause of your anger. Approach your colleague calmly and express your concern in this way: "I don't want to be angry with you. I want us to get along and work together effectively to reduce stress for both of us. If you could complete the tasks related to my work, it would help alleviate my stress, and I would greatly appreciate it. If there's anything I can do to make your job easier, please let me know, and I'll be happy to help." You'll be surprised at how often honesty and kindness are met with a positive response.

By being honest, you will find ways to resolve issues. When honesty becomes part of your personality, you will become an expert at resolving conflicts because you learn not to tolerate injustice. If injustice still prevails, you leave the toxic environment in search of a healthier one.

In this example the mirror effect of honesty operates in this manner: If you ignore your colleague who caused you stress, they will likely ignore your concerns and continue their behavior, reinforcing the issue. If you shout and yell at your colleague, they probably retaliate, exacerbating the situation and causing you even more stress. However, if you speak with kindness, you are more likely to be met with a kind response.

Kindness and honesty kindle the first rays of light within your heart, radiating across your mental landscape and casting clarity across the shadowy recesses of your mind. This light of honesty gently guides you into the dark void within—a place you may have long avoided, filled with fears, doubts, and uncharted corners of your psyche. Honesty acts as a beacon, opening your inner eyes and allowing you to truly see yourself for who you are. It uncovers your strengths, your flaws, and the intricacies of your character, offering you the profound gift of self-awareness.

At the same time, honesty shines outward, dispelling the darkness that surrounds you. It pushes away toxic people and hostile environments, exposing falsehoods and revealing hidden intentions. Honesty brings the light of truth into your life, guiding you, step by step, closer to your goals and your soul.

Let's summarize what we have discussed so far. Honesty entails the truthful outward expression and representation of your feelings, thoughts, words, and actions without filters, or modifications. Embracing honesty offers several advantages. It helps you become comfortable in uncomfortable situations. You become better equipped to handle challenging situations, allowing you to perform better during tough times.

Honesty also encourages you to take ownership of your actions, to be unafraid of others' judgments. It empowers you to express yourself authentically and seek people and places that are supportive and soothing. This helps you stand against adversity without resorting to lies and deceit.

Additionally, honesty has a mirror effect. When you express your true feelings, thoughts, actions, and intentions, you receive genuine responses from the outside world. If you act kindly, you receive kindness in return; if you act unkindly, you receive unkindness in response. This feedback allows you to see your own image more clearly, recognize your flaws and shortcomings, and create opportunities for growth and maturity. Honesty amplifies your internal state, enabling you to see your inner light and darkness more vividly and become more intimately knowledgeable about yourself. This self-awareness through honesty is an essential tool in your path to enlightenment.

Truth in the light encompasses two core attributes: honesty and integrity. We've discussed honesty; now, let's define integrity. Integrity means staying true to your moral values and keeping your words, beliefs, and actions in line with each other. It means doing the right thing even when no one is watching and staying committed to moral principles in all aspects of life. Integrity is the harmonious alignment of one's words, actions, and beliefs. Another meaning of integrity is the state of being whole, and you can only achieve wholeness by living out your dreams and upholding the promises you make to yourself.

Imagine you promise yourself to exercise and eat healthy food tomorrow. When tomorrow arrives, you feel too lazy to work out and pass by a restaurant with tempting food you want to avoid. What will you do? Will you honor your promise to yourself and maintain your integrity, or will you succumb to temptations and desires? Modifying, postponing, or disregarding your goal after committing to it indicates a lack of integrity.

If you cannot keep the promises you make to yourself, you are unlikely to keep promises made to others. Broken promises generate negative emotions and cause you to feel a sense of failure and shame. They dim the light in your heart as you become untrustworthy in the eyes of others and, most importantly, you begin to lose trust in yourself. Failing to uphold your promises leads to self-doubt, making you believe you are incapable of achieving your dreams, or that your goals are unattainable. At the same time, lacking integrity toward others causes them to doubt your abilities, reenforcing your self-doubt.

There is a specific practice you can integrate into your life, one that can help you build integrity, strengthen self-trust, and begin to believe in yourself. This practice is simple but profound, and it unfolds in two steps.

First, think of something you do every day that you dislike about yourself—something you've wanted to stop for a long time. It doesn't have to be monumental; in fact, it's better to start with something small and manageable. Maybe you overeat and feel unhappy with how your body looks in the mirror. Instead of planning a grand overhaul with extreme diets and long hours of daily exercise, which often leads to burnout, start with a small promise to yourself. For example, decide that you will not eat anything for two hours before going to bed.

This small change won't instantly reshape your body, but that's not the point. What matters is that you hold onto this promise, night after night. By keeping this commitment, you begin to build the foundation of integrity—proving to yourself that you can trust your own words. Cultivating integrity in this way becomes the stepping-stone for more significant changes later.

The second part of this practice involves adding something positive to your daily routine—something you've always wanted to do but haven't yet incorporated into your life. Ideally, this new habit should complement the one you're working to eliminate. Imagine you've been meaning to read more books but never find the time. Tell yourself that every night, instead of opening the fridge to snack, you will read for at least 15 minutes before bed. Now, the time you once spent feeding an unwanted habit is transformed into something constructive.

These small steps may seem insignificant at first. Not eating before bed won't immediately make you feel like you're in the best shape of your life. Reading for 15 minutes a day won't help you finish a book in a week. But they will make a difference, however slight. More importantly, they will teach you discipline. You'll learn to resist the pull of hunger when you know you shouldn't eat, and you'll force yourself to read even when you don't feel like it.

As these habits become second nature, something remarkable happens—you begin to crave progress. You'll find yourself wanting to push your boundaries. Perhaps you'll decide not to eat for the first two hours after waking up and fill that time with a morning jog. These adjustments will come naturally as your confidence grows. Over time, these incremental changes will shape you into the person you've always wished to become.

This transformation doesn't happen overnight. It takes time—weeks, months, maybe even years. But slowly and surely, by committing to this practice, you will build the integrity to tackle greater challenges. Each small promise kept, each habit added or removed, becomes another step forward on the path to becoming your best self. One day at a time, you'll find yourself growing stronger, more disciplined, and more aligned with the person you aspire to be.

If you stumble one day—eating before bed or falling asleep without reading—don't lose hope. One misstep, or even several, is not a sign of failure. True failure is only found in giving up on your dreams and abandoning the promises you've made to yourself. If you falter, accept it for what it is—a moment, not a verdict. Use it as fuel to reignite your determination the next day, ensuring you don't miss another opportunity to try again.

Even if you miss more days than you'd like, don't give in to despair. Keep going. If the promises you've made to yourself feel too overwhelming, don't be afraid to adjust them. Make them smaller, more manageable. Find the strength you currently have and start from there. Build on that foundation, no matter how small it seems, and let your progress grow step by step.

Above all, don't give up on yourself or allow thoughts of self-doubt to take root. If you've failed, it doesn't mean you're incapable—it simply means you haven't yet discovered your boundaries or your true strength. Experiment with your plans. Adjust your promises until you find what works for you, and then build your confidence one brick at a time. Every small success, no matter how minor, is a step forward. Keep moving, keep trying, and trust that with persistence, you will grow into the person you're striving to become.

By implementing this practice, you will cultivate a strong sense of integrity that boosts your self-confidence, strengthens your accountability, and earns the trust of others. When you demonstrate integrity, people naturally trust you because you live by your words and take responsibility for your actions. You develop a clear understanding of what you want and approach promises with care, whether they are to yourself or others.

Practicing integrity helps you discover your inner strength and what you are truly capable of achieving. Once integrity becomes an integral part of you, your character transforms and evolves profoundly. Before committing to anything, you thoughtfully assess your abilities. Once you give your word, you dedicate every ounce of effort into honoring it. By being deliberate in your words and actions, you cultivate a character that inspires both admiration and respect.

To attain and uphold integrity, you have to swim against the current of adversity and difficulty in life. Consider promising yourself that you will exercise every day. This commitment means you must exercise when you feel good, when you don't feel good, when you're tired, when you're unmotivated, when you're sick, on vacation, injured, partying, drinking, or smoking. No matter the circumstances, you must keep your promise to yourself. By doing so, you will witness real transformation in your body. Integrity is the essence of true transformation in any endeavor. It builds new habits, opens doors to new opportunities, transforms personalities, and changes lives. To attain integrity, you must develop resilience, consistency, perseverance, commitment, and accountability.

Here's another technique you can integrate into your practice to develop integrity through small, realistic, and specific goals. Let's say you want to build a habit of daily exercise. Instead of making an indefinite, overwhelming commitment, start with something manageable. Promise yourself to work out for just 30 minutes a day for the next seven days with two rest days. This goal is small, realistic, and specific, giving you a clear path to success.

Once you've completed that week, you'll have built confidence and momentum. Use that to set your next goal—slightly bolder but still achievable. For instance, commit to exercising for the next two weeks, allowing yourself two rest days per week. If you meet that goal, stretch it a little further: a month of exercise with ten rest days. By breaking your larger aim into short-term goals, you'll create a series of achievable steps that move you steadily forward.

Rarely will you need to make promises that last longer than 30 days. Short-term commitments give you the chance to recalibrate, adjust, and build upon your successes. Each small victory reinforces your self-trust and strengthens your integrity. By focusing on achievable increments, you'll avoid the frustration of setting goals that feel overwhelming or out of reach.

Success in life is often achieved incrementally, and so too should be the goals that lead to success. Baby steps may seem small, but they are the foundation of meaningful, sustainable progress. Over time, these small, specific promises will add up, taking you closer to your larger aspirations while building the discipline and confidence needed to achieve them.

Grand and aggressive promises, if followed through and achieved, can bring about radical change and rapid improvement. That is wonderful. However, the issue with such grand and vague promises is that they often set you up for failure. For example, someone who has never exercised but suddenly declares they'll work out for two hours every day "forever" usually loses steam after a few days, weeks, or months. The goal is too broad, too overwhelming. This pattern is even more pronounced when it comes to overcoming addictions.

Take quitting smoking, for example. If you've tried to quit cold turkey and failed many times, it's important to shift your approach to something more manageable. Instead of committing to quit forever, start with a small, specific promise each morning: commit to not smoking just for that day. This approach breaks the overwhelming challenge into something achievable, allowing you to focus on succeeding in the short term without the pressure of a lifelong commitment. The key is to tackle the challenge one day at a time.

If one day feels particularly difficult and the thought of staying smoke-free feels overwhelming, hold on to your promise until the next morning. When the new day comes, you may no longer feel the urge to smoke, and you can commit to another smoke-free day. But if the craving persists and you feel overwhelmed, before making a promise for that day, give yourself permission to smoke one or two cigarettes just for that day—without guilt or shame. Allowing this small flexibility isn't a failure; it's a tool. It reduces the overwhelming pressure and gives you room to regain your footing.

What matters most is honoring your promise when you make it. If you commit to staying smoke-free for a day, keep that promise. Then, when the next day arrives, make the same commitment. One day at a time, you'll find yourself building momentum and resilience. Over time, the smoke-free days will start to outnumber the days when you need a break. Each day is a manageable step forward, and every small victory brings you closer to your ultimate goal of becoming fully smoke-free. This method allows you to navigate the process with flexibility and self-compassion, while steadily moving toward lasting change.

This approach works because it breaks down the process into achievable steps, rather than expecting instant transformation. Success on a single day builds confidence and proves to you that change is possible. Over time, those single days add up, and you begin to build a sense of control over the addiction.

You can incorporate this technique to overcome any drug addiction or bad habit. Create your own model and personalized promises, as long as they are realistic, achievable, and incremental—aligned with your current mental strength. With persistence, you will prevail.

One of my earliest memories is of my father smoking a hookah. I must have been no more than two or three years old. I remember reaching for the hookah, and to my surprise, my dad handed it to me. I took a puff and felt a sudden wave of lightheadedness. My dad gently took the hookah from my small hands, bringing it to his lips. He inhaled deeply and exhaled a thick cloud of smoke that swirled and danced in the air. I was immediately mesmerized, captivated by the way the smoke curled and twisted. It was beautiful in its own way—hypnotic and otherworldly. From that moment, something about smoking captured my attention—a strange, unexplainable allure. I fell in love with the smoke.

By the time I was seven, I wasn't just watching anymore. I had become a regular hookah smoker. In Iran, where I grew up, smoking hookah was a deeply ingrained cultural practice. It wasn't viewed as harmful, and it was readily available. Restaurants served hookah alongside food, and it was a social activity people enjoyed together. I remember asking my father if my brother and I could have our own hookah during these outings. At just seven and ten years old, my brother and I could finish an entire hookah ourselves. For most people, a single hookah was shared among several adults—but not for us. We didn't just keep up; we craved more.

By the time I turned eleven, smoking hookah had become a weekly ritual. At eleven, I also took my first step into cigarettes, picking up discarded butts from the ground, lighting them, and experimenting. At nineteen, I was smoking a pack a day. By twenty, I couldn't get through a single day without buying two or three packs at a time. Smoking had taken over my life. On nights I partied with friends, it wasn't unusual for me to go through four or five packs in just 24 hours. Deep down, I knew I was harming myself, but I couldn't stop. I didn't even know where to begin.

The first time I tried to quit was when I was nineteen. I lasted just ten hours before lighting up another cigarette again. Over the years, I kept trying. Sometimes I managed a day, maybe two, but never more. At twenty-eight, for the first time, I managed to stay smoke-free for three weeks. I thought I had finally conquered it, but then I relapsed. Each failed attempt left me more frustrated, but it also taught me something valuable. I started to notice patterns—what triggered my cravings, the excuses I made, the times I was most vulnerable. I began to understand that quitting wasn't just about willpower; it was about changing my entire approach.

At thirty-seven, I accomplished something I once thought impossible: I stayed smoke-free for over two months. But even then, I relapsed. This time, however, felt different. I had discovered a method that worked for me, the very technique I've shared with you. Yesterday, I didn't smoke. Today, I promised myself the same. Tomorrow, I'll wake up and make that promise again. One day at the time.

Since then, I've learned how to overcome not just smoking but other challenges in my life. There were times when I felt hopeless, convinced I could never quit. But I didn't give up. I eventually stopped smoking, and if I can do it, so can you.

This isn't just about quitting smoking—it's about reclaiming control over your life. Whether it's a harmful habit you want to quit or a positive one you wish to cultivate, the process is the same. Break it down into small, achievable daily promises. Focus on today. Don't overwhelm yourself with thoughts about the future.

The key is to focus on the journey, not the destination. Success doesn't come from wishing or waiting an end result—it comes from winning today. And if you can win today, you can win again tomorrow. Over time, those small victories will build into something remarkable: the life you truly want for yourself.

Success today puts you in a stronger mental state to make and uphold tomorrow's promise. It also brings you joy to see yourself succeed. You'll sleep better after a productive day, and that rest will give you an edge as you tackle the next day with renewed energy. Grow into the person you aspire to be, one promise, one day, and one step at a time.

An old tale speaks to this way of approaching life's difficulties—the story of the man and the mountain. A man once stood at the base of a towering mountain, its peak hidden above the clouds. He had dreamed of standing at the summit, basking in the view from above, but now that he was here, doubt crept into his heart. The mountain was massive, its path steep, the journey so long and treacherous.

"How will I ever reach the top?" he muttered to himself. "The journey is too long, the climb too hard. What if I fail? What if I run out of strength before I reach the top?"

Just then, an old traveler appeared, leaning on a weathered staff. His face was lined with the wisdom of many journeys, and his eyes held the calm of someone who had conquered many mountains of his own. He observed the man's hesitation and smiled.

"Why do you look so troubled?" he asked.

The man sighed, rubbing the back of his neck. "I want to climb this mountain, but just looking at it makes me feel exhausted. The peak is so far away, and I don't know if I have it in me to go all the way."

The traveler chuckled softly and tapped his staff against the ground. "Then don't climb the whole mountain."

The man frowned. "But isn't that the whole point?"

"Not today," the traveler replied. "Today, just take one step. And when you've done that, take another. You don't need to conquer the entire mountain right now—just focus on what's right in front of you. Keep your mind on the next step, not the peak."

The man hesitated but took a deep breath and stepped forward. Then another. The peak still seemed impossibly distant, but he kept walking, focusing only on the ground beneath his feet.

Days passed. The climb was difficult, but instead of being paralyzed by the enormity of the journey, he only asked himself one thing each morning: "Can I take just one more step today?" And every day, the answer was yes.

One evening, as he rested on a ridge, he gazed behind him and was stunned by how far he had come. The base of the mountain was barely visible. His doubts had faded, replaced by quiet confidence. And then, on a morning like any other, he took a step—and realized there were no more steps to take. He had reached the summit.

This principle applies not only to yourself but also to your commitments to others. If a friend asks you to work out together every day, agree to a one-week promise. Take only one step with your friend toward working out together. After that week, reassess and make a new promise if you wish to continue. Avoid open-ended commitments, whether to yourself or others, as they often lead to disappointment.

Another essential aspect of integrity is setting clear conditions. If your friend asks for daily workouts, agree to one week with conditions—for instance, you won't be able to exercise if your tasks at work run late. By establishing conditions, you manage expectations and ensure both you and others understand what to expect of you.

This is how you cultivate trust and integrity, both in your own eyes and in the eyes of others. Those who make bold, sweeping promises may seem exciting at first, but they often disappoint. In contrast, those who make small, steady promises may seem cautious and boring, but they are reliable and earn lasting trust.

Do you remember the chapter where we talked about logical balance—and how your way of thinking and living is like a chain, with each link connecting a different aspect of your life? We also explored how broken, missing, or weak links in that chain can hold you back from growth and success.

Now, if you've taken the time to identify those weak or missing links, this is your opportunity to put them to good use. Apply the practice we discussed earlier to strengthen those weak links in your logical chain, cultivate positive habits, eliminate harmful ones, build upon your integrity, and deepen your sense of self-worth. Bit by bit, as you repair the chain—through awareness, intention, and consistency—you'll notice your path becoming clearer, your character more grounded in your devotion, and your life more aligned with your goals.

Now, here is the single most important aspect of cultivating integrity: you must ensure your integrity is grounded in sound morality. Without a foundation of high morality, integrity becomes a destructive force. It will lead you to success, but success in all the wrong ways. If your moral compass is skewed or rooted in falsehoods, your integrity will only guide you deeper into darkness. Like honesty, integrity is a double-edged sword—it will cut you if you fail to wield it with precision and care.

For instance, if you believe that white lies are acceptable, that revenge is a sign of power, that suppressing others demonstrates strength, or that profiting at the expense of others is justified, then your integrity, though lead you to success, will ultimately increase your suffering. You will become rich and powerful, but your suffering will grow alongside your wealth.

You may accumulate wealth, influence, and power, but these gains will come at a cost. As your success grows, so too will the emptiness and turmoil within you. Integrity without morality is like building a sturdy ship with a flawed design—it may sail, but it will ultimately steer you toward disaster.

In other words, the impact of integrity on your life depends on the nature of your belief system and your moral understanding. While integrity always leads to success, its spiritual effects can be either harmful or beneficial, depending on the foundation upon which it is built. Without a solid moral foundation, the devil becomes your only guide to success. It will grant you all the wealth and power you desire, but it will drag your soul into its dark den, tormenting and torturing it endlessly.

This is yet another reason why it's crucial to approach enlightenment in the right order. If you don't first deconstruct your misguided belief systems rooted in falsehoods and societal norms, practicing integrity will bring no meaningful progress on your path to enlightenment.

Now that you understand how to wield both honesty and integrity with precision, you are on the brink of learning how to use these twin virtues together to uncover the wisdom of truth. However, before you pick up these double-edged swords of light to confront your inner demons, it is essential to examine what happens to those who try to embrace one virtue while neglecting the other. Cultivating one without the other is not just incomplete—it is dangerous and perilous.

Possessing integrity without honesty often lays the groundwork for narcissism. When a person has ambitious goals and unwavering integrity to achieve them but relies on dishonesty to reach those ends, they resort to manipulation. This Dishonest manipulation stems from a self-serving hidden agenda—an effort for personal gain. This combination of self-serving ambition and deceit becomes the root of narcissism.

Narcissists are exceptionally harmful to society. Dishonesty shapes deceitful characters, while integrity becomes the tool that guides these characters to success. Together, dishonesty combined with high integrity is a potent potion of darkness, enticing those willing to sell their souls to the devil for earthly glamours and glories.

Consider a person who is successful and respected. He is a man of his word, accountable for any promises he makes. He appears virtuous, often extending financial help to those in need. Yet, his generosity is not driven by a sincere desire to help others but by a hunger for recognition, respect, and fame. While his actions outwardly display integrity, the dishonesty in his intentions feeds his ego and sense of self-importance.

Beneath this seemingly altruistic facade lies a concealed agenda. His generosity is transactional, a barter where wealth is exchanged for the admiration he seeks. Humility is missing from the essence of his personality. Such a person is not, and cannot be, on the path of enlightenment and is ultimately harmful to society.

You might wonder, "What's wrong with wanting a little attention and admiration if he's helping people in need?" The answer is that the harm caused by this behavior far outweighs the good it appears to accomplish. The image of generosity he projects is hollow, devoid of authenticity. His craving for respect stems from narcissistic traits, and when people admire or respect him because of his money, they unintentionally reinforce narcissistic behaviors.

From his own perspective, he may believe he is living in the light, associating himself with virtues like generosity and benevolence. Receiving admiration confirms, in his mind, that others see him as a good and noble person. He becomes a person of influence and people become blind to his inflated ego and narcissistic tendencies. People begin to see such traits as admirable, even desirable, and seek to emulate them. This perpetuates a societal cycle where narcissism is celebrated and empowered, allowing others with similar tendencies to rise to positions of influence, fostering a culture where self-interest and narcissism reigns supreme.

When those in positions of power and influence are driven by self-serving interests, it inevitably leads to chaos and conflict. Their actions are driven by personal gain, and anyone who stands in the way of their ambitions becomes an obstacle to be removed. This relentless pursuit of self-interest eventually leads to power struggles that fracture communities, destabilize societies, and perpetuate suffering on a larger scale.

Unfortunately, this phenomenon is all too common in the world today. We frequently admire individuals we should not, mistaking their wealth, charisma, or influence for genuine virtue. The allure of material success and the confidence they exude often blind us to their underlying motives. In elevating these individuals, we unknowingly enable the very traits that lead to division and conflict.

Individuals who possess integrity without honesty often present a facade of kindness and respect, outwardly adorned with a beautiful image. On the surface, they appear successful, virtuous, and commendable, having mastered the art of concealing their true motivations and character. These individuals define themselves by the meticulously and carefully crafted image they project to the outside world, creating an illusion that is misleading and deceivingly appealing. Narcissism is a complex human behavior that is difficult to spot, especially in highly intelligent people. Their cleverness allows them to hide their narcissistic traits behind actions that seem generous, kind, or even commendable.

This form of deceit is not a random occurrence; it is a strategic and deliberate choice. Those with integrity without honesty are experts at manipulation. They selectively reveal aspects of themselves that serve their interests. Their actions are driven by a desire for personal gain, fueled by vanity, greed, and a thirst for power. Possessing integrity allows them to succeed in any endeavor, while their dishonesty enables them to cheat their way to the top with remarkable speed. Since their dishonesty stems from narcissistic tendencies, they often strive for positions of power and influence within society.

Politicians who sacrifice the welfare of their own people to gain power, spiritual leaders who steer followers toward conflict rather than harmony, and business executives who prioritize profits at the expense of their employees' well-being—these examples often reflect individuals with high levels of integrity but lacking honesty. They excel in their roles, achieving success and influence, and amassing followers, yet their true motivation lies in personal gain and glory.

The danger lies in their ability to ascend the ladder of success rapidly. Their skillful deceit allows them to navigate complex social structures and gain influence at the expense of truth and moral principles. Their proficiency in presenting lies that closely resemble truth can be particularly perilous for society, as it becomes challenging to discern truth from the carefully crafted narrative they weave.

The current state of the world highlights the prevalence of such individuals who have integrity without honesty in positions of power across various sectors, including politics, religion, spirituality, business, television, motivational speaking, online influencing, and other branches of so-called success in almost every country. These people pursue power, wealth, and earthly glory at the expense of others. They are the ones who cast darkness over the world, fueling the conflicts we witness today. Unfortunately, their manipulative abilities enable them to maintain control over the less fortunate, holding onto their power and influence. These highly intelligent individuals, with their dark interior concealed by a virtuous exterior, pose a significant risk to the well-being of the communities they serve.

On a smaller scale, the less intelligent and less successful narcissists are the ones we encounter daily. They are the ones who make life unnecessarily difficult for those around them. These "average narcissists" are often the byproducts of highly influential narcissists. When society admires and emulates narcissistic leaders and influencers, it inadvertently normalizes these traits, leading many to adopt them without the cunning sophistication required to conceal their toxicity.

These "average narcissists" are the overly controlling type of people—the apartment complex managers who seem to always find a reason to make life harder for tenants whose lifestyles differ from their own. They are the managers at work who create a hostile environment by nitpicking anything that doesn't align with their personal preferences. They are the team leaders who insist that collaboration means unquestioningly following their lead. Their actions are not driven by a desire to serve the greater good but by self-serving interests and self-glorification, often at the expense of others' peace of mind.

These individuals create friction in day-to-day interactions, turning what could be harmonious relationships into constant battles of control. While their outward appearance may suggest order or diligence, their true impact is one of disruption, leaving a trail of frustration and discontent in their wake.

Let's explore another scenario involving the least cunning types of narcissists. Imagine two individuals employed by the same company, assigned identical responsibilities, and completing an equal number of tasks. However, the motivation behind their hard work varies significantly. One person diligently performs their duties, believing that they must earn their income through hard work, while the other is driven by self-interest.

The individual driven by dignity becomes readily noticeable. Their service is pleasant, exuding positivity, and their dedication is evident in every task. For them, hard work is not merely a requirement but a source of pride and dignity. They consistently give their best effort.

Conversely, the person motivated by self-interest operates at the minimum threshold required to retain their job. While they complete assigned tasks, their efforts stem from a fear of unemployment rather than genuine commitment. Usually, their interactions with colleagues are unpleasant, contributing to a toxic work environment that affects everyone around them. If they perceive themselves as hard workers, they are deceiving themselves—practicing a form of integrity without honesty, as their true motivation remains concealed and ultimately self-serving.

Let's summarize the impact of possessing integrity while lacking honesty. Anyone driven primarily by dishonest self-serving motivation to achieve success is, to some extent, a narcissist. Deep down, they know that if it becomes clear they only care about themselves, they will not be accepted and respected by their community. This awareness compels them to conceal their true motives.

As a result, they grow more dishonest over time, refining their ability to deceive and developing ever more cunning tactics. Over time, this repeated practice of manipulation not only helps them achieve their goals but also reinforces and enhances their narcissistic traits. Dishonesty becomes a skill they sharpen, allowing them to mask their true intentions more effectively and manipulate others with greater precision.

To shield themselves from exposure, they cultivate a polished exterior—a facade of confidence, beauty, and toughness. However, this outward image is rooted in falsehood. Beneath the surface, they are neither truly tough nor beautiful but fragile, insecure, and hollow. Their hard shell conceals the emptiness within.

When authenticity and honesty is lacking, fear takes root. Dishonesty creates hollow personalities, leaving a void within—a void that is filled with fear. This fear stems from the constant threat of exposure, the dread of others uncovering their true nature. Dishonest people live in a state of perpetual anxiety, fearing the loss of their jobs, friendships, relationships, and social standing should their deceit come to light.

This fear keeps growing, feeding on itself and spiraling into an unrelenting cycle. The more dishonest they are, the more their fear intensifies. They fear being seen for who they truly are, fear the collapse of their carefully constructed facade, and fear the judgment and rejection that might follow. The worry about negative consequences causes them to twist the truth even further, creating and enhancing a facade that aligns with what they believe others want to see, rather than expressing themselves authentically. Their fear makes honesty feel like a dangerous vulnerability.

They counterbalance their fear by projecting an image of strength and confidence, concealing the underlying fear beneath their facade. However, despite their outward display of assurance, this endless cycle of fear becomes a defining feature of their lives, dominating their thoughts and actions. Dishonest people live in the shadow of their own making, constantly fearing—and then fearing some more.

If and when their true nature becomes known, it emerges as toxic behavior, exposing traits like manipulation, gaslighting, entitlement, and narcissism. That is why they fear authenticity—it lays bare the darker aspects of their personality that they work so hard to conceal. But this fear of being authentic comes at a significant cost: it prevents them from forming genuine, meaningful relationships. They may have family and friends, but within their own mind, they are isolated—disconnected from the world around them. Vulnerability, the foundation of trust and connection, remains elusive to them, leaving them isolated in their carefully constructed facade, unable to experience the depth of genuine relationships that authenticity brings.

Fear is the poison of the mind that erodes honesty, promotes suffering, and annihilates genuine connections. Every lie you tell plants a seed of fear in your heart—a silent, creeping force that takes root and grows over time. With each lie, you bury the truth deeper, yet the deeper it lies, the more terrifying it becomes should it ever come to light. In this way, fear becomes your guiding force, and truth transforms into your greatest nightmare.

Avoid dishonesty as much as you can, for its impact grows over time. Fear, born of deceit, begins to dictate your choices, influence the paths you take, and erode the authenticity with which you live your life.

It becomes a shadow that looms over every aspect of your existence, holding you back from your true potential.

The first step to overcoming fear is a stride of honesty. Honesty forces you to confront your fears head-on, no matter how uncomfortable the situation may be. When you choose to be honest, you have nothing to hide. You expose yourself fully and vulnerably. In that vulnerability, you find strength. You no longer fear those who try to undermine you, nor do you dread attacks on your reputation.

Fearlessness and honesty go hand in hand. When you are fearless, you refuse to compromise your honesty for the fleeting illusion of security. The pursuit of truth, guided by honesty, gradually diminishes the power fear holds over you. Honesty requires prioritizing truth above earthly power, wealth, respect, or acceptance by others. It demands that you live in alignment with your inner values, even when it's inconvenient and challenging. Honesty always prioritizes truth, and it is through this unwavering commitment to truth that fear loses its grip.

Truth has the power to liberate you from fear. However, to attain and understand the truth, you need both honesty and integrity. Honesty alone can make you fearless, but only to an extent. Integrity is equally essential, as it enables you to embody bravery and act in alignment with the truth. True fearlessness comes from the balance of both—honesty to face the truth and integrity to live by the truth.

Those with integrity but without honesty often fall into the realm of narcissism, blinded by their own self-serving motives. They act with purpose and discipline, but their lack of honesty prevents them from seeing and embracing the truth. On the opposite end of the spectrum are those who are honest but lack integrity. They, too, fall short of truth, leading to a different type of misalignment.

Honesty without integrity leads to hypocrisy. Basically, every honest person who lacks integrity is, to some extent, a hypocrite; their actions, words, and beliefs do not align. They say one thing but do something else. While they may speak truthfully, lacking integrity to live by their own spoken words transforms those words into empty echoes. They proclaim virtues they do not practice or criticize behaviors they themselves indulge in. Such individuals lose their credibility and descend into a hollow life where their truth-telling becomes meaningless.

Consider individuals who genuinely value monogamous relationships but lack the integrity to resist the temptations of lust. In their daily interactions, they succumb to fleeting desires and cheat on their partner for momentary gratification. They may feel genuinely sorry the next day, regretting their actions, and promising never to cheat again. They truly mean what they say at the time. However, when they feel unhappy or emotionally vulnerable, they find themselves cheating again.

These individuals may be honest in their promises, but they lack the integrity to uphold their promises through time and life's ups and downs. They are hypocrites, not wanting their partners to cheat on them while they continually cheat on their partner. This type of hypocrisy is not limited to romantic relationships but extends to business partnerships, friendships, and any interaction with other people. Whether tempted by lust, money, fame, power, or other desires, they cheat or betray those who care for them. People who lack integrity cannot be trusted.

There are other types of honest people who lack integrity, often found among addicts. Those suffering from addiction often sincerely express a desire to quit. However, when the moment arrives, they fail to resist their cravings for the drug. They succumb to their desires even though they know these desires are harmful. People who possess honesty without integrity lack the discipline to live the life they believe is best for them. Consequently, they unwillingly hurt themselves and those around them.

Consider those addicted to alcohol. They genuinely love their family and friends, but they consistently choose alcohol over their loved ones. Even when they know their addiction is causing pain to whom they care about most, they are unable to put down the bottle. They repeatedly choose what they hate over what they love. In this way, they are hypocrites.

People who possess honesty without integrity often hurt themselves and those around them. They lack discipline and are unprepared to face the consequences of their actions or pay the price for their past wrongdoings. These individuals are not in control of their own lives; they are slaves to their own temptations and desires.

Those who are honest but lack integrity are weak individuals. Despite their efforts, they consistently fail to overcome the adversities and challenges of life. They adopt a victim mentality, blaming the world for their lack of perseverance. They perceive life as excessively dark, cruel, and difficult. Because every life challenge seems insurmountable, they never truly enjoy a good quality of life. They surround themselves with like-minded individuals who reinforce their belief that others are to blame for the darkness in their lives. Whenever they take one step forward, they take two steps back, remaining stuck in a vicious cycle of failures and victimhood mentality.

Honesty without integrity and integrity without honesty both fail to grasp the truth. Let's examine both in a nutshell. Those with honesty but lacking integrity are hypocrites who unwillingly hurt and betray themselves and those around them. They may have good intentions, but their actions are consumed by darkness. They are beautiful on the inside but rotten on the outside. Conversely, those with integrity but lacking honesty harm others to achieve self-satisfaction through power, respect, and wealth. They always have a hidden agenda. Their intentions are self-serving. They project a beautiful image of themselves, but their hearts are consumed by darkness. They are beautiful on the outside but rotten on the inside. Both groups fail to distinguish between light and darkness. They have not understood the truth and have fallen into darkness.

Those who have fallen the farthest are devoid of both integrity and honesty, making them the most miserable of all. Without integrity, they lack the discipline and resolve to achieve meaningful success, enslaved by their desires and unable to rise above their animalistic impulses. Without honesty, they become manipulative and deceitful, seeking to fulfill their desires even at the expense of others.

In the most extreme cases, this absence of integrity and honesty manifests as deeply destructive behaviors. These are the rapists, murderers, sociopaths, and psychopaths—individuals whose actions leave devastation and suffering in their wake.

Such individuals are hypocrite-narcissists with self-serving hidden agendas, driven by a twisted pleasure in harming others. They derive enjoyment from inflicting pain and are comfortable in their own darkness. They despise the light. They suffer from the chaos in their minds, continuously swinging between dysphoria and euphoria. They are slaves to their own chaos, desires, and darkness. The voices in their heads scream loudly. They suffer from relentless mental unrest.

The hand of destiny placed me in this category of people from a very young age. For the majority of my life, I was a hypocrite-narcissist with self-serving hidden agendas. I never murdered anyone or caused great physical harm, ironically thanks to my own weak and cowardly nature. But in my mind, I had already committed unspeakable acts. I fantasized about vengeance, destruction, and even death.

My parents weren't bad people; in fact, I grew up in a relatively decent household. Yet, in the grip of my rage and the darkness that resided within me, I wished for my parents' deaths countless times. If I could wish death upon my own parents—the very people who gave me life—imagine how many others I wished to see suffer. And when I did witness suffering in others, it brought me an unsettling sense of satisfaction. It made me feel even with the world, as if I wasn't alone in my torment. Pain and suffering were the only constants in my life, and in my twisted perception, I wanted others to feel the same. If I couldn't escape it, why should they?

For so long, the theme of my existence was weakness and helplessness, compounded by a deceitful nature I had carefully crafted to survive. I lied to protect myself, manipulated to gain favor, and wore masks to ensure no one could see the disgusting reality of who I truly was. I thrived in darkness because, in my mind, it was the only place I could exist.

As I shared earlier in this book, I despised myself for feeling mentally inadequate, carrying a lifelong sense of being "less than others." Except for a brief period during elementary school, most of my childhood and adolescence was engulfed in darkness. Pain and suffering dominated my early memories. I always saw myself as a victim, and growing up in a third-world country only fueled my resentment. I hated the government and blamed them for everything missing in my life. By the age of 11, I was joining riots and throwing stones at the police as an outlet for my seething anger.

Physically, I was no better off. I grew up painfully skinny—so much so that my friends nicknamed me "deadly skinny." I was even thinner than any girl my age, and that was hard for me to accept. I remember standing on a scale when I was 14 years old, surrounded by neighborhood kids. Most boys weighed between 40 to 60 kilos (90 to 135 pounds), while the thinner ones were around 35 kilos (77 pounds). When I stepped onto the scale, it read a measly 27 kilos (59 pounds). Everyone laughed, and I hated myself for it. I hated my weak, frail body, just as I hated my mind for feeling inadequate.

At 11, my family moved to a small city, and I attended a school that could only be described as brutal. Teachers frequently resorted to severe physical punishment, sometimes beating students so harshly that they were sent to the hospital straight from the classroom—whether for failing a test or simply being too loud. The kids were just as violent, carrying knives and forming cliques for protection. To survive, I befriended the most ruthless kid in school, using deceit and manipulation to gain his trust. I developed a dishonest character, using it as a survival mechanism to protect myself. In many ways, it was like living in a prison. When I watch prison movies now, they don't feel so bad; they remind me of my middle school and high school years.

When I moved to America at 17, I seized the chance to create a completely new identity. With no one to verify my past, I lied about everything. I fabricated stories about my childhood, portraying myself as someone I admired but had never been. My best friend had an entirely illusionary image of me, one built on deceit. I would recount experiences I envied in others and claim them as my own. My dishonesty knew no bounds, and my emotions were equally stunted. I felt excitement and joy when playing games and hanging out with friends but little else. Anger, sadness, and despair filled the rest of my days. My only other outlet was smoking and drinking, numbing myself from the harshness of reality.

As a young adult, I projected my anger onto others, especially my mother. I blamed her for everything wrong in my life. I yelled at her until she cried, walking away with an evil smile of satisfaction. Breaking her heart gave me a twisted sense of power. I enjoyed causing emotional pain, not just to her but to my siblings and friends, especially when I felt they had wronged me. I was an ungrateful brat, drawing strength from the darkest parts of myself. Too weak to inflict physical harm, I resorted to mental and emotional torment.

I smoked incessantly, drowning every childhood dream in parties and distractions. Despite being drawn to spirituality and high moral ideals, my life was the opposite. I spoke boldly, trying to mask my hollow personality, but my actions never aligned with my words. My lack of self-esteem drove me to pretend I was someone I was not. I lived a life steeped in hypocrisy, embodying everything I despised.

In an ironic twist, looking back at my life, I realize I used the excuse of being a victim of the world to contribute to its darkness. I blamed the world for its cruelty while creating and spreading darkness myself. I hated dishonesty and lack of integrity, yet I lived by them every day. I can tell you from experience, nothing good comes from this path. It leads only to more pain, more suffering, and deeper darkness.

Now, let's make an observation: everything discussed in this chapter about the lack of honesty or integrity ultimately leads to suffering—either for oneself, for others, or often for both. In essence, the absence of honesty and integrity always manifests as some form of suffering. If you take a moment to reflect on your own struggles, you will find that they frequently arise from a lack of these qualities.

Whether you find it difficult to express yourself freely, feel held back by fear, struggle with confidence, face challenges in staying consistent, or find it hard to achieve the success you desire, these shortcomings add to your suffering. However, by cultivating and strengthening your honesty and integrity, suffering gradually diminishes over time. Honesty allows you to express yourself freely without reservation, unshackling you from the chains of fear. Integrity fuels your dedication and determination, helping you achieve success through consistent effort and unwavering ambition.

Fear dissipates when replaced by the courage that honesty brings. Fear diminishes even further as life's challenges lose their daunting edge, while integrity strengthens your resolve and motivates you to persevere.

Do not burden yourself with thoughts about how far you still have to go to achieve greatness or enlightenment. Instead, focus on today, taking small, meaningful steps to cultivate honesty and integrity in every moment. Precision in your direction matters more than the perceived distance to your destination. If you are moving in the right direction, you are inevitably drawing closer to your ultimate goal.

On the path to enlightenment, the focus is not on how far you must go to end your suffering. The goal is to suffer less each day than the day before. As long as you reduce your suffering day by day, you become more enlightened than you were yesterday. Achieving this is as simple as consistently enhancing your honesty and integrity, one day at a time.

There will never be a time when everything is perfect and free of challenges, but that does not mean you cannot continuously live in a state of bliss. Bliss is a relative term. If you feel better than you did yesterday and continue this trajectory throughout your life, a sense of bliss will follow you every day. It will feel as if you are consistently in a state of bliss, regardless of the challenges you face.

You suffer less by finding the courage to say what you've always wished to say, to do what you've always wished to do, to pursue your goals and dreams, and to become a better person than you were yesterday. Each day, strive to be a bit more honest and to uphold more integrity than the day before. Your suffering dwindles as you improve yourself. Then, a sense of contentment naturally follows. There is no other way to end suffering; there is no other path to bliss.

Honesty and integrity are attributes of light that, when practiced and cultivated, begin to radiate from your heart. With this inner light, you can venture into the darkest corners of your being in search of your soul. This inner light empowers you to confront fears, endure adversities, and rise above difficulties wherever and whenever they appear. This light guides you through the narrow pathways of devil's den, illuminates the darkness within you, helps you face and overcome your inner demons, and leads you to rediscover your true self. With this light, you can navigate life's roughest terrain while preserving your peace and tranquility.

A state of bliss is not a life devoid of challenges; rather, it is a life filled with the greatest possible challenges at all times. This is why those who seek the light of truth are strong and powerful. Consider the superheroes in your fairy tale stories: they are the ones who face challenges that no one else dares to confront, who make the impossible possible, and who achieve success against all odds. Real life is no different. You must become the superhero of your own life story. An easy life is never a good life, and a good life is never easy.

If you seek to end your suffering and mental agony, if you seek the truth, if you aim to find the best version of yourself, then be prepared to face the toughest challenges in life, challenges that may even surpass your darkest imagination. Only then is there hope for a life full of bliss and tranquility. Remember the concept of contradiction in duality that we discussed at the beginning of this book. You can't have one side of duality without the other. If you seek light, you must understand darkness. If you yearn for bliss, you must endure deep suffering. If you desire a good life, you must embrace a tough life.

Possessing both honesty and integrity means having sincere thoughts and feelings that align with your words and actions while maintaining consistency in your values and beliefs according to your moral understanding. In other words, honesty and integrity together represent a harmonious integration of one's genuine thoughts, feelings, words, and actions, all guided by personal beliefs, values, and moral principles.

This fusion of honesty and integrity creates a synergy that fosters a holistic approach to truth. It is a steadfast commitment to upholding a moral compass, ensuring that decisions and behaviors are congruent with deeply held values. This way of being ignites a light within your heart that brightens your path during your darkest days.

When you possess both honesty and integrity, you become brave and fearless. By being honest and never lying, you become an expert at detecting deceit and are not easily fooled. You become careful and deliberate in your words and actions. You only say what you truly intend to do, and you express yourself authentically. Your integrity gives you dedication and a sense of purpose, keeping you steady and unswayed by the whims of others. You know what you want and work hard to achieve your goals and dreams. You focus on improving yourself day by day, without comparing yourself to others. You will not betray or cause suffering to others. Your primary motivations will no longer be driven by money, fame, or power. If you become wealthy or powerful, you remain genuinely generous and use your influence to help others achieve their dreams. You become a warrior of light, bringing safety and security to the hearts of those around you.

Honesty and integrity are not simply on or off switches; they are not qualities that you either possess or lack entirely. Everyone can exhibit honesty and integrity to some extent. What truly matters is how consistently you apply these virtues. Are you honest all day, every day, and in every situation with everyone? Are you honest with yourself? Do you maintain integrity at home, at work, in social gatherings, and within your communities? Do you uphold integrity in the pursuit of your personal dreams?

The challenge many people face with honesty and integrity is their situational bias. They tend to be honest when it suits them and demonstrate integrity only when compelled to do so. Sadly, many willingly compromise honesty and integrity in exchange for safety and security.

Imagine waking up one day to hear that the government in your country will no longer be enforcing any laws and that there will be no police. No one will be punished for theft, rape, murder, or any other act of violence. Picture a country where anarchy reigns. No shop, bank, or home would be safe from invaders. Imagine how people would react in such a situation. Do you believe people would maintain honesty and integrity based on high moral standards, or would they disregard these virtues and vandalize, take, and destroy everything in their path?

Obviously, there would be both types of people in any society. However, those with good virtues would be in the minority. Crime rates would undoubtedly spike. Streets would become unsafe, shops and stores would be broken into, and massive theft, rape, and murder would take place. People would invade each other's personal spaces. The fear of uncertainty would cause many to lose their honesty, and the greed for survival would cause them to lose their integrity. In such a scenario, the depth and purity of one's honesty and integrity would be truly tested.

Would you sell your honesty and integrity for any prize? Would you trade them for safety and security? Would you exploit others if it benefited you? Would you betray those around you for momentary ecstasy and satisfaction? Would you lie to get ahead in life? Would you abandon your moral standards for money, fame, or power? Do you have a price tag on your honesty and integrity?

Let's consider an example where the value of honesty is tested. Imagine you're dining at a restaurant, and when the receipt arrives, you notice that some of the items you ordered and enjoyed are missing from the bill. You realize that if you say nothing and pay as it is, no one will notice.

Now, let's add another layer. Perhaps you're struggling financially—your rent or mortgage is due soon, and you're short on funds. This extra money could make a difference in easing your burden. On the other hand, the restaurant's owner is wealthy, and this small amount won't impact their financial status in any meaningful way. With all this in mind, the temptation to stay silent grows stronger.

But is it worth it? Is it worth selling your honesty for a small, fleeting financial relief? Would your justification of blaming your dire financial situation or the owner's wealth make it any less dishonest? Honesty is not about circumstances; it is not about whether the other party can absorb the loss or whether your reasoning feels justified. It's about remaining true to your moral values and principles, even when no one is watching and even when it costs you or hurts you.

Your moral values are worth more than a few extra dollars. Yes, it may sting in the short term, especially if finances are tight, but the price of dishonesty is far greater. By compromising your honesty, you compromise your self-respect and entangle yourself deeper into the web of darkness.

Now, consider an extreme example. Imagine a banking error results in one billion dollars being deposited into your account without a trace. You know you could keep the money, and the bank would never find out. Keeping the money would be dishonest but returning it would be incredibly difficult.

Would you stand by the truth and inform the bank of the error in their system? Would you value truth and honesty over a billion dollars? This would be an extremely challenging situation, especially if you're already struggling with the daily cost of living. This money could transform your life, providing luxuries you could only dream of. It could change the lives of your family, friends, and those around you. You would never have to work another day.

Is a billion dollars the right price tag to abandon truth and honesty? If your answer is to keep the money, then you are not walking the path of enlightenment. However, if you can muster the courage to return the money, the respect you would gain for yourself would outweigh the luxuries the money could provide. Some might believe that a billion dollars would end their suffering, but in reality, those who possess far more still suffer today. Money, fame, and power cannot alleviate mental agony. If the goal in life is to not suffer, you must value truth above all else. Obtaining truth through honesty and integrity is what ultimately defies suffering in life.

As for myself, if I were presented with a billion dollars without any consequences, I genuinely cannot predict my actions. However, I understand what the right thing to do would be; I know that I would have to return the money. I know that revealing the truth in any situation is the only righteous course. Retaining money that I have not rightfully earned does not contribute to my journey toward enlightenment. Ideally, I hope I would stand by the truth and return the money. I hope you, too, would willingly return the money and never trade truth and honesty for any worldly possession.

There is a famous quote that states, "If you do not sacrifice for what you want, what you want becomes the sacrifice." If you aren't willing to sacrifice everything for the truth, then the truth will inevitably become the sacrifice for everything else in your life. Upholding honesty and integrity is extremely challenging, but it is the only path to truth. The question then arises: how deeply do you seek the truth in your life? How much are you willing to sacrifice to preserve your honesty and integrity? The ultimate question is, are you willing to give up everything you cherish to find the truth? This may include your health, family, friends, loved ones, beliefs, faith, comfort, wealth, fame, power, or even your life. If your answer is no, then the path of enlightenment may not be for you.

Your true path is defined by what you are willing to sacrifice. If you are willing to sacrifice truth for power, then your path is one of power. If you are willing to sacrifice truth for money, then your path is one of wealth. If you are willing to sacrifice truth for your family, then your path is one of family and so on. Ultimately, the thing you are most willing to sacrifice everything else for determines your ultimate path in life.

Willing to sacrifice everything for truth does not necessarily mean you will always have to give up everything—it means that when faced with a choice between truth and any other aspect of life, you will choose truth, no matter the cost. If your job conflicts with your moral values, you must be ready to find another job. If your partner or children choose a path of destruction and align themselves with darkness, you must separate your path from theirs. However, this does not mean you should hate or resent them. You must continue to love them, extend compassion, and offer kindness. You must even help them if they ever genuinely seek redemption. But you cannot participate in their darkness, nor can you compromise your values for their sake. Even if truth requires the ultimate sacrifice—your life—choosing it remains the most righteous path.

Consider a scenario: you are living in Poland in 1942 in a small village. The German police, Reserve Police Battalion 101, arrive in your village. Your Jewish neighbors, who have always been kind to you, flee as the police approach. The Nazi officer asks you, "Which direction did your Jewish neighbors flee?" What will you do?

If you reveal the direction, you betray your integrity by facilitating the capture and likely murder of your kind neighbors. If you lie, you compromise your honesty, undermining your commitment to truth. What is the right course of action that upholds both honesty and integrity? In such moments, you must think beyond conventional choices. Sometimes, the only way to uphold the truth is through ultimate sacrifice.

You could respond to the officer in this way: "If I tell you the direction, I betray my moral values and help you plunge deeper into darkness by assisting in the murder of my neighbors. If I give you false information, I betray my honesty and risk angering you, which might provoke harsher actions against me, my family, my neighbors, or even the village. This, too, would worsen the situation for everyone. Therefore, I choose silence. I will not provide the answer you seek because I believe it does not serve the greater good. Do what you will with this decision, but I will not assist your inquiry."

This response may result in your imprisonment, torture, or even death. It could endanger your family, or it could lead the officers to let you go unharmed. The outcome is beyond your control. However, by standing firm in both your honesty and integrity, you embody the ultimate expression of truth. You show unwavering courage, prioritizing what is right over personal safety and comfort. This is how honesty and integrity make you fearless: even in the face of death, you stand tall, resolute, and unshaken.

This is what it means to become fearless through honesty. This is what it means to uphold integrity rotted in the highest moral values. This is what it means to sacrifice everything in the pursuit of truth. Standing for truth is not a grand act performed for recognition but a profound, yet quiet stand for moral values and justice. Such a choice elevates your character, turning you into a real-world superhero—someone who exemplifies the highest values of humanity.

Truth in the light reveals both your beauty and your flaws. It unveils reality. With the light ignited within your heart, it dispels darkness, lies, and confusion. By practicing truth in the light, you learn to see through deception. You become confident and clear-minded. Your vision becomes sharp, and your accuracy increases. Honesty provides you with clarity, while integrity grants you determination, consistency, and purpose. You become the ultimate fearless warrior.

Only then will you be strong enough to confront your own weaknesses and imperfections. Only then can you truly transform and improve. Truth in the light leads you to your soul, enabling you to reunite with the best version of yourself.

When you are fully connected and in harmony with your soul, every moment of life is imbued with a sense of completeness, even during the darkest days when the outside world seems unbearable to others. Living in alignment with the soul is so fulfilling that it erases past regrets and future worries. When you are one with your soul, you do not fear the darkness. You remain mentally unaffected by the whims of destructive human behavior. Even if your physical body is imprisoned and tortured, your mind stays healthy, free, and intact.

Pitesti Prison Reeducation Experiment, also known as the "Pitesti Phenomenon" took place in Romania between 1949 and 1951. This experiment was designed by the communist regime to forcefully re-educate political prisoners and dissidents into adopting communist ideology through systematic physical and psychological torture.

The aim was to break down individuals mentally and physically to reshape their minds into obedient supporters of communism. Prisoners were subjected to severe methods of torture, including beatings, starvation, electric shocks, and forced to stand in small pits for hours. Torture was carried out not only by guards but also by prisoners who had been broken and re-educated, turning victims into perpetrators in this cycle of violence.

While the primary goal was to create loyal communist supporters, many prisoners either died, went insane, or suffered profound psychological trauma. A few prisoners, however, were labeled as successes of the experiment as they became perpetrators and bowed down to the communist tyranny of the time. Eugen Turcanu, initially a victim, was transformed by the regime into one of the chief torturers at Pitesti, brutally torturing his own friends.

However, some other individuals, despite the extreme conditions, emerged with strengthened faith and unimaginable moral convictions. Father George Calciu, an Orthodox priest, survived the Pitesti experiment and spent the rest of his life promoting love and peace. He not only lived to tell his story but also forgave his captors and torturers.

His life was marked by acts of forgiveness, spiritual leadership, and advocacy for freedom and human dignity.

What distinguished Eugen from George? Eugen, having lost touch with his soul during the brutal days of torture, descended further into darkness until he became one of the most ruthless torturers himself. He sacrificed truth and dignity to regain his physical comfort. In contrast, George kept his soul intact. While his physical body was broken down, his mental strength and soul grew stronger each day. He became a symbol of resilience, and his life story is one to admire. George never spoke of regretting the past, fearing the future, or experiencing trauma and psychological breakdowns. Instead, he emerged mentally stronger, happier, and claimed to have achieved a higher state of serenity and peace after enduring the tortures.

When you are not in harmony with your soul, life feels dark even on the brightest days. Conversely, when your soul is intact, even your darkest days seem bright, filled with growth and wisdom. If you ever feel anything remotely negative, the issue does not lie in the external world but within yourself and your level of connection with your soul.

In summary, we have discussed three types of truth in the last three chapters. Let us reiterate each one briefly. Truth in the darkness is about accepting that you can never know the whole truth. Be humble, remove your vanity and arrogance to understand the depth of your mental suffering. There is more to learn than the whole of humanity can ever fully comprehend. Reality is vastly complex. Keep your mind open, your beliefs flexible, and your outlook susceptible to change. Do not uphold rigid beliefs as if what you believe is the absolute truth. Encourage yourself to continually examine, re-evaluate, and refine your belief system—from its very roots to the fruits it bears. Use this as a catalyst for change, growth, and transformation. Be brave, face your fears, and do not shy away from your own darkness but challenge it and become comfortable with its chilling nature.

Knowing the truth in the shadow is all about balance between light and darkness. While suffering is great, the power of humanity is greater. Choose your path wisely. You have the capability to endure any hardship in life, be grateful, and accept life as it is given to you. Your happiness does not lie in some distant future but exists within everything you already possess.

Anything permanent and of the highest value can only exist within you and cannot be found in the outside world in any shape or form. The outside world is temporary and consistently changing; therefore, nothing external can ever be permanent and unchanging. Emotions and thoughts, like the second law of thermodynamics, strive for equilibrium, meaning you are impacted by the emotions and thoughts of those around you. To maintain a stable inner state, exert enough energy to counterbalance opposing emotions and thoughts of others.

Do not cling to fleeting joyful moments as they hinder your journey toward tranquility, just as holding onto past pain will weigh you down, impeding your growth and well-being. Hone the skill of timely release and letting go of emotions and thoughts attached to your memories, whether of joy or pain. Shed your burdens. Become weightless to be able fly in the sky of consciousness.

Strive to gain true intelligence, the power to discern light from darkness, the ability to see the intention behind any action, and the capacity to avoid being fooled by lies and deceptions. Do not envy those more fortunate than you or look down on those less fortunate. See all of humanity and every individual as equal. Do not judge, nor compare.

Knowing the truth in the light is about upholding honesty and integrity at any cost. With upholding honesty face your fears and become comfortable in uncomfortable situations. Do not tolerate injustice and always strive for an environment where honesty is valued and supported. Do not fear consequences in life or trade your honesty for security and comfort. Embrace honesty's mirror effect. Be kind, so the world be kind to you. Know that unkindliness perpetuates unkindly.

Upholding integrity develops resilience, consistency, predictability, and accountability. Integrity builds your character and allows you to transform into the person you aspire to be. Uphold both honesty and integrity simultaneously. Without these twin virtues, you cannot generate the inner light needed to illuminate the darkness within you.

Be cautious not to sell your integrity at any cost. Those who possess honesty but lack integrity are hypocrites. They are weak in their determination and fail to achieve their goals in life. They appear beautiful on the inside but are ugly on the outside.

Be cautious not to sell your honesty at any cost. Those who possess integrity without honesty have a hidden and self-serving agenda. They are the narcissists. They project a beautiful image of themselves to society, appearing generous and kind on the outside, but are dark and deceitful inside. They are successful and admired by society, but their success comes at the cost of their morality and peace of mind.

And never sell both your honesty and integrity. Those who lack both honesty and integrity are among the worst people in the world. They are narcissistic hypocrites with self-serving hidden agendas. They take pleasure in inflicting pain and causing suffering. They are comfortable in their own darkness, and they despise the light.

Strive to possess both honesty and integrity. Be truthful and become someone who others can rely on. Do not be motivated by wealth, fame, power, or respect, nor be interested in using others to achieve success. Uphold high moral values and be driven by an inner desire to improve yourself and become the better versions of yourself day after day. Strive to eradicate your suffering to attain an eternal state of bliss. Be fearless, accountable, trustworthy, and kind, and sacrifice anything in pursuit of the truth. Gain clear vision and understand your purpose in life.

Take the time to develop your honesty and integrity. Practice them daily. To end your suffering, you must understand the depth of your suffering. A good life is filled with challenges and overcoming them is what generates your happiness. Strive to be better than you were yesterday and continue on that path, until you attain a lasting sense of happiness, tranquility, serenity, and peace in life.

Chapter 12: Layers of Truth

Truth is omnipresent, existing in every nook and cranny of existence. It is woven into our world layer by layer. Consider these layers of truth like the different ways we study layers of light and its properties. We use light to observe physical reality, whether through our naked eyes, a microscope, or a telescope.

Through a telescope, we explore the vastness of the cosmos, gaining insights into astronomy, cosmology, astrophysics, astrobiology, and so on. It allows us to see distant stars, galaxies, and the very fabric of the universe. This way of observing light through telescopes represents a layer of reality that pertains to the macrocosm, the grand scale of existence.

Through a microscope, we delve into the finer details of the natural world, uncovering the intricacies of biology, chemistry, nanotechnology, and so on. These fields of study reveal the cellular structures and molecular interactions that form the foundation of our world. Observing light through a microscope represents another layer of reality, one that pertains to the microcosm, the detailed aspects of existence.

With our naked eyes, we observe the world around us directly, gaining insights into geology, anthropology, archaeology, and more. This immediate perception allows us to interact with our environment and understand the social and physical landscapes we inhabit. Observing light through direct eyesight represents yet another layer of reality, one that pertains to our immediate surroundings.

Thus, depending on the method we use to observe light, each method reveals a different aspect of reality. Each layer provides unique insights and contributes to our overall understanding of the world we inhabit. While light imparts knowledge about the physical and visible reality, truth reveals the depths of the moral and invisible world. Truth has layers similar to light, with each layer unraveling different aspects of reality. These layers of truth consist of internal self-truth, external self-truth, and external truth. Studying different layers of truth will equip you with various abilities and skills to understand reality more comprehensively.

No matter which layer of truth you are exploring, the practice remains the same. It is the practice of honesty and integrity. It involves learning humility, gratitude, confidence, bravery, consistency, and all the other attributes we have discussed so far.

The inner layer of truth, or internal self-truth, is about knowing yourself. To know yourself, you must see yourself exactly as you are. It is important to acknowledge both your beauty and your flaws, without glorifying your beauty or hiding your imperfections. The more clearly you see who you are, the more accurately you come to know yourself.

To truly get to know yourself, cultivate the habit of spending time with yourself multiple times throughout each day. Being alone with yourself means turning your attention inward and attending to your physical, emotional, and psychological needs. It means creating moments where you can disconnect from external distractions and engage in deep self-reflection.

It's about listening to your inner voice, understanding your emotions, and recognizing the signals your body and soul are sending to you. Sounds simple. Yet, many people overlook these signals. Dehydrated alcoholics reach for another beer instead of a glass of water. Over stressed workaholics double down on their workload, adding even more stress to their pursuit of wealth. Those in toxic relationships continuously engage in destructive arguments with their partner, further fueling their mental turmoil.

People often fail to address their own needs because they become consumed by the demands of the external world. They strive to meet societal expectations, fulfill obligations, and live up to the standards imposed by others, all while neglecting the quiet cries of their souls from within. Over time, this neglect leads to mental illnesses, pulling them further away from the inner peace and tranquility they seek.

If you find yourself struggling to maintain your mental health and inner peace amidst your daily challenges, know that you have the power to break this cycle. The key lies in turning your attention inward and spending more time with yourself to understand your own needs. By cultivating self-awareness, you will significantly reduce your mental agony and foster a deep sense of inner peace. This awareness will also help you to detect early signs of distress and respond appropriately, preventing minor issues from escalating into serious problems.

It would be ideal if you could dedicate days, weeks, months, or even years to complete solitude—separating yourself from friends, family, social media, work, and all other distractions that pull your attention outward. In this sacred silence, you could direct your focus inward, exploring the depths of your psyche and becoming intimately acquainted with the landscape of your mental construct. When practiced with intention and discipline, long-term solitude holds immense potential for self-realization and personal growth.

However, such an opportunity is neither feasible nor realistic for most people. Very few have the privilege to retreat from their responsibilities for extended periods, and even fewer are willing to venture so deeply into themselves. The thought of such prolonged solitude can be intimidating, and the sacrifices it demands deter most people.

Recognizing this, the focus here is not to push you toward an unrealistic ideal but to explore how you can integrate the profound benefits of solitude into your daily life. By carving out moments of quiet reflection, even amidst the chaos of modern life, you can begin the journey of turning inward. This practice, while simple, can still lead to significant transformation of your character and a deeper understanding of who you are.

Finding time for introspection and being alone is possible for everyone, regardless of the lifestyle. Whether you have a busy schedule with family and children, or you work multiple jobs to cover your expenses, or even if you are famous and constantly surrounded by people, none of these circumstances should prevent you from carving out moments of solitude each and every day. No matter how hectic your life may be, there are always opportunities to create space for yourself.

If you seek solitude, opportunities to find it exist every day, even amidst the busiest of lives. During moments like a shower or bedtime, you can turn your attention inward and attend to your own needs. All you have to do is to stop thinking about the outside world. While it's impossible to fully control your thoughts and emotions, you do have the ability to guide and redirect them with intention. By focusing inward, your mind gradually begins to reflect more of your internal state rather than being consumed by external circumstances.

Whenever you find a quiet moment alone, try this simple practice. Begin by focusing on your breath. Take slow, deep breaths through your nose, allowing your diaphragm to expand, gently pushing your belly outward, and then exhale slowly. Keep your attention on the rhythm of your breathing. Visualize the air moving in and out through your nostrils, and feel your lungs expanding and contracting with each breath. This simple practice helps draw your mind away from distractions.

Next, try to feel your heartbeat. Scan your chest, neck, and head to see if you can sense it anywhere. If you can't feel your heartbeat naturally, gently place your index finger just below your jawline, beneath the curve where it angles upward near the ear. Press against your neck and notice the faint pulse of blood flowing through your veins. Stay connected to your breath and heartbeat simultaneously. Whenever your mind wanders off, gently bring it back to these sensations.

After a few seconds or minutes, something remarkable will happen. For a fleeting moment, your mind stays entirely with you, grounded in the present, without wandering. In that stillness, you'll sense a calmness washing over your mental landscape. It could last only for a fraction of a second. It's subtle yet noticeable when it comes. Once you reach this state of relative calmness, start talking to yourself gently and kindly, as though addressing an old friend: "Hey there, I'm here with you now. How are you? Are you doing okay? Is your life all right? What can I do to make things better for you? Everything is going to be okay. I am here to take care of you."

In this state of introspection, let your thoughts and emotions flow freely. You may uncover a deep sense of sadness and find yourself crying. Let the tears come; don't resist them. Simply observe. Alternatively, you might feel a surge of joy and delight. Don't try to cling to it or amplify it; just let it move through you.

You may even experience a wave of anger rising within you—a surge of heat coursing through your body, quickening your heartbeat and tightening your muscles. Resist the urge to fight or suppress it. Instead, stay relaxed and focused on your breath and heartbeat. Let the rage wash over you like a wave, noticing its intensity as it builds and then gently fades away. Whatever arises, allow it to exist without judgment or analysis, observing until it naturally subsides.

You may not feel anything at all, and that's okay. Simply try to remain in the moment, gently bringing your mind back to the present whenever it wanders. Stay with it as a silent companion, allowing yourself to just be.

All the while, also listen to the voice of your soul—the whispers that emerge from the deepest recesses of your mind. Listen intently, with patience and openness. If your soul asks for something, make a mental note to honor its request, then continue to listen. Simply listen and remember. Let your mind speak to you, instead of filling it with your own thoughts.

These whispers of the soul have a profound purpose. They will help you understand the emotions you experience, revealing the roots of your mental and emotional struggles. They will shed light on the source of your pain, your fears, and even your joy. Through these quiet murmurs, your soul will guide you toward awareness, offering clarity about your mental state and emotional landscape. In listening, you gain an understanding of who you truly are.

It is impossible to truly know yourself through critical thinking alone. The information you possess about yourself is incomplete and fragmented. You cannot fully remember the early years of your life—formative moments that played a significant role in shaping your character. Many experiences have faded from your memory with time, slipping into forgetfulness, and some traumas may be buried so deeply that you have no conscious access to them. These forgotten and hidden layers of your life are critical to your journey of enlightenment.

Furthermore, you are an exceedingly complex creature, far more sophisticated than what science, logic, critical thinking, or any form of external analysis could ever fully comprehend. No external tool or practice can fully unravel the depths of who you are.

The only part of you that truly knows you entirely is your soul. Your soul is not bound by forgetfulness. It remembers your past completely and holds the keys to every experience that has shaped you. Unlike you, your soul is not traumatized or fragmented. It understands your wounds, carries the wisdom to heal them, and always remains completely aware. It is an infinite well of insight and guidance.

When you take the time to listen to your soul, it gently whispers the roots of your struggles, illuminating the unseen wounds you carry. It guides you through hidden traumas and unresolved conflicts, showing you a path toward healing and understanding.

To unlock this wisdom, you must give your soul the time and space to speak. Learn to tune in to its subtle voice and let it teach you about who you are. This quiet, patient listening will reveal truths about yourself that no amount of analysis or external insight could ever uncover. Through this practice, you can begin to heal, grow, and discover the profound depths of your own being.

This entire practice takes no more than a few short minutes. It can be done almost anywhere—while taking a shower, lying in bed, waiting for the next train, sitting at a restaurant before your friend arrives, or any time you find a quiet moment of solitude. There's no need for elaborate preparation or unrealistic conditions.

There's also nothing more you need to do—no analysis and no overthinking. Just make a mental note of everything you heard and felt within you. They will begin to make sense as you continue this practice. It's simply a practice of self-awareness, a moment to reconnect with your soul. These small, intentional pauses can bring clarity and balance, grounding you amidst the busyness of day-to-day life. To experience the full effect, practice this regularly. Make it a daily habit—Its simplicity belies its power, and over time, it can profoundly enrich your life.

Now, imagine yourself at a party with friends and family, where conversations fill the air and music blares in the background. It might seem impossible to find solitude in such a bustling environment, but solitude is more about where you direct your attention than your external circumstances. Even in the midst of the party, sitting on the couch between your friends and family, you can choose to be alone.

To achieve this, turn your attention inward. Start by closing your eyes and taking a deep, slow breath through your nose for 3 to 5 seconds, allowing it to fill your abdomen. Focus on your inner self and hold your attention there, then exhale. If your focus feels fuzzy, take another deep breath in the same way. Breathing deeply through your nose and abdomen helps center your mind wherever you direct it. With intention, shift your focus inward. Then, open your eyes. Observe everything around you without focusing on anything in particular. Simply become a passive observer through your senses. In this brief moment, you've transitioned your awareness from the external world to your inner self—completely hidden from the eyes of others while sitting among them.

The redirection of attention is so subtle that most people won't notice it. While everyone continues chatting and engaging with each other, you will be sitting among them, yet alone with your thoughts and feelings. This practice allows you to create a bubble of introspection. If you stay in this state for too long, others may eventually notice you're not fully present with them. However, in most situations, just a few seconds to a few minutes is enough to explore your inner truth. Unless someone calls your name, asks you a question, or directly engages you, you can remain in this state, attending to yourself and listening to what your body and mind are trying to tell you.

Now, it's time for internal insights. Unlike the quiet solitude where you connect deeply with your soul and address yourself in the second person, this moment calls for speaking to yourself in the first person. In the midst of a lively party or chaotic environment, access to your soul will not be granted, but you can still step back and observe yourself. While this level of awareness may not delve as deeply, it remains profoundly valuable. The purpose here isn't to unravel childhood wounds or dissect your psyche amidst the party. Instead, it's about ensuring that you're not causing yourself any harm, becoming mindful of your actions, and aware of their potential repercussions.

Silently ask yourself, "How am I feeling? Am I okay?" Assess if you've done anything wrong at the party. "Have I been drinking too much? Smoking too much? Talking too much? Eating too much?" Consider your bodily needs. "Am I thirsty? Hungry? Tired? Am I relaxed or stressed?" Reflect on your feelings. "Am I angry? Sad? Happy? Content?" Analyze your thoughts. "Are the voices in my head too loud? Are they in harmony or discord?" Finally, ask yourself, "Do I truly want to stay at the party longer, or do I want to leave?" By asking these questions, you are scanning your thoughts, feelings, and physical body.

Follow whatever your body and mind tell you to do. If your inner self urges you to leave, then go home. If your inner self is content staying longer, then stay. If it wants you to stop drinking alcohol, grab a bottle of water next. If it tells you to stop eating, refrain from munching on the snacks. When you turn your attention inward, it becomes easier to do the right thing because you become aware of your true needs and hear the voices from within.

By turning your attention inward, you become the passive observer of your own character rather than an active or reactive participant. Being a passive observer means being in the world and seeing the world, but not being part of its distractions. It means being of the world but not consumed by the world. By practicing introspection, you learn to maintain a balance between passivity and activity. You learn to remain passive unless life situations prompt you to take action.

In the hustle and bustle of a busy life, you may find yourself constantly active or reactive. Being reactive is the most stressful and the worst way to live because it means you are constantly being tossed around by life's circumstances. When you are reactive, you are swayed by the outside world rather than guided by your own volition and will. Even being constantly active causes mental and physical stress as you deal with life's struggles from all directions. In a state of stress, you cannot achieve inner peace and tranquility, as peace is the opposite of stress. The best way to reduce stress is to practice introspection. Redirect your attention inward throughout each and every day and take a passive stance in life whenever possible and feasible. This doesn't mean always being passive, but learning when to be passive, when to be active, and almost never being reactive.

Therefore, the natural state of being should always be passive, calm and collected. In this state, you observe and absorb the world around you without immediate reaction, allowing for a deeper understanding and connection with your inner self and the world around you. When life demands action, you can then transition into an active state with intention and purpose, responding thoughtfully rather than impulsively. This approach ensures that your actions are deliberate and aligned with your values. By cultivating this balance between passive observation and mindful action, you maintain inner peace and gain profound clarity.

Practicing internal self-truth teaches you the essential skill of self-control. It enables you to observe your own thoughts and emotions, allowing you to understand their impact on your behavior. Internal self-truth provides clarity of your unmet needs and unresolved issues, guiding you toward appropriate actions and decisions. This process is about recognizing and understanding your emotions and thoughts rather than suppressing them.

As you deepen your understanding of yourself, you become adept at discerning the next step you need to take at every moment in your life, similar to the example we discussed about knowing what to do next while sitting with friends and family at a party. This guidance helps you align your actions with your core values and long-term goals, ensuring that each step you take is purposeful and informed by self-awareness.

Anytime throughout the day when life does not demand immediate action from you, take a moment to reflect internally and scan your entire being to recognize your current state. Ask yourself, "What is the most appropriate action I should take at this very moment?" Consider whether you should work, rest, exercise, drink, eat, socialize, pray, meditate, or any other option available at that moment. Then, listen to yourself—not to your superficial desires but to your inner voice and emotions. Follow the guidance that comes from the deepest part of your being. The greatest teacher you could ever hope to find resides within, always offering you the best possible path forward at any given moment.

These practices take only a few seconds to a few minutes each time, but their impact is profound. By incorporating the habit of introspection multiple times a day, you will notice that your actions become more aligned with your core beliefs and life goals. As you continue this practice, you become more attuned to your true self, finding greater comfort and confidence in your own skin.

However, it is extremely important to always practice honesty and integrity simultaneously at all times. When practicing internal self-truth, you must be brutally honest with yourself and uphold your integrity to the highest moral standards. This is because, without honesty and integrity, the insights and decisions you derive from within will be flawed and untruthful.

If you are not honest with yourself or lack integrity, your own thoughts and feelings will deceive you. Remember the mirror effect of honesty: it applies not only to the outside world but also to your inner world. If you lie to yourself, your own self will lie to you in return in the form of thoughts and feelings. This distortion creates a cycle of self-deception that can severely impact your mental and emotional well-being. Recall the differences between emotions and feelings: emotions are the sensations of the soul, while feelings are the sensations of the body.

If you lie to yourself, you create a mental space for your inner demons to settle between your soul and your physical body, between your emotions and feelings, between the voice of the soul and your active thinking. Your inner demons will distort and twist the emotions and messages of the soul, preventing your thoughts and feelings from accurately reflecting what your soul wishes to communicate. As a result, when you turn inward to listen to your inner self, the messages you receive through your thoughts and feelings will not be grounded in truth. You will hear the voice of the devil rather than the whisper of the soul. You will deceive yourself causing confusion, poor decision-making, and a deep sense of dissatisfaction.

For example, if you convince yourself that you are content with your current life situation, when, deep down, you are not truly satisfied, those superficial feelings of contentment will quickly fade. Over time, disconnection from your soul manifests as anxiety, depression, or a persistent sense of dissatisfaction. Simply put, without honesty and integrity, practices like prayer, meditation, introspection, and self-reflection will do more harm than good.

Practicing honesty and integrity is essential for closing the gap between you and your soul. When you commit to being truthful with yourself, you begin to clear the fog of self-deception, reducing the influence of inner demons on your internal state. At the same time, integrity allows you to build a strong, trustworthy relationship with yourself. Practices of meditation and introspection from this state of clarity will naturally propel you forward toward your true purpose and values.

I cannot emphasize enough how critical it is to walk the path of enlightenment in the correct order. Any misstep or deviation will cause more harm than good. Enlightenment is only effective if pursued in the precise sequence, much like opening a lock. Even one incorrect step in the pattern will prevent the lock from opening.

The first and most essential step is to cultivate humility. Without humility, nothing else works. Humility helps you shed arrogance and rigid beliefs, creating space for growth and understanding. Once humility is established, you can build gratitude—learning to appreciate the gift of life, however it is given to you.

With gratitude as your foundation, the next step is to gain true intelligence. True intelligence is the ability to see everyone as your equal, stripping away vanity and pity. It is the lens through which you perceive the deeper truths of humanity.

Only then can you effectively practice honesty. Honesty requires the humility to admit your flaws, the gratitude to accept your life as it is, and true intelligence to see equality among all. At the same time, use the wisdom of true intelligence to see beyond surface appearances to cultivate a strong moral understanding. This morality becomes the framework for proper integrity.

When your honesty is paired with integrity built upon a solid foundation, you can finally engage in genuine self-reflection. This self-reflection enables you to confront your inner darkness and bring your soul closer to light.

If you attempt to skip steps or take shortcuts, no amount of meditation, prayer, introspection, or even years of complete solitude will bring lasting relief from your suffering. Every step must be taken in its rightful place, one leading naturally to the next. Only then will the gate of enlightenment open, and only then will your suffering truly begin to dissipate.

Now, let's explore another aspect of internal self-truth: people often behave better when they feel they are being watched. For example, imagine your house is a bit messy one day, and your friend calls to say they're coming over. Suddenly, the thought of being judged for the mess motivates you to tidy up the house before they arrive. This response is a natural human tendency—to present yourself better when you believe you're being watched or potentially judged.

By practicing internal self-truth and observing yourself, you become the one watching and judging your own behavior. This self-reflection turns you into a passive observer of your own actions, prompting you to act as you would if others were watching.

When you embrace this practice, you cultivate a heightened sense of self-awareness and accountability. You begin to watch yourself closely and maintain a more orderly and conscientious approach to your daily life. This continuous self-monitoring encourages you to uphold higher standards of behavior and integrity, even when no one else is around.

This initiates a chain reaction of personal transformation. You become cleaner, better dressed, more well-behaved, more articulate, a better listener, a more dedicated worker, a more considerate partner, and so on. Improvement happens through self-observation and self-reflection. Furthermore, when you reflect internally, when you become the passive observer of your own life, and learn to live up to your own standards, you begin to lose interest in how others judge and perceive you.

You become content with who you are because you become the judge of your own life. This self-assuredness builds an invisible, impenetrable wall around your mental landscape, making you unaffected by other people's judgments. As a result, you become more united with yourself and more consistent in your actions, behaving the same way whether you are alone or with others. You are no longer swayed by external opinions or societal pressures, as your self-worth is rooted in your own perceptions and standards.

There was a story I once read in third grade that I never thought much of—until years later. One crisp morning, a grandfather and his young grandson set off on a journey, leading their horse with a heavy bundle of luggage strapped securely to its back. The boy was excited, and the old man was experienced but weary, knowing that the road ahead was long.

As they entered the first village, townspeople gathered around, eyeing them with disapproval.

"What fools!" one man scoffed. "They have a strong horse, yet they're walking on foot while making it carry nothing but luggage?"

Hearing this, the grandfather and grandson exchanged a glance. Maybe the villagers had a point. So, the old man hoisted his grandson onto the horse while he continued walking alongside it.

They hadn't gone far before they entered the next town, where the villagers again gathered and whispered among themselves.

"What an ungrateful little boy!" a woman muttered. "Riding in comfort while his poor old grandfather walks? Where's the respect for elders these days?"

Embarrassed, the grandson quickly got off, and the grandfather took his place on the horse.

Not long after, they entered another village. The moment the locals saw them, they shook their heads in disapproval.

"That selfish old man!" they said. "Riding like a king while the poor boy struggles on foot? Shameful!"

Frustrated, the grandfather sighed and reached down, pulling his grandson onto the horse so they could ride together.

They continued their journey, relieved that they had finally found a reasonable solution. But as they passed through the next town, they were met with gasps of horror.

"Have you no mercy?" a merchant cried. "Both of you riding at once? That poor horse is carrying your weight and the luggage! You're exhausting the poor creature!"

Completely exasperated, the grandfather rubbed his temples. He mumbled to himself: "No riding, no walking, no anything is ever right, is it?"

After a moment of thought, he had an idea—a foolish one, but an idea nonetheless.

Determined not to upset anyone anymore, he and his grandson dismounted. Together, they lifted the luggage off the horse and onto their shoulders. Step by step, they staggered under its weight, huffing and stumbling toward a narrow bridge that crossed over a rushing river.

People stared, laughing, pointing, and jeering.

"Look at these two! Carrying their luggage while they have a perfectly good horse! Have you ever seen such fools?"

Sweat dripped down their faces as they struggled under the sheer weight of the load. Their legs wobbled, their backs strained, and just as they reached the center of the bridge, their balance gave way. They stumbled sideways, crashing into the horse.

Startled, the horse let out a panicked neigh and stumbled backward. Its hoof landed awkwardly, and its weight pressed against the wooden railing. The old, weathered beams groaned under the strain before suddenly splintering apart. With nothing left to support it, the horse lurched sideways and tumbled over the edge, plunging into the river below.

The grandfather and grandson lay sprawled on the bridge, their luggage scattered around them. They could only watch as the rushing current carried their loyal companion away, its cries fading into the distance.

A long silence followed.

Finally, the grandfather let out a weary sigh and turned to his grandson.

"You see, my boy," he said, "if you try to please everyone, you'll lose what truly matters to you."

And with that, they gathered what they could of their scattered belongings and walked on—this time, not stopping to listen to what anyone else had to say.

Internal self-truth will teach you to stay grounded in your own volition, to trust your inner voice, and to seek guidance only from your soul. It liberates you from the shifting whims and burdens of others' judgments, allowing you to live according to your own discernment rather than being swayed by external influences. When you align with your inner truth, you no longer seek validation, nor do you fear rejection. Instead, you navigate life with clarity, making decisions that resonate with your deepest values rather than bending to societal expectations or the fleeting opinions of others.

The final aspect of internal self-truth is to keep your thoughts and feelings in check, ensuring you remain grounded in reality rather than fantasy. While fantasy helps you explore and express yourself creatively, it must be balanced with a firm grasp of reality. Stories, movies, and artwork often use the imaginative realm of fantasy to convey complex ideas, truths, emotions, and experiences in ways that deeply resonate with us. When used wisely, fantasy becomes a source of inspiration, teaching, and entertainment. Fantasy as artistic expression can offer new perspectives, stimulate creativity, and provide a safe space to explore different ideas.

However, it is crucial to distinguish between fantasy and reality. The danger arises if you blur the lines between them. If you start believing in the illusions created by your fantasies, you find yourself disconnected from the real world. This disconnection will lead to unrealistic expectations, unmet desires, and a deepening sense of dissatisfaction.

For example, if you constantly fantasize about an idealized version of yourself—one without flaws or struggles—you will become dissatisfied with your current reality, leading to feelings of inadequacy and disappointment. Similarly, if you fixate on an ideal partner, you will continually face disappointment in your relationships. The truth is, no one is perfect, and expecting otherwise only sets you up for frustration.

To live a more fulfilling life, respect both yourself and others as they are—with all their strengths and flaws. Do not let your fantasies override the reality of human imperfection, whether in how you view yourself or in your expectations of others. Even the best version of you will still have imperfections. "Best" doesn't mean "perfect". When you respect the imperfections in yourself and those around you, you ground your aspirations in reality, creating a foundation for genuine and realistic connection.

Let's consider another common example where people mistake fantasy for reality: advocacy for world peace and the end of all wars and conflicts. While the idea of global harmony is undeniably appealing and beautiful, it remains a distant fantasy rather than a tangible reality. People who advocate for love and peace on a global scale frequently fail to practice these principles in their daily lives.

They may have ongoing conflicts with their own loved ones, constantly engaging in arguments with their friends. They may experience tension with their neighbors, face disputes with coworkers, and nurture grudges against those who have wronged them, such as a friend who betrayed their trust or an ex-partner who was unfaithful. They fantasize about peace on a global scale while failing to achieve it in their own personal lives. How can they believe global peace is possible while they find it impossible to find peace within their own circle of friends and family?

In truth, the peace they lack is not global. It is internal. They grapple with their own thoughts and feelings. It is not the terrorists or enemies they despise; deep down, they despise their own actions and inner turmoil. It is not world peace they truly seek but peace within themselves. However, because they are not honest with themselves, they misinterpret the desire for inner peace as a need for more peace in the world. They externalize and fantasize their inner needs. They project their judgment outward, blaming the external world for what they lack within.

This is the danger of living in a world of fantasy rather than reality. Reality forces you to take tangible steps toward creating a better world, while fantasy shifts responsibility onto others to magically provide what you lack. The devil is a trickster, and this is yet another one of its deceptions—leading you into disappointment through the idealized, fairy-tale world of fantasy. Meanwhile, it keeps you distracted from the turmoil that lies at the root of your suffering.

By practicing internal self-truth, you come to realize that many things you wish to change in the world are actually reflections of what you lack within yourself. It forces you to focus on transforming your inner world rather than demanding change from the outside world.

When you shift your focus inward, you uncover the roots of your dissatisfaction and conflict. By addressing these internal issues, you cultivate a sense of inner peace and harmony that naturally extends outward. This outward reflection of your internal state will naturally cause a positive change in the external world. In doing so, you contribute to world peace by first cultivating peace within yourself and then sharing that peace with the world, rather than expecting it to come from others.

Now, imagine a world where everyone thinks exactly like you, believes what you believe, and follows the same ideology and way of life. It sounds peaceful, doesn't it? A world free from opposing views, from ideological clashes and the friction that comes with diversity. Many people dream of such a world, convinced that true harmony can only exist when everyone shares their beliefs. But this fantasy is a dangerous trap—one that has fueled some of the bloodiest conflicts in human history.

Religions, political systems, and ideologies all fall into this trap. Muslims believe that the world would be a better place if everyone embraced Islam. Christians believe the same about Christianity. Capitalists argue that free markets and competition are the only viable path to prosperity, while communists envision a world where wealth is shared equally, free from class struggles. This mindset is not limited to religion, politics, or economics—it extends to any belief system that refuses to acknowledge the legitimacy of other ways of thinking. When people refuse to accept diversity, they inevitably see those who think differently as obstacles to peace rather than fellow human beings. And what happens when those "obstacles" refuse to convert, comply, or submit? Tensions rise. Accusations fly. Communities divide. Soon, the desire for ideological unity turns into something far darker: a justification for conflict.

This is how wars begin. What starts as a well-intentioned wish for a "better" world escalates into bloodshed, destruction, and suffering. And when war erupts, it does not remain an abstract concept—it becomes deeply personal. Your own life could be at risk. Your family members might be tortured or executed. Women could be brutally raped. Children could be stolen and trafficked. Famine and starvation would spread, leaving millions to suffer. Entire civilizations could collapse into chaos. And for what? A world that was supposed to be "united"?

Your enemies won't just disappear or comply with your ideology simply because you demand it. That's the part so many fail to understand. People will never simply vanish because you disagree with them. They will fight with all their might for their own right to survive, just as you would if someone tried to erase your beliefs, your culture, and your identity. So before falling for the fantasy of a world where everyone thinks like you, ask yourself: Are you willing to pay the price? Are you ready to watch the world burn just to enforce your version of "peace"? Because history has shown time and again—when people fight to erase others in the name of peace, they only cause further destruction. Even if you have been a victim of war and have seen death, famine, and chaos, wishing for more of it will not solve your problems. You can never extinguish fire with more fire.

This cannot be the desire of the soul. The soul only advocates for true love and peace, which means harmonious coexistence. Such a desire for ideological unity stems from the vanity of the physical body, not the essence of the soul. If you cannot coexist in perfect harmony with someone who holds a radically opposing ideology to yours, then you are not truly advocating love or peace by any measure.

This is how dangerous the world of fantasy can be when people attempt to impose their unrealistic ideals onto reality. Many advocate for world peace while harboring unresolved conflicts in their own personal lives. They expect external forces—governments, leaders, and society at large—to fix the world's problems, all while refusing to address the disharmony within themselves and their own household. Worse yet, they do not seek peace in its true form but rather a version that aligns with their personal worldview—one in which others conform to their beliefs and values. This illusion of peace, rooted in control rather than understanding, only breeds further conflict. On a larger scale, such rigid idealism escalates into societal division, political strife, and even war, as opposing visions of an imagined utopia collide, causing the very chaos they claim to oppose.

Every time you have a thought or feeling, take a moment to consider the consequences if it were to become reality. Don't just focus on the end result; think about the process and the sacrifices necessary for your thoughts and feelings to come true. Envision the journey, not just the destination, and reflect on the impact it may have on you and those around you. Make sure you are not fantasizing about something unrealistic or undesirable.

In times of conflict, even with enemies, strive not to destroy them but to foster mutual understanding and peaceful coexistence. Your soul yearns for harmony, forgiveness, and collaboration to build a better future. Unlike the earthly conflicts among humans, the soul of humanity has never been divided. Every human soul craves love and peace. If you can connect deeply enough—soul to soul—conflicts will dissolve, allowing love and peace to prevail. Begin by becoming intimate with your own soul, then reach out to connect with others on that deeper level. Shake their hands, touch their heart, and eventually, connect with their soul. This is the only way to truly end conflicts—not only with those around you but even with your enemies.

Practicing internal self-truth involves understanding your inner self, your soul, and the boundless love and peace residing within you. Your soul inherently seeks to resolve conflicts through empathy, compassion, and understanding. When you align your thoughts and feelings with the true emotions and voice of the soul, you contribute to a more peaceful existence, both internally and externally.

By basing your thoughts and feelings on the true emotions and voice of the soul, you can progressively improve your life. The truth will liberate you from suffering, but the principles of truth must be practiced with precision. There is no other path to truth but the truth itself.

Let's summarize internal self-truth. At its deepest level, introspection is about establishing a real connection with your soul. It requires setting aside moments of solitude each day to truly tune in to the soul, allowing the wisdom and insights of your soul to come to the surface. Practice honesty and integrity to accurately interpret the emotions and voice of the soul as they manifest in your thoughts and feelings. Your soul holds the key to understanding and resolving your traumas and alleviating your suffering.

On a more surface level, internal self-truth involves becoming a passive observer, turning your focus and intention inward, and truly listening to your inner self. This practice of self-reflection allows you to recognize your physical and mental state in any given moment, enabling you to make the best possible decisions in any situation. By practicing self-awareness consistently, you pave the way for meaningful and positive transformation.

This is the message of the internal self-truth: Discover your true self. Become intimate with your soul, its emotions, and its voice. Become the passive observer of your own reality and the judge of your own character; build an unbreakable mental barrier, unaffected by the judgment of others. Do not wander too far into the realm of fantasy and always return to reality. Focus on addressing what is lacking within yourself rather than dwelling on the flaws of the outside world. Embrace the uniqueness of your own character, and respect the individuality of others, even when it differs from your own. Within you lies a vast, inexhaustible reservoir of love and peace. Tap into this source, let it overflow within you, bring these qualities into your daily life, and radiate them outwardly.

The next layer of truth is external self-truth. To understand this, let's revisit the example of the party. You are sitting on a couch surrounded by friends and family, immersed in conversation and music playing in the background. You decided to take a moment for yourself: you closed your eyes, took a deep breath, and turned your attention inward. As you opened your eyes and exhaled, you started to scan your state of being, listening to your body and mind.

In this state of introspection, you became attuned to your inner self, recognizing your true needs in the moment. Perhaps you realized the need to stop drinking or overeating. You found comfort within your own skin, relaxing your body and quieting your mind. Now, you are calm and collected, even amidst the bustling environment around you.

However, suddenly, you hear your name being called. A friend is asking for your opinion on a topic. This moment requires you to shift your attention from your inner world back to the external world.

As you were sitting on a couch, for a few moments, you were the observer of your own reality. Now, as a friend asked for your opinion, you find yourself in the spotlight with others observing you and awaiting your response. Your practice of internal self-truth has transitioned to the practice of external self-truth. How will you respond to your friend? Will you be completely honest, articulating the truth as best you can, or will you add a bit of a white lie to spice up the conversation and grab the audience's attention?

When you finish speaking, others will join in to share their thoughts. Will you listen carefully and give them your full attention, or will you be preoccupied with formulating your next response, merely pretending to listen?

As you shift your attention outward to respond to your friend, do so with the awareness gained from your internal reflection. Share your opinion authentically, listen intently to the ensuing conversation, and engage with empathy.

External self-truth integrates your inner truth into interactions with those around you. It maintains a balance between your internal awareness and your external engagement. It enhances the quality of your relationships and reinforces your inner truth. Integrate your inner insights into your outer actions. Live a life that is both true to yourself and positively impactful on those around you.

Here is the challenge with external self-truth. You might be tempted to present yourself to others as better than you truly are, desiring that others think highly of you. However, feeling the need to present yourself as more competent than you actually are is both deceitful and untruthful. This behavior not only misleads others but also creates a false image that you must constantly maintain, adding to your stress and sense of unrest.

You may find yourself pretending to be better than you truly are, driven by a deep craving for respect and admiration from others. This desire for validation drives you to create a facade that aligns with societal ideals of success and virtue. This is when you distort the truth to appear more captivating, competent, or mysterious. However, this behavior stems from insecurities that make you dependent on social validation to feel worthy.

It's a natural human tendency to seek acceptance, especially from those you care about, but sacrificing truth for external approval is the wrong way to go. You don't need anyone's validation to be worthy. The only approval you truly need is your own. You must become worthy in your own eyes. If you face your naked truth with honesty and accept yourself as you are, then if others fail to see your value and accept you, that's on them, not on you.

However, if you find that you are not happy with who you are, take it as a signal that genuine change is needed in your life. This is precisely where authenticity and honesty come into play. Authenticity lays you bare, exposing your weaknesses while igniting within you the motivation needed to work on those very weaknesses and bring about a true and lasting transformation, freeing you from the need to hide behind a facade.

Don't undermine yourself by crafting a false image just to appear interesting to others. Let honesty strip away the mask you hide behind and push you toward meaningful change. This transformation won't happen overnight. You must face your own naked truth day after day, becoming intimately aware of your inadequacies until you can finally overcome them. But by pretending to be more than you are and avoiding your true self from rising to the surface, you unconsciously delay the very change you need. The mask provides comfort, shielding you from the inner discontent you feel about yourself. It dulls the urgency to improve, making procrastination and stagnation seem acceptable. Drop the mask, embrace the truth, and let that truth propel you toward the person you truly want to become.

Avoid distorting reality, especially when recounting stories or responding to an inquiry. When sharing an experience or describing past events, resist the temptation to embellish your role or omit less flattering details. If you saved a leg, don't claim you saved a life. If you contributed to a minor task, don't assert that you revolutionized the entire project. Exaggerating your contributions for the sake of admiration chips away at your authenticity and leads to a disconnect between who you are and who you project yourself to be.

Equally important is avoiding selective omissions of the story to hide shameful aspects of your past. Shame is a powerful force, leading to distorted storytelling as a defense mechanism to shield yourself from vulnerability. While it may seem easier to conceal embarrassing details, confronting and sharing them truthfully—when appropriate—can be transformative. Experiencing the shame again through honest recounting will feel difficult, but it forces you to confront the actions that caused the shame in the first place. This self-awareness sparks a real change in you, motivating you to avoid repeating those actions in the future.

When you commit to honesty, something powerful happens: the next time you are about to make a mistake, you will pause. You will remember that you no longer have the luxury of hiding behind a mask. You know you have to face your own truth and expose your actions to the light, no matter how shameful they may be.

This awareness becomes a force of accountability, making you think twice before engaging in an act you would later regret. When you know that your honesty will not allow you to sweep your mistakes under the rug, you naturally become more mindful of your choices. In this way, honesty acts as both a shield and a guide, protecting you from making impulsive decisions while steering you toward a path of self-respect and authenticity.

On the other hand, if you consistently hide your shame from others, you will also unconsciously hide it from your own awareness as well, making you more likely to repeat the very actions that caused it in the first place. Without bringing the root cause to light, the necessary change to break the cycle will remain undiscovered. Avoiding uncomfortable truths traps you in a pattern of recurring mistakes. Life has a way of presenting you with the same challenges repeatedly until you learn the wisdom they offer. As long as you hide your shame and deny the lessons embedded in your past experiences, you'll find yourself facing similar situations over and over again.

When I was struggling to quit smoking and failing repeatedly, I began sharing my challenges with a close friend—a brother on the path of enlightenment. Every day, I would talk to him, explaining my plan to quit. Without judgment, he would always ask, "Did you smoke today?"

Knowing that he wouldn't condemn me, I tried to be as honest as I could. Even then, admitting something like: "I relapsed last night, bought a pack, and smoked it all in a day" felt shameful. He never judged me, nor did he undermined my ability to quit; instead, he encouraged me to try again. Yet, despite his kindness, each admission of failure forced me to confront my own shortcomings—my lack of discipline, my hypocrisy, and the uncomfortable truth of my own weakness.

Ironically, it was in those moments of shameful honesty that I found the motivation to try once again and finally quit for good. The more I had to confess my failures, the harder it became to light another cigarette. Every time I reached for one, I would immediately remember that I would have to tell him the truth. That awareness, that accountability, made smoking feel like a conscious act of self-betrayal rather than just a habit. Without him, I might still be smoking today.

In the end, my friend helped me quit, but it wasn't just his support—it was the act of stripping away my own illusions, removing the mask, and speaking the truth that truly set me free.

Revealing your shame, facing it honestly, and breaking free from the cycle of repeating mistakes is what liberates you from re-experiencing that same shame. Authenticity is the key to ending these vicious cycles of suffering. By embracing your true self and sharing your honest experiences with others, you empower yourself. You no longer need to maintain a facade or live in fear of exposure. Instead, you step into the light, a life of honesty and freedom, where personal growth and deeper connections replace the weight of hidden shame.

Think about it—if you have to modify reality to make yourself look more appealing or hide your shame, you are not only deceiving others but also disrespecting your true self. Every time you alter the truth, you silently tell yourself that who you are is not enough. This undermines your own worth, creating a deep disconnect between your inner self and the image you project to the world.

By hiding the truth, you might receive praise or validation for a fleeting moment—but at what cost? You are stabbing yourself in the back, weakening your self-trust, and shattering your self-worth. The admiration you gain from others through lies will never fill the void left by betraying your own truth.

Find your worth in an authentic and genuine manner, rooted in the truth of who you are, rather than in a false image crafted through exaggerated heroism or the omission of your shame. True worth comes from embracing both your strengths and your flaws, from acknowledging your achievements without inflating them and facing your mistakes without hiding them. Authenticity is the foundation of self-respect and inner peace, while pretense creates only a fragile sense of self-worth—one that is hollow and crumbles over time.

In most cases, when you choose to tell the truth and reveal your shame, your friends will not only understand but also support you in overcoming the insecurity and discomfort you feel inside. By exposing your vulnerabilities, you open the door for others to become the support system you might not even realize you need. Instead of battling your shame in isolation, you may discover that by sharing your insecurities, a friend might step forward with exactly the insight or reassurance you've been searching for. They might even say, "I've been through that struggle too," sharing their own experiences of shame and giving you valuable guidance on how to move forward.

Additionally, the fear you have about revealing your imperfections is often far more daunting than the truth itself. When you confront and express the reality of your shame, you'll likely discover it isn't as frightening and overwhelming as you imagined—especially when you see how many people respond with empathy and understanding, offering help instead of judgment.

However, if your friends laugh at you and judge you for sharing your shame and insecurities, then they are not your true friends. Their judgements and laughter reveal their true nature and prove they lack the genuine support and compassion that real friendship requires. In this moment of vulnerability, you uncover an important truth about them—one that might have otherwise remained hidden.

Your honesty provides you with the clarity to see who truly values you for who you are and who does not. You will know who your true friends are and who are not. Friends who mock or belittle your vulnerabilities are not just unkind and unfriendly—they actively create a toxic environment that stifles your progress and reinforces feelings of inadequacy and shame. In this way, honesty reveals the toxicity that surrounds you.

By distancing yourself from such individuals, you make space for healthier, more uplifting relationships. True friends don't judge or ridicule you when you open up; they listen, empathize, and offer encouragement. These are the relationships worth nurturing—the ones that help you grow and empower you to embrace your true self.

Letting go of false friends can be difficult, especially if they've been part of your life for a long time. But this process is essential for your well-being. Surrounding yourself with people who respect and support you allows you to flourish emotionally, mentally, and spiritually. Seek out new, genuine friends who appreciate your honesty and vulnerability, and who stand by you as you strive to become the best version of yourself. These are the connections that will truly enrich your life.

Having a few genuine friends who support your growth is far more valuable than maintaining many superficial connections that do not serve your best interests. Genuine friendships are built on mutual respect, understanding, and a shared commitment to each other's well-being. Sharing your vulnerabilities helps you grow and also acts as a measure of the quality of your relationships.

Moreover, while honesty and vulnerability are valuable, it is not always wise to share your deepest insecurities with just anyone. You need to be mindful of your audience and consider who you are speaking to before revealing personal struggles. Not everyone will respond with kindness and understanding. If you expose your shame and insecurities on social media, for example, chances are you will face ridicule, judgment, or even outright attacks. Instead of helping you heal, this can leave you feeling even more wounded.

When your audience is not receptive to your truth, silence is the better choice. Choosing silence empowers you to uphold honesty and integrity while protecting yourself. It allows you to remain authentic without making yourself exposed to unnecessary harm. Silence is not the same as wearing a mask; you are simply choosing when, where, and with whom to share your truth.

Silence is not a sign of weakness; on the contrary, it signifies great internal strength. When you master the art of silence, you will understand when to speak and when to remain quiet. You will respond to the world on your own terms.

Wisdom recognizes that not every situation requires a response. Words, once spoken, cannot be taken back, and engaging in unnecessary or harmful conversations only pulls you further away from your core truths. Silence protects inner peace.

It is perfectly acceptable to choose silence and refrain from discussing sensitive topics that you are not comfortable sharing with certain people. Perhaps you are not ready to confront your shame publicly, or maybe you are simply uncomfortable with your audience. In such a scenario, you can politely state that you do not wish to talk about the subject.

Choosing silence in such situations is a valid and respectful approach to managing your personal boundaries. It allows you to maintain control over your narrative and protect your emotional and mental well-being. When you politely decline to discuss certain topics, you are exercising your right to privacy without distorting the truth.

When an uncomfortable truth about yourself causes shame or regret, the first step is to internally acknowledge and accept yourself just as you are. Embrace who you are and how you are, without judgment. Once you accept the truth about yourself, you become better equipped to address your insecurities. Silence can then serve as a protective measure, offering the time and space needed to process your thoughts and feelings. However, it is equally important to eventually share your insecurities with the right audience, in the company of those who genuinely care for you and are willing to listen without judgment. This act allows you to confront the fear of vulnerability and helps you shine light on the root cause of your struggles. In doing so, you stop hiding behind your shame and begin to fully embrace who you are, no matter how uncomfortable it may feel. And through this self-awareness, you will eventually grow and transform.

There is another aspect of external self-truth to consider. Imagine a scenario where a fight breaks out between a friend and a stranger. Whose side do you take? Would you instinctively support your friend? What if your friend is in the wrong, will you still tend to support the friend over the stranger?

This raises an important question about the nature of your loyalty. Should your loyalty lie with friends, or should it be with the truth? If you are seeking enlightenment, then your loyalty should always align with the truth, not with any individual person or group. External self-truth challenges the tendency to favor a friend over a stranger. In any situation, what should matter most is your commitment to truth and justice, always siding with what is right, regardless of whether it benefits a friend or a foe. This unwavering alignment with truth is about choosing loyalty to what is fundamentally good and just.

If your friend is genuinely a good and virtuous person, they will value truth and justice even if it comes at their own expense. True friends will respect you for siding with truth, and they will stand with you because both of you share the same commitment to justice and righteousness.

Authentic connections are not built on blind loyalty to one another but on shared values and mutual respect for what is right. When you prioritize truth and justice above all else, you attract and cultivate friendships rooted in integrity—relationships that support your growth and also the collective pursuit of a better and more just world.

This brings us to the concept of justice versus favoritism. Truth stands impartial, seeking justice above all. On the other hand, favoritism stands in opposition to justice. Favoritism disregards justice by unfairly favoring one side over the other. If you choose favoritism over justice, it will inevitably lead to more suffering. Have you noticed that you are often hurt more profoundly by those closest to you? This pain stems from favoritism.

When you like someone, you may naturally tend to overlook their flaws and idealize their strengths, failing to see their true character. Your personal bias causes you to disregard the truth about who they really are, preventing you from making a fair and accurate assessment of their character and favoring them simply because you like them and have feelings for them. This tendency to favor their strengths over their weaknesses skews your perception of their true character, leading you to trust them more than you should. Consequently, you build unrealistic expectations of them. When they eventually act in ways you dislike, the disappointment cuts deep because your expectations have been shattered.

The only reason your loved ones can hurt you so deeply is that you hold biases and unrealistic expectations about them. You want to believe that they are better than they truly are. When reality contradicts your beliefs, the resulting pain is intense. Additionally, people often hide their darker sides. If you overlook someone's bad behavior due to your biases, and they simultaneously conceal their flaws, you have no chance of truly knowing them, setting yourself up for inevitable disappointment and suffering. The only way to avoid being hurt is to accept the truth, remain unbiased, and be just in your assessment of their character.

I grew up believing my parents were the smartest, wisest, and all-knowing. I placed them on a pedestal, seeing them as figures of absolute authority and perfection. Whenever I noticed flaws in their behavior, I tried to justify them, twisting reality to fit the image I needed to believe in. But every time they failed to meet my unrealistic expectations—every time they revealed their imperfections—it hurt me deeply.

As I grew older, I carried this silent disappointment within me, feeling as though my parents had somehow failed me. I expected them to be more than they were capable of being, and when they inevitably fell short, I resented them for it and even hated them. The contradiction was painful—I loved them deeply, yet I couldn't accept them as they were. I judged them harshly, blaming their shortcomings for everything that went wrong in my life, seeing their imperfections as the root of my own struggles.

It wasn't until I finally saw my parents for who they truly were—two average people doing the best they could—that my resentment dissolved completely. And beneath that resentment, love remained. They didn't change; my perception did. When I accepted the painful truth—that they were flawed human beings, just like everyone else—I was freed from my anger. The truth, though difficult, was what set me free.

Paradoxically, seeing my parents as less than the idealized figures I once imagined them to be—accepting them for who they truly were—improved our relationship. There was no longer a need for arguments or disappointments because I had stopped expecting them to be something they were not. I no longer felt betrayed by their shortcomings, nor did I need to fight to change them. Instead, I recognized their patterns, understood their limitations, and made peace with the fact that they will always act within the bounds of who they are.

Even though many of their actions still aren't ideal, they no longer hurt me. I have freed myself from the cycle of expectation and disappointment. The truth about them, as harsh as it was, has set me free.

While the truth itself can be painful, it only hurts once. Accepting that someone you love—whether a family member, friend, or partner—is not truly a good person, or at least not as good as you once believed, brings an initial wave of pain. This moment of painful clarity is intense but temporary. As you begin to adapt to reality, the pain fades, and healing begins.

Conversely, if you deny reality and continue to believe that this person is inherently good despite their actions, you subject yourself to ongoing emotional harm. Every time they act contrary to your idealized image of them, the pain resurfaces with increasing intensity. This cycle of repeated disappointment and pain is far more damaging than facing the truth. By denying reality, you trap yourself in a loop of suffering, unable to move forward and find peace.

Accepting the truth, though initially painful, allows you to break free from this cycle. It enables you to set appropriate boundaries, protect yourself from further harm, and seek out relationships that are healthier and more supportive.

Your parents, siblings, partner, children, or even your best friend may not be as good as you think—or may not be good people at all. It's a harsh truth, but one worth confronting. You may have unknowingly lived a lie, growing up in a toxic family—surrounded by individuals who cause you more harm than good. It is okay—even necessary—to distance yourself from them, regardless of the closeness of your relationship. This isn't an act of hate or rejection but a declaration of self-preservation and a commitment to truth and growth.

Even your own children may turn toward darkness, forcing you to create distance to protect your integrity and peace. It's a difficult step, but one you may have to take. If, one day, they choose to seek truth and justice, they will find their way back—not just to you but to the light you've embraced. Until then, you must not allow their darkness to consume you simply because of the roles they've played in your life. Once you accept the truth and endure the sting of harsh reality, disappointment no longer follows.

True transformation begins with your willingness to step away from what no longer serves you. If you genuinely want to change for the better, everything around you must also change and evolve—better people, better environments, better habits, and better goals. This doesn't mean abandoning love or compassion for those you leave behind. It means creating the space needed to thrive and grow, while extending an open hand should they decide to join you on the path of truth and enlightenment.

The greatest weakness of darkness is that it vanishes in the light of truth. If you practice truth and radiate light from your heart with honesty and integrity, then whenever darkness approaches, it will disappear, revealing what it sought to hide. This principle also applies to understanding people's true personalities. If you live by truth, the veils of darkness surrounding those who come close to you will be removed, allowing you to see their true selves, no matter how cunning and deceitful they may be.

Every time you have been mistreated by someone else, it might be true that they have been deceitful, but the real mistake lies in your failure to carry enough light of truth to see through their deception. The only time you can be deceived is when you fail to see the truth, and often the reason for this failure is your own biases and favoritism.

Favoritism implants bias in the mind, diverting you from the path of truth. If you aim to perceive the world with clarity, you must eliminate favoritism from your judgment, whether it pertains to minor preferences or significant decisions in life. This includes favorite colors, weather, places, foods, and even friends. Blue is as beautiful as red or any other color, sunny days are as vital as rainy days or any other day, and mountains are as magnificent as oceans or any other place. Every type of food has its role in the larger ecosystem. Friends should be valued based on their commitment to truth rather than mere personal preferences.

For instance, if your desire tells you that a sunny day at the beach is better than a cold, rainy day in the mountains, the truth tells you that both are equally important. Without rainy days, everything would dry out, and without sunny days, the Earth would be perpetually flooded. The balance between sunny and rainy days is what makes life beautiful, not one over the other. When you accept truth as your guiding principle and set aside your desires, you realize that both sunny days and rainy days have their own merits and drawbacks. Moreover, if you refuse to appreciate rainy days as much as you enjoy sunny days, there will always be disappointing rainy days in your life. This is an unnecessary self-inflicted misery.

Think of it this way: if you like sunny days, that's perfectly fine. If you prefer to decorate your house with everything in blue, that's also fine. What is important here is to understand that just because your house is blue, it does not mean blue is better than any other color. Similarly, if you love living by the beach and enjoying sunny days, it does not make rainy days any less beautiful.

You can choose what you like, but do not let your preferences lead you to dislike something else. Respect the beauty and importance of everything that isn't your first choice. When you encounter it, take the time to admire, appreciate, and even learn to enjoy it, just as you should with rainy days. Embracing this mindset enriches your experiences and helps you find value and joy in a variety of things, broadening your perspective and deepening your appreciation for the world around you.

Implementing this principle in your life requires you to choose the truth over your own desires. Throughout your life, you have been told and conditioned to choose your favorites—whether it's a favorite color, place, food, etc. This conditioning makes it difficult to appreciate things that are not your first choice.

However, embracing inherent beauty in all things demands a shift in perspective. It means recognizing that your preferences do not inherently make something better or worse. Your preference is just your preference; it holds no bearing on truth or reality. By recognizing truth and broadening your appreciation, you cultivate a more balanced and fulfilling life. You learn to find joy and beauty in a wider array of experiences, making your life richer and more varied. This mindset enhances your ability to connect with others, understand different viewpoints, and navigate the complexities of life with greater wisdom and compassion.

Sometimes in life, you must endure rainy days. Take this as a metaphor for uncomfortable and undesirable situations in life that test your resilience. These are the dark days of your life. In such moments, remember that the entire universe has always existed and continues to exist in perfect balance. From your limited perspective, life may seem imbalanced and unfair at times, but this does not alter the fundamental truth of the universe's perfect equilibrium. If you trust the truth, then accept that the injustices you experience happen for reasons that lie beyond your understanding—and that's okay. There will always be rainy days, undesirable situations, and moments of darkness in your life. And that, too, is okay. In its own way, it is still beautiful, as it brings balance and promotes appreciation and gratitude for the brighter days to come.

On a grander scale, you are neither obligated nor capable of grasping the reasons behind all the darkness and suffering in the world. Different belief systems, ways of life, wars, and catastrophic events each possess their own unique beauty, contributing to the grand scheme of the universe's perfect design. Embrace the idea that every element, no matter how perplexing or painful, has its place in the larger tapestry of existence. Cultivate a deeper sense of peace and resilience within you. Navigate life's challenges with grace by understanding that there is, indeed, a perfectly acceptable and godly reason behind all hardships.

Furthermore, whenever you find yourself in a deep, dark, scary, and frightening place, find your way out of this darkness with the light from your own heart. You possess the power to generate light within yourself, like a shining star. The darkest of the darkest places are not dark enough to keep out the light that you can ignite within your heart. The light of truth grows from within you, and no one can stop it from shining except for yourself. Never surrender to darkness and allow it to suffocate the light within you.

Through practicing internal self-truth, you come to know your true self, enabling you to transform your character for the better. By practicing external self-truth, you gain an understanding of how you interact with those around you, thereby shaping your identity from an external perspective.

Now, let's examine the outer layer of truth: the external truth. This encompasses societal, cultural, political, and religious teachings, which often stand in stark opposition to objective truth. In nearly every country, societal doctrines are crafted to serve the interests of a powerful minority ruling over the majority. These social teachings are meticulously designed to maximize wealth, power, and control for the elite. Consequently, the general populace is misled and manipulated into accepting distorted versions of reality that benefit the ruling class. This manipulation perpetuates inequality and obscures the true nature of justice and fairness. Understanding this layer of truth requires critical examination of the systems and structures that shape our societies and cultures.

Favoritism plays a significant and insidious role in this layer of truth as well. Here, we will delve into another facet of favoritism, one specifically crafted to empower the ruling class. This form of favoritism is meticulously designed by societal teachings to keep you ensnared in their schemes, serving their profit, power, and interests.

In sports, for example, you are conditioned to pick a favorite team and, almost instinctively, to dislike the other teams. Competitiveness has long surpassed its healthy threshold, transforming sports into arenas of battle where the winner is glorified, and the loser is scorned. You are encouraged to participate in this battle by taking a side, further contributing to this competitive toxicity.

When played in a friendly manner, without the intervention of the ruling class, sports serve as a way to stay healthy, spend time with friends, and develop personal skills through an appropriate balance of competitiveness and cooperativeness. However, at the elite level, sports are no longer about health, or true enjoyment of time spent.

Instead, they have become instruments of profit and control. The commercialization of sports prioritizes profit over genuine athleticism and camaraderie, turning athletes into commodities and fans into mere consumers.

Competitor athletes often damage their bodies in the quest to reach the top, suffering injuries that affect them for the rest of their lives, seldom achieving their goal of becoming the best. Even those who reach elite professional levels are not spared; they often develop serious injuries later in life. Consider injuries related to soccer as an example. Soccer players often develop neurodegenerative diseases such as dementia, Parkinson's disease, CTE, ALS, and Alzheimer's.

More aggressive sports such as American football, boxing, and UFC see even higher levels of injury due to their inherently aggressive nature. These sports today have transformed into giant businesses where athletes' health is sacrificed for the sake of profit. Players are pushed beyond their limits to put on a better show, thereby increasing revenue. Meanwhile, audiences indulge in unhealthy food and drinks at the games, eating hot dogs and drinking soda, becoming less healthy themselves. The sport, originally meant to improve health, has morphed into a business that profits by compromising the health of both athletes and fans.

Stadiums are filled with commercials and branding. They are adorned with advertisements from major brands, and broadcasts are interspersed with commercials. This constant exposure not only generates significant revenue but also reinforces brand loyalty among fans.

Fans are encouraged to express their loyalty through consumerism by spending money on gadgets, clothing, memorabilia, and other merchandise associated with their favorite teams and players. Special edition items and limited time offers create a sense of urgency and exclusivity, driving sales. The sports industry has turned fandom into a lucrative market.

Athletes themselves become brands. Their jerseys, shoes, and other merchandise are marketed and branded heavily by giant corporations. Endorsement deals with major corporations further commercialize their image.

This situation is a carefully crafted scheme by businessmen who sell favoritism. From a young age, you are trained to choose a side, love one team, and despise the others. Sports marketers capitalize on the emotional investment of fans. By promoting fierce rivalries and encouraging fans to pick a side, they ensure a loyal and engaged audience. This emotional connection drives merchandise sales, ticket purchases, and viewership. Businesses further exploit these rivalries by sponsoring events and creating exclusive content.

Today, through engineered favoritism, sports serve as a divisive force among people, a means to extract and concentrate wealth, and a tool for brainwashing through branding and promoting consumerism. This is all accomplished by programming people's minds with favoritism. Sports empty your wallet, fill your belly with junk food, plant the seeds of division between you and others who support a different team, and brainwash you into believing that whatever they are selling is worth buying.

Let's examine engineered favoritism in politics. Unlike in sports, where money is the primary goal, the main objective in politics is power. Favoritism in politics accumulates power for the elite.

Governments claim to serve the public, and through favoritism, they manipulate you into believing they have your best interests at heart while actually serving their own agenda of power accumulation. Through favoritism, they sell the idea that all the problems in the country stem from the other side or the other countries, regardless of which side or country you support. This creates a perpetual cycle of blame, where there is always an opposing party to fault.

Politicians use this tactic to serve their own purpose of accumulating power at the expense of their citizens. Whenever people complain, politicians deflect by blaming the other party or other countries and asking you to join them in the blame. When power shifts, the blame shifts with it, but the main goal of power accumulation remains constant.

Take America, for example. Do you think it is merely a coincidence that power consistently shifts between the Democratic Party and the Republican Party every four to eight years, never gravitating toward a third party? This pattern is not random. Since 1828, political power has remained concentrated within these two dominant parties. Engineered favoritism toward the two dominant parties ensures that a third party never rises to prominence—preventing the introduction of new, innovative ideas that could potentially shift the concentration of power within the branches of government. It is a calculated mechanism designed to maintain the illusion of choice and democracy while ensuring that power remains concentrated, constantly swinging back and forth between the two dominant parties.

This cyclical shift of power is accompanied by a corresponding shift of blame. With each election, the party out of power can blame the party in power for the country's problems, creating a constant back-and-forth that obscures long-term accountability. If one party were to stay in power for too long, their mismanagement and failures would become too apparent, potentially leading to public unrest and uprising.

However, the regular alternation of power between the two parties prevents any single party from being held accountable for too long. It also fosters a perpetual state of false hope, with each election presenting the illusion of change and the promise of a better future. This system keeps the populace engaged in a never-ending cycle of blame and anticipation for a brighter future, diverting attention from systemic issues and preventing substantial political reform.

If you buy into political favoritism and hold an unwavering bias toward your favorite political party, believing they will ultimately solve your country's problems, you are falling into their trap—clinging to a false hope that will never materialize.

Even if a benevolent politician rises to power with genuine intentions to bring about meaningful change, the deeply entrenched system—the so-called "shadow government"—ensures that no single leader can disrupt the established order. The political stage is carefully constructed so that even the most well-meaning figureheads are bound by the invisible chains of bureaucracy, corporate influence, intelligence agencies, and economic structures that serve those in true power.

This system is designed not to serve the people but to maintain control over them. The ultimate goal is to keep the populace powerless, divided, and distracted, regardless of which politician or policy is in place. On August 12, 1986, Ronald Reagan famously said in a speech, "The nine most terrifying words in the English language are: I'm from the government, and I'm here to help." He captured this idea in just a few seconds.

Elections and political debates create the illusion of choice, giving people the belief that they have control over their government. However, behind the scenes, the real decisions are made by those who have been in power long before any elected official took office—and will remain in power long after they leave. In this way, radical change that would return power to the hands of the people is systematically neutralized before it can take root.

Furthermore, favoritism is also deeply embedded in religion, exploited by those in power to create conflict and division among people. The elites have engineered religious exclusivity, ensuring that religions operate in ways entirely contrary to the messages preached by their prophets. Instead of fostering unity and compassion, as the original teachings intended, religions are manipulated to sow division and perpetuate control. Each faith claims to be the true religion and denounces others as either crafted by the devil or, at the very least, less favorable.

Choosing any religion that helps you become a better person on your personal and spiritual journey is perfectly acceptable. However, believing that your religious doctrine is superior to all others means you have fallen into the trap set by those who seek to divide and control through division and hatred. This form of favoritism promotes conflict and misunderstanding among people who are essentially on similar quests for meaning and spiritual fulfillment. Just as you cannot say that any one color is inherently better than another simply because it resonates with you, you cannot claim the superiority of one religion over another. Certainty in religious doctrine is a carefully crafted scheme by malevolent forces that peddle vanity, hatred, and division under the guise of divine liberation.

Each faith, when practiced with love and compassion, has the potential to enrich one's life. It can promote empathy, compassion and unity among fellow human beings. However, the same faith, if practiced with a sense of superiority, will lead to hatred and division. No true religious leader has ever promoted division and hatred; on the contrary, they have all advocated for compassion, unity, and understanding. Unfortunately, over time, the elite and those in positions of power have morphed these religions into doctrines of division and control. By instilling favoritism and a sense of superiority and exclusivity, powerful elites have promoted loyalty to one religious doctrine while opposing others, labeling them as inferior.

In education, favoritism is evident as well; the prestige of the school from which you graduated matters more than the actual knowledge you have accumulated. Favoritism imposes standards that prioritize appearances and affiliations over genuine merit and effort. There is no aspect of society where favoritism is not rigorously imposed.

If people were to unite, governments and powerful elites would have no choice but to succumb to our demands and provide a better life for all. Unity is a formidable force. When people come together with a shared vision and purpose, they can challenge and disrupt entrenched systems of power. Favoritism, however, fosters intolerance and keeps us divided—powerful tools used by those in power to maintain their control. By encouraging us to focus on our differences and engage in conflict with one another, they distract us from the larger issues at hand and prevent us from organizing effectively.

Whether it's through allegiance to different sports teams, political parties, or religious doctrines, these divisions weaken our collective power. As long as we fight among ourselves, we remain divided and in conflict, diminishing our ability to enact meaningful change. Disunity ensures that the elite maintain their power, controlling our lives according to their own interests and preferences.

The elite have spent centuries perfecting the art of crafting governmental and societal systems designed to maintain their grip on power. They have mastered the division of the masses, ensuring that people remain fragmented across countless ideologies, beliefs, and affiliations. Whether in religion, politics, entertainment, or social movements, they manufacture enough variations—different flavors of the same fundamental structures—so that no single group becomes powerful enough to unite and create meaningful change.

These divisions keep people distracted, constantly arguing over their differences rather than recognizing the underlying system that keeps them all in place. While the masses fight over political parties, religious doctrines, sports rivalries, and social issues, the true rulers remain untouched, their control unchallenged. It is a game designed to ensure that power remains in the hands of the few while the many remain too divided to ever pose a real threat.

There is no favoritism in truth. Truth is impartial and unbiased. It does not favor one side over another. Truth aligns with justice, wherever and whenever it is found. Truth serves everyone, not just a select few. If you seek to understand the truth in the world, you must first relinquish your loyalty to favoritism in all aspects of life. Stand by the side of justice rather than aligning with any particular politics, religion, or sport. Practicing external truth means understanding the external world for its true value and purpose, rather than the one crafted by the ruling class to manipulate and control you.

Do you recall that the truth in the darkness required dismantling old belief systems? If you now see how favoritism has manipulated you in sports, politics, religion, and all other aspects of life, then prepare yourself to shatter any beliefs rooted in favoritism. This realization demands a radical shift in your perspective. Get ready to unlearn everything you have ever been taught. Embrace the challenge of questioning long-held assumptions and biases. Only by breaking free from these ingrained patterns can you begin to understand the world through the lens of impartial truth. Journey toward enlightenment requires courage and an open mind.

Another aspect of external truth is that you mirror the outside world into your inner world and vice versa. Your perception of the world closely mirrors the internal world you create within yourself. If you view the external world as chaotic and unfair, you are likely to experience a similar level of chaos and distress within your mental landscape. Have you ever noticed how those with an angry mindset often find themselves in fights and arguments with others? If you find yourself in conflict with others, it stems from an unresolved conflict within yourself. If you feel intolerant toward others in sports, politics, religion, or any other aspect of life, it is a clear indication that there is a part of yourself you refuse to accept. Favoritism creates external divisions, but these divisions are a reflection of internal struggles. Those in power know your weaknesses and exploit them to serve their own agenda.

When you align yourself with a particular group or ideology to the exclusion of others, you do so to validate your own beliefs and sense of identity. When you join a community that reinforces your beliefs, it makes you feel better about yourself. This need for validation and feeling better stems from unresolved insecurities and a lack of inner peace. You project your internal feelings and thoughts onto the external world and, in turn, absorb the external world's perceived reality into your mental landscape.

If you are internally driven by greed for money, then you see no problem with the commercialization of sports. If you are internally driven to achieve success even at the cost of others, then you will see no problem with your favorite political party. If you have narcissistic tendencies, you see no problem with viewing your own beliefs and religion as superior to all others. Each time you justify and support the flaws in the external world, it is because you possess the same deficiencies within yourself. However, if you find peace within yourself, you will no longer add to the conflicts of the outside world. You will refuse to partake in their scheme.

Furthermore, one of the most widespread problems in the world today is the sense of loneliness. A life that embraces individualism in the outside world leads to internal loneliness. Despite the proliferation of social media and numerous ways to connect, the lack of genuine human connection is evident everywhere. Do you ever feel lonely? Do you ever feel that people around you do not truly understand you? If you do, you are not alone. In fact, you are part of the vast majority of people who feel the same way.

Society encourages you to embrace individualism, personal space, competition, success, wealth, and winning as the main goals in life. Society insists that you must prioritize your own interests for the sake of your personal security and well-being. This prompts you to strive for a so-called better life, constantly trying to look better, make more money, become more intelligent, accumulate more knowledge, buy more gadgets, and live up to societal standards.

This relentless pursuit leaves you feeling restless, caught in a perpetual rat race. The belief that life is all about your success and improvement leaves little room for genuine connections with others. You may live with your family or be surrounded by people, yet still feel lonely. This loneliness stems from a life outlook rooted in individualism. If your internal world revolves around you, then your external world will reflect this, leaving you isolated.

This is another drawback of favoritism—self-favoritism. Self-favoritism inevitably leads to a sense of loneliness and a lack of genuine connection. If your life is primarily about you, then you cannot expect others to prioritize anyone but themselves, creating a self-centered society. In such a society, where everyone lives their own lives independently, everyone ends up alone on their journey. In social gatherings, there may be a fleeting sense of relief from loneliness. However, this relief is temporary, and the sense of isolation soon returns due to the absence of genuine connections and deeper bonds.

Unfortunately, in today's world, individualism is widely promoted and glorified. Many people strive to be independent, but for all the wrong reasons. True independence comes from within—it's about not relying on external factors to provide a sense of happiness and joy. This inner independence is a positive way of being self-reliant. However, what we see in our societies today is the opposite: a focus on external independence. Everyone strives to have personal space, personal time, personal finances, personal hobbies, personal goals, personal achievements, personal social media profiles, personal self-care routines, and personal entertainment preferences.

These pursuits, while seemingly empowering, actually contribute to a growing sense of isolation and loneliness that permeates modern societies. And isolation by definition weakens our collective power. The more you focus on "personal" everything, the more you distance yourself from meaningful connections and community, leading to a fragmented society where genuine human interaction and mutual support are increasingly rare. This is yet another carefully crafted scheme by the elite to ensure we stay isolated and in conflict with one another, diminishing our collective power by promoting self-favoritism and individualism.

The elite class encourages us to prioritize our own interests above all else, fostering a culture of competition and mistrust rather than collaboration and unity. This strategy ensures that we remain in conflict with one another, distracted by our personal pursuits and disconnected from the potential strength we could harness as a unified collective.

While truth sometimes requires you to focus inward and attend to your personal growth and well-being, it also calls to direct your time and energy toward others. Truth does not advocate strict individualism; rather, it emphasizes the importance of balancing personal and communal interests. This balance creates a sense of community and connectedness that can help eradicate feelings of loneliness. In a community where everyone is committed to maintaining strong, supportive relationships, a sense of unity and wholeness naturally emerges, benefiting every individual within it.

Such a community provides a safe space for its members to openly share their thoughts and feelings, allowing them to draw positive energy and support from one another, which enhances the overall mental and emotional health of the group. Just as you should strive to move your soul toward collective consciousness, where love, peace, and connections are abundant, you must replicate that same deep connection in the material world, as it is key to overcoming isolation and loneliness. By shifting your focus away from self-centered goals and self-favoritism to include the beliefs, benefits, and well-being of others, you cultivate meaningful relationships and build nurturing communities. This interconnectedness brings a deeper sense of purpose and belonging, ultimately leading to a more fulfilling and harmonious life.

Life is not about trying to get ahead, feeling good, achieving success, being better than others, accumulating wealth, becoming more intelligent, or being more desirable. True quality of life is only achievable through meaningful connections. The most important connection is the one with your own soul. From there, it extends to connections with others through collaboration rather than competition, achieving success together rather than pushing others down to be first. If you achieve success at the expense of others, you also sacrifice a part of yourself along the way. Don't sacrifice your well-being based on societal standards. Do not favor yourself just because society tells you that everyone is out for their own interests.

Prioritize genuine, heartfelt connections and strive for a balance that respects both your own needs and the well-being of those around you. By doing so, you cultivate a life enriched by mutual respect, shared achievements, and deep, meaningful relationships. This approach not only enhances your quality of life but also fosters a sense of interconnectedness with the entire world that far surpasses the hollow victories of individualism and competition.

Inclusion and cooperation are far superior to separation and competition because truth becomes most visible and understandable in an environment of peace and harmony. When race, competition, and conflict arise, deceit and darkness follow. For example, people tend to cheat more often when they are forced to compete rather than when they are encouraged to cooperate. Conflict creates a fog that obscures the truth from view.

Practicing external truth is about bringing people together, regardless of their social, economic, political, and religious backgrounds.

It is only through inclusion and cooperation that you can understand truth on a macro level. Inclusion fosters an environment where diverse perspectives can be shared and appreciated.

External truth bears the fruit of selflessness and unity, creating a foundation for a more just and interconnected society. When people come together in harmony, collective wisdom and truth that emerge can lead to transformation of the entire society which enhances individual lives and also builds stronger, more resilient communities. Embracing inclusion and cooperation paves the way for a brighter future where the inherent worth of every individual is recognized and valued, thereby eliminating the sense of loneliness from the hearts of individuals within society.

Truth is omnipresent; it exists everywhere, within everything, at all times. Each of us holds a portion of the truth, yet none of us possesses the truth in its entirety. Instead of clashing over selfish interests or truths we only partially understand, let us set aside our differences and unite as brothers and sisters, mothers and fathers, sons and daughters. Together, we can piece together the fragments of truth each of us holds, revealing a higher and more comprehensive understanding. Let us embrace and love one another despite our differences, building a better future where every person is valued and every voice is heard, guided by the universal principles of love and compassion.

The spectrum of truth begins deep within you and extends far beyond your surroundings. When you comprehend this end-to-end spectrum of truth, you gain true wisdom. Through the diligent practice of honesty and integrity, you cultivate the fruits of light that grow from the tree of truth and radiate from your heart. You become humble, righteous, courageous, and confident. You gain clear vision and see through the fog of lies and deception.

One immutable aspect of truth is its unchanging nature. When you grasp the truth, you understand timeless concepts. You build a solid and resilient personality, un-swayed by external forces. You remain steadfast and composed, even when confronted with darkness. Your mind is strong, and your presence is commanding. Integrate honesty and integrity into your daily life to embody these qualities. The pursuit of truth is not a fleeting endeavor; it is a lifelong commitment.

Let us rewind and revisit the big picture we are drawing in this book. We seek truth because it ignites a light within our hearts, guiding us through the darkness of the devil's den to rediscover our soul. At the same time, truth nurtures the growth of the soul, helping it become stronger and more resilient. Earlier in the book, we compared the soul's needs to those of an apple tree, drawing parallels between their growth processes. Just as a tree needs light to thrive, the soul requires truth. And just as a tree depends on water for sustenance, the soul depends on love.

Now, let us focus on the meaning of love and how it can be obtained in a way that never decays over time. True love, like truth, is eternal, unchanging, and everlasting. To understand this, consider the analogy of diamond and coal. Both are made from carbon, but the difference lies in the purification process. A diamond is forged through extreme pressure and heat over an exceedingly long period. Although it is fundamentally the same as coal, a diamond is much stronger, more durable, and vastly more valuable. The same can be said about love. Common love is like coal: plentiful and superficial, whereas true love is like a diamond: rare, precious, and forged through the trials and tribulations of life. True love is extremely rare, but it is infinitely more powerful and valuable than common love. When you understand and embrace pure love, it becomes eternal, shining brightly throughout your life without ever fading.

Up to this point, we have explored why we suffer and have discussed various strategies and techniques for self-improvement. In the next chapter, we will delve into how to achieve these goals. Truth provides you with the "why", while love provides you with the "how." Truth tells you why you need to overcome adversities, traumas, and the wrong choices of your past. Love shows you how to surmount these difficulties. Truth reveals that you need qualities like bravery, strength, gratefulness, humility, honesty, and integrity. Love, on the other hand, guides you in cultivating these qualities. Knowing the truth is the theory of life; knowing love is the practicality of life. If truth ignites a light within your heart, showing you the direction you need to take, then love is what guides your steps along the path illuminated by the light of truth.

Truth gives you clear sight to see reality through the fog of deceptions, making the path to enlightenment visible and revealing the tools and attributes you need to walk that path. Love, on the other hand, shows you how to walk the path of enlightenment and how to use the tools attained by understanding the truth. If you comprehend the truth, you have all the tools in your inventory to walk the path of enlightenment. Now, it is time to begin treading that path and truly experience the bliss that comes with attaining true love.

Up to this point, you have ventured deep into the darkness of your mental landscape, confronting your inner demons. You have faced your insecurities, shames, and regrets. You have uncovered the deceptions cast by the devil, compounded by societal pressures that obscured your understanding of reality. In this journey, you have ignited the light of truth within your heart by cultivating honesty and integrity—a beacon guiding you through the narrow, dark passages of the devil's den to rediscover your soul. By embracing the truth, you have found your soul amidst the darkness of your mind. Now, as your soul stands illuminated by the light of truth, it begins to heal and grow. Yet, you remain within the devil's den. Truth has brought you to your soul and ignited the light to nourish it, but the next challenge lies ahead: you must emerge from the tunnel and rise above your inner darkness while united with your soul. The power of love becomes the force that pushes against adversity, lifting you out of your inner darkness and into the divine light. It is time to understand what love is and what it can do.

Chapter 13: Meaning of Love

A common mistake people make is defining love solely through their past experiences. People define love based on their interactions with partners, parents, children, or friends. While these relationships may reflect certain aspects of love, they do not capture its full depth and true essence. If you attempt to understand love only through the lens of your daily interactions, you will limit your perception of its boundless nature.

Love is timeless, limitless, and universal—a fundamental force woven into the very fabric of existence. It is the purest form of energy that has shaped and constructed the entire world. Love exists everywhere, in every particle, in every living being, and even in non-living entities. Your soul, too, is crafted from the fabric of love and is deeply dependent on it to thrive.

Just as your body, composed largely of water and requires water to survive, your soul is largely made of love and needs a continuous flow of love to sustain itself. Without love, the soul experiences a form of "dehydration," resulting in spiritual, psychological, and emotional suffering. To overcome this suffering and find lasting peace, you must truly understand the essence of love and consciously nourish your soul with it. Without love, the cycle of suffering will never end.

Before we delve into the deeper meaning of love, let us first examine how love manifests in human experience. One of the most profound examples is a mother's love, which is considered one of the highest forms of love in our physical reality. A mother's love is unique in its intensity and depth, as it comes close to unconditional love. But what makes this love so powerful? How does a love so enduring and selfless come into existence?

When a woman begins her pregnancy, she embarks on a journey filled with numerous challenges, sacrifices, and profound transformations, both physical and emotional. From the very start, her body begins to undergo significant changes to support the developing fetus, leading to various forms of physical discomfort and complications.

In the early stages of pregnancy, many women experience morning sickness, characterized by nausea and vomiting, which can range from mild to severe and, in some cases, result in a condition called hyperemesis gravidarum, where persistent vomiting leads to dehydration and significant weight loss. As the pregnancy progresses, hormonal changes can lead to iron deficiency anemia, which causes fatigue and weakness; or she may develop gestational diabetes, where elevated blood sugar levels pose risks to both the mother and baby. Furthermore, some women develop preeclampsia, a serious condition characterized by high blood pressure and damage to organs, like the liver and kidneys. Complications with the placenta can result in excessive bleeding, posing life-threatening risks to both the mother and the fetus.

As the baby grows, the physical strain on the woman's body increases. Back pain are common due to the added weight and the shift in the center of gravity, causing discomfort and sometimes debilitating pain. The pressure of the growing uterus can also lead to varicose veins, hemorrhoids, and frequent urination. Sleep becomes challenging, particularly in the later stages of pregnancy, as finding a comfortable position becomes difficult due to the size of the belly and the baby's movements, which tend to intensify over time.

Pregnancy is not only a physically demanding experience but also a significant emotional and psychological journey. Many women experience heightened emotions due to hormonal fluctuations, which can lead to anxiety and depression. The anticipation of childbirth, concerns about the baby's health, and the impending transition to motherhood amplify stress levels.

In addition to these challenges, pregnancy can also impact a woman's social and professional life. The physical limitations and need for frequent medical appointments can disrupt work and social interactions, sometimes leading to feelings of isolation or frustration. The societal expectations surrounding pregnancy and motherhood can further contribute to a woman's emotional and psychological burden.

And then comes the intense and demanding ordeal of childbirth, a painful and unpredictable process fraught with risks for both mother and child. Labor can last for hours or even days, involving excruciating contractions, intense physical strain, and the uncertainty of potential complications. Also, childbirth can result in significant physical damage for the mother, including tearing, surgical incisions, or the need for a cesarean section, each carrying its own set of risks and a longer recovery period. For some, childbirth can lead to more severe complications such as hemorrhage and infection, all of which can be life-threatening.

After enduring the painful yet beautiful process of childbirth, she is handed a crying baby that demands comfort and feeding. In the early days and weeks, a newborn wakes up every few hours and cries late into the night. This relentless demand for attention and care can leave a mother sleep-deprived and emotionally overwhelmed. Newborns require constant feeding, diaper changes, clothing, bathing, and soothing, all of which place immense physical and emotional demands on a mother.

After childbirth, a mother's beauty also decays. The skin on her stomach has stretched to accommodate her growing baby, resulting in loose skin and stretch marks. Weight gain during pregnancy can linger, reshaping her figure and making it challenging to return to her pre-pregnancy body. Hormonal changes can lead to hair thinning or loss, and even the texture of her hair and skin may change. Varicose veins may appear on her legs as a result of the increased blood flow and pressure during pregnancy. Breastfeeding can leave breasts sagging or uneven as they lose firmness. Some women experience diastasis recti, a separation of abdominal muscles that can permanently alter her posture and core strength. These changes can affect how a mother perceives herself. Society's unrealistic beauty standards can amplify feelings of inadequacy, making her hyper-aware of her physical imperfections.

Raising a child also brings significant financial strain. The costs of childcare, medical expenses, diapers, formula, and other necessities quickly add up. For mothers who were previously employed, the decision to return to work is fraught with challenges. Some need to temporarily or permanently set aside their careers to provide full-time care for their newborn, resulting in lost income and, potentially, lost professional opportunities. This can lead to a sense of loss of identity and financial independence.

Raising children demands significant investments of money, time, and personal sacrifice. Despite these challenges, many women find motherhood to be an incredibly rewarding journey, filled with moments of joy, fulfillment, a profound sense of connection and real contentment. From a purely logical perspective, having a child appears to bring nothing but hardship and struggle. Yet, a mother's love transcends these difficulties; she cherishes her baby above all else, finding deep meaning and fulfillment in the experience. What might seem like absolute madness from a logical standpoint is viewed as one of life's greatest blessings from a moral perspective.

How, then, can such deep suffering be seen as a blessing and love? What truly defines love, and why is it so profound? To love means to rise above life's greatest challenges with grace, joy, and contentment. Childbirth is just one example of the hardships love demands. Any genuine expression of love carries difficulties that match, if not surpass, the challenges of raising a child. Love is a journey meant for the strong and determined, not for those with faint hearts. If you learn to love and live in a state of love, no matter how challenging your life may seem, you will navigate it with grace, fulfillment, and contentment—much like a mother who finds joy in raising her child.

Mother Teresa deeply understood the essence of love, and she beautifully expressed it when she said, "I have found the paradox, that if you love until it hurts, there can be no more hurt, only more love."

Let's examine the features of love, one at a time, to better understand the true meaning of love. A key characteristic of love is that it is always a one-way road. Some people mistakenly think of love as a two-way street: "You love me, and I love you." However, love that demands something in return isn't truly love; it resembles an exchange or a transaction rather than an authentic act of love. Pure love has no expectations; it gives freely and willingly without asking for anything in return.

A mother's love is a one-way road. She loves her child regardless of any circumstances—even when the baby wakes her up in the middle of the night. This love is pure and unconditional, especially in the early years when the child is still very young.

As soon as mother's expectations enter the picture, the once pure love becomes tainted, causing distance between mother and the child. What begins as unconditional love in early childhood, over time, becomes clouded by a mother's growing expectations as her child matures. This shift is the beginning of tension and arguments between a mother and her child.

For example, when a child doesn't get good grades in school, the mother's disappointment creates a rift in their bond. The child internalizes this disappointment as a sign of conditional love, believing that their worth is tied to meeting certain standards. As a result, the emotional distance between them grows, weakening the pure love they once shared.

A mother's love that is tainted by expectations leads to disappointments. Similarly, a child experiences conditional love, shaped by rules and standards. The unconditional and pure love that once existed between mother and child in the early years has now transformed into a less pure form, diluted by the complexities of life.

As the child progresses through adolescence and into young adulthood, the mother's expectations continue to expand. Whether it's about academic success, career choices, behavior, or life decisions, each unmet expectation provides fertile ground for arguments and conflict. These conflicts, repeated over time, erode the bond between mother and child. The mother feels that her child is not living up to her hopes, while the child feels stifled and misunderstood, leading to mutual disappointment.

By the time the child reaches young adulthood, the relationship develops into a love-hate dynamic, where both mother and child still care deeply for one another but are frequently at odds. The unconditional love of early childhood still exists, but it has become overshadowed by feelings of unmet desires, unrealistic expectations, and unresolved conflicts. Both begin to harbor a sense of resentment.

This is why pure love can never truly be a two-way road. Love remains pure only when it gives without expecting anything in return. It is the very act of selfless giving that defines and gives meaning to true love. When love begins to demand or expect something in return, it loses its purity and transforms into a transaction or an exchange.

Another feature of love is that it inherently sacrifices itself to protect and nurture what it cherishes. Love is a protective force that willingly endures hardship to provide safety and comfort to the beloved, often at the cost of its own ease. Think of a father who works tirelessly day and night to provide shelter, food, and security for his family. A selfless father will pick up a sword and a shield to fend off any threat that dares to harm his loved ones. This father is willing to fight enemies and lay down his life, if necessary, to protect and defend his family.

Exhausted and wounded after the battle, all the father longs for is to see his family safe and well. At the very first sight of them, his love instantly deepens. These sacrifices, made consciously and willingly, strengthen his bond with his loved ones.

Similarly, a mother sacrifices her beauty, comfort, time, and energy to nourish and care for her child. From the moment she becomes a mother, she willingly puts aside her own needs and desires, often giving up her career, hobbies, or personal aspirations to ensure her child's well-being.

The demands of parenthood are constant, requiring them to invest countless hours in caring for the child—whether it's through sleepless nights, endless nurturing, or simply being present in the child's life day after day.

As the years pass, parental sacrifices accumulate—physically, emotionally, and mentally—but instead of depleting the parents, these acts of giving deepen their love for their child. Each moment of sacrifice strengthens the bond between them, and through this selflessness, their love continues to grow. It is precisely through these selfless sacrifices that the parent's love finds its truest form of purity, as long as it does not become tainted by expectations and conditions.

Let's explore the other side of love. Love is not something to be taken; it is something to be received. Taking stems from selfishness and entitlement, while receiving requires openness and acceptance. The true receiver of love stands at the end of a one-way road, where love flows freely.

When love is demanded, it loses its purity, becoming shallow and unfulfilling. Forced love is not willingly given, and without willingness, it cannot be true love. Paradoxically, the more one expects to receive love, the further they distance themselves from experiencing love in its purest form.

To receive true love, one must practice patience and let go of the expectation to be loved. Only when this expectation fades away does love find its way naturally, freely, and genuinely to the receiver. True love cannot be chased or claimed—it must be allowed to flow, unbidden and unconditional.

Love, at its core, is about spreading goodness and kindness, creating a space of safety, comfort, and well-being for the one who receives it. When love is given and received with sincerity, it often becomes a source of joy and contentment. Love seeks only what is best for the beloved and never inflicts deliberate harm. However, even pure love can sometimes be difficult or unpleasant for the lover and beloved, yet it is never harmful.

Consider the example of a child taking bitter medicine from their mother. The taste may be unpleasant, and the experience may be difficult, but the mother's intention is not to cause harm. On the contrary, it is an act of love meant to bring healing and well-being to the child. In this way, love sometimes requires difficult actions and tough decisions, but always with the ultimate aim of nurturing, protecting, and fostering growth of the beloved.

Love also gives meaning to forgiveness. True love does not harbor grudges, regrets, or resentments; it transcends these burdens entirely. Such negative feelings arise from unmet expectations, but true love, free of expectations, remains untouchable by disappointment or hurt. Love is inherently whole, requiring no validation, no reciprocity, and no reward.

Even when love is met with indifference, rejection, or harm, it does not cease to flow. It may redirect its attention, but it never stops giving unconditionally. Love does not waver in the face of adversity because its essence is unbreakable. Love is an energy that knows nothing but love itself—steadfast, resilient, and self-sustaining.

This is precisely why love triumphs over all odds. Its strength lies in its simplicity and purity, transcending the complexities of human feelings and expectations. Love endures because it is not bound by the limitations we place on it. It forgives, not out of obligation, but because forgiveness is simply an extension of its nature.

Unlike the fleeting and fragile feelings tied to the physical world, pure love resides in the spiritual realm, impervious to harm. No act of cruelty, injustice, or malice in the material world can penetrate the spiritual sanctity of love. Throughout history, individuals who embodied true love and understood the profound meaning of forgiveness have shown us the enduring strength of love.

Even in his final moments on the cross, Jesus spoke words of pure love directed at those who had tortured him and sought to take his life: "God, forgive them, for they don't know what they do." Despite the immense suffering inflicted upon him, he chose forgiveness over resentment. Similarly, Gandhi, with his last breath, forgave the man who shot him. Both exemplified love's capacity to transcend even the ultimate betrayal.

Martin Luther King Jr. championed this transformative power of love in the face of hate: "We must meet hate with love. Remember, if I am stopped, this movement will not stop because God is with the movement. Go home with this glowing faith and this radiant assurance. Be concerned about your brother. You may not like what he does, but you must love him. Love is greater than like." In another powerful moment, he told his oppressors: "We shall match your capacity to inflict suffering by our capacity to endure suffering. We will meet your physical force with soul force. Do to us what you will, and we will still love you."

The Prophet Muhammad forgave even those who had tortured and killed his family and friends. When he rose to a position of power over his enemies, he chose to protect them, granting them safety and dignity instead of revenge.

Mother Teresa, in her simple yet profound words, taught that "Forgiveness is a decision, not a feeling. It is an act of love." She always said, "If you really want to love, you must learn how to forgive."

These figures faced immense suffering, cruelty, and injustice, yet they responded with unwavering love and forgiveness. Their actions serve as a testament to love's invincibility, its capacity to endure beyond the physical world. Their love transcended personal pain, reflecting the boundless, spiritual nature of pure love—a force that triumphs over even the greatest darkness, illuminating the path to peace and unity.

Love's purity makes forgiveness not only possible but inevitable. When love is pure, it recognizes that harm inflicted in the physical world cannot diminish its spiritual essence. Forgiveness flows naturally because love remains untouchable, unbroken by the injustices of the material realm. It is this unyielding strength that makes love, alongside peace, one of the most powerful forces in existence. Love forgives not because it is weak but because it is strong beyond imagination and completely invincible.

In a nutshell, pure love is characterized by several key criteria, each interwoven to form its unique and profound nature.

First and foremost, love is a one-way road—it gives freely without expecting anything in return. True love is not transactional; it is free of burden and obligation.

Secondly, love is deeply rooted in selflessness. It prioritizes the well-being of the beloved above all else, with no thought of personal gain or reward. Love's focus is always on the beloved, seeking to nurture and protect.

Thirdly, love thrives and grows through conscious and voluntary sacrifices. These sacrifices are not born of duty but of a heartfelt desire to support, uplift, and strengthen the beloved. Love is an act of devotion.

Fourthly, love is inherently beneficial to the receiver. While it may sometimes bring discomfort as it fosters growth and healing, its ultimate aim is always the well-being of the beloved. Love seeks to uplift, even when it requires temporary difficulty.

Fifthly, love cannot be demanded or coerced. It can only be received with an open heart. Demanding love diminishes its purity, as love must flow freely to remain pure.

Lastly, love always forgives. Its core remains untouchable, leaving no room for grudges, regrets, or resentments. Forgiveness is not a compromise but an extension of love's unshakable purity.

For true love to flourish, all these elements must work in harmony, each reinforcing the other. Pure love is not just a simple human emotion; it is a universal force—the most powerful energy in entire existence.

Within you lies an infinite reservoir of love, waiting to be tapped into and understood. To truly comprehend what love is, you must learn to generate and harness this love from within. Love is not simply a passive emotion but an active energy that, once cultivated, can be brought into physical reality. When you possess love in this way—internally generated and consciously harnessed—you can begin to manifest it in your day-to-day life.

Let's reimagine the invisible realm and the role of love within it. Picture the invisible realm of consciousness as being woven from the fabric of truth. Truth itself is made of love and peace, and these qualities permeate through the entire invisible realm. Your soul, being a creature of the invisible realm, is crafted from love and peace, existing naturally in a state of collective consciousness where love and peace are abundant and ever-present.

However, when you are deceived by the devil, your soul begins to drift toward the region of the collective unconsciousness—a place where love and peace, while still present, are far less abundant. The journey from collective consciousness to collective unconsciousness passes through what I call the devil's den—a narrow, dark, labyrinthine pathway that distances your soul from the collective consciousness and the love and peace it longs for. This separation creates a sense of disconnection, making it harder for you to access your soul.

No matter how deeply your soul may be lost in the darkness of the devil's den, your connection to your soul is never entirely severed and you can still hear its faint whispers and sense its emotions in your mind. However, the further your soul wanders into the collective unconsciousness, the harder it becomes to grasp its presence. Love, which flows through your soul, is always accessible, but when your soul is consumed by darkness, love becomes harder to reach and less abundant in your life.

As you navigate the dark, narrow pathways of the devil's den to reconnect with your soul, two powerful forces guide the way: truth and love. When you embrace and understand the truth, you move toward your soul, illuminating the darkness as you go. At the same time, when you understand and embrace love, your soul moves toward the light of truth. While you move toward your soul by embodying truth, love draws your soul closer to the light of your truth, closing the gap.

To put it another way, with truth, you mentally traverse the collective unconsciousness to find your soul. Truth shines light into the shadows, moving deeper into the darkness to expose it. This is why we mentioned earlier that people often fear the naked truth—because truth inherently leads you to confront the darkest parts of yourself, others, and the broader reality as a whole. And people are afraid of the darkness.

Love, however, works differently. It draws your soul out of the collective unconsciousness and into the collective consciousness, moving it from darkness toward light. This is why you might have heard people say, "Where there is love, there is light."

Paradoxically, truth-seekers who rely solely on logic fail to grasp the full depth of truth, as truth's essence far surpasses the boundaries of logic and is intricately embedded in the morality of love and peace. While they may illuminate many paths with their intellect, they will miss the essence of truth that resides beyond pure reasoning. This oversight leads them into a darkness from which they never recover, leaving their souls lost and unfulfilled.

History offers us many examples of brilliant philosophers, like Nietzsche, who, despite their extraordinary intellect, ultimately found life devoid of inherent meaning. By exploring the corridors of truth solely through logic, they ventured deep into the devil's den, only to miss the location of their own soul within it. Deceived by the devil's cunning, they searched in all the wrong places, mistaking intellectual illumination for ultimate understanding. Though they illuminated the devil's den with the light of their intellect and provided humanity with invaluable insights, they themselves perished in the darkness of their own minds, unable to transcend it. They perished before reaching the light of truth, their brilliance obscured by the absence of love.

Without love, their understanding of truth became slightly skewed, veering toward emptiness and despair, with nihilism as their final destination. Truth, without the power of love, cannot be understood, leaving the seeker adrift in a sea of meaninglessness.

The reality is, you don't need to be a genius or exhaust every avenue of intellectual exploration to uncover the essence of truth. Simply walking the path of love reveals enough truth to guide you toward enlightenment. If you truly understand love, your wisdom will surpass that of the most brilliant scientist or philosopher in human history. Intellect, no matter how profound, pales in comparison to the boundless power of love. Love is a powerful arbiter, the beacon that shows you how to go about traversing the spiritual realm. Love is the bare minimum requirement for enlightenment, and without it, enlightenment is impossible—even for the greatest minds of all time.

Now, if you combine the wisdom of truth with the power of love, something extraordinary happens. With love, you bring your soul into the light, and with truth, you shine the light into the depth of darkness. Together, they allow you to reach the highest levels of enlightenment. The takeaway is that the power of love—is the bare minimum requirement for enlightenment. Paradoxically, while truth holds the wisdom to guide you to the highest realms of enlightenment, truth without love ceases to be true and can only lead you deeper into darkness.

With this image in mind, let us delve into how the power of love can be harnessed. As you practice spreading love in the physical realm, your soul, in the inviable realm naturally ascends from the collective unconsciousness toward the collective consciousness, gravitating toward regions rich in love. By doing so, your soul draws from the boundless love of the invisible realm, channeling it back to you so that you can manifest it in your physical reality. This cyclical process of harnessing and spreading love creates a continuous flow of love energy between you, your soul, physical reality, and the larger collective consciousness.

As this happens, your soul draws closer to you, allowing you to sense its true needs, hear its voice more clearly in your thoughts, and sense its emotions more vividly. These internal shifts gradually ripple into the physical realm, manifesting as positive feelings, mental clarity, and an overall sense of well-being.

The more you spread love, the more adept your soul becomes at harnessing and collecting love, growing stronger and more capable in the process. This ongoing work of the soul—constantly seeking, gathering, and sharing love—is what allows it to grow and mature.

The boundless reservoir of love is always available, but it requires conscious effort to access and channel it. By learning how to generate love from this limitless source, you ensure that you and your soul have an unending supply of love. Through empathy, kindness, and compassion, your soul learns to harness the energy of love.

Furthermore, while receiving love from others is soothing and pleasant, it is not what enables your soul to grow. Receiving love from others can be compared to being handed a glass of water when you are thirsty. It provides temporary relief, quenching your thirst for the moment, but without regular access to water, you will soon find yourself thirsty again. In contrast, if you possess your own source of water, you will never suffer from thirst, as you can draw from it whenever you need. The same principle applies to love. You must tap into the infinite reservoir of love and harness it continuously, as much as possible, so you never sense a deficiency of love at any moment in your life.

Love cannot be demanded, and it is not always readily available to be received. Trying to fill yourself by receiving love from others leaves you dependent on external sources, which are unreliable, limited, and often unavailable. When you receive love, it momentarily lifts your spirit and makes you feel better, but your soul cannot thrive on a limited and external supply of love. Unfortunately, in today's world, love is in short supply. Greed, hatred, and anger dominate many aspects of our lives, creating a serious deficit of love in physical reality. Striving to receive love as a means of feeling better will leave you unfulfilled.

The solution to this scarcity lies within each of us. You and I are responsible for generating and spreading more love than we receive, contributing positively to the abundance of love in the physical world. The greatest achievement in life is learning to generate love from within and manifesting it into the visible world. In doing so, you not only nourish your own soul but also contribute to spreading love that the world so desperately needs.

Through consistent acts of giving love—without the expectation of receiving it in return—you elevate both your own soul and those around you. This process of harnessing love from within and sharing it outwardly ensures that the energy of love continues to grow and thrive, counteracting the negativity that is so prevalent in the world today. In this way, you become a source of love, and through your actions, you create a ripple effect that positively impacts everyone around you.

You possess an infinite capacity to bring love into the world through the goodness and kindness within your heart. Love, though immensely powerful, often reveals itself in the simplest actions—offering a ride to a coworker, sharing a smile with a child, or petting a dog. These small gestures are profound because they transform everyday moments into opportunities to spread love. Through such actions, love flows effortlessly into the world. Everyone has something to give as an act of love. In this way, everyone has the ability to experience love.

Love is not measured by the quantity of what is given but by the quality of the intention, willingness, and sacrifice behind it. For instance, consider a person who struggles with daily living expenses yet still finds ways to help those less fortunate. Their act of giving holds the same measure of love as that of a wealthy person who, with pure intention, helps others on a larger scale. In both cases, it is the purity of the intention, not the amount of wealth or resources given, that defines the depth of love. In this way, love transcends material measures; it is the spirit of sacrifice that reveals love's true essence.

No one holds a unique privilege or greater right to experience love more than anyone else. Love is an equal opportunity for all, unrestricted by wealth, status, or circumstance. It can only be found in the willingness to spread goodness with pure intention. The fountain of creation pours love endlessly into existence, and it is available to anyone who is willing to draw from it. All that is required is the openness to receive this infinite love, and the willingness to share with others.

Love is not only possible in times of peace and ease but also in moments of deep struggle and adversity. Love is a choice, one that transforms not just individuals but entire societies. Nelson Mandela endured a life filled with immense hardship and decades of facing hatred and oppression. During his 27 years in prison, he received very little love and was often met with cruelty and indifference. Yet, despite the harsh conditions and the injustice he suffered, Mandela made the conscious choice to continue spreading love. Every day, in the face of hostility and adversity, Mandela deepened his commitment to love, showing the world that love is not dictated by circumstances but by the choices we make. After he seized power, he extended compassion and forgiveness even to the prison guards who held him captive.

As it has been said, one day after Nelson Mandela became President of South Africa, he went to a restaurant with his security team. Among the customers, he noticed a man sitting alone at a nearby table. Mandela extended an invitation for the man to join them.

The man accepted but appeared deeply stressed. His hands trembled as he ate, his demeanor filled with tension and nervousness. But as the meal went on, Mandela's warmth and kindness began to have an effect. Slowly, the man relaxed, his trembling subsided, and eventually, he even smiled and laughed, finding unexpected joy in the presence of the former prisoner-turned-president.

After the meal, one of Mandela's security guards, curious about the man, asked Mandela about him. Mandela explained: "This man was one of the prison guards who was rough on me during my time on Robben Island. I invited him over so he could see for himself that I hold no hatred for him. That I love him as a fellow human being and that I have forgiven him."

Mandela's life serves as a powerful reminder that love is always within our control, no matter how dark or difficult the situation. If you choose to love, nothing and no one can stop you from doing so. Love is always available as a choice, independent of the treatment you receive or the conditions you face. Even in the midst of suffering and injustice, love remains a suitable option.

The capacity to love comes from within and is not contingent on external validation or reciprocation. If you desire to love, you will find a way to love, no matter the obstacles. In the darkest of circumstances, love is a powerful force that moves against adversity that can guide you through your daily struggles. Mandela's life stands as proof that even when faced with the worst of humanity, you still have the power to choose love.

Up to this point, we have explored the manifestation of love in physical reality—the outward expressions of love through our interactions, sacrifices, and acts of kindness. Yet, love holds a deeper meaning that transcends what is visible. In the invisible realm of consciousness, love is a moral energy and a fundamental principle that upholds the entirety of existence.

At its deepest level, love means peaceful coexistence with the entirety of existence in perfect harmony. In this way, peace and love—the divine duality of truth—must be cultivated simultaneously. Love is about aligning yourself with the universal flow of life. When your soul seeks to tap into the infinite reservoir of love within the collective consciousness, it requires you to exist in a state of peace and harmony with the world around you. This harmony opens the faucet to the boundless source of love, allowing your soul to gather and harness its power.

But how can you coexist peacefully in a world filled with conflict, chaos, and division? This is precisely what makes pure love so rare and embracing it so challenging. To live in love, you must learn to love not just the parts of the world that you find agreeable or familiar, but all of existence. True love is not selective or conditional—it encompasses all things, without discrimination. While it is natural to surround yourself with those who share your beliefs and values, this should not diminish your love for those who are different from you, or even for those who may oppose you.

Jesus perfectly encapsulated this idea when he said, "Love thy enemy." You can only truly understand love when you are able to love your enemies from the bottom of your heart, free from any resentment or hatred. When you reach this state of peace with the entirety of the world, you tap into the essence of pure love. At this point, the infinite reservoir of love pours into your being, filling you with a sense of fulfillment and bliss that surpasses your wildest imagination—an experience so profound that no words can come close to truly capturing its serenity.

If you practice selective love, choosing only to love those who agree with you or make you feel comfortable, you limit your access to the boundless love available to you. The more narrowly you choose to love in the physical world, the more you restrict your soul's access to the infinite love of the invisible realm. This self-imposed limitation leads to greater inner conflict, suffering, and discontent. On the other hand, the more you extend your love—even to those who may hate or hurt you—the more your soul taps into the universal source of love. As your capacity for love expands, your experience of suffering diminishes, replaced by a profound sense of peace and fulfillment.

In essence, the key to unlocking the infinite reservoir of love lies in your ability to love universally, without boundaries or conditions. The more you open yourself to love, the more it flows into and through you. When you learn to coexist peacefully with the entirety of existence, you have truly learned how to love.

In the previous chapter, we discussed how truth provides the "why," while love offers the "how" to cultivate virtues such as humility, gratitude, resilience, and bravery. Understanding and embodying these virtues requires continuous practice and a commitment to serving others in the name of love, a journey that calls for vulnerability.

To fully understand love, you must also understand the role of vulnerability in your service to others. We've already touched on the idea that love is a one-way road of giving without expecting anything in return, requiring selflessness and sacrifice. However, the deeper layer of this practice is embracing complete vulnerability, meaning you willingly put yourself in a position where you may be harmed or misunderstood in your effort to serve. It is through this vulnerability that you learn and internalize virtues like bravery, resilience, and humility.

Consider this: if you serve others while keeping yourself shielded or in a "safe" place, you never truly become braver. If you avoid the possibility of harm, discomfort, or discrimination, you miss the opportunity to cultivate resilience. True service, rooted in love, demands that you expose yourself to risk—whether it's emotional, social, or even physical. When you offer love and service in a state of vulnerability, you develop what could be described as a "spiritual thick skin," one that becomes stronger and more impenetrable over time.

This process mirrors the way the immune system functions. When exposed to a virus, your body learns to create antibodies that protect you from future illnesses. Similarly, in the realm of spirituality, when you expose yourself to harm and challenge out of love, your soul builds resilience and strength. Over time, this fortifies you against future moral, emotional, and spiritual harm. The paradox here is that it's through exposure to difficulty in the name of love that you develop the inner strength to withstand adversity.

The critical point is that you must be in a state of love when exposed to harm in order for this transformation to occur. If you are harmed without cultivating and maintaining a mindset of love, the result can have the opposite effect—making you bitter, defensive, and filled with resentment. It is only when love is at the core of your vulnerability that experience leads to growth and strength, rather than emotional or spiritual injury.

In essence, vulnerability in service—rooted in love—is the pathway to developing the virtues you strive for. It challenges you to step outside of comfort and safety, to risk your own being for the sake of others, and to allow yourself to be transformed by that risk.

Imagine a scenario where a close friend is severely ill with a contagious virus. You know that your friend has no one else to care for them, and you have the time and energy to step in and help. However, the fear of contracting the illness might cause hesitation, holding you back from offering the support your friend desperately needs. Yet, if your love for them is stronger than your fear, you will choose to serve—tending to your friend until their health is restored.

Imagine your two-month-old child falls ill. Would you keep your child at a six-foot distance, quarantine them in a locked room for two weeks, and prioritize your own health over theirs? Of course not—it would be unthinkable. Your love for your child eclipses any fear of getting sick yourself. Your only concern is their well-being, and you'd do anything to see them recover, no matter the risk to yourself.

Now, imagine it's your friend who is sick. If love is truly your driving force, there should be no difference in how you approach the situation. Love knows no boundaries or conditions. It compels you to face your fear, set aside your self-interest, and prioritize the well-being of another. In love, whether it's for a child, a friend, or a stranger, the response is the same—you choose to act out of care and compassion. True love dissolves the distinctions we create between relationships, because the essence of love is universal.

This act of love, service, and vulnerability in the face of fear strengthens your courage. True bravery doesn't come from the absence of fear, but from choosing to face your fear. And if your love is pure, even if you do become ill after helping a friend, you will not regret your actions. Instead, you will find peace in knowing that you were able to help when your friend needed you most. That is the sacrifice that deepens your love, enhances your bravery, strengthens your resilience, and enriches your moral understanding. Love, when genuine and selfless, can overcome even the most paralyzing fears.

Unfortunately, society teaches you to distance yourself from those who are unwell—to keep six feet away and to isolate both them and yourself. This approach fuels fear, keeping you paralyzed, disconnected, and lonely. Society's message ensures that fear maintains its grip on you, preventing genuine connection.

Do not follow this path. Instead, embrace the transformative power of love. Face your fears directly and open yourself to vulnerability and genuine connection. It is through this courage that you will find true fulfillment, a sense of belonging, and inner peace. Love is the antidote to isolation, and only by choosing love over fear can you break free from the loneliness that society imposes.

Moreover, when you spread love to help others without any expectation of return, you free yourself from the emotional weight of their response. Even if those you serve respond negatively, your lack of expectation protects you from disappointment. By not seeking validation or appreciation, you build resilience, instead of building resentment. In this way, you no longer perceive mistreatment as an obstacle but as an opportunity to elevate your character and nurture your soul. You are no longer affected by negative responses toward you.

Over time, this practice fosters emotional and spiritual maturity, transforming challenges into opportunities for growth. This is precisely how you move through life's challenges with grace, maintaining your lasting peace all along. This method builds an impenetrable fortress of peace around your mental landscape, shielding it from darkness. Within this protected space, you can cultivate a lasting state of bliss and happiness.

If you want to be completely free from suffering, you must cultivate an extraordinary level of moral, spiritual, and emotional strength. However, attaining this strength is not an overnight process; it requires deliberate effort and gradual growth over time. And this growth occurs through exposure to harm and adversity. Every challenge, criticism, or setback becomes an opportunity to fortify your inner resolve. Over time, by consistently choosing love, kindness, forgiveness, compassion, and understanding in the face of hardship, you train yourself to rise above the pain inflicted by the outside world.

The path of enlightenment demands vulnerability and a commitment to selflessness, but the result is true freedom from suffering. You will no longer be swayed by external forces or circumstances because your strength will come from within. Resilience, when cultivated with love, creates a barrier against suffering, empowering you to face life's difficulties with peace and unwavering inner strength.

Serving others with love and vulnerability also eradicates vanity by stripping away any sense of superiority as you attend to the needs of others. In humbling yourself to serve anyone, regardless of their status or circumstances, you confront the reality that no one is inherently better or worse than anyone else. This act of service reveals your shared humanity with others, fostering profound humility. Through selfless service, you transcend ego and pride, recognizing that true strength lies in compassion and equality—not in superiority and hierarchy.

In serving others, you gain an intimate understanding of life's struggles and hardships. For instance, when you care for someone who is ill, you become acutely aware of the health challenges they face, from physical discomfort to emotional distress. If you assist someone with financial difficulties, you begin to comprehend the weight of their financial burdens and the constant stress that accompanies them. When you provide support to someone grieving the loss of a loved one, you begin to understand the depth of their sorrow, the emptiness they feel, and the strength it takes to move forward each day. If you mentor a child struggling in school, you become aware of their frustration and the fear of failure they carry. Each act of service reveals to you the gaps in people's lives—the areas where they lack support, stability, or well-being. By stepping in to fill those gaps with your time, energy, and abilities, you experience the suffering of those you help, granting you the power of compassion.

You learn to put yourself in other people's shoes, seeing the world not only through your own eyes but through the eyes of everyone you have served. As you progress in this endeavor, you begin to see the world through the collective lens of humanity, and ultimately, through godly vision. This is the power of compassion.

This process of walking in other people's footsteps—seeing and addressing their struggles—grants you yet another perspective: one rooted in gratitude. By opening your eyes to the sufferings and challenges around you and actively working to ease those sufferings, you naturally begin to value the blessings in your own life. Things you may have once taken for granted—your health, financial stability, or even basic comforts—become infinitely more meaningful when you recognize that others may lack these very things. This newfound awareness fosters a profound sense of gratitude, helping you cherish even the smallest details of your life that others might go without. In this way, serving others not only provides relief to those you help but also enriches your own spirit, deepening your appreciation for what you have.

Every time you serve others with love, you place yourself in unique situations that challenge you to refine different aspects of your moral character. Each act of service out of love calls upon a specific virtue, whether it be gratitude, humility, generosity, or resilience. For example, you practice humility when helping someone of a lower social class, setting aside judgment or prejudice; gratitude when recognizing the lack in others' lives compared to the abundance in your own; bravery when tending to someone who is ill, confronting your own fear of sickness; and generosity when sharing your resources without expecting anything in return.

Through each act of service, you are called to embody a different virtue and strengthen it in practice. These moments push you beyond surface-level of reality into depths of morality. When an action is driven by self-serving motives, it doesn't truly enhance your moral character, as it ultimately serves your own benefit. In contrast, when an act is performed out of pure love, with no expectation of reward, your morality is genuinely tested—and as a result, your moral understanding deepens and grows. Morality is not something you can simply read about and learn—you must live it to truly understand it.

Morality originates from the invisible realm and is deeply rooted in truth. As your moral understanding deepens through acts of service, your awareness of truth expands as well. This growing understanding helps you identify the gaps in your own character, the areas where certain virtues are lacking. Each act of service compels you to confront and challenge those gaps, strengthening the attributes that foster your growth. Through selfless service, you uplift others and also cultivate a more complete and virtuous version of yourself, firmly grounded in truth, love, and morality.

Let's summarize the essence of love. Love is a one-way road of giving—voluntarily, consciously, and wholeheartedly. It is a selfless act that expects nothing in return and grows stronger through sacrifice. Love always forgives because it cannot be truly harmed. Love can be received but never demanded, as it must flow freely. The purpose of love is always to benefit the beloved, making it an act of service that genuinely fulfills the needs of others.

True acts of love must be carried out with complete vulnerability, free from any reservation. Any harm that may arise from giving through pure love does not lead to resentment; instead, it fosters resilience, strengthens character, and deepens moral understanding. Over time, this development, rooted in love, creates a fortitude that shields the giver from moral harm. This mental fortress of peace becomes a sanctuary for lasting bliss and happiness. Acts of service born from love unveil the suffering of others, nurturing compassion in the heart of the giver. Through the consistent practice of pure love, one builds an unshakable strength, deeply connected to understanding of truth and morality.

Earlier, we mentioned that truth has the power to liberate you from fear. Love, as one of the building blocks of truth, is also an essential step in this process. When you embody honesty and integrity in your pursuit of truth and act out of love to comprehend the highest levels of morality, you ultimately free yourself from fear.

Love and fear are like light and darkness: when there is no light, darkness dominates; when there is a little light, shadows emerge; and when there is abundance of light, darkness dissolves entirely. The same applies to love and fear. Where there is no love, fear dominates. When love is mixed with fear, attachments form. But where there is pure love, there is freedom—and no fear.

When you embody love, live with honesty, and act with integrity, every confrontation with fear becomes an opportunity for transformation. No matter how terrifying the fear might seem, pure love acts as a light that dissipates the darkness, leaving no room for fear to take hold. Each time you face your fears, armed with love and truth, fear will inevitably dissolve, bestowing upon you the strength and freedom that come with living in alignment with your true essence.

Love and fear are two sides of the same coin—an undivine duality in creation, much like light and darkness or truth and falsehood. Love is the single most powerful and fundamental energy in the invisible realm of existence, while fear is merely the absence of love-energy, just as darkness is the absence of light. In this way, everything you have ever experienced in your life is either rooted in love or in its absence, manifesting as fear. All your emotions and feelings, as well as your personality and character, have always been—and will forever be—shaped by love or fear. Positive attributes such as bravery, generosity, serenity, and compassion arise from love, while negative attributes like hate, anger, greed, and jealousy are born from fear.

Imagine a newborn baby. Emerging from the safety of the womb, the baby enters an entirely new and unknown world. The first breath a newborn takes is accompanied by a cry—a response to the fear of the unknown, a signal to the surrounding world that it needs love and care. When the mother holds and nurtures her baby, showering it with her love, the baby becomes quiet and stops crying. Within the first few minutes of life, the newborn experiences two emotions: the fear of the unfamiliar world and the love of its mother. The baby knows no other emotions. Newborns do not understand anger, hatred, jealousy, or even positive emotions like happiness or serenity; they do not even know how to smile. At birth, the only two emotions a newborn experiences are fear and love. At the core of your being, fear and love are the most primal emotions, and you inherently understand them. Every other emotion is learned and shaped through life experiences, stemming from these two fundamental emotions of love and fear.

Fear lies at the root of all negative emotions and traits in humanity. It drives behaviors that divide, harm, and disconnect us from one another. For example, the fear of terrorism fuels hatred toward those perceived as threats. A soldier's anger in the heat of battle is born from the fear of losing or dying. When one sees others as more capable or successful, fear of inadequacy manifests as envy and jealousy.

A deep fear of losing control or feeling inadequate can contribute to narcissistic tendencies, as narcissists cope with these fears by seeking validation, superiority, and dominance in their relationships. Moreover, A persistent fear of powerlessness contribute to a victim mentality, particularly when individuals internalize a belief that they have little control over their circumstances.

Fear fuels all negative traits like greed (stemming from fear of scarcity), dishonesty (fear of consequences), and aggression (fear of vulnerability). At its core, fear creates a defensive mindset, causing people to act in ways that prioritize self-preservation—at the expense of others or their own values. Fear is the foundation of division, conflict, insecurity, and despair, bringing out the worst in humanity and perpetuating cycles of negativity.

In contrast, love is the root of all positive emotions and virtues. Love fosters generosity, encouraging you to share your time, energy, and resources with others. It nurtures compassion, allowing you to connect deeply with others' struggles and extend kindness. Love inspires bravery, enabling you to face challenges for the sake of those you care about. It brings happiness, filling your life with joy and warmth through meaningful relationships. Love teaches patience, helping you endure difficulties with grace and understanding.

Love also sparks creativity, channeling passion into art, innovation, and new ideas. It instills hope, providing strength and optimism even in the face of adversity. Love shapes humanity's greatest qualities. In every way, love elevates you, revealing the best of who you are and fostering a sense of purpose and fulfillment.

Every decision you have ever made, and every decision you will ever make, is either fear-based, love-based, or a mixture of both. When your actions are driven by fear, you begin to build walls around yourself—physically, psychologically, and emotionally. For instance, you might install heavy locks on your door out of fear of intruders, shutting yourself off from the outside world. You may close your heart to avoid emotional pain, choosing to keep others at a distance rather than risk being hurt. Fear of betrayal might stop you from forming close relationships, eroding your trust, and leaving you isolated even when surrounded by people. Fear promises safety behind these walls, protecting you from harm and discomfort, but in doing so, it isolates you and disconnects you from your true desire for genuine connection.

Furthermore, fear might cause you to avoid taking risks in your career, trapping you in a job you dislike because you fear failure or financial instability. Fear can lead you to suppress your words, thoughts, and emotions, hiding behind a false facade out of fear of judgment or rejection. In small daily choices, like avoiding a new experience or declining an opportunity, can stem from a fear of the unknown, keeping you confined to your comfort zone. Even in your inner world, fear builds barriers that keep you from exploring your true self, silencing your dreams and desires. Over time, these walls grow higher and thicker, creating a fortress of isolation that separates you not only from others but also from yourself.

Paradoxically, in a world rife with chaos and conflict, no matter how tall or thick the walls of fear and insecurity you build, they will eventually crumble, leaving you exposed. These walls, which you construct to shield yourself from harm, only create a false sense of safety. Whispers of fear promise protection, but in truth, it delivers pain.

By isolating yourself behind these barriers, you don't escape the turmoil of life; you only delay the inevitable. The world's unpredictability will find its way through the cracks, breaking down the very defenses you thought would keep you safe. Instead of offering solace, fear amplifies your suffering, chaining you to the very pain you sought to avoid.

Love, on the other hand, is open, vulnerable, and liberating. When you make decisions based on love, you break down barriers that confine you, allowing yourself to experience genuine connections and freedom. Love encourages you to trust others, giving them opportunities to show their true selves. Even in the face of betrayal, love does not harden your heart; instead, it teaches you to grow stronger, transforming pain into wisdom while keeping your heart open.

Instead of harboring bitterness, love enables you to build resilience that does not rely on walls for protection. Over time, your spiritual skin becomes impenetrable—through wisdom gained from the power of openness and vulnerability. Nothing, no matter how harsh or cruel, can cause you emotional or psychological harm when you are grounded in love.

When Jesus said, "But I say unto you, that ye resist not evil: but whosoever shall smite thee on thy right cheek, turn to him the other also." it was not a call to weakness or passivity. Quite the opposite—it was an invitation to embody true strength. Turning the other cheek signifies a profound spiritual power: standing firm in your truth, so resilient and unyielding in your inner peace that even the most powerful adversaries cannot disturb your foundation. It means being so fortified by love and clarity that, even when struck with all the force of hatred and malice, your spirit remains untouched. The adversary may lash out, but they will fail to leave so much as a bruise on your spiritual skin.

This is the paradox of love's vulnerability: it appears open, vulnerable, and delicate, yet it harbors the ultimate strength. By choosing love, you don't just protect yourself—you transcend the need for protection altogether, standing firm in a state of fearlessness and unshakable grace.

Love fuels honesty, empowering you to express your thoughts and ideas openly, without fear of judgment. It gives you the courage to follow your passions, explore your creativity, and cultivate your greatest talents. When love is the driving force, you prioritize your dreams over doubts, taking risks to pursue what truly matters to you. Love inspires you to leave behind the comfort of security to pursue a path that brings you true joy and fulfillment.

In relationships, love fosters patience and understanding. It encourages you to accept others as they are, nurturing their growth without conditions or demands. Love drives you to share your vulnerabilities, creating trust and intimacy. In challenges, love inspires bravery, helping you face difficulties with grace and resilience, keeping your actions aligned with your values.

Fear, unfortunately, is humanity's default for decision-making because it acts as a defensive mechanism, offering a false sense of protection and security. It keeps you anchored in your current situation, trapped in a comfort zone that feels safe, familiar, and predictable. While this might seem reassuring on the surface, it comes at a significant cost. Fear robs you of your dreams and a true sense of peace, creating a life that may feel comfortable but never truly fulfilling.

Instead of providing relief, fear keeps you in a constant state of stress. Deep down, you know you are capable of more—that you have untapped potential and dreams waiting to be pursued. Yet fear shackles you, paralyzing you with doubts and anxieties. It convinces you to settle, whispering that risks are too great and failure too daunting. This inner conflict leaves you restless: yearning to grow and evolve but held back by the chains of fear. Fear doesn't just keep you where you are; it prevents you from becoming who you could be. It feeds self-doubt, fosters regret, and perpetuates a cycle of longing without action.

On the other end of the spectrum, love-based decisions are bold and transformative, yet they require a high level of awareness and a conscious choice to implement. Love's vulnerability can seem daunting and frightening, as it demands that you lower your walls of fear and expose yourself to the possibility of pain. Unlike fear, which offers a false sense of security with little effort, love asks you to take risks, confront your fears, step into the unknown, and endure the pain.

Love does not come without its challenges. It brings pain and suffering because you have no barriers to shield you. But it is through this exposure that you grow stronger. Love compels you to face your vulnerabilities and endure discomfort, and in doing so, it transforms you. It builds resilience, fosters clarity, and strengthens your spirit. Over time, you rise above your suffering, finding a sense of inner peace and fulfillment that fear could never provide. Your suffering ends when you reach its deepest depths through love. You live and endure unimaginable pain until nothing remains but love. The process of making love-based decisions is not easy—it will be painful and unsettling. Yet the results are unbelievably good.

Love envisions a brighter future and inspires you to take risks and embrace radical changes in pursuit of your dreams. It propels you forward because staying in the same place for too long erodes your sense of satisfaction, contentment, and fulfillment. Love urges you to open new doors, tackle new challenges, and live a life rich with adventures and meaningful experiences. Where fear clings to the past and the familiar, love thrives in the possibility of the unknown, always pushing you toward challenges that lead to a brighter future.

Moreover, most people make decisions as a mixture of love and fear. Rarely is a choice purely driven by one or the other; instead, love and fear often intertwine, shaping our actions and their consequences. The problem is that when decisions contain even a trace of fear, they create attachments, obligations, and unseen emotional burdens—both for ourselves and for those we try to help.

Let's go back to the example of a friend who has contracted a highly contagious virus. Many good-hearted people would step in to help. They might deliver food, check in regularly, or offer emotional support. But at the same time, they remain cautious. They wear masks, sanitize themselves before and after each visit, and keep their distance—doing their best to be kind while also minimizing their risk of getting infected. Their actions are commendable and reflect a sense of responsibility, yet they do not fully transcend fear.

This is where the deeper problem lies. While these people face their fear of illness, they do not overcome it. It's like entering a race but never reaching the finish line. They gain experience, but they do not achieve true success in moral or spiritual growth. Their walls of fear do not grow taller, but neither do they crumble. Fear remains, lingering quietly in the background, shaping their decisions in subtle ways.

Beyond that, their sense of obligation—the feeling that they should help because it's the right thing to do—places an unspoken burden on the sick friend. The friend, now feeling indebted, may struggle with guilt or feel pressure to reciprocate the kindness once they recover. Obligations create attachments, and attachments create invisible chains that bind people to one another—not in a way that deepens love, but in a way that weighs them down.

Even though these actions are helpful and admirable, they do not truly enhance one's ability to tread the path of spiritual enlightenment and moral growth. Decisions that are a blend of love and fear may serve a practical purpose, but they do not elevate the soul. True growth requires moving beyond obligation, beyond attachment, and beyond fear—to act purely out of love, free from hesitation, self-protection, or expectation of something in return.

Hug your sick friend. That hug might do more for their recovery than the medicine you bring. Touch has power. It carries warmth, reassurance, and healing that no pill or prescription can replicate. When you embrace them, you are telling them, I am here. I am not afraid. You are still you, and I still love you.

Sit with them. Talk with them. Look them in the eyes and speak to them as you always have. Do not treat them like they are fragile or broken. Do not let their illness define them. Let them feel, even for a moment, that life is still normal, that they are still part of it, that they are not isolated or cast aside.

Do not hesitate. Do not shrink away. If you act uncomfortable around them, they will feel it. If you keep your distance, they will notice. The last thing they need is to feel like a burden, like their presence is something to be endured rather than embraced. Make them feel loved, not avoided. Make them feel valued, not pitied.

You are not just there to offer medicine or practical help. You are there to offer presence. Real presence. The kind that says, I see you. I accept you. I am not going anywhere. Because love is the most powerful healing force of all.

The next time you're faced with a decision, ask yourself, "Am I making this choice out of fear or out of love? Am I clinging to what is, or am I embracing the potential of what could be? Am I fully committing, or am I holding back, hesitant by fear to align my actions with my deepest values and purpose?" Know that if your decision is rooted in fear, you will likely feel trapped and unfulfilled. However, if you face that same fear and make your decision with love and vulnerability, you will overcome it, and in the process, you will make better choices that lead to a sense of satisfaction and fulfillment.

Love is always within your reach. No matter the challenges you face, you can choose love—love for yourself, love for those around you, and love for the life that has been gifted to you. Let love guide your perception: see through love, hear through love, and sense the world through love. When you choose love, you unlock the best version of yourself, closing the gap between you and your soul, and bringing your soul into the light.

We could discuss the meaning of love until the end of time, but even eternity would not be enough to fully define it. Love is too vast, complex, and labyrinthine to be entirely grasped by the human mind. What we have explored so far offers only a glimpse into the essence and characteristics of love. The only way to truly understand love is to open your heart and your mind to its radiant light, and let yourself experience the warmth, comfort, and transformative power that love brings.

Chapter 14: Orders of love

Just as truth weaves its way through reality, layer by layer, so too does love. Just as understanding of truth begins within, so too does love. The path of enlightenment is an inward expedition—a journey where the understanding of any concept must first take root in the self. And at the heart of this journey lies self-love, the first step toward understanding love in its purest form.

What would it feel like to truly love yourself? To cradle your entire being in the warm, unconditional embrace of love? Love is neither selective nor conditional. It does not demand perfection, nor does love withhold itself until you become someone better. Self-love begins with acceptance—embracing every part of who you are today.

True self-love does not discriminate. It does not cherry-pick the traits that seem worthy. Instead, it asks you to stand in the light of your strengths and the shadow of your flaws, to face both your triumphs and your failures with equal compassion. True self-love invites you to acknowledge the imperfections, the wounds, and even the darkness within you—not to deny or hide them, but to embrace them as integral parts of your character.

To love yourself is to claim all of you. It is to see beauty in the messy, the broken, and the whole, knowing that together they form who you are today. Self-love gives you the clarity and strength to see your own naked truth. Stop fighting against your own nature and start accepting it. Recognize your flaws and imperfections with clarity. This acceptance is not surrender or complacency—it is the foundation of authentic growth. In other words, loving yourself is not about settling for your flaws but to create a space where meaningful change can flourish.

Instead of feeling ashamed or guilty about your imperfections, approach your weaknesses with kindness. Shift your perspective from self-criticism and rejection to acceptance and compassion. Let this love take root in the deepest corners of your being—allow it to flow into the parts of yourself you struggle to accept. Let it soften the hard edges of self-judgment and heal the fractures of self-rejection.

Stop fighting with yourself, as if you must be someone other than who you are at this very moment. You are here, now, exactly as you are—and that is okay. Each of us carries flaws, imperfections, and aspects of ourselves we wish to change. This shared struggle is part of the human experience; you are not alone in it.

Paradoxically, the parts of yourself you dislike most are the ones most deserving of love. The flaws you criticize, the weaknesses you try to hide, the mistakes that haunt you—these are not signs that you are unworthy. They are the parts of you that are wounded, seeking healing, waiting to be acknowledged with kindness rather than condemnation.

Think about a child who is struggling, acting out, or feeling lost. Would you scold them endlessly, push them away, and tell them they don't deserve love? Or would you comfort them, help them understand their struggles, and guide them with patience? Your rejected parts are no different. They are not obstacles to be destroyed—they are wounds to be healed.

You cannot hate yourself into becoming a better person. Self-rejection does not lead to growth—self-acceptance does. When you embrace your imperfections instead of running from them, you create space for transformation. When you offer love to the parts of yourself you once shunned, they begin to soften, evolve, and integrate into a healed version of you.

Paradoxically, your deepest struggles are your greatest opportunities for growth. Love is not reserved for the perfect—it is the very thing that makes healing and growth possible. The moment you stop seeing your flaws as proof of your unworthiness and start seeing them as parts of yourself in need of compassion, you begin the journey toward true self-acceptance.

To strive for goodness, to live with integrity, is no small feat—and everyone grapples with it. You are no different, no less deserving of love than anyone else. If anyone in this world deserves love, so do you. Self-love understands how challenging the path of enlightenment can be and encourages you to be patient with yourself.

So, lay down the burden of self-criticism and rejection. Accept yourself as you are—not to stay the same, but to build a foundation for growth that is rooted in love and understanding. Let love be the force that guides you forward, embracing every part of who you are.

Once you fully accept yourself for who you are and become comfortable in your own skin, the next step is to believe in yourself. Believe in your potential to grow. Self-belief is more than just confidence; it is the unshakable trust that you are capable of growth, that your efforts matter, and that your journey holds meaning. It is the force that drives you forward even when the path is unclear, even when doubt whispers in your ear.

To believe in yourself means to trust in your ability to evolve. It is the understanding that who you are today is not the final version of you. You are a work in progress, and every effort, every failure, every moment of struggle is shaping you into something greater. Strive to be better today than you were yesterday. Growth is not about proving your worth to the world; it is about honoring the potential that already exists within you.

Trust in the possibility of change and in the promise of a brighter future. Even when the world seems to weigh heavily against you, hold onto the belief that within you lies the strength to overcome any obstacle. There will be moments of doubt, times when it feels like progress is slow or nonexistent. But self-belief is not about never doubting—it is about choosing to move forward despite the doubt. It is about replacing fear with trust, replacing hesitation with action, and replacing self-judgment with patience and perseverance.

Believe in your ability to rise. Believe that you are capable of transforming your life. Believe that, no matter how many times you fall, you have within you the power to stand again. Powered by love, fueled by purpose, strive to become the person you are destined to be. Not because you lack anything now, but because within you already exists everything you need to grow, thrive, and transcend.

Acceptance and self-belief together create a psychological force so powerful it can reshape your life. They give you the courage to transform, the clarity to see what needs to change, and the strength to act. With self-acceptance as your foundation and self-belief as your motivation, no challenge is insurmountable.

In an experiment conducted in 2016, known as the "Batman Effect" students were given an impossible puzzle to solve. The students were unaware that the task cannot actually be completed. One group wore ordinary clothing, while the other donned "hero capes" of their favorite superheroes.

The results were astonishing. Those in ordinary attire gave up quickly, resigning themselves to the task's difficulty. But those in hero capes persisted far longer. Fueled by a sense of empowerment, they clung fiercely to hope, demonstrating remarkable resilience and determination. They came up with incredibly creative tactics to solve that impossible puzzle.

Life often feels like that impossible puzzle. Achieving your dreams requires a strength that sometimes feels beyond your current capacity. This is where the power of acceptance and self-belief steps in. They are your mental superhero cape, equipping you with resilience and determination to keep moving forward, no matter how tough the journey might be.

So, every day, put on your invisible superhero cape. Accept yourself as you are, love yourself, and believe in the boundless potential within you, waiting to be unleashed. Meet life's challenges head-on, not with fear or hesitation, but with hope and determination. You have everything you need to fight for your dreams—now, rise and turn your dreams into reality.

Your body and mind together form a sacred temple that you dwell within, and you are also the devoted caretaker of this temple. Your body and mind deserve your utmost care, respect, and affection. Self-love calls upon you to fulfill this sacred duty by nurturing yourself in ways that honor your well-being. However, self-love whispers caution, reminding you that indulgence is not the same as care. Make sure you are not mistaking self-love for something it is not.

It's easy to confuse momentary pleasures with acts of self-love. Hours lost in the phone screen, impulsive shopping sprees, overeating, or overdrinking may feel like comfort and joy in the moment, but these fleeting distractions are not the essence of self-love. Even treating yourself to extravagant vacations, delicious meals, or luxurious outings doesn't align with self-love. These are illusions—temporary escapes, the devil's whispers of, "You deserve this ease. Indulge in pleasure." Pleasure is not love. Fleeting desires and momentary temptations are not self-love. Desires and pleasures may promise fulfillment, but they deliver only a temporary sense of relief—accompanied by lingering dissatisfaction. But real love, whether for yourself or others, is not about ease or comfort; it requires sacrifice through hardship before the reward.

Love is forged in the crucible of hardship. Without facing challenges, you cannot truly understand or cultivate love. It is after the darkest hours of the night that the sky begins to brighten. It is only after pushing your limits during a workout that your muscles feel healthier and stronger. It is only after resisting the allure of unhealthy foods that your body thrives.

The principles of love are no different. Love is priceless. No amount of money or pleasure can ever buy you love. You must endure hardship before you can truly access love. Self-love and self-discipline are inseparable companions, while temptations, momentary pleasures, and fleeting desires stand as adversaries to true self-love.

Every time you resist the temptation of short-term gratification and choose the path of effort and discipline, you are practicing self-love. Love is found in the willingness to sacrifice immediate pleasure for lasting growth. Love reveals itself in the choices that nurture your body and mind.

True self-love uplifts you. It strengthens you from within and prepares you to face life's challenges with grace. To love yourself is to honor the temple of your being with actions that align with your highest values. Caring for yourself, rooted in discipline, is the ultimate act of self-love.

Self-love doesn't mean giving up on life's pleasures; rather it requires a shift in perspective on how you perceive pleasure. It's not about denying yourself joy but redefining what brings you joy in a way that aligns with your well-being. Numbing your mind with drugs, alcohol, lust, overeating, or elevating your social status through greed and vanity are not acts of self-love. These fleeting pleasures ultimately drain you rather than nurture you.

True pleasure that stems from self-love lies in appreciating life's simplest joys. Can you savor the refreshing taste of a glass of water rather than craving a sugary soda? Can you find satisfaction in eating a wholesome salad instead of indulging in a greasy cheeseburger? Can you feel the beauty of waking early to watch the sunrise instead of rolling around in bed all morning?

Self-love finds joy in the choices that nourish your body, mind, and soul. It delights in the effort it takes to exercise, knowing the vitality it brings, rather than sinking onto the couch for hours of idle comfort. It appreciates the challenge of reading a thought-provoking book, expanding your mind, rather than passively consuming endless episodes on Netflix.

Pleasure born of love demands effort—it asks you to choose what is challenging and ultimately rewarding over what is easy but meaningless. It's not about deprivation; it's about elevation. The secret to self-love is to turn even the simplest things in life into sources of joy and satisfaction.

The song "Somewhere Only We Know" by Keane captures this concept beautifully, weaving its message into a melody that speaks to the heart. The lyrics begin with simplicity: "I walked across an empty land. I knew the pathway like the back of my hand. I felt the earth beneath my feet, sat by the river and it made me complete." These words evoke an image of serenity, not in extravagance or adventure, but in the quiet appreciation of life's little moments.

He walks across an empty land, not some magical, faraway place; It's ordinary, with little scenery. The path isn't a new trail filled with surprises and wonders but one he has walked countless times, as he knew the pathway like the back of his hand. He talks about feeling the earth beneath his feet—something we all experience daily but rarely notice. Then he sits by the river, finding a profound sense of completeness in that simple act. This isn't a scene of extraordinary luxury or excitement. What brings him fulfillment is the unadorned beauty of being present, sensing peace within, and connecting with the small, simple things that we often take for granted.

As the song continues, the tone shifts, laced with a subtle sadness: "Oh simple thing, where have you gone? I'm getting old, and I need something to rely on." These lines resonate deeply with many people. Keane, despite their fame and fortune, reflect on a universal truth: the more we chase external pleasures—money, comfort, recognition—the further we seem to drift from the true sources of joy. The simplicity that once brought wholeness now feels distant, overshadowed by the distractions of earthly glamour. Keene members are now rich and famous but when they talk about real joy, they talk about the simple things.

Ironically, what many of us believe will bring us happiness—more wealth, more possessions, more comfort—is actually the root of our discontent. Fame and riches, though alluring, can dull our sensitivity to life's simple joys. Keane's longing for that quiet completeness by the river reminds us that real happiness isn't found in material abundance but in the ability to appreciate life's unassuming moments.

The song serves as a poignant reminder to pause and reconnect with the simple things we often overlook: the feel of the ground beneath our feet, the gentle murmur of a river, the serenity of a familiar path. These are the moments that ground us, bring us peace, and make us feel whole. This is the essence of self-love.

When you love yourself, you become both the caregiver and the one being cared for. You start making choices that support your health, growth, and happiness, choices that are unconventional and often challenging. While many people seek to escape difficulty for comfort or trading simplicity for the busyness of a complex life, you can choose to move in the opposite direction. Simplify, slow down, and embrace the path less traveled—not because it is easier, but because it matters and holds deeper meaning.

When you become disciplined in making choices that truly benefit you—like eating healthier or avoiding harmful habits—you start to find joy in those decisions, even when they are difficult or go against your immediate desires. Over time, you realize that living a disciplined life, making sacrifices, and finding joy in little things fulfill you far more than any Earthly glamours.

We've all heard the saying, "You are what you eat," but even more powerful is the truth that you are what you think and feel. Your thoughts and feelings shape your inner world, directly influencing your mental landscape and well-being. To truly love yourself, actively cleanse your mind and heart of negativity and safeguard yourself against the intrusion of harmful thoughts and feelings.

One of the devil's greatest deceptions is to make you believe that you're not good enough—not attractive enough, not worthy of love, not deserving to be accepted. These thoughts weigh you down, making you feel out of place in your own life, burdened by shame and insecurity. These negative thoughts and feelings stem from a deep-seated desire to be accepted by others.

The truth is, no one is perfect, and perfection isn't the key to love or acceptance. No one can ever be accepted by everyone. There will always be those who disapprove of you or misunderstand you. If you constantly seek validation and acceptance from the outside world, you will find yourself trapped in an endless cycle of disappointment and inadequacy. Relying on others for your sense of worth will always leave you feeling like something is missing, as if you are unloved or unworthy.

The way to break free from this cycle lies within you. Create love within yourself, for yourself. Become the source and receiver of your own love. You deserve your own love, no matter what flaws or imperfections you believe you have. No one can take self-love away from you except you. It is a gift you give yourself, and it is yours to protect.

The world's opinions, judgments, and standards do not define your worth. No matter what others think or say, you are worthy of your own love. You are not too flawed, too imperfect, too ugly, or too unlovable to not deserve your own love. Self-love isn't about achieving an ideal image or meeting society's standards—it's about accepting who you are, as you are, and choosing to treat yourself with kindness and compassion.

When you embrace self-love, you free yourself from the need for external validation. You begin to fill the void within you that no amount of approval from others can ever truly fill. Loving yourself will fulfill you more than anyone else ever could because you realize that your worth is not defined by anyone else but you.

Humanity has a tendency to outwardly project its inner self. What we believe about ourselves often becomes the lens through which we view the world and others. For example, a liar assumes that everyone else is also a liar, and a cheater believes that everyone cheats. This is because we mirror and reflect what is inside of us onto the outside world. When someone tells you that you are ugly or unworthy, it is often a reflection of how they see themselves. Their words are not truly about you; they stem from their own inner struggles and insecurities.

When people say you are unlovable or not good enough, it's because they see themselves in that way. Their criticisms are projections of their own misery, their own unresolved pain. On the other hand, those who love themselves encourage you to love yourself too. People who see beauty within themselves, they see your beauty as well.

However, be mindful not to fall into the trap of self-delusion. True self-awareness requires you to see your own image reflected in the mirror of reality. Acknowledge your flaws and embrace your strengths, but do so with honesty and humility. Avoid the pitfall of toxic positivity—don't sugarcoat your weaknesses or pretend they don't exist in an attempt to maintain an idealized image of yourself. Also be wary of those who shower you with excessive and unrealistic praise, cloaked in toxic positivity. Pay close attention to the person offering the praise. If they carry a self-inflated image of themselves—exuding arrogance or a detachment from reality—their comments, no matter how positive they appear, are not going to benefit you.

Praise disconnected from reality is ultimately harmful, even when it seems beneficial on the surface. It feeds illusions and creates a false image of yourself. True self-love is rooted in authenticity and knowing your genuine self, not an illusory version of who you are.

Toxic negativity reflects the inner struggles of those who wield it, while toxic positivity reveals a denial of reality. Neither serves your growth or well-being. Instead, anchor yourself in the realm of reality and truth. Surround yourself with those who speak honestly, authentically, and positively, as truth is the foundation upon which meaningful growth and genuine self-understanding are built.

This understanding is crucial: what others say about you often reveals more about them than about you. You have the power to choose how you respond. Ignore the toxicity, whether negative or positive. Instead, open yourself to the positivity of those who radiate self-love and kindness based on truth. Surround yourself with people whose words and actions uplift you and reflect the positivity you want to nurture within yourself.

Even though the words of others cannot change who you are at your core, positive words grounded in truth can inspire you. Positive words act as a spark, encouraging you to cultivate enough self-love and inner strength to transform yourself from within. True change always comes from within, but the encouragement of others who radiate truth, love, and positivity can be a guiding light on your journey toward self-acceptance and growth.

In January 2007, world-renowned violinist Joshua Bell participated in a social experiment orchestrated by The Washington Post. Dressed inconspicuously in jeans and a baseball cap, Bell performed six classical pieces on his $3.5 million Stradivarius violin at the L'Enfant Plaza Metro station in Washington, D.C., during the morning rush hour. Over approximately 45 minutes, more than 1,000 commuters passed by; only seven stopped to listen, and 27 people contributed a total of $32.17.

Just days earlier, Bell had played the same repertoire to a sold-out audience in Boston's Symphony Hall, where ticket prices averaged $100 each.

Remember, context and perception influence the recognition of talent and beauty. If Bell had confined his performances to subway stations, he would have perceived himself as an average musician, sensing a lack in his talent. However, by performing in venues where audiences value and understand his artistry, his exceptional talent is acknowledged.

Similarly, the people you surround yourself with significantly impact your self-perception. If you're among people who consistently undervalue or dismiss your abilities, you will start to internalize these negative beliefs. If you surround yourself with egotistical and narcissistic people who praise you out of arrogance, you will build a delusional image of yourself and inevitably fall short when confronted with reality. Conversely, surrounding yourself with those who recognize your potential will help you value your true worth and capabilities. Choose your environment and associations wisely.

As you take care of your physical appearance, remember to also invest time and energy in cultivating your inner beauty. Work on becoming more compassionate, speaking and acting with kindness, and embracing authenticity in everything you do. Self-love is a lifelong journey of growth and self-discovery. Strive to become a better version of yourself each day.

Take a moment to ask yourself: Am I surrounding myself with people who value inner beauty? Am I more compassionate, authentic, and kind than I was before? Am I gaining more control over my impulses and actions today than I did yesterday? If your answer is yes, then you are deepening your love for yourself. Keep walking this path, and you will continue to discover the unimaginable beauty and strength within you.

Self-love is the foundation from which you radiate love to the world. The love you give to others can only match the love you hold for yourself. If you cannot love yourself, it becomes impossible to love someone else—you cannot offer something to someone that you do not possess yourself.

When you learn to love yourself—when you accept both your strengths and weaknesses, embrace who you are without judgment, and forgive yourself for your mistakes—you open the door to loving others in the same way. By approaching your own imperfections with compassion and kindness, you develop the capacity to accept others as they are. You begin to see both the good and the bad in them without rejection, to forgive them for their wrongdoings, and to meet them with the same compassion and understanding you have shown yourself. By nurturing love within yourself, you create a wellspring of kindness and empathy that flows freely into your relationships, enriching your life and the lives of those around you.

As you cultivate self-love, it's equally important to practice loving others. The key to loving others is to let go of expectations. Expectations not only dilute the purity of love but also harm the ones you care about. Consider the example of a mother and her child.

At first, the mother's love is unconditional—pure and selfless. But as the child grows, expectations begin to creep in. The mother starts to expect good grades, acceptable behaviors, and achievements that align with her hopes and dreams. What was once pure love becomes conditional love. The mother, perhaps unknowingly, ties her love to the fulfillment of her desires for her child's success, turning love into a burden of obligation.

This shift places immense pressure on the child, who may feel trapped by the weight of these expectations. Conflicts arise as the child struggles to meet the demands of love that has become conditional. The father may behave in similar ways, adding to the pressure. The once-loving family environment becomes strained, and light of love begins to fade under the shadow of expectations.

Children respond to this tainted love in one of two ways. Some comply, becoming overly obedient, striving to meet their parents' demands to gain approval. These children grow into adults as people-pleasers, constantly seeking validation from others at the expense of their own happiness. Their lives become marked by an unrelenting effort to live up to expectations that never truly satisfy.

Other children rebel, rejecting the authority that feels oppressive. They turn to drugs, alcohol, or destructive behaviors, lashing out against the rules of the house and the expectations placed upon them. These children feel unaccepted for who they are, harboring deep anger and resentment toward their family and, eventually, society. They rebel against authority regardless of whether it is the law of the house or law of the land.

Both paths lead to psychological wounds. These children carry the scars of conditional love, struggling with feelings of inadequacy, resentment, and confusion. They develop complex relationships with their family members—loving and hating them simultaneously. These conflicts leave them uncertain and confused about their feelings, unable to reconcile the love and hurt they experience from the same person.

Love is the most powerful and transformative force in existence. It has the capacity to heal, uplift, and bring profound beauty to life. Yet, as magical as love is, if it becomes tainted by darkness, it turns into a force of destruction and chaos. When people let their love carry the shadows of their own unresolved pains, insecurities, and inner darkness, they pass that tainted love to others.

The beloved consumes the darkness of the tainted love. They become psychologically confused to receive something in the name of love that is so cold and dark. Instead of feeling cherished, they feel burdened and wounded.

This is why it is so vital to be mindful of how you love. Love purely, unconditionally, and without expectation. Love should never become a weight that your beloved has to bear; it should set them free. True love, when it asks for nothing in return, nurtures growth, fosters trust, and becomes a source of healing and connection.

By letting go of expectations and purging your love of any selfishness and darkness, you allow it to remain untainted. Such love uplifts those you care about, creating bonds that are genuine, supportive, and liberating. Seek only to give, not to gain.

Love is the ultimate servant. It gives freely, serves others with enthusiasm, and finds joy in the act of giving—all without asking for anything in return. When you carry pure love within you, you naturally offer it to others, accompanied by a willingness to sacrifice in the name of love. True love transforms service into a source of joy.

This selfless love creates a protective aura around you, shielding you from feelings of dissatisfaction and dysphoria. When you are rooted in pure love, you become nearly impossible to anger or upset. How can you become angry if you have no expectations? Pure love makes you whole. You become complete on your own and do not rely on others to define your worth.

Furthermore, when you give love purely, you open yourself up, vulnerable and exposed. Those who dwell in darkness will perceive your vulnerability as weakness, seeing your kindness as an opportunity to exploit you. However, in this openness, something remarkable happens—you begin to see people's true personalities. Love acts as a mirror, reflecting their hidden intentions. You will notice who stays by your side as a genuine friend and who lingers only to take advantage of your generosity.

Pure love sharpens your intuition, making you adept at recognizing the motives of those around you. When you realize someone is exploiting your kindness, love naturally guides you to protect yourself.

Without anger or resentment, you distance yourself from those who mean you harm. This act of distancing is not just a safeguard for you; it is also a lesson for them.

When they lose access to the gift of love they once received from you, they lose something profoundly valuable. This absence may compel them to reflect on their actions, reevaluate their choices, and perhaps even aspire to change for the better. Pure love transforms you into a better person and inspires those who come into contact with you to strive for self-improvement—even those with the darkest of hearts.

Do you remember how we discussed the importance of loving your own flaws and imperfections with compassion rather than rejection? How the most insecure parts of you are the ones most in need of your love? The same principle applies to others. If someone seems truly bad or lost, it's often because they've never experienced what real love is. Perhaps they've gone through life without ever receiving unconditional love—love free from expectations or judgments. These individuals, the ones who seem the furthest from love, are the ones who need it the most.

Imagine you have food to share—would you give it to someone who just finished a hearty meal or to someone who hasn't eaten in days? The same logic applies to love. Share your love with those who've been starved of it, even if they appear angry, bitter, or aggressive. Sometimes, the love you show them can spark a change, planting a seed that may grow and transform them forever.

However, if their aggression or negativity becomes harmful to you, it's okay to protect yourself by creating distance. Do so with kindness and understanding, showing them that your boundaries are not born from hatred but from self-respect. Let them see that even as you step away, you do not despise them. This approach leaves the door open for them to reflect, heal, and perhaps learn what love truly is.

Never give up on love. Even if you do not receive kindness in return, your pure love will leave an indelible mark on the hearts of those you encounter. Pure love has a way of lingering—it plants seeds of warmth and compassion that may one day grow, even in the most unlikely places. Your love can become a powerful legacy that touches others in ways they may not realize until much later.

Pure love holds the power to transform the world for the better. It has the potential to end wars, resolve conflicts, and bring joy and prosperity to the lives of every individual. Yet, despite its boundless potential, pure love remains one of the rarest treasures. And as with anything rare, its value is immeasurable. This is why we create countless songs, poems, and stories about love. Love is something we all long for, yet so few of us truly experience enough of it. The scarcity of pure love is why its presence is so deeply felt and why its absence is so profoundly missed.

True love is rare because it is often mistaken for things it is not. Love is not about pleasing others, obeying their demands, or seeking their approval. It is not lust, affection, or dependency. Nor is it the reliance on someone else to fill the emptiness within. Love cannot even be found in happiness or comfort.

The way most people analyze and understand love is often through the lens of romance. While romance can sometimes mirror love, in many cases, it stands in stark contrast to what love truly represents. Modern-day romance, as promoted by society, frames romantic love within the confines of lust, affection, dependency, and expectations.

These societal teachings contribute to the prevalence of broken families and relationships in our world today. Many relationships begin with the fleeting spark of lust and are built upon the fragile foundation of expectations and mutual dependencies. Partners demand many things from one another—financial support, emotional reassurance, acceptable behaviors—and over time, these demands grow. With rising expectations comes rising tension, leading to unresolved arguments and conflicts. Each clash becomes more heated, less tolerable, and further erodes the relationship's stability.

In such relationships, what keeps them going is not love but mutual dependency. The comfort of familiarity, the intensity of lust, or the illusion of security is frequently mistaken for love. The relationship becomes unhealthy when expectations overshadow mutual respect and support morphs into obligation. This is not love; this is a bond of dependency, built on need rather than genuine connection.

Many toxic relationships persist in a state of perpetual conflict, where arguments and dissatisfaction never seem to end. Those who remain together endure a constant cycle of clashing expectations, while others eventually separate, leaving both partners hurt and broken. Tragically, the aftermath of these separations often leads each partner to seek a new relationship with even more rigid expectations and demands, mistakenly believing that such conditions will lead to a better outcome. They fail to realize that it was precisely these expectations and dependencies that eroded their previous relationships in the first place.

This pattern reflects how most people experience what they call "love." They believe they loved their previous partners, not recognizing that true love was never present in their relationship. What they experienced was a mixture of fleeting lust, illusions of security, and emotional dependency. True love has a defining marker—it never fades. Love cannot turn into hate or indifference. Once love is genuine and present, it becomes a permanent state, unshaken even by separation. Love doesn't diminish or alter its perception of the beloved.

Real romantic love begins with genuine affection, not lust. Affection stems from a sense of true connection and bond. Sexual intimacy, within this context, is not merely a physical act but a profound spiritual union. True lovers are not entangled by emotional voids or unmet needs. They do not look to their partners to fill an emptiness they sense within or to use them as the source of their happiness. Instead, they are whole and content on their own, sharing their joy and smile with one another without expectations.

Such a relationship is built on generosity, not demands. Each partner focuses on what they can give rather than what they can receive. Their support is offered freely from a place of love, not as a response to obligation or dependency. The relationship thrives on openness and vulnerability. Partners feel safe sharing their insecurities, fears, and weaknesses, knowing they will not be judged or shamed. There is no pretense or hiding; everything is laid bare in truth.

True love also respects individuality and independence. Both partners are strong and capable of walking away if the relationship becomes irreparably toxic, yet they stay—not out of fear or dependency, but because they genuinely desire to be together. The door is always open for either partner to leave at any time, without needing to justify their choice. Yet, they make a deliberate choice to be with one another, every day, not because they must but because they want to. This freedom strengthens their bond rather than weakens it, as it is rooted in mutual respect, trust, and autonomy.

Even so, challenges are inevitable, even in the healthiest relationships. Arguments and conflicts will arise, but in relationships grounded in true love, these moments are handled differently. Disagreements are not fueled by unmet expectations but by shared struggles. They are resolved through understanding, open communication, and compromise. Instead of breaking the bond, such conflicts ultimately strengthen it, deepening the connection and reaffirming the choice to walk the path of love together.

When a relationship is rooted in trust, truth, and unconditional love, it becomes unshakable. Its foundation is stronger than anything external forces could break. Such a bond weathers the storms of daily struggles, standing strong. A relationship built on true love is rarer and stronger than a diamond.

What was described above is not limited to romantic relationships. True love transcends boundaries and can exist in any type of partnership or connection. Love can thrive between two people or among billions. It can flourish in friendships, business partnerships, sports teams, religious communities, music bands, or any group that shares a common bond.

Love is not confined by labels, roles, or circumstances. It exists wherever there is a willingness to give freely, without expectation, and to nurture trust, respect, compassion, and kindness. When love is present, it strengthens connections, fosters unity, and builds a foundation of mutual support and understanding. Whether it's a team working toward a common goal or a community seeking harmony, love has the power to uplift any relationship. True love knows no bounds and recognizes no barriers. You have the power to offer love to anyone, anywhere, at any time.

The best way to practice love is to start with small, everyday acts. If you give a coworker a ride, don't expect gas money or a favor in return.

If you cook dinner for your partner, don't expect them to do the dishes. When you visit a friend, don't expect to be fed. If you give money to someone in need, don't anticipate being repaid. Even when you speak, let go of expecting your audience to listen. By removing expectations from your daily life, you begin to understand and experience the true essence of giving love.

The responsibility to bring more love into this world rests on our shoulders—yours and mine. It is up to us to let go of our differences, cast aside our egos, and offer love freely to one another. Let us humble ourselves before the immense power of love and embrace the role of its servant. To serve one another in the name of love—what could possibly be more meaningful or more noble?

Expectations act as barriers to love, stopping its natural flow. The less you expect, the greater your capacity to love. And as more people learn to give love freely, the world will naturally be filled with more love to be received.

When love for yourself merges with the love you extend to others in your daily interactions, you reach an elevated awareness of love, which I call the *higher order of love.* At this level, love brings you profound peace. You are no longer weighed down by disappointment or dissatisfaction caused by unmet expectations. Love will fill the void you sense within and removes all your emotional and psychological dependencies on others. You achieve mental stability, and your mood becomes more balanced. You embrace the world as it is, with all its imperfections, finding peace in the act of loving without conditions. And that peace born out of love brings you eternal joy and happiness.

Love can expand into an even more abundant and boundless form, reaching a state where it truly knows no limits. At this highest level, you see everything as interconnected by love. You love all things—regardless of labels or distinctions. King or peasant, good or bad, living or non-living—it all becomes one in your eyes. These differences no longer matter because you recognize divine perfection in all creation.

You begin to view the world as a masterpiece crafted by God, seeing through what can only be described as divine vision. The 13th-century mystic Meister Eckhart captured this profound truth when he said, "The eye with which I see God is the same eye with which God sees me." He understood that God perceives creation through the lens of pure love. Everything that has ever existed and everything that will ever exist is born of God's love. Therefore, the only way to truly sense God is through love.

When you learn to love yourself—not with vanity, but with compassion—and extend that love to those around you, to nature, and to all that has ever existed, both the beautiful and the painful, you begin to glimpse at the divine. Loving without reservation or condition allows you to see life as God sees it: through the lens of love.

As this love flows through you, it transforms your perception. The world, with all its flaws and wonders, becomes a reflection of divine beauty. Your heart becomes filled with an unshakable peace, joy, and connection—a sense of unity with all of existence. In that moment, you are no longer just a spectator in the divine masterpiece; you are a part of it, experiencing life as God intended: through love, for love, and as love.

In this state of awareness, everything becomes a reflection of divine love. You no longer judge or separate things but instead embrace all as part of the same wondrous creation. To see and understand the world in this way is to live fully within love, viewing all of existence through the lens of unity and compassion.

In this level, you will embody love, even when faced with the darkest challenges or adversaries. Even in the presence of the devil himself, your love remains unwavering. One of the most profound examples of this level of love is the story of Jesus.

There is a reason why the story of Jesus has endured through the ages, shining brightly across centuries, even to this day. Whether you are a believer or an atheist, whether Jesus was a historical figure or a fictional character in an old story, the truth at the core of his story remains undeniable. It carries an eternal and unchanging message that transcends beliefs and interpretations.

Jesus's life is the story of love in its purest form. It teaches the depth, resilience, and boundless nature of love—a love that forgives, embraces, and sacrifices without expectation or condition.

At this level, fear, hate, and anger dissolve completely in the power of love. You no longer see differences between a friend and a foe—love flows unconditionally to all. Love becomes a servant of the entire world, bringing compassion and kindness to everyone it touches. It smiles at a friend with the same warmth it smiles at an enemy. It loves an enemy just as deeply as it loves a friend.

True love embraces every soul that has ever existed and will ever exist. It is untouched by darkness, shining with a brilliance that transforms everything it touches. Where love resides, darkness cannot remain. Love illuminates with its radiant glory, driving away shadows and leaving only light.

In this state, love becomes the ultimate force of harmony. It replaces chaos with peace, bridging divides and soothing the turmoil of the world. Light of love brightens even the darkest corners.

Eyewitnesses recount that when Mahatma Gandhi faced his assassin, he did not turn to run or shield himself from harm. Instead, he stood firm, bowing his head in a gesture of forgiveness. He met his fate with grace, taking three bullets to the chest. Many, driven by fear or anger, might have turned away, taking the bullets in their back, but Gandhi chose to face his assassin with the power of love and compassion. With his final breath, he forgave the man who shot him, embodying the ultimate expression of love even in the face of death and betrayal.

Gandhi's understanding of love did not end with him. When the assassin and his co-defendants were captured and sentenced to death, Gandhi's sons, Manilal and Ramdas, appealed to the court to commute their sentences. Inspired by their father's teachings, they too showed an extraordinary measure of love and forgiveness.

Mahatma Gandhi understood what Jesus meant when he said, "Love thy enemy." In his final breath, Gandhi demonstrated the depth of his understanding of love. He lived and died by its principles, showing the world that even in the darkest of moments, love has the power to prevail over fear, anger, and hate.

When love transcends all boundaries and reaches a state of infinite expansion, it dissolves every anxiety and worry. Even the fear of death loses its power, for true love brings a profound, unshakable peace that nothing can take away. Whether in life or in death, true love remains calm, steady, and unwavering. It becomes a shield for the soul, impenetrable by anything. Even the devil itself is powerless and without a weapon in the presence of love.

This is what I call *the supreme order of love*. When you attain this level of love, you are filled with an unparalleled sense of peace. You no longer experience anger or hatred, for such emotions have no place in a heart that overflows with infinite love. Your calmness and serenity become a reflection of your inner transformation, a testament to the highest state of being that any human can achieve.

To reach this supreme order of love is to reach the pinnacle of inner peace, where nothing external can disturb the harmony within. Siddhartha Gautama, known as the Buddha, understood the supreme order of love when he said, "The path of enlightenment is the end of suffering." He revealed that the only way to end human mental suffering is to find true peace, and to find peace, one must understand the highest orders of love and truth.

When you achieve absolute peace, your mind becomes a tranquil sanctuary. The inner turmoil of mental arguments fades away, and the voices in your head grow calm and quiet. Chaos, anxiety, excessive stress, sorrow, and even sadness lose their hold on you. You enter a state of bliss where peace and happiness govern your daily life. In this state, whether you dwell in a king's castle or a king's dungeon, your happiness remains unshaken. You are no longer influenced by the outside world because your peace and joy come from within.

The supreme order of love is so powerful, so profound, that its essence is beyond the understanding of most people. Yet, for those who grasp and live by it, love transforms their lives entirely. To embody this love is to transcend suffering and embrace a state of unparalleled tranquility and fulfillment.

There is nothing easy about attaining truth and love in life. To reach them, you must possess a burning, unwavering desire and dedicate every moment of your life to this pursuit. Truth and love demand continuous practice and commitment; only through such effort do you stand a chance of obtaining them. On the path to enlightenment, there are no shortcuts.

If you allow yourself to be led by fleeting desires and temptations, the path to truth and love will remain out of reach. Luck plays no role in understanding the higher concepts in life. Enlightenment is not a matter of chance; it is the result of deliberate choice, discipline, and perseverance. Only those willing to dedicate themselves fully to this journey will uncover the profound beauty of truth and love.

Let's step back and revisit the picture we're painting here. As we discussed earlier, a tree needs light, water, and fertile soil to thrive and grow. In much the same way, the human soul requires truth, love, responsibility, and good intention to flourish and come into the light. In this comparison, if light represents truth and water symbolizes love, then soil is responsibility and intention.

Truth and love do not reveal themselves to just anyone—they present themselves only to those who embrace the role of responsible warriors with good intentions. Responsibility and good intentions are the foundation upon which truth and love can be understood. Just as an apple seed cannot grow and harness the benefits of light and water without the grounding support of soil, you cannot fully embrace and utilize truth and love without first taking responsibility with good intentions for yourself and your life. Responsibility and good intentions anchor your soul, making it possible for truth and love to help your spiritual growth.

A tree must grow strong roots in the soil to support its weight, absorb water and nutrients, and lift itself toward the sky. When your personality is firmly rooted in responsibility and good intentions then you gain the strength to withstand the weight of daily struggles, draw upon the transformative power of love, and fuel your spiritual growth toward the infinite sky of truth.

Without roots, a tree cannot stand tall; likewise, without a personality grounded in responsibility and good intention, you cannot sustain the journey of spiritual growth. These roots of personality anchor you, nourish you, and give you the strength to rise above challenges, allowing your soul to stretch toward the boundless heights of enlightenment.

Truth gives you the "why"—the reason you must walk the path of enlightenment. Love shows you the "how"—the way to navigate this journey. Responsibility, paired with good intention, provides the "what"—the actions you must take to move forward.

When you take full responsibility for your life, every piece of the puzzle comes together. You understand exactly what you need to do at this moment to ease your suffering. You know how to approach each problem through the lens of love; and truth gives you the clarity to understand why you are doing it, even in your darkest days.

With truth, love, responsibility and good intention working together, you gain a complete guide: the purpose, the method, and the action. Knowing why you walk, how to walk, and what steps to take, you tread the path of enlightenment with confidence and clarity.

Chapter 15: Responsibility and Intention

Like everything else on the path of enlightenment, responsibility begins with the self. So, what are your responsibilities to yourself? The simple answer is "everything." You are responsible for every aspect of your life—your current situation, your failures, your successes, and every good and bad thing that has happened to you or will happen in the future. Responsibility for your entire life rests with you.

It's true that many bad things have happened and will continue to happen to you that are not your fault. But just because something isn't your fault, it doesn't mean you are not responsible for addressing the mess you find yourself in.

Let's consider an extreme example. Perhaps your parents abused or abandoned you, or you grew up in an orphanage where you were mistreated and neglected. Such experiences leave deep emotional, psychological, and even physical scars. You may carry traumas imposed upon you by others that ignite anger within you, chronic depression that lingers, or anxiety attacks that grip you without warning. All these struggles may stem from the terrible hand you were dealt with as a child.

You are not to blame for being treated unjustly as a child. But here's the hard truth: that does not relieve you of the responsibility to heal yourself. If you are sad and depressed because of what others did to you, it is not their responsibility to fix you. In most cases, they won't and can't fix you. The responsibility to climb out of the swamps of sadness lies with you alone. You must find a way to control your anxiety, address your trauma, and reclaim your peace—because no one else can do it for you, even if they want to.

People can and often will hurt you and break you, but they can never fix you. Healing is a deeply personal journey, one that requires you to take ownership of your pain and transform it into strength. This is not an easy path, but it is the only path to true liberation. Responsibility is about recognizing your power to change and grow despite what has happened to you. Only you can take those steps forward.

Some of us were born into this world with disadvantages and disabilities. Perhaps you are missing a limb, have physical features that society deems less attractive, or face physical challenges like the inability to hear or see. Maybe you live with a genetic or neurological condition such as Down syndrome or cerebral palsy. If you are one of these individuals, you have started life with a unique set of challenges—a disadvantage in a world that often values perfection.

But do not feel pity for yourself, and do not seek pity from others. Pity will not serve you or empower you. Though you may have a disadvantage, it does not diminish the tremendous power that exists within you. That power—the essence of your spirit—is just as potent as it is in anyone else. Your physical limitations have no bearing on the strength of your soul.

Rise above your disabilities and embrace the truth of who you are. You have the capacity to contribute, to create, and to inspire. Claim your rightful status in the world, not by focusing on what you lack, but by harnessing the incredible potential that lies within you. Your journey may be more challenging, but it is no less meaningful—and your ability to rise above challenges is what will make you extraordinary.

Consider the inspiring example of Sean Stephenson. Born with Brittle Bone Disease, his bones were so fragile they could break from something as simple as sneezing. Doctors believed he wouldn't survive beyond 24 hours after his birth, yet he defied the odds and lived for 40 remarkable years. Standing just three feet tall, with small, crippled arms and legs and a funny-looking face, he could neither walk nor lift anything heavier than a book. Nearly every bone in his body had been broken at some point, subjecting him to excruciating pain—pain so intense it surpasses anything most of us could ever imagine.

Despite these challenges, Sean achieved extraordinary accomplishments. He worked for Bill Clinton and an Illinois Congressman, wrote several books, and became a successful motivational speaker, inspiring countless people around the world. He even managed to get married. Sean was a strong man in a fragile body, who claimed to experience a level of happiness and peace beyond what most people could fathom. Though his life was filled with pain, it was also filled with purpose, joy, and fulfillment. He lived a painful but happy life. If Sean Stephenson could live a fulfilling life despite his circumstances, so can you.

In his TEDx talk, "The Prison of Your Mind," Sean powerfully highlighted the detrimental effects of pity—whether directed at oneself or others—and how it hinders personal growth. He began by stating, "If somebody pities me, they're wasting their time, because I have chosen a life of strength." Sean urged his audience to reject pity and instead embrace personal strength and resilience. He further emphasized that self-pity is the "worst drug that ever hit the human race," as it leaves individuals "completely frozen in potential."

Sean introduced three transformative concepts in his speech. The first is: "Never believe a prediction that doesn't empower you." He shared the story of how doctors predicted he wouldn't survive beyond 24 hours after his birth. Yet, more than 30 years later, he stood—or rather, sat in his wheelchair—before his audience, defying that prediction.

You, too, shall refuse to let others' pessimism or doubt bring you down. The predictions and judgments of others do not define your potential. Instead, focus on beliefs and actions that uplift and empower you to rise beyond limitations, just as Sean did.

The second concept Sean highlighted was: "You are not your condition." Born with Brittle Bone Disease, Sean refused to let his condition define or limit him. Instead, he chose to celebrate life and pursue happiness and success, reaching heights that many only dream of.

You, too, shall refuse to believe that your conditions or life circumstances define your potential. Your limitations are self-imposed illusions, not genuine barriers. Your potential is infinite, shaped not by the challenges you face but by the strength, resilience, and determination you bring to overcome them. Believe in your boundless capability and pursue the life you deserve.

Sean concluded his talk with a profound message: "The only prison is in your mind." He explained, "The real prisons do not have guards. The real prison is up here," he said, pointing to his head. "And we all got it." He went on, "When you love yourself—whether you're sleeping on a prison cot or in a mansion, whether you have food in your belly or don't know when your next meal is coming—when you learn to master your emotions, then and only then are you free."

This mental prison you live in is entirely self-created. You are both the prisoner and the warden. And here's the truth—your prison door has always been open. And the choice to walk out... that's yours to make. You have the ability to walk out of your mental prison. Free yourself from the self-limiting beliefs that keep you confined. The key to your freedom is in your hands. Embrace the strength within you, step out of the mental constraints you've built, and live a life defined by possibility, courage, and boundless potential.

Refuse to indulge in pity—whether for yourself or for anyone else. Pity saps strength, stifles growth, and chains you to stagnation. Do not let the negativity or pessimism of others drag you down and hold you back. Reject the notion that your circumstances or conditions dictate your identity and potential. Most importantly, avoid constructing a mental prison out of your own self-imposed limiting beliefs.

Now, let's look at responsibility from a different angle. It's easy to point out problems and assign blame to others, but it's far more challenging—and meaningful—to seek solutions. Once, there was a talented artist who wanted to understand how people viewed his work. He decided to conduct a little experiment. He painted a beautiful picture—a masterpiece he was proud of—and placed it on a busy street. Beside the painting, he left a note that said, "If you see any mistakes, please point them out by marking the painting."

Then, he left it there and walked away.

When he returned the next day, his heart sank. The painting was filled with marks. People had scribbled all over it, pointing out flaws everywhere. Some marks were on areas he hadn't even considered problematic. His once-beautiful painting was now covered in criticism.

The artist was heartbroken but determined to learn something from this experience. He went back to his studio, cleaned up the painting, and decided to try again. This time, he added a twist.

He placed the same painting on the same street, but now, the note read, "If you see any mistakes, please fix them yourself."

Then, he left it and waited.

When he returned the next day, to his surprise, the painting was untouched. Not a single person had tried to fix anything. The same people who had been quick to criticize the painting before, now didn't bother to do anything when asked to take action.

It's easy to criticize and point out flaws, but when it comes to solving problems or making things better, most people hesitate or simply don't act.

Pointing out flaws in a painting is similar to a victimhood mentality. There is never a shortage of victims who are quick to criticize and judge the flaws of others. However, when it comes to offering tangible solutions, they never step forward. In contrast, those with a responsible mindset are far fewer, but they focus on finding solutions rather than merely highlighting problems. Complaining only adds to the problem, while taking responsibility makes you part of the solution. Always strive to be part of the solution, not part of the problem.

The greatest obstacle to success is adopting a victim mentality—focusing on flaws and blaming the world, destiny, circumstances, or others for one's lack of achievement. Those who fall into this mindset see others as villains while portraying themselves as powerless, helpless, and innocent bystanders. They believe that politicians are robbing them of their freedom or that business leaders are stealing their opportunities for success. Victims perceive the world as a hostile place filled with bad people, intent on using and abusing them. They drown themselves in self-pity.

This mindset becomes a convenient way to shift blame onto others for all the problems in their lives and the world. By pointing fingers and casting others as responsible for fixing their issues, they absolve themselves of the obligation to take meaningful action. In doing so, they stagnate their own growth and miss the opportunity to create positive change for themselves and others.

This mindset is disempowering and a significant barrier to progress. Do not adopt a victim mentality. Blaming your parents for their lack of support, society for the challenges you face, or your friends for your bad habits may feel justified, but it robs you of the opportunity to take control of your life. Shifting blame onto others demotivates you from taking action and creates a false sense of helplessness. Focus on what you could have done better so you can learn and grow, rather than searching for where others fell short.

The truth is, you cannot change your parents, your society, or anyone else in the world. The only true power you have is to make changes to your own life. Acknowledge the problems within yourself and take responsibility for addressing them. Only by changing yourself for the better will your life truly improve.

If there exists a problem and you are not actively working to address it, then you are part of the problem. This is the irony of victimhood: victims are quick to point out all the issues in the world but fail to see how their own inaction contributes to the very problems they criticize.

Victims often say, "I didn't cause this; whoever did should fix it." But with that mentality, nothing ever gets resolved. Those who create chaos and destruction aren't going to suddenly turn into angels and undo what they have done. Waiting for someone else to clean up the mess is futile. Instead, it falls upon you and me to take responsibility for addressing and improving any issue in the world that affects our lives.

If there is something in your life that bothers you, it is your responsibility to either change yourself or change your circumstances so that it no longer troubles you. Waiting for someone else to rescue you, teach you, or provide the life you dream of is a futile gamble. Don't wait for miracles to occur, make them happen yourself.

Taking responsibility is about reclaiming the power to improve your life and contribute positively to the world. Growth and progress begin when you stop waiting for change and start creating it. Responsibility is not a burden—it is your liberation. Embrace responsibility, and you unlock the potential to create the life you truly desire.

Throughout your life, you truly have only two choices: take responsibility or embrace victimhood. Responsibility is the path to freedom, growth, and fulfillment, while victimhood only chains you to your struggles. You hold the reins, and the choice is yours. If you choose responsibility, you will live a tough but quality life. You will gain the power to make your own decisions and shape your own world.

Now, you may ask, how do I rise above the struggles and traumas I have battled with all my life? Let's consider an example. Suppose you were abused as a child, and each act of abuse filled you with anger. As a child, that anger may have served as a defense mechanism—a way to shield yourself from pain. But as an adult, that same anger arises whenever you witness injustice, reactivating your inner traumas that harm you more than they help. Anger, which once felt protective, now exacerbates your struggles and holds you back.

To rise above this, take responsibility for your anger. First, acknowledge its presence and accept it as part of yourself without judgment. Then, make the conscious decision to take control of it. Reflect and think of a solution that works for you and write it down. For example, you might write: "Every time I feel anger rising within me, I will close my eyes, take a few deep breaths, and stay silent. I will not express my anger outwardly while enraged but will reflect inwardly, extinguishing the flame of rage before it consumes me. Then, once I am calm, I will seek a solution to the issue that triggered my anger and address it with clarity and composure."

Commit to following this solution. Keep the note with you, and each time you feel anger rising, read it. If you've memorized it, close your eyes and repeat it in your mind. Practice this daily. Each time anger surfaces, stick to your commitment. Over time, this deliberate effort will rewire your reactions and transform your relationship with anger, allowing you to gain control over emotions that once dominated you.

If you lash out at the world when anger consumes you, you only amplify the rage within and worsen the situation rather than addressing the root of the problem. To truly understand the cause of your anger, you must confront it in moments of calmness, not while under its influence. When you control your emotions and allow yourself to settle, you create the mental space to examine the triggers of your anger with clarity and composure.

In this state of calmness, your mind naturally begins to seek solutions to the sources of your frustration. With time and patience, your mind will uncover the root causes of your suffering and develop strategies to resolve and remove them. This process teaches you self-control and trust in your ability to reflect and solve your problems. This is how you take responsibility for your situation—by seeking solutions instead of contributing to the problem.

The process is not instant, but with persistence, your mind will adapt, and the anger that once controlled you will lose its power. Rising above your struggles is about consistent, conscious effort—acknowledging your pain, taking responsibility, and creating actionable solutions to heal and grow.

Now, imagine you struggle with procrastination. Perhaps, as a child, you avoided responsibilities, and this habit became ingrained in your behavior. Now, as an adult, procrastination continues to hold you back, keeping you from reaching your goals and leaving you feeling stuck.

Start by taking responsibility. Recognize that procrastination isn't an external problem—it's a pattern within you that you can change. Write a simple action plan: "Every day, for the next seven days, I will tackle one small task that I've been avoiding, no matter how insignificant it feels. I will spend at least 20 minutes working on it, without distraction." This small commitment helps break the cycle of avoidance, building momentum over time.

When you take responsibility for your weaknesses, your mind naturally begins to search for solutions. These solutions may not come instantly, but with consistent effort, your mind will adapt and find innovative ways to overcome the challenges you face. It's a process of trial and error. Even if you're unsure how to address a problem, the key is to take action. Don't worry about whether your first attempt will succeed or not. Just try.

As the saying goes, "You miss 100% of the shots you don't take." Each attempt brings you closer to finding a solution that works. Whether it's overcoming anger, procrastination, or another challenge, persistence is your greatest ally. By taking responsibility and making deliberate efforts, you address your weaknesses and also build resilience and confidence that carry you forward. Success is not about perfection—it's about taking consistent action and learning from each step along the way.

Part of embracing responsibility is being ready to fail. Failure is a natural part of growth, especially when you're trying something new.

Most successful people in the world have one pattern in common. They have failed repeatedly. Michael Jordan, one of basketball's greatest legends, famously said, "I've missed more than 9,000 shots in my career. I've lost almost 300 games. Twenty-six times I've been trusted to take the game-winning shot and missed. I've failed over and over and over again in my life. And that is why I succeed."

Failure has been a part of your life since the beginning. As a child, you fell countless times before you learned to walk. You probably stumbled off a bicycle before mastering balance. You may have been rejected in job interviews but landed a position eventually.

Each time you failed, you got back up and tried again. So, why stop now? Success isn't about avoiding failure—it's about rising after every fall and continuing to move forward. Perseverance turns setbacks into stepping-stones, and every stumble brings you closer to where you want to be.

Imagine a child, after falling a few times, decided, "Maybe I'm not meant to learn to walk." With this mindset, no child would ever take their first step. It's the determination to rise after every fall that teaches a child to walk. Adulthood is no different. If you try something, fail, and convince yourself, "This isn't for me," or "I'm just not talented enough," or "I don't want to look foolish again," you will never succeed.

Embrace failure and be grateful for it. Every failure is a step closer to success. Each stumble is an opportunity to learn, grow, and refine yourself. Responsibility demands that you take ownership of your actions and persist through setbacks.

Moreover, responsibility is a powerful source of motivation. When you take responsibility for something, it pulls you off the couch and away from distractions, compelling you to take meaningful action in your life.

For example, if you're unhappy with your body and feel overweight, take responsibility by telling yourself, "I am responsible for my body, and it is my duty to care for it and not neglect it." This statement becomes a powerful call to action, shifting your mindset from blame to empowerment.

Next, create a personalized plan that works for you and build upon it over time. Start with small, actionable steps, like writing a note that states: "I will begin my day with a light and healthy breakfast for a week." If you stumble, don't give up—try again until you succeed. Once you feel more confident, expand your plan: "I will also avoid eating after sundown and eliminate processed foods from my diet."

Commit to following your plan consistently. Over time, as you stick to your plan, you will begin to see positive changes—not just in your body, but in your confidence and discipline.

Responsibility doesn't leave room for excuses. It pushes you to resist temptations—like late-night snack binges—and stand firm against desires that undermine your goals. Most life struggles stem from giving into desires and temptations and satisfying more of your desires will never solve your problems. If you want a different outcome, you must become a different person. Change happens when the old version of you perishes and a new version of you that thinks and acts differently takes its place.

In a nutshell, never adopt a victim mentality. It avoids responsibility and lacks the power to create meaningful change. Those who see themselves as victims perceive life as beyond their control, leaving them feeling helpless and powerless. To create solutions and move forward, focus on taking responsibility and reclaiming your power to make a difference.

You are responsible for every aspect of your life—whether it's the trauma you experienced in childhood, the injustices inflicted upon you by others, or the consequences of the wrong choices you've made. If you want to change your life, you must take full responsibility for making that change a reality.

Responsibility drives you to step out of your comfort zone, to do what you've never done, and to become someone you've never been. It sparks motivation and innovation, encouraging you to try new approaches and explore different paths until you uncover a solution to your challenges.

Responsibility also demands persistence. It teaches you not to view failure as a final destination but as a stepping-stone toward success. Every failure carries a lesson, offering insights into your missteps and guiding you closer to your goals. In every aspect of life, responsibility is not about blame—it's about stepping up, finding solutions, and making a difference.

Once you take responsibility for your own life, you must also extend that responsibility to the people and environment around you. If a friend is sick and has no one else to help them, and you have the time and energy, it becomes your responsibility to step in. If your workplace is toxic, it is your responsibility to reduce that toxicity in whatever ways you can. If you've been betrayed by your partner, responsibility calls for taking action to find the root cause of your own missteps toward betrayal to ensure it doesn't catch you off guard again. Even if you are dissatisfied with your country's leadership, it becomes your responsibility to find constructive ways to advocate for change.

As mentioned earlier, you have only two choices in life: to take responsibility or adopt a victim mentality. If you choose responsibility, another decision lies ahead when facing struggles. In any situation, as a responsible individual, you typically have two constructive options: if the issue doesn't concern you, walk away. However, if you decide to stay, you must take full responsibility and commit to improving the situation.

For example, imagine you land a job and initially feel excited, but over time, you realize the work environment is toxic and draining. If your workplace is harmful to your mental health, it is your responsibility to make the necessary changes to restore your peace of mind. Complaining about the toxicity won't change anything; it will only amplify your dissatisfaction and make your workplace feel worse, exacerbating your mental health.

The worst mistake you can make is pretending the toxicity doesn't bother you. Suppressing your feelings and ignoring the problem won't make it go away; in fact, it will only allow it to grow larger, entangling you further in toxicity. Denial might offer a temporary escape, but it's not a solution and does nothing to alleviate your mental suffering.

You have two options: leave or stay. If you decide to leave, it may come with setbacks like a temporary loss of income or career instability, but taking responsibility means accepting the price of change. You don't like your job? Then take the leap—accept the cost and pursue a new career that better suits you. If you choose to stay, then focus on improving your work environment in whatever capacity you can.

First and foremost, stop complaining. Don't go around talking to your coworkers about how toxic the workplace is—that will only make you part of the toxicity, fueling it further with your complaints. While you probably won't have the power to change the entire organization, small acts like approaching coworkers with kindness, praising them for their good work, completing your tasks diligently, and bringing positivity in whatever ways you can to those you work with can make a tangible difference.

These changes may seem minor, but they are not insignificant. When you act with positivity and radiate it to others, you are more likely to receive positivity in return, helping to counteract the overall toxicity in your workplace. Let your positivity overpower the toxicity, preventing it from creeping into your mind and causing mental distress.

Now, imagine a different scenario—one where you have been betrayed by your partner. Rather than assigning all blame to your partner, reflect on your own role in the relationship. Were there warning signs you ignored? Did you fail to nurture the relationship or address issues when they arose? If your partner is truly incompatible with you, then take responsibility for having chosen them in the first place and learn from the experience to make wiser decisions in choosing your future partner. Perhaps you neglected your partner, or maybe you didn't nurture the relationship with enough love and care to keep it healthy and strong. Reflect on what may have gone wrong from your side—identify the root cause of the issue with your personality. Use this to ensure that the situation does not repeat itself.

Now, consider dissatisfaction with your country and government. Again, you have two options: leave or engage. If you dislike your home country, consider moving to another country and starting a new life elsewhere. This may involve challenges such as learning a new language, adapting to a new culture, and accepting setbacks in career opportunities. These are the new challenges you'll face as a result of leaving your old problems behind.

On the other hand, if you choose to stay, work to improve your country in any capacity you can. Avoid adding to division by blindly taking sides in political or ideological arguments. Instead, foster understanding and build bridges by encouraging dialogue and highlighting common grounds. Real solutions do not come from trying to force others to think like you, but from approaching differences with empathy and a willingness to understand the other side.

Do not fell for the trap of favoritism, assuming that those who think differently are "the problem." Often people believe the solution is to make others think like them or simply suppress opposing viewpoints. This approach not only adds to division but creates a cycle of conflict. As we discussed in the chapter about truth, favoritism blinds you to the complexities of reality. The truth is, we are inherently diverse, and there will never be a time when everyone shares the same exact values and perspectives.

The real solution lies in finding common ground. When discussing politics with friends or family, highlight the strengths and weaknesses of each perspective. Focus on bringing people closer together rather than deepening the gap between opposing sides. Take the time to hear the other side, to truly understand where they are coming from, and to show empathy. When you take one step closer to someone through understanding, they are more likely to take a step closer to you. Empathy and mutual respect are the foundations for meaningful dialogue and lasting solutions.

Perhaps you cannot resolve all political conflicts or bring harmony and understanding to an entire country, but you can create more harmony among your friends and family. This is your duty and responsibility as a member of your community and your country. Positive change begins on a small scale, and by fostering understanding, compassion, and respect within your immediate circle, you contribute to the greater good.

This principle applies not only to politics but to any conflict. If you resist and fight, others will fight back, often with even greater force, creating a destructive cycle that leaves both sides damaged. However, when you approach with compassion, patience, and a willingness to listen, you open the door to resolution and progress. Just as in mathematics, where problems with multiple terms require finding a common denominator, conflicts among people require finding common grounds, shared values, and similar goals.

Responsibility also means recognizing your own limitations. Approach every situation with humility, acknowledging that your perspective may not always be the best or the only valid solution. By staying open-minded, you allow for a broader understanding and greater collaboration. Real solutions take time, patience, and consistent effort to formulate. They require resilience to overcome setbacks. It demands honesty and integrity to earn the trust and respect of those involved. Instead of viewing your idea as the ultimate solution, treat it as a starting point to create a practical resolution that benefits everyone.

Ultimately, whether you're navigating personal relationships, workplace challenges, or societal tensions, the key is to act with good intention, compassion, and a commitment to finding solutions. When you take responsibility with good intentions to foster connection and understanding, you contribute to a more harmonious world—one step closer to peace and progress for everyone involved.

Whatever action you engage in, do so with good intention. When discussing politics with a friend, resist the urge to dominate the conversation with your logic. This will only feed narcissistic tendencies within you. Instead, approach the dialogue with humility and a genuine desire to understand their perspective.

If your friend makes a valid point, acknowledge it with sincerity. If you notice a flaw in their reasoning, point it out kindly and respectfully, not to undermine them but to help them see a potential blind spot.

Be just with your words. Be gentle with your tone. Be kind with your actions. Be understanding with your heart. Be patient with others' flaws. Be compassionate in your judgments. Be generous with your forgiveness. Be steadfast in your love. This is how you harbor good intentions.

If your friends need your help, approach the situation with love and sincerity, not out of obligation or a sense of being forced. When you help others out of obligation, it diminishes the joy and connection that genuine acts of kindness bring. Instead, offer your assistance from a place of compassion and a clear heart. Let your actions be driven by love, not weighed down by reluctance or the sense of burden.

True kindness is not about fulfilling an obligation—it is about willingly choosing to be there for someone because you care. If you find yourself feeling reluctant or resentful, take a moment to reflect. Ask yourself, "Am I helping because I genuinely want to, or because I feel like I have to?" If resentment is present, reconsider your actions. Do not act and do not help anyone with reluctance, as it undermines the authenticity of your intention. If you choose to act, do so with love and sincerity. By aligning your intentions with love, your actions will have a deeper, more authentic impact—both on others and on yourself.

Have compassion for people around you, your community, and all of humanity. While you may not bring global peace to the entire world, you can bring peace to your home, your workplace, and your circle of friends and family. You are not responsible for what lies beyond your abilities, but you are responsible for the incredible abilities you do possess.

These responsibilities do not require grand achievements measured by material or societal standards. Your greatness is not defined by worldly accolades but by the purity of your heart and the virtues you cultivate. It is in the honesty of your communication, the integrity and dignity you uphold, the sincerity of your love, and your unwavering commitment to truth. Your greatness lies in understanding and becoming one with your soul. Responsibility, when guided by good intentions, radiates passion, love, and patience as you pursue your life's duty and purpose.

The question now is, how are you going to achieve such greatness? Create a healthy daily ritual for yourself that reflects your commitment to growth and discipline. Tame the wild beast within you, face your inner demons, and take control of your life. Write down your ritual, read it every day, and hold yourself accountable. Keep practicing your ritual until it becomes second nature.

For example, you might start your day with the following morning ritual: wake up and make your bed, drink a glass of water, wash your face and groom yourself, meditate for five minutes, clean your room, exercise for at least 15 minutes, eat a healthy breakfast, take a shower, and meditate again.

If you commit to starting each day with a ritual like this—or one tailored to your own needs—you'll naturally set the tone for a better day, every day. Your body will be nourished, your mind will be calm, and your surroundings will be clean and organized.

The key is to design a ritual that works for you while ensuring it genuinely benefits your well-being. It should include habits that nurture your physical, mental, and emotional health. Whether it's exercise, meditation, hydration, or tidying up your space, ensure each component contributes to your overall well-being. At the same time, ritual has to be something you can see yourself practicing for the rest of your life. The beauty of such a routine lies in its timelessness and the lasting benefits it brings to your life. Choose activities that will remain valuable no matter your circumstances.

If you commit to starting each day with the ritual I just mentioned or something similar, you will naturally set yourself up for a better start of the day, every day. Your body will feel nourished, your mind will be calm, and your space will be clean. Design a ritual that works for you and brings genuine benefits. Make sure it's not something you might abandon due to changing life circumstances. Instead, choose something that, at least in theory, you can practice every day for the rest of your life—something that will always be beneficial.

Imagine waking up late for work, your alarm blaring as you scramble out of bed. In your haste, you don't even glance at yourself in the mirror before rushing out the door to face life's challenges. Your heart races, your mind spins with stress, and your day feels chaotic before it even begins. Now, picture an alternative. Imagine making yourself responsible for waking up an hour earlier than needed to attend to your daily ritual. This small decision forces you to prioritize your bedtime, avoiding late-night parties or excessive drinking, giving your body the rest it craves. Already, you're setting yourself up for a better night's sleep and a more peaceful start.

You wake up early, greeted by the calm quiet of the morning. You make your bed, a small act that instantly brings order to your space. You tidy your room, clearing the clutter not just around you but in your mind. Next, you do a quick workout, getting your blood flowing and energizing your body. You step into the shower, feeling the warmth wash away the remnants of sleep. Then, you take a few minutes to meditate, grounding yourself, calming your thoughts, and setting your intentions for the day. All of this takes less than an hour.

Now, imagine heading to work after this morning ritual. Your mood is lifted, your mind is sharp, and your body feels refreshed. Compare this to the rushed, disoriented start you had in the first scenario—waking up hungover, rushing to get dressed, and running out the door without so much as a glance in the mirror. The contrast is stark. One choice leads to chaos and stress; the other cultivates calm, order, and readiness.

This simple, consistent morning routine not only transforms your day but reshapes your mindset, setting the tone for a life where you feel in control, balanced, and prepared for whatever comes your way. It's a small shift with a profound impact.

In your daily ritual, be sure to include moments for self-reflection, times when you turn inward to connect with your true self. Whether you meditate, pray, or simply sit with your eyes closed, these moments are essential to understanding yourself. Keep yourself clean, and ensure your surroundings are tidy as well. An organized room reflects an organized mind. Nurture your body—eat well, but don't overeat.

Write down your daily rituals and responsibilities and read them every day to remind yourself. As forgetful creatures, we often fail to remember the promises we made to ourselves. By writing down your rituals and responsibilities and revisiting them, you stay on track. Attend to each responsibility with love in your heart and peace in your mind. This is how you develop consistency and perseverance.

When you encounter daily struggles beyond your routines, face them with confidence, determination, and, most importantly, good intentions. Approach life with the courage to fly, not the fear to crawl. By following this path, you strengthen your mind and see yourself as more capable. Every day, practice self-love; put on your invisible superhero cape by accepting yourself as you are and believing in your ability to achieve greatness in life. Your mental superhero cape has real power. It empowers you to conquer challenges in ways that may even surprise yourself. Your superpowers aren't visible, but they are real and reside within your soul.

To harness superpowers, you must confront and master your own demons. Venture into every corner of the devil's den—the narrow, dark passages of your inner world—searching for your soul. With the light of honesty and integrity, shine through the darkness and confront your own demons. Acknowledge and respect the darkness within you, but do not succumb to its temptations. The devil's goal is to distract you from discovering your soul, to hold it captive, and drain it of its superpowers. When the devil possesses your soul, it siphons the strength and harness the power meant for you, leaving you weakened and crawling through life. But your soul is yours—take it back. Reclaim what belongs to you and regain your superpowers.

Truth is your guide. Never lose sight of it, for without truth, you risk wandering aimlessly, lost forever in the devil's den. Let truth illuminate your path and lead you to your soul.

As you search for your soul with truth, use the light of love to draw your soul closer to you. Love illuminates the path for the soul, toward the light of truth shining from your heart. Live each day filled with love, and refuse to let anger, hatred, or despair darken your journey. Allow love to draw your soul back to you so you can once again feel the superpowers that lie within.

When you become one with your soul, you step into the boundless realm of infinite love—even amidst the chaos of this world. This sacred union transforms your life, infusing it with peace, strength, and a profound sense of purpose at every step of your journey.

Your greatest responsibility in life is to become one with your soul. Begin by identifying the responsibilities that will help you in this endeavor. Write them down, as they represent the rules you impose on yourself to stay aligned with your higher purpose. These rules are your guiding principles, designed by yourself for yourself to keep you focused and to guard against the distractions and deceptions of the devil—your inner fears, temptations, and doubts. When you discover better ways of living, update your rules and rewrite them. keep revisiting and rereading your own rules to keep them fresh in your memory.

Live by your own written rules with unwavering dedication. Obey them not out of obligation but as an act of love for yourself and your soul. Be hard on yourself when it comes to accountability, but temper that hardness with kindness and compassion. Recognize your flaws but approach them with patience and a commitment to self-improvement. Acknowledge your inner darkness, but never let it dictate your actions. Respect its presence, for it is part of you, but choose to follow the light of truth and love instead.

In the dense forests of Thailand, there is a long-standing tradition among monks in the Thai Forest Tradition to spend time meditating in the wilderness, surrounded by the raw beauty—and dangers—of nature. Among the stories passed down is the tale of a monk who once lived deep in the jungle, where tigers roamed freely.

One evening, as the monk sat in meditation under the shelter of a simple umbrella tent, he heard the unmistakable sound of a tiger approaching. The ground trembled lightly with its steps, and the deep, guttural growl of the beast echoed in the stillness. Most people would have panicked, perhaps screamed or tried to flee. But the monk did neither. He remained calm, his breath steady, his heart open.

He didn't see the tiger as an enemy or a threat but as a fellow being of the forest. Instead of fear, he felt respect and reverence for the creature. Maintaining his stillness, the monk silently projected thoughts of peace and goodwill toward the tiger, acknowledging its presence and his shared place in the ecosystem.

The tiger circled his tent for hours, its eyes gleaming in the moonlight. It sniffed the air and even brushed against the monk's shoulder, but it never attacked. Instead, as dawn broke, the great cat quietly walked away, disappearing into the jungle. The monk had survived not because of weapons or defenses but because of his respect for nature and his refusal to view the tiger as an adversary.

The tiger represents the darkness and demons within you—ready to attack and tear you apart mentally and emotionally. Just as you would stand no chance against a tiger with your bare hands, you cannot overcome your inner demons with brute force or sheer willpower. They are countless in numbers and fueled by infinite rage, hatred, and vanity; fighting or fleeing from your inner demons only strengthens their hold over you. Instead, you must respect the devil but respect yourself more. Do not heed its demands.

Your devil commands your demons, encircling you from every angle, testing your resolve. To avoid being torn apart, you must remain vigilant. Like the monk who faces fear with calm composure, you must confront your inner darkness with understanding, respect, compassion, and above all, love. In doing so, you teach your demons to respect you. Like wild creatures, your demons sense fear. They know when you are weak. They circle you, sniffing for insecurities, waiting for a moment to strike. But if they sense love, they dare not to come close. They recognize the power of love—a force so intense and pure that it dissolves their infinite darkness upon contact.

Demons only attack when you are fearful, anxious, and unsteady. Responsibility with good intention is what anchors you, giving you the confidence to stand eye-to-eye with your inner demons and hold your ground. It equips you with the strength to face your devil, to look at it directly in the eye without trembling or faltering. When you stand firm in the light of love, rooted in truth, the devil cannot mentally harm you. Instead, it is forced to respect the power greater than itself.

The devil disrespects those who are weaker than it, but it respects those who stand resolute in their truth and love. The choice is yours. Will your devil respect you, or will it overpower you?

Finally, the apple seed finds its place, resting quietly in the darkness of the soil. It senses the warmth of sun rays penetrating through the dirt, gently drying its shell. Water pours down from above and the shell gets moist again. Meanwhile, seed observes the world from a tiny space inside the shell. It is not aware of the outside, but it has a desire to know. Moist from the water and heat from the sun slowly work their way through the shell. With an effort from the seed, shell cracks open and light shines in. The seed sees for the first time what resides outside of its bubble. The world looks beautiful but scary. Anything can hurt the seed. It is vulnerable and alone. It wants to stay but it has a desire to grow. Water drops down from the crack, lifts the seed upward and teaches it how to defy the relentless power of gravity. Through the help from water, warmth from the sun, and support from the ground seed begins to trust the world. It comes out of the shell and feels the heavy weight of dirt on its back. Slowly, it learns to jerk from side to side and maneuver through the pebbles of dirt. By the time it masters the skill of breaking through dirt, it has already surfaced. A new challenge starts. Now it has to grow through air and not dirt. It feels the fear again, the fear of unknown. It can't go back. It looks down and sees the roots that have grown on its feet. It pushes itself upward and reaches for the infinite height of sky. It grows tall and becomes a tree. Then it learns to pay respect to life. It creates shade for animals. It provides housing for birds. It lets insects eat its leaves so later they become food for the soil that is underneath. It grows beautiful flowers then comes the fruit that holds many seeds just like itself.

Recap

Let's summarize everything we've discussed in this book and fill in any remaining gaps to delineate the full picture.

At the beginning, there existed *God*—the state of *singularity*. In this state, everything existed within God, yet paradoxically, nothing existed. There were no dimensions, no time, no space, no reality—nothing that the human mind can conceive. It was a state of absolute oneness.

From this singularity, God initiated creation. To create, God introduced the concept of *information*, which allowed for distinction and differentiation. This marked the emergence of *separation*, the foundation upon which all creation would be built. God then imbued information with the attribute of *ground zero awareness*—the ability to exist, persist, and evolve. This fusion of information and ground zero awareness gave rise to the most fundamental form of *consciousness*.

Using the concept of separation, God extended itself from the state of singularity into *duality*, creating two opposing realms of consciousness: *the visible* and *the invisible*. God assigned the attribute of *light* to the visible realm, birthing the potential for physical reality, and the attribute of *truth* to the invisible realm, laying the foundation for spiritual reality. Moreover, light was given the attribute of *logic* and truth was given the attribute of *morality*, establishing the basis of *quantity* and *quality*.

At the next stage of creation, duality was further employed. When applied to light, it gave rise to matter and energy—the fundamental building blocks of the physical universe. Similarly, when duality was applied to truth, it gave birth to love and peace—the essence of spiritual existence.

At this stage, *time* and *dimension* came into being in their purest forms—*zero time* and *zero dimension*—where everything and nothing existed simultaneously. Zero time is when the clock has not yet ticked—when there is no future, no present, and no past. Similarly, zero dimension is the absence of form, distance, and movement.

Up to this point, everything existed in a state of pure divinity. Information, separation, ground zero awareness, consciousness, the prime dualities of visible and invisible, light and truth, physicality and spirituality, logic and morality, quantity and quality, matter and energy, love and peace—all were unified in essence with God while simultaneously distinct from singularity. Time and dimension, though present in potential, had not yet begun to unfold. Zero time and zero dimension encompassed all moments and no moments, all forms and no forms—an existence that was *everything* and *nothing* at once. This was the first stage of creation: the emergence of all that is and all that is not. A paradoxical reality where unity and separation coexisted harmoniously.

Creation, though still unmanifested, held the seeds of everything that was to come. This state, marked by infinite potentiality, transcends human language. Words, no matter how precise or poetic, fall short of conveying the depth and totality of these concepts.

The only "language" capable of expressing these realities is the *language of silence*. In silence, the mind quiets, and the deeper layers of consciousness begin to awaken, allowing for a glimpse of the indescribable. Similarly, the only "action" capable of revealing these truths is *stillness*. In stillness, the distractions of the physical world fade away, and the essence of existence becomes perceptible.

Silence and stillness are the gateways to understanding the infinite and the eternal. They are the means by which the human spirit reconnects to the highest levels of divinity. Through silence, you hear everything; through stillness, you see everything. In this state, your existence transcends duality, becoming both everything and nothing simultaneously. You gain the wisdom of log*ical and moral contradiction*, the ultimate understanding of *unity in separation*. It is only in this state that you truly sense singularity and the presence of God and receive the wisdom of the inner workings of all existence.

This is the moment when the seventh chakra, the *Sahasrara*, opens, and you come to experience pure divinity. This state is beyond words; it can neither be fully explained nor described—it can only be *sensed* and ultimately *become*.

The opening of the seventh chakra is an extraordinary and nearly unattainable state. It is so rare that perhaps fewer than a handful of individuals alive today have ever experienced it, if that. This state of pure divinity and ultimate awareness is inherently unstable. Even for those who reach it, the experience is often brief, a fraction of a second; they cannot remain in this heightened state for long before descending to a less elevated level of awareness. Yet, the wisdom and insight gained from even a brief glimpse of this state are infinitely more profound and powerful than anything words can describe.

Those who achieve this state experience the true end of suffering in this lifetime. They attain clarity, serenity, and mental stability that transcend the limitations of ordinary human existence, entering a realm of unity, peace, and understanding beyond description.

A few of greatest spiritual figures in history have likely attained this state, including Moses, Jesus, Muhammad, Siddhartha Gautama, Lao Tzu, and Shams. These enlightened individuals used the wisdom gained from opening their seventh chakra to illuminate the path for humanity. Their teachings, rooted in profound truths, continue to guide countless seekers of enlightenment, serving as eternal beacons of light in the quest for divine understanding.

At the next stage, time moved from a state of zero-ness, yet it had not yet begun to tick. This marked the creation of the past, present, and future, all existing in a single instance. Simultaneously, space began to stretch, but it had not yet formed anything—giving rise to dimensions and the framework within which creation could unfold.

With time and space now active, light and truth began their divine work, defining the world through their offsprings—the dualities of matter and energy, as well as love and peace. These divine forces orchestrated the creation of the visible and invisible realms, weaving the first fabric of reality itself.

However, with this first spark of creation, concepts less than divine came into existence. As light began to emerge, it was given by God its undivine counterpart: darkness. Similarly, as truth manifested in creation, it was endowed with its opposing duality: falsehood. These undivine elements further enhanced the balance of God's perfect creation, forming the evolving multiverse.

At this point of creation, there existed only a *flash of light* and a *hint of truth*—concepts brimming with potential yet devoid of tangible form. Nothing had yet fully materialized; time and space were in their rudimentary forms—barely stirring yet holding infinite potential within them. The interplay between divinity and undivinity was present and active but unmanifested, suspended in a delicate balance. Light and truth carried the promise of creation, while darkness and falsehood loomed, waiting to assert their counterforces. Think of it like a car that has been turned on and activated, but not yet moving.

In this state, the universe was poised at the edge of creation, where every possibility hung in a delicate suspension. The first subtle movements of time and space hinted at the immense unfolding yet to come, setting the stage for the dynamic interplay of forces that would shape existence.

When you come to truly understand the totality of this pre-existence—when you grasp the essence of light and truth alongside their counterparts, darkness and falsehood—you achieve a profound level of awareness. This state of enlightenment bridges the divine and undivine, revealing their interconnectedness and interdependence at the foundation of all that is. It is through this awakening that you understand the interplay of opposites and the infinite wisdom contained within them. This was the second step of creation, the moment where potential began to stir, and the first glimpses of existence prepared to take form.

At this stage, your sixth chakra, the *Ajna* or third eye, will open. This awakening allows the fundamental wisdom woven between divinity and undivinity to flow into your consciousness.

The opening of the sixth chakra is an incredibly rare and profound experience. While it is not as elusive as the seventh chakra, very few people ever reach this state of being. Achieving such a high level of awareness requires an unwavering dedication to the path of enlightenment and a willingness to sacrifice everything along the way.

Without this relentless commitment, the full wisdom of the sixth chakra will remain out of reach.

If you attain this state, you will experience a transformation so profound that suffering becomes almost nonexistent. Even if your physical body were subjected to relentless torment and pain, your mind would remain intact, immersed in a state of bliss. The peace and love you sense within you would become unshakable. No external force would be powerful enough to disrupt the calm and harmony radiating within you. You would exude an aura of serenity and strength.

However, this state is highly unstable. If you ever manage to open your sixth chakra, be prepared to lose it within moments—seconds or minutes at most—before falling back to a lower level of awareness.

Yet, even fleeting moments in this state leave a lasting imprint. The wisdom gained during this experience transforms your life, almost eradicating suffering and reshaping your understanding of existence. While the state itself may not be permanent, the profound insight it imparts will stay with you forever.

At the very next step of creation, the world began to take form as time marched forward and space stretched and expanded. This was the moment when, if the Big Bang theory holds true, the initial bang occurred, booming creation into existence.

While light evolved and transformed itself into the vast cosmos we inhabit today, truth also expanded, giving rise to the spiritual dimension. Light became the foundation of external physical reality and truth became the foundation of internal spiritual reality. In this dual unfolding, the visible and invisible realms began to complement one another. The physical world we see and interact with became the counterpart to the spiritual reality we sense and experience within. Together, these realms established the interconnected structure of existence, each influencing and reflecting the other. This pivotal moment was the true beginning of the manifested universe, both seen and unseen, born from the interplay of light and truth.

Then, inevitably, life began to form—first as single-celled organisms on Earth, and possibly on other planets. At this stage, the *second level of awareness*, which I call *autonomous survival awareness*, came into existence. Life forms, even in their simplest forms, were fundamentally different from any other form of existence that had come before them. Their complexity was unparalleled, and with this complexity came the concept of *intelligence*. Even the simplest organisms, such as viruses, demonstrated astonishing levels of intelligence in their ability to adapt, survive, and evolve.

However, the story of life's evolution is not limited to physical reality. Each creature was created through duality, having counterparts in the invisible realm of consciousness with a comparable level of awareness. These spiritual beings—mystical creatures of the invisible realm with *autonomous survival awareness*—are mostly unknown to humanity at this point in time. As far as I have explored, there is little to no information about these beings in the written works of humanity.

These spiritual entities are beyond the scope of this book to describe in detail. However, what is essential to understand is that they serve as the building blocks of life forms in the spiritual realm. Their existence generates the flow of primal spiritual energies, which we define as emotions. Much like single-celled organisms, such as bacteria, that permeate every corner where material life is found, their counterparts in the invisible realm extend throughout all spaces where spiritual life exists.

As life evolved in both the visible and invisible realms of consciousness, it began to specialize in order to survive and evolve. In the visible realm, single-celled creatures evolved into multi-cellular organisms, developing distinct cells with specialized functions. This specialization led to the creation of complex creatures composed of these specialized cells. These creatures attained a higher level of awareness, which I call *instinctive survival awareness*.

Creatures with instinctive survival awareness encompass all animal kingdom, plant kingdom, and all other forms of life. These beings operate with innate drives and instincts that guide their survival and shape their personal character. Their awareness is more advanced than the autonomous survival awareness, enabling them to develop unique personalities and interact with one another in increasingly complex ways.

Simultaneously, as these beings evolved in the visible realm, their counterparts emerged in the invisible realm of consciousness. These spiritual entities, created with the same level of instinctive survival awareness, are commonly referred to as spirits. Just as insects, animals, and plants exist to fulfill roles in the physical ecosystem, these spiritual beings play their roles in the moral and spiritual ecosystems of the invisible realm.

Each form of a spirit carries within it the essence of a moral attribute. There are spirits of light and spirits of darkness—some embodying divinity, while others represent undivinity. Yet, at this early stage of creation, they all coexisted in perfect harmony. There was no conflict between them, no opposition or struggle—only balance. Darkness did not seek to consume light, nor did light attempt to banish darkness. Light spirits and dark spirits lived together in peace and harmony. Each simply existed, fulfilling its purpose in the grand design of creation.

Up to this point, everything in existence operated under the pure will of God. All living and nonliving entities, both in the visible and invisible realms, adhered to God's will with absolute obedience. Even though the world was imbued with both divinity and undivinity, it existed in absolute peace without conflict, as God's will is inherently flawless and unshakable.

At this level of awareness, the interplay of divinity and undivinity is not seen as conflict but as a unified whole, perfectly orchestrated to sustain the equilibrium of existence. When you gain the wisdom to grasp the totality of this balance—the seamless unity within the opposing dualities in action—you will feel an unshakable peace and a deep sense of unity with all of existence.

Achieving this level of insight opens your fifth chakra, the *Vishuddha*, or throat chakra. This is the gateway to understanding the deeper harmony within the apparent contrasts of existence. Through this awakening, you come to realize that even the undivine serves a purpose within the grand design, and you perceive the interconnectedness of all things. This profound wisdom allows you to see unity within duality, bridging the gap between what is divine and what is undivine, and understanding them as essential parts of a greater, perfect whole. This level of spiritual understanding, while not as elusive as the sixth and seventh chakras, is still exceedingly rare, with very few individuals able to attain it.

At this stage, you transcend many of the emotional struggles that plague most people. Hatred completely ceases to exist within you; anger and sadness become rare and fleeting. While you may still encounter minor frustrations or moments of discomfort that bring small traces of suffering, the overall burden of suffering in your life is nearly eradicated.

In this state, you likely dwell in a more or less permanent sense of bliss, serenity, and happiness. Your mind remains calm and balanced, and your outlook on life is marked by peace and understanding. The wisdom you gain at this level allows you to see the interconnectedness of all things and to live harmoniously, both within yourself and with the world around you. It is a profound state of being, where the light of spirituality guides your thoughts, emotions, and actions, creating a life that is deeply fulfilling and meaningful.

Then the next step of creation began. God introduced the concept of *choice*, a concept that marked the evolution of creation into an entirely new form of life: humanity. Unlike any other creature, humanity was bestowed with a godly gift—the *power of will*. This unprecedented ability allowed humans not only to choose but also to alter reality in ways no other being had been permitted to do up to this point.

Up until now, all existence adhered perfectly to God's will, maintaining a delicate balance between divinity and undivinity, light and darkness, truth and falsehood. However, balance itself requires its undivine duality: the potential for imbalance. By giving humanity the freedom to choose, God allowed for the possibility of imbalance within the harmony of existence. This decision was not an imperfection but an extension of the duality that defines perfect creation. Humanity's ability to choose brought with it immense responsibility—the potential to create both beauty and chaos, harmony and discord.

This power of will, bestowed upon humanity by God, brought forth a new level of awareness, which I call *intuitive progressive awareness*. This level of awareness transformed humanity but also entered the realm of spirituality, granting dark spirits the power of will as well.

One spirit that was granted the power of will was *Lucifer*. As one of the archangels, Lucifer belonged to the order of dark spirits, standing at the highest ranks of the dark forces. He was an entity that existed at the very threshold between light and darkness, neither fully consumed by darkness nor entirely belonging to light. It is this unique position that has earned him his well-known titles—the Light-Bringer and the Morning Star—names that reflect the paradox of his nature.

As a being at the cusp of two realms, Lucifer embodied both illumination and obscurity, a presence that was neither wholly absent of light nor fully defined by darkness. This duality is intrinsic to his essence. His role in creation was one of transition—a creature that creates channels between the two realms of light and darkness.

Lucifer used the gift of free will to tempt humanity into exploring darkness, luring them away from the light. Humanity, driven by curiosity and the pursuit of knowledge, accepted Lucifer's offer and willingly strayed from the higher path. Lucifer became the gateway through which humanity descended from the divine realm. Together, they plunged into an undivine reality—falling into lower realms of existence.

Lucifer initially existed as a dark spirit, dwelling in peace within the kingdom of God. However, after misusing his power of will—committing to darkness and creating imbalances in reality—he descended into the lower realms of existence. Lucifer lost its divine powers and came to operate solely through undivine and dark forces.

Stripped of its divine powers and divine light, Lucifer transformed into what is now known as *the devil*. With this shift, many dark spirits who were also granted the power of will aligned with Lucifer's undivine nature, embracing darkness and falsehood. As a result, they too descended and lost their divine powers. They fell into the realm of the devil and came to be known as *demons* or *fallen angels*.

The devil and his army of demons embody the imbalance that prevails in the lower realms, perpetuating suffering, injustice, and chaos. Their dark influence stands in opposition to the light of truth that humanity is called to seek and restore.

This imbalance, paradoxically, created yet another perfect balance within creation. As many dark spirits descended from the divine realm, higher realms became dominated by the forces of light. Meanwhile, the lower realms, now home to the fallen spirits, became enveloped in darkness. The light spirits that remained in the higher realms upheld the purity of divine harmony, while the dark forces that filled the lower realms embraced chaos and falsehood.

In this way, the higher and lower realms came to perfectly counterbalance one another, creating yet another duality within the grand design of existence. The divine realm, radiant with truth and purity, stood in stark contrast to the darkened lower realms, where suffering, deception, and chaos reigned. Yet, despite their opposition, they existed in perfect harmony within the greater order of reality—each reinforcing the existence of godly order, like two opposing poles of a vast cosmic equilibrium. In this way, the imbalance created by the lower order became yet another force that reinforced the perfect balance of the higher order.

Furthermore, humanity was initially created as a light spirit in the divine realm, but by aligning itself with Lucifer, it too lost its divine powers and descended to the lower realms of existence. The spirit of humanity then split into two forms: body and soul. The body became the dark side of humanity, suffering in the physical realm and enduring the evils of this world, while the soul became the light side, holding humanity's spiritual essence yet suffering in the lower levels of spiritual realm, where the devil and demons reign.

Additionally, light spirits were assigned by God the task of helping humanity against the dark forces in the lower realms of existence. These light spirits descended into the lower realms, becoming known as *angels*. Together, humanity and the army of angels stand in opposition to the devil and its legion of demons. Thus, the perfection of creation remained intact once more, even amidst the duality of balance and imbalance.

In ancient times, the nature of these spirits, angels and demons was defined in the mythologies of civilizations such as the Egyptians, Mesopotamians, and Norse—and even in Hindu traditions in modern times—along with many others. These mythologies and religions interpret these mystical entities not as spirits, angels or demons, but as gods embodying forces of nature.

Over millennia, as human spiritual and moral intelligence evolved, we came to understand that these mystical beings are not creators themselves, but rather part of the greater creation. Thus, we began to recognize their true nature, assigning them more appropriate roles and characteristics rather than worshiping them as gods.

With God granting humanity and Lucifer the power of will, they misused this gift, plunging into darkness and deepening the imbalance. Thus, a profound twist in creation began to take shape. Up to this point, light and darkness, truth and falsehood existed in perfect balance. However, the introduction of imbalance in reality disrupted this harmony. The dark forces began to exert more influence than the light forces in the lower realms.

Truth, initially countered only by falsehood, now faced opposition from darkness as well. Light, similarly, was opposed by both darkness and falsehood. These four forces—light, darkness, truth, and falsehood—merged and intermingled, creating a complex, imbalanced reality of the lower realms where undivine forces became more palpable and pervasive than divinity itself. The light of truth became obscured beneath the veil of falsehood and darkness.

There is an old story that demonstrates the lopsided nature of reality in the lower realms, where dark forces hold greater sway. One day, a student approached his master and asked, "Oh master, if I have a clean and holy garment and put a filthy object within the garment, will my object become clean, or will my garment become filthy?" The master replied, "Indeed, your garment will become filthy."

The student then asked, "What if I have a filthy garment and put a perfectly clean and pure object within the garment?" The master responded, "Still, your pure object will become filthy."

The master went on to explain, "The state of the entire existence in the lower realms leans toward impurity. Filth will always overpower purity if the two are mixed in any shape or form. Things can only remain pure by staying separate from filth."

Humanity, endowed with the power of will, became the central figure in this unfolding drama. With the ability to choose, humanity has the power to either strive to restore balance by aligning with the light of truth or further create imbalance in reality by succumbing to darkness and falsehood.

This imbalance was imbued with the attribute of *suffering*. Every time humans acted in ways that disrupted the harmony of existence—through choices rooted in darkness and falsehood—they experienced suffering as a consequence. Conversely, every time they chose balance, aligning with light, truth, and a deeper understanding of existence, their suffering diminished.

In this way, suffering became a kind of gauge—a divine "knob" that regulates the intensity of one's inner turmoil. It serves as both a warning signal and a teacher, guiding humanity toward greater awareness. When imbalances arise, suffering increases, urging individuals to reassess their actions, thoughts, and choices. When balance is restored, suffering recedes, offering peace and clarity.

This mechanism was woven into the fabric of reality—not as a punishment, but as a natural consequence of existence's interconnectedness. Suffering became a human sensation that measures the level of imbalance in reality and a force that drives humanity to strive toward higher states of understanding and harmony.

If there were no suffering, we would be no more than animals—living, breathing, reacting, but never truly evolving. Pain alone does not create progress. A wolf feels hunger, a deer feels the cold, but neither builds civilizations. They experience discomfort, but they do not suffer in the way we do. They do not look at their pain and ask, *Why must it be this way?* or *How can I change this?* They simply endure it, and when the pain passes, they move on.

Humans, however, are different. We do not merely feel pain—we suffer because we recognize what pain means. We anticipate it, reflect on it, and fear its return. We imagine a world without pain and wonder how to make that world a reality. It is this very suffering that has propelled us forward.

The first humans did not just feel the sting of winter's cold; they suffered from it. They did not simply endure hunger; they longed for a way to escape it forever. They were not content with pain fading and returning in cycles—they wanted control over their fate. And so, they sought warmth beyond summer times, creating shelter. They sought food beyond the hunt, planting seeds, farming, and cultivating livestock. Every great human innovation—medicine, architecture, philosophy—was born from the unique human ability to suffer. And, in suffering, humanity refuses to accept things as they are.

And so, suffering is not merely an unfortunate side effect of life—it is the very engine of human evolution. Without it, we would still be sitting in the cold, waiting for the sun to rise. Without it, we would have no reason to build, to think, to change. Without it, we would not have reached for the stars, questioned the meaning of existence, or searched for something greater than ourselves.

We do not love suffering. We do not seek it. But paradoxically, it is suffering that has given us the power to transcend suffering itself and reach enlightenment.

By navigating this elegant dance of balance and imbalance through suffering, humanity was given the opportunity to rise above its struggles, gain wisdom, and evolve in physicality and spirituality through alignment with the divine purpose of creation.

However, instead of working to restore balance, humanity has collectively deepened this imbalance thus far. Through choices that align with darkness and falsehood rather than light of truth, we have tipped the scales further, granting dark forces even greater influence over our physical and spiritual reality.

As we observe the state of the world today and throughout history, it becomes evident that humanity's contributions have empowered darkness and falsehood far more than truth and love. The imbalance has manifested widespread suffering, conflict, and moral decay. If you seek to rise above worldly conflicts and suffering, you must purify your heart and mind, for in a world tainted by filth, the heart and mind are easily corrupted upon contact.

Keeping oneself pure is a delicate and challenging process. To achieve this, you must actively maintain balance by choosing truth, love, and light to resist the pervasive pull of dark forces that dominate our reality.

The devil now stands as a dark force between humanity and divine order, weaving veils of darkness and falsehood that obscures the light of truth. This creates a formidable barrier for those seeking to ascend toward divinity, turning the path of enlightenment into a journey through darkness and deceptions—a passage through *hell* itself, the *devil's den*. This hell, forged by darkness and falsehood, lies between humanity and the divine, a realm of torment and turmoil.

For those unable to pierce through this abyss, the consequence is eternal entrapment in darkness, where chaos and discord reign, perpetuating endless suffering. Yet, for those who muster the strength to confront the devil and its legions of demons, there is hope. With the light of truth, you can navigate the dark tunnel of the devil's dominion and emerge victorious into the radiant light of truth.

In this light, you find yourself in the kingdom of divinity—a sanctuary of ultimate peace and eternal bliss, reserved for those who overcome the trials of darkness. This is not merely a vision of the afterlife; it is a reality to be achieved in this lifetime. The choice is yours: to continue suffering in the remaining days of your life or to step into a state of bliss. The crossroad lies before you—choose your path wisely.

At your core, you are a light spirit, split into soul and body. Your spirit is the essence that resides within your mind—the space where your body and soul converge. In essence, you are three things. You, the one reading this, are a light spirit. The eyes and ears through which you perceive these words belong to your body, while the emotions and sensations that stir within you arise from your soul. All three—body, soul, and spirit—meet and coexist within the realm of your mind.

Think of it this way: your spirit is the driver, your body is the vehicle, and your soul is the passenger, navigating the winding roads of your mental landscape. However, your journey is not without obstacles. Your body is beset by the forces of evil, your soul is opposed by the devil, and your spirit—caught between the two—struggles against their weight. The devil feeds on division, keeping your body and soul disconnected through suffering, thereby weakening your spirit. In this way, the innate superpower of your spirit is harnessed by the devil and used against you, leaving you fragmented, lost, and yearning for wholeness.

But within you lies the ability to restore your full strength, to reclaim your superpowers. The key is to merge your body and soul into one, to break free from the illusions that keep them apart, and to awaken to the true nature of your spiritual existence. Thus begins your spiritual journey—an eternal dance between light and darkness, where every step forward is a step toward reunification, toward truth, and ultimately, toward the divine.

The soul, tethered to the divine, yearns to ascend beyond the physical realm, striving for unity with the spirit and *collective consciousness*—a state of enlightenment, truth, and harmony where divinity reigns supreme. It whispers to you, urging you to rise, to seek wisdom, to move toward the light. Yet, the devil stands in opposition, weaving illusions of fleeting pleasures and false comforts, luring you into complacency. Each moment of indulgence in these temporary distractions tethers you further to the material world, pulling you downward, away from your soul's true calling.

Thus, the devil drags the soul of humanity into the depths of *collective unconsciousness*—its den, a realm of darkness, ignorance, chaos, and suffering, where undivine forces hold sway. It is a slow descent, disguised as comfort, wrapped in deception. The more you succumb, the more distant you become from you own light—the very essence of you as a light spirit.

This cosmic struggle defines human experience. Every thought you harbor, every action you take, and every decision you make serves to align you with one of these opposing forces. It is within this eternal tug-of-war that the journey of the spirit unfolds—a battle between divine transcendence and dark descent. And it is within this battle that your purpose is forged, as you navigate the thin line between illusion and truth, between suffering and liberation, between separation and oneness.

With every decision you make and every alliance you form—whether with the soul or the devil—you actively empower one side. Acts of love, compassion, and truth nourish the soul, drawing you closer to divinity and aligning your essence with the higher realms. In contrast, actions born of selfishness, deceit, or harm strengthen the devil, pulling you deeper into chaos and imbalance.

This is the profound essence of the gift of will and choice bestowed upon humanity—a divine power enabling you to chart your course within the grand design of existence. Whether you ascend toward unity, enlightenment, and divine harmony or descend into division, despair, and darkness depends entirely on how you wield this sacred gift of will.

Each moment presents an opportunity, a crossroads where you decide your own spiritual journey and also contribute to the collective fate of humanity. With every choice, you leave a mark on the tapestry of creation, shaping the world around you as much as the journey within you.

When you come to understand the perfectness of reality—both in its balance and imbalance—you begin to see existence in a new light. You realize that even what appears unbalanced or flawed is, in fact, part of a flawless design. This understanding allows you to perceive beauty not only in what is good and harmonious but also in what is evil and chaotic, recognizing both as expressions of God's creation.

This profound realization enables you to see that every aspect of existence, whether divine or undivine, serves a purpose in the grand design. When you reach this level of awareness, your fourth chakra, the *Anahata*, or heart chakra, opens.

With this awakening, a surge of unconditional love fills your entire being. This love is so powerful, so transformative, that it becomes the single greatest experience of your entire life, surpassing all other emotions and connections you've ever known. It binds you to the world in a state of unity, acceptance, and profound compassion.

This unparalleled experience of love will remain your most treasured memory unless you ascend even further and reach higher levels of spiritual awareness by opening additional chakras. Each level builds upon the last, but the opening of the heart chakra serves as the first step and the cornerstone for the deeper understanding that follows.

This love becomes your guiding force, connecting you deeply to yourself, others, and the world. It is love that sees harmony within chaos and balance within imbalance. In this state, you no longer resist the existence of darkness or evil but embrace it as part of the tapestry of existence, empowering you to live with compassion and acceptance.

This state of being, marked by the opening of the fourth chakra, is closely associated with common spirituality and many religious experiences. It is often described by those who feel they have encountered God, angels, Jesus, Buddha, Muhammad, other prophets, or other divine entities. Additionally, many individuals who undergo dramatic personal transformations—such as former criminals or satanists who suddenly dedicate themselves to a spiritual or religious path—often describe a brief but overwhelming experience of pure love. This is the hallmark of their first encounter with the opening of the fourth chakra and divinity.

Reaching this state is challenging, but some people manage to achieve it. Among them are religious and spiritual individuals who are genuinely good-hearted and strive to live by their beliefs. These people aim to help others with positive intentions, extending kindness and compassion wherever possible. They are pleasant to be around, make great friends, and understand how to give and receive love. Their lives are marked by a sense of purpose and a reduced level of suffering compared to others.

These individuals have found comfort in their spirituality and accept life's hardships as part of the divine will, even if they don't understand it. They are content and grounded in their faith, experiencing a moderate level of serenity and satisfaction with life.

However, despite their spiritual growth, they do not reach the state of permanent peace and bliss. The struggles of physical reality still affect them, and they remain vulnerable to the emotional turbulence of life's ups and downs. While they have attained a significant level of spiritual awareness, their journey is not yet complete—they have yet to achieve the higher states of enlightenment that bring unshakable peace and mastery over life's challenges.

Unfortunately, many of these good people, emboldened by their transformative spiritual experiences, lose the humility that initially guided their journey. Believing they now understand the true nature of reality, they develop a sense of superiority regarding their beliefs. This rigid self-assurance closes their fourth chakra and plunging them down to the lower states of awareness, as their closed-mindedness limits their growth.

As a result, they frequently spend the remainder of their lives dwelling within the framework of their established beliefs and religious doctrines, unable to move beyond them. While they promote unity among those who share their views, inflexibility in their beliefs contributes to division with those who think differently. Their unwavering certainty creates barriers rather than bridges, even as they genuinely strive to live virtuously and promote unity.

Despite these shortcomings, they remain fundamentally good people. They are kind, compassionate, and admirable in their dedication to their spiritual journey. Their lives are marked by sincerity, and their presence is generally pleasant and uplifting. However, their spiritual growth stalls, leaving them unable to access the higher states of awareness that could lead to greater understanding. Nonetheless, they serve as an example of devotion and kindness within their realm of understanding.

As profound as the experience of opening the fourth chakra may be, it can also mark the downfall of many on the path of enlightenment. While this state of heightened awareness offers a glimpse to divinity and boundless love, it is inherently unstable. Many who reach this level soon falter, descending back into lower states of awareness. For some, this descent becomes permanent and exceedingly dangerous.

At this stage of awareness when the fourth chakra has been activated at least once, the devil's influence becomes most relentless, for it recognizes the immense potential of those who stand at this threshold. Their awareness and wisdom, if corrupted, can serve dark purposes with devastating effect. Should the devil succeed in manipulating them, these individuals can become its most powerful human allies, wielding the knowledge they have gained to sow darkness and imbalance rather than light and harmony. Thus, the fourth chakra represents not only a gateway to spiritual ascension but also a battleground where the stakes are higher than ever.

When individuals at this stage allow their arrogance and a sense of superiority to reach the level of narcissism, they quickly fall to lowest levels of awareness. Though they may continue to present themselves as enlightened, they are not. These are the *false prophets* who exploit the wisdom gained from opening the fourth chakra to accumulate worldly possessions and fulfill their earthly desires for fame, wealth, and power.

Many contemporary gurus, mages, yogis, zen masters, priests, imams, rabbis, and spiritual leaders fall into this category. Having experienced the wisdom of the fourth chakra, they know how to speak convincingly about love, peace, and enlightenment, attracting large audiences and devoted followers. Their words are beautiful and, to a significant degree, truthful, yet their intentions are tainted by darkness. Manipulated by the devil, they give in to their desires, using spirituality as a means to build personal empires of wealth and influence.

They may speak of peace and serenity, but their actions sow darkness and chaos in the world. Despite their modest appearance and eloquent words, their greed for material possessions, fame, and power betrays them. They charge exorbitant fees for speeches, conferences, and retreats, amassing tremendous wealth while continuing to acquire more in the name of love, truth, spirituality, and God. In this way, darkness, in its most deceptive and powerful form, masquerades as light, leading many astray under the guise of divinity.

They amass followers with alluring words of encouragement, promising light and divinity, weaving a narrative that captivates hearts and minds. Yet beneath this facade, their worldly greed seeps into the hearts of their followers, entangling them further in the web of earthly glamour and material desires.

Rather than guiding their followers toward liberation from suffering, they anchor them in a state of greed and attachment, perpetually chasing an elusive promise of peace and bliss. Trapped in anticipation and suffering, the followers remain blind to the truth, their journey stalled by the very forces they sought to transcend. This cycle of deception ensures their dependence on the material world, turning a path meant for enlightenment into one of endless anticipation and disillusionment.

These leaders and their followers remain deeply entangled in the physical realm, unable to transcend its limitations, and thus, true enlightenment eludes them. Be especially cautious when you encounter someone who claims to be enlightened, for many of them serve as messengers of the devil. They wield immense wisdom, speaking eloquently of love, peace, and goodness, and their words may resonate deeply with your heart. However, do not follow them blindly. Hidden within their truths are meticulously planted lies, carefully crafted to derail your spiritual journey.

This deception works subtly yet powerfully. When you follow them without question, you ingest the vast truths they offer along with the small but potent lies embedded within. That single lie can corrupt your entire understanding, leading you astray. Consider this analogy: imagine being served a large, healthy meal—full of nourishing ingredients—but hidden within is a single morsel of poison. It doesn't matter how nutritious the rest of the meal is; consuming the poison could make you severely ill or even kill you. Such is the devil's strategy: it tells you 99 truths to get you to accept one deadly lie. Keep your ears, eyes, heart, and mind open, and approach their words with discernment.

Their darkness often disguises itself as light, and learning to recognize this deception is essential for your spiritual growth. When you learn to read between the lines, distinguishing moments of genuine truth from cleverly masked falsehoods, you strengthen your own wisdom and elevate your awareness. Interacting with such individuals—who are, in essence, the devil's most powerful human allies—is a high-risk, high-reward endeavor. You can gain invaluable insights, but if your understanding falters and you fail to discern the truth from lie, the descent into illusion can be a swift and devastating freefall.

To safeguard yourself, always strive to find your own path. Your soul is your greatest teacher, far surpassing any external guide. It holds the key to ultimate reality and is always prepared to lead you—if only you choose to listen. Trust in your inner wisdom, for it is your purest connection to the divine and the most steadfast source of truth on your journey toward enlightenment.

Moreover, if you desire to walk the path of spirituality beyond the fourth chakra, you must understand that while religion or spirituality can serve as a starting point on the journey to enlightenment, reaching higher states of being requires transcending the boundaries of religion or any specific method of practicing spirituality.

By its very nature, religion creates separation. It is rigid in its doctrines and does not tolerate differing sets of beliefs, thus limiting its ability to foster true unity. For this reason, religion alone cannot open the fifth chakra, which is fundamentally about understanding and embodying unity. The fifth chakra requires a perspective that embraces all existence as one interconnected whole—a vision that transcends the divisions created by religious systems and structures.

With that said, you can embrace your preferred religion as a guiding light on your spiritual journey, drawing strength and wisdom from its teachings. However, it's crucial to understand that your religion's value lies in how it resonates with you personally—it does not make it inherently better or superior to any other faith. Each religion holds profound truths that guide individuals toward higher understanding in ways that align with their unique perspectives and experiences.

Practicing your religion with an open mind allows you to transcend personal biases that create division, enabling you to reach higher states of awareness and understanding. You can be a Jew, Christian, Muslim, Taoist, Buddhist, Hindu, or follow any other religion and still open all your chakras as long as you understand in your heart that, while your religion may be the best spiritual path for you, it might not be the best path for someone else. Respect others' spiritual paths as equally valid as your own.

Paradoxically, if you cling to the belief that your faith is superior to others, that very sense of superiority becomes a barrier to enlightenment. Such rigidity fosters division and blinds you to the wisdom found in diverse paths. True spiritual growth flourishes in a state of humility and openness, where the recognition of universal truths surpasses the confines of individual belief systems. Only by letting go of the need to compare and judge can you move closer to supreme understanding and unity with the divine.

The reason all religions face inherent limitations is that, while their foundation rests on truth, their structures have been shaped by the devil's influence. No true prophet in history ever claimed to establish a new religion. No spiritual leader ever wrote a sacred text or declare any written words to be holy. Muhammad did not pen the Quran nor create Islam. Jesus did not write the Bible nor establish Christianity. Moses did not author the Torah nor found Judaism. Lao Tzu did not compose the Tao Te Ching nor originate Taoism. Siddhartha Gautama did not inscribe the Teachings of Buddha nor create Buddhism.

Every so-called "holy book" was later proclaimed sacred by corrupt powers seeking control and domination over earthly realms. Every organized religion was established by corrupt leaders to manipulate and control the masses. This is why religious texts, while containing infinite wisdom rooted in the truths of the prophets, are flawed in their structures, promoting division and obscuring the light with darkness. Religions can serve as valuable tools for navigating the initial stages of enlightenment, offering guidance through their infinite wisdom. However, to reach higher levels of spiritual awareness, one must transcend the mental constructs of religion and delve into the essence of the prophets' teachings, free from the limitations imposed by the institutions built in their names.

To ascend further on your spiritual journey, trust in your soul and surrender completely to God. Your soul is your most authentic guide, a compass attuned to divine truth. Soul, your ultimate source of all wisdom and love, is the only constant on the path to enlightenment. No teacher, system, or religion can illuminate your way as purely and clearly as your own soul.

This path demands faith in yourself and in the divine, free from the constraints of external authority. By letting go of reliance on external structures and embracing the guidance of your inner being, you step closer to understanding unity, balance, and the divine reality that lies beyond all divisions. The journey is yours alone, and only by surrendering to God and listening to your soul can you ascend to the higher realms of spiritual awareness.

There is an old tale in Rumi's poems that speaks to the problem with rigid beliefs. This retelling, though inspired by the original, is not an exact translation.

In the vastness of the desert, where the earth kissed the horizon, Moses wandered, seeking solitude and communion with God. As he walked, his ears caught a peculiar sound—a voice, raw and fervent. Curious, he followed the voice to its source.

There, under the shade of a lone tree, sat a simple man. His clothes were tattered, his hands calloused, but his face glowed with sincerity. He spoke aloud, addressing God as though speaking to a friend.

"My Lord," the man said, his words filled with tender devotion, "if only I could serve You! I would mend your shoes, wash Your feet, bring you milk, comb your hair, kill your lice, make your bed ready when you want to sleep. Oh, how I wish to care for You, my beloved God."

Moses, hearing these words, he approached the man, his voice stern and commanding. "What are you saying?" he demanded. "Do you not understand that God is beyond human form? God has no feet to wash, no hair to comb, no hunger or thirst to satisfy! Your words are an insult to God's divinity. Stop this blasphemy at once!"

The man, startled and ashamed, lowered his head. His voice faltered, and he fell silent. He tore his shirt in a fit of self-disappointment and ran off. Moses, thinking he had corrected the man's misguided devotion, walked away with a sense of duty fulfilled.

But as the desert wind stilled, a voice thundered from above, striking at his heart. It was the voice of God.

"Moses," God said, "what have you done? Why have you silenced the love of one of My servants?"

"Lord," Moses replied, confused, "he spoke of serving You in ways unworthy of Your majesty. He offered to wash Your feet and comb Your hair as if You were a man! I thought it was my duty to correct him."

God's voice echoed in Moses's heart: "Moses, you speak of My majesty, but you forget My mercy. I do not look at the words. I look at the heart. That man's love was pure, and his devotion reached Me with his simple words. You see blasphemy, but I see sincerity. You see error, but I see love. Let each of My servants praise Me as their heart leads them, for all paths of love are sacred to Me."

Moses stood in silence, humbled and ashamed, he turned and retraced his steps. When he found the man, Moses fell to his knees before him. "Forgive me," he said. "I was wrong. God has told me that your love and devotion are precious to Him. Speak to Him in the way that feels right to you, for your heart is true."

The message here is clear: spirituality is deeply rooted in morality, and the quality of morality is not measured by its precision or adherence to specific rules but by its intrinsic value and purity. A pure heart, filled with love, compassion, and integrity, holds infinite worth—far surpassing any religious doctrine or structured belief system. It is the purity of your heart that illuminates your spiritual path, not the meticulousness with which you follow a particular set of teachings.

If you mistake the structure of your religious doctrine for its moral value, you will hinder your spiritual growth. Rules and rituals, while meaningful, are merely tools; they are not the essence of spirituality. They point the way but are not the destination. Let your soul be your compass. Nurture its purity and allow it to guide you.

The first three chakras—*Muladhara* (root), *Svadhisthana* (sacral), and *Manipura* (solar plexus)—are deeply rooted in physical reality and based on overcoming fear. The details of these chakras, while extremely important in the path of enlightenment, are beyond the scope of this book. All you need to know is that by overcoming fear with love, you will ascend these three layers.

However, those who never rise above their fears and above the third chakra are bound to a life of suffering, even if they achieve material wealth and power. While they may outwardly seem successful, they are never truly at peace within themselves. Their minds remain restless, their hearts unfulfilled, and their lives driven by desires and fears tied to the physical world.

These individuals may or may not be religious or spiritual, but regardless of their outward practices, they never experience the profound sense of pure love that comes with higher states of awareness. If they do engage in religion or spirituality, they risk becoming devoted followers of the misguided leaders previously mentioned. These individuals are drawn to such leaders because their own understanding remains limited to the physical realm, where appearances, authority, and material promises hold sway.

If your higher chakras remain unopened and you still find yourself burdened by fear and suffering, do not be disheartened. The path to spiritual awakening is always within reach. If you long to open your chakras and feel the profound love that radiates from the heart, if you wish to personally step into and experience the divine reality, you can achieve this by aligning your lifestyle with the true needs of your soul.

The path of enlightenment is not reserved for a select few; it is available to everyone—regardless of age, circumstances, or where you stand on your spiritual journey. No matter how distant divinity may seem, when you commit to walking this path with sincerity and determination, success is inevitable. The journey is challenging, but the promise of enlightenment, peace, and divine connection awaits all who persevere.

Before discussing the path of ascension toward the divine realms of reality and higher levels of awareness, let us first explore the process of human creation. You were initially brought into existence as a light spirit, a being of divine essence, untainted and whole. Yet, through the intermingling with Lucifer, you became bound to its undivinity. You descended from the divine realm, becoming fragmented into two undivine dualities that you now share with Lucifer, plus one divine duality—representing the core of your being as a light spirit.

Your first undivine duality lies within you: the spiritual interplay between your soul and the devil. This internal conflict manifests as the opposing forces of light and darkness within your thoughts and emotions. It grips you with the struggle between your passive thoughts and active thinking, as well as the tension between emotions and feelings. The inner struggles you face—between love and fear, truth and falsehood—are born of this eternal tug-of-war between your soul's divine aspirations and the devil's undivine pull.

Your second undivine duality resides in the external, physical realm. Here, good and evil manifest as the forces of duality, shaping your earthly existence. Evil is the devil's manifestation into the material world and takes form in chaos, injustice, and suffering you may experience in your daily life. You are called to leave the world better than you found it, spreading goodness rather than darkness.

Beyond these two undivine dualities lies your pure, divine duality: the sacred connection between you and your soul. This duality, unlike the others, is balanced and harmonious by design. It is the essence of your true nature; it's your spirit, untainted and pure, calling you towards unity with the divine.

Now, to elevate your awareness, to ascend into higher realms of consciousness and divine experience, you must first transcend the dualities that lie at the core of your creation. You must first rise above your undivine dualities before you can confront and navigate your divine duality.

Your undivine dualities, though integral parts of your being, are not meant to dominate you. To rise above them, approach both ends of the spectrum with understanding and respect. Stop resisting evil in the material world and battling the devil within. Instead, honor their existence without succumbing to the temptations and Earthly desires.

The path of enlightenment has been illuminated by the examples of great spiritual teachers throughout history. Learn from the way they lived their lives; embrace the wisdom in their actions and gain the lessons from their teachings. Jesus, for instance, never fought against the evil in this world with physical resistance. He spoke against injustice, but he waged no war. Even in the face of death, he did not resist, for his mission was complete, and his purpose fulfilled. Similarly, Siddhartha, known as the Buddha, lived in peace, embodying principles akin to Jesus. He embraced compassion and understanding without succumbing to the chaos around him.

If you find yourself in a country marred by conflict and war, the example of Prophet Muhammad offers profound lessons. When he began to speak his truth, he faced violence and hostility. People hurled stones at him, vandalized his business, and tortured his followers. Yet, he did not fight back. When his life was threatened, he fled to Medina. Even then, when his enemies pursued him with armies, he only picked up the sword in self-defense, as his mission was not yet complete. Muhammad's approach to battle was guided by strict principles: never act out of anger or hatred, and never attack beyond what is necessary to preserve one's rights. He instructed his followers to show mercy—if an enemy dropped their weapon, they were not to kill them; if they fled, they were not to be chased. Even captured prisoners were treated with dignity, walking unchained, eating the same food, and receiving kind words and treatments. Muhammad strictly forbade inflicting any form of pain or discomfort on prisoners of war.

One tale attributed to Ali, Muhammad's nephew, captures the essence of fighting with a pure heart. During a battle, Ali disarmed his enemy and was ready to deliver the final blow. But when the enemy spat on his face, Ali stopped, lowered his sword, and withdrew. Later, when asked why he hadn't seized the moment, he replied, "When he spat on my face, I became angry. I could not continue the fight until I regained my composure and remembered why I was fighting. A battle fought for the preservation of love and truth cannot be waged with anger." Only after mastering his emotions did Ali resume the fight, eventually triumphing over his opponent.

As time passed, enemy soldiers began to refuse to fight against Muhammad, recognizing the goodness in him. Some of his former enemies, who had once tortured and killed his followers, later became followers themselves and even joined his army. When Muhammad and his army finally marched toward Mecca, not a single drop of blood was shed. Muhammad personally forgave his enemies, including those who had tortured and killed his loved ones. He did not strip them of their property or punish them; instead, he protected them. They lived under his rule with the same safety and freedoms they had before.

Moses, too, navigated a mission fraught with conflict. When he approached Pharaoh, he spoke with kindness, urging him to follow the path of righteousness or to let his people go. Pharaoh resisted, and calamities ensued, but Moses never sought to destroy him or his army. His goal was to bring Pharaoh and his people into the light of God. Yet when they resisted and pursued Moses and his followers, their own actions led to their downfall as they drowned in the sea—so the story goes.

Moses and Muhammad did not confront their adversaries with hatred or vengeance. They approached with kindness, extending a hand even to those who opposed them. They defended themselves only when necessary, always keeping their greater mission at the forefront—the fulfillment of divine purpose.

There is a profound common thread woven through the lives of all true spiritual leaders: they did not resent the darkness or evil of this world. Instead, they acknowledged its presence without succumbing to its influence. If you live in a relatively peaceful place, where your home is not under siege and your skies are free from bombs, then take inspiration from Jesus and Siddhartha. Respect those who oppose you; yet stand firm in your truth. Let evil rule the material world if it must, but never bow to it. Live a life of peace and compassion, avoiding harm to others—even those who may seek to harm you.

Jesus did not even harbor anger toward Judas. Even in betrayal, his love for Judas remained unwavering. Look also at Mahatma Gandhi, who, as he faced death, bowed to his assassin and forgave him for the act of taking his life. These leaders remind us that strength lies not in retaliation but in steadfast love and unshakable truth.

However, if you find yourself in a land torn by chaos, where your life and the lives of those you love are under constant threat from malevolent forces, then let Muhammad and Moses guide you. Defend yourself, but never take the offensive. Be a warrior, but do not unsheathe your sword first. Fight not out of hatred or vengeance, but with love and compassion. Even if your enemies inflict pain upon you and your loved ones, do not let hate poison your heart. When they cease their aggression, lay down your arms. If they fall into your mercy, treat them with kindness, protect them, and show compassion.

Demonstrate that you embody love and truth above all else, and make it clear that your actions stem not from malice, but from a desire to safeguard what you hold sacred. Let your life stand as proof that, even in the face of darkness, your heart remains unshaken, filled with the light of understanding, peace, and divine purpose.

Learn to respect and love your enemies, even the evil itself that exists in this material world. If that evil finds itself at your mercy, protect it, for this act reflects the depth of your compassion and understanding. As long as you harbor resentment, anger, or hatred while fighting against the darkness, you remain bound to that very darkness, unable to transcend. Paradoxically, evil seeks to make you fight darkness with hatred and anger, planting its dark emotions in your heart. It deceives you into believing that fighting darkness in this way will lead you to light, while in reality, it drags you deeper into its abyss.

True spiritual wisdom lies in seeing beyond the surface of good and evil, understanding their roles in the grand duality of existence. Through this perspective, you come to realize that the undivine dualities of the external, physical world are not to be eradicated with malice but understood with clarity and embraced with the light of love. Only by rising above anger and hatred can you begin to free yourself from the chains of this earthly reality and step toward higher consciousness.

Just as you must approach the external world with compassion and understanding, so too must you do the same with your inner reality—your inner devil. Do not wage war against your desires or resist yourself with hostility. When you falter, avoid self-pity or self-punishment. Instead, choose to understand yourself. Acknowledge your mistakes, correct them, and rise again with renewed purpose. Be strong in your mission and steadfast on your path. Keep your mind sharp and clear; Hold firm against the devil's temptations.

The devil and its army of demons will come at you from every direction, testing your resolve. But know this: only the power of love can shield you. Love yourself as you are, flaws and all, and protect yourself from succumbing to the darkness within. Stay true to your essence and hold yourself accountable but treat yourself with kindness. Do not hate the devil, for hatred only binds you to it. Instead, shine the light of truth into its darkened depths. From the darkness, gain wisdom—let the devil teach you what you must never become. See the devil not as an enemy but as a guide that warns you of danger. Yet, heed this wisdom without following devil's path.

This understanding of the devil and your inner demons allows you to see the imbalance of undivine duality of your spiritual reality. By getting to know the darkness within, you gain profound insight into your inner imbalances, empowering you to master yourself.

When you couple this inner knowledge with an awareness of the imbalances of the external world, you begin to ascend. You move toward deeper layers of consciousness and approach the divine realms of existence. Understanding the undivine dualities of your being—the physical and spiritual, the body and evil, the soul and the devil—opens the gateway to living in a state of love. This is what leads to everlasting bliss.

When this wisdom becomes clear and you align with it fully, the energy of your heart awakens. The fourth chakra—the heart center—opens, allowing divine love to flow into your being. In this sacred space of love, you will feel a deep connection to the infinite, and the bliss of divinity will fill your soul.

In this state, you no longer experience reality through the filters of your mind or personal interpretation. Instead, you are touched by a divine intervention—an experience beyond your creation. The power of this encounter will be so profound that the emotions and thoughts you experience will be entirely new, unfamiliar, and otherworldly—yet soothing and inviting, as if they were gifted to you from a realm beyond this world. For the first time, you will feel the gentle touch of the divine and the angels who are here to help you.

The next step on your journey to enlightenment is understanding unity—a realization that bridges the internal and external worlds into a single, seamless reality. Now that you've learned not to resent evil in the external world and not to resist the devil within, you possess the prerequisites to grasp an even deeper truth. This is where you encounter the concept of the trinity: the mirroring of the inner realm into the outer realm and the outer back into the inner. Everything you see outside yourself is but a reflection of your internal state, just as your internal state mirrors your external experiences. We've talked a lot about the mirror effect. Here is the very root of it all.

If your surroundings are chaotic, it reflects the chaos within your thoughts. If your feelings swing wildly, it mirrors the conflict present in your external habits. When you feel oppressed by the world around you, it reveals that you suppress your own passive thoughts and emotions internally. If you are an angry person, know that it is your anger toward yourself manifesting outwardly.

To truly ascend, you must understand that your external world and your internal reality are, at their core, one and the same. What you consider external is not external at all; it is simply a projection of your mind. Your senses deceive you into believing you perceive the outside world, but in truth, all you see, hear, smell, taste, and touch is the creation of your mind.

The eyes, for example, do not truly "see"—they are merely receptors, sophisticated tools that collect light and pass on information to the brain. When light enters the eye, it first refracts through the cornea and lens, creating an image onto the retina at the back of the eye. The retina contains specialized light receptor cells—rods and cones—that detect only a narrow bandwidth of light called visible light, which accounts for less than 1% of the actual light that enters your eyes. Arguably, the remaining 99% goes entirely unnoticed, as our eyes lack the receptors to perceive it.

Once the rods and cones absorb visible light, they trigger a biochemical reaction, converting light into electrochemical signals. These signals travel through the optic nerve to the brain, carried by ions such as potassium (K^+) and calcium (Ca^{2+}).

Interestingly, the image that strikes the retina is upside down and reversed due to the way light bends when passing through the lens. However, you do not perceive the world as inverted. Instead, the brain's visual cortex, located at the back of the brain, processes these signals, reconstructing the image and correcting its orientation. Furthermore, your visual cortex filters out another 99% of the visual data it receives, presenting only a fraction of the information as the final image you perceive. In reality, you are consciously aware of less than 1% of the total visual input your eyes detect.

Therefore, what you "see" is not the world itself—it is a representation built by your brain projected into your mind, using the limited data provided by your eyes and the processing system of your brain, which captures less than 1% of the 1% of the actual light.

Think of it this way. Look around you right now. Imagine that 10,000 things exist in your immediate environment. Given the limitations of your visual perception, the best-case scenario is that you see only 1 out of those 10,000 things that exist around you. This means that 9,999 things are happening around you right now that you are completely unaware of. And this doesn't even account for the microscopic and quantum world—entire hidden dimensions of reality filled with countless organisms, particles, subatomic particles, and strange interactions that remain invisible to you. If we were to include the unseen microscopic and quantum scale, your visual perception would shrink to detecting less than 1 in trillions of things happening around you at any given moment.

Thus, you have never seen the external world as it truly is; you have only experienced your mind's extremely primitive interpretation of it. This concept holds true for all your senses. Your hearing, touch, taste, and smell—like your vision—are primitive tools, each capable of perceiving only a modified, fraction of reality. Your senses are extremely inadequate to capture the full scope of reality, offering only a narrow and incomplete glimpse of it. What you perceive as "external reality" is, therefore, not an absolute truth but a construct—a mental image synthesized from the signals your receptors can detect and transmit.

The same is true for your inner world. You might ask: is the world within you real? The answer is no—not in the way you might think. Your internal reality is composed of thoughts and feelings, but they too are filtered and manipulated. Your feelings are interpretations of the pure emotions of your soul, yet these emotions are distorted by the devil within. Similarly, your thoughts are not pure but skewed versions of the voice of your soul. The devil manipulates your mind, ensuring you neither hear the soul's voice clearly nor experience its emotions in their untainted form.

In this way, both your external and internal worlds are merely perceptions—limited, imperfect recreations of reality within your mind. The external world is how your mind interprets what it perceives outside of you, and the internal world is how your mind interprets what's within you. Neither reflects true reality; they only point to what your limited mind can comprehend. Your internal and external realities coexist in the very same space, intertwined within the landscape of your mind.

Now let's look at this concept from a different angle. When you dream, you experience the dream world as if it exists outside of you. The people, landscapes, and emotions feel vivid, convincing you that you are moving through a real space. Yet, in reality, everything you see, hear, and feel is not happening outside of you at all—it is merely a projection of your own mind, an internal reality mistaken for an external one. Your actions within the dream are shaped by the cues you perceive from this seemingly "outside" world, even though it is entirely within you.

Similarly, when you wake up, the physical reality you experience is just another interpretation—this time, of another form of external reality. Your mind constructs your external world based on the sensory input it receives. Every decision you make, every reaction you have, is dictated by the cues from your environment, processed and framed within the limitations of your perception.

In this way, you are always dreaming—whether it is a night dream, woven from your subconscious mind, or a daydream, constructed by conscious part of your mind. Yet, in both cases, everything you experience is filtered through the mind. You have never existed outside of your own perception and your own mind, whether awake or dreaming. Your entire existence—your joys, your fears, your understanding of reality—resides within a tiny bubble of your own creation, shaped by the intricate workings of your mind and your individual consciousness.

When you fully grasp this concept, you realize that the division between the inner and outer worlds, as well as the separation between waking life and the dream world, are all merely part of one grand illusion. They all exist within you, created by the same mind, and are fundamentally one. What happens within you mirrors the external world, and what occurs externally is a reflection of your internal state at all times. When you no longer see these as separate, when you allow all perceptions to merge into one unified understanding of reality, something profound occurs: you step closer to truth.

This merging of worlds—inner and outer, waking and dream—opens your fifth chakra, the center of unity and higher perception. The trinity becomes clear: seemingly two opposite realities are in fact one higher reality. You no longer perceive your inner and outer experiences as separate, nor your dream and waking states as different, but rather as layers of the same truth, creating a broader and less limited understanding of existence.

When this wisdom takes root, you realize that suffering is a perception. Your suffering arises from how you interpret the world, both within and without. Whenever your perception of reality is not grounded in truth, you suffer. Shift your perspective and align it with truth, and you will transform your experience. Shift your perspective from suffering to peace, and you will feel peace. In this way, the opening of the fifth chakra diminishes your suffering to its smallest form, you see that suffering was never external to you, nor a part of you—it is a universal divine knob designed to align you with truth and divinity.

By merging the internal and external into one unified reality, you transcend the illusion of duality through the process of trinity. You step into a clearer understanding of yourself, the world, and existence itself. Here, as you step closer to truth, your suffering nearly dissolves, making way for peace to flow in its place—a peace born not of the earthly realm, but of the higher realms. This is the path of unity, the revelation of the trinity; and peace is the gift of the fifth chakra.

With the opening of the fifth chakra, you once again encounter another otherworldly experience—an experience of divine intervention, beyond anything your imagination can comprehend, even more profound than the activation of your fourth chakra. You gain the profound wisdom of the unity of all things, realizing that every opposing force in reality is, in truth, one and the same.

This realization fills you with a deep and lasting peace, as nothing appears contradictory anymore. Even forces that seem to oppose one another are revealed to work in perfect harmony, operating beyond the limits of ordinary human understanding. This insight dissolves inner conflict and brings you into a state of serene acceptance, where unity and peace reign within you.

With the opening of your fourth chakra, you have come to understand love, and through the fifth chakra, you have attained peace. Now, you are ready to step onto the next level of your path to enlightenment—understanding truth itself, which emerges as the perfect union of love and peace. It is through merging love and peace—wisdom from fourth and fifth chakra—that the journey toward your soul's most intimate depths begins.

This is where the concept of trinity reappears—a union of previously distinct forces into one: love and peace. You found harmony with the devil within and the evil outside through love. You merged the world within with the world without through peace. Now, you are ready to merge love and peace into a unified understanding of truth.

This process reveals your soul as it truly is—a being of love and peace. When you come to know your soul at its most fundamental level, your conscious mind begins to merge with the soul. Through this Trinity, love and peace converge to form the wisdom of truth, and your conscious awareness unites with your soul, activating your higher self—the most profound essence of your being: your spirit.

However, this merging is not without consequence. To unite fully with your soul means that the spiritual realm—the dimension in which the soul resides—will merge with the material world of your physical body. When dimensions intertwine in this way, it is both a powerful and perilous experience. You become exposed to angels, demons, energies, and forces beyond human scope. This heightened state of awareness demands precision, caution, and purity of intent. Any misstep here can possibly lead to irreversible mental damage, for this is a realm where there is no going back. Mistakes are often unforgiving.

But if this path is walked wisely, the rewards are extraordinary. Wisdom flows into you from the spiritual world, surpassing anything you have ever known. You reach the boundaries of the divine realm and begin to see not through your own limited perceptions, but through the vision of beings more powerful and wiser than yourself. You start to sense the true, unskewed emotions of the soul, and its voice becomes crystal clear in your mind. This is when your third eye opens, bestowing upon you *multidimensional* vision—an awareness that transcends space, time, and ordinary human understanding.

With your third eye open, the eye of the spirit, you come to know collective consciousness, accessing knowledge that defies intellectual comprehension. This is the realm of might and magic. This is where concepts such as clairvoyance, precognition, retrocognition, and intuition originate. These abilities, however, are not enlightenment themselves. Some individuals are naturally born with *interdimensional* abilities, allowing them to perceive or connect with spiritual dimensions. But this is not the same as becoming multidimensional—a state achieved only through merging with the soul and attaining enlightenment.

There are many ways to open the third eye, but if it is awakened through means other than the path of enlightenment, its function will be limited and incomplete. The third eye may activate, allowing access to interdimensional states, but it will not function at its full capacity—preventing you from reaching multidimensional awareness.

Interdimensional individuals exist outside looking in, peering into the spiritual world but remaining separate from it. Multidimensional beings, on the other hand, exist inside looking out, living within the unified reality of all dimensions.

Those who possess interdimensional abilities are especially vulnerable to darkness if they do not seek to walk the path of enlightenment or misunderstand the wisdom behind their natural gifts. The devil relentlessly pursues them, seeking to use their gifts to ensnare their souls. Many people with interdimensional abilities who make their living as palm readers, fortune-tellers, or spirit mediums are often not communicating with light forces but with dark forces, exchanging earthly gains for their spiritual gifts. Light spirits do not engage with those whose intentions are corrupted by material attachments. Instead, the devil thrives here, offering illusions of power and glamour to pull them deeper into darkness.

The interdimensional and multidimensional realms represent the devil's highest domain. Beyond this point lies the realm of divinity, a level of awareness where the devil is not permitted to enter by God's will. However, it is here, right behind the boundaries of divinity, that the devil's power is at its greatest.

It is best to avoid opening portals to the spiritual realm through interdimensional abilities, especially when a fortune teller, spirit medium, or similar figure requests money, gifts, or put their powers on display. Material gain and exchange is strictly forbidden in these realms. Such transactions and performances are dangerous and invite dark forces beyond your understanding. Even those who walk the path of enlightenment and reach this heightened state of awareness with pure heart and enter into multidimensional realm must proceed with extreme caution.

Constantly purify your body and mind, for even the smallest trace of darkness can be your undoing. At this level, the devil will try to deceive you with promises beyond imagination—offering wealth, power, and the entire world in exchange for your soul. The devil will stop at nothing here, for its greatest triumph is capturing souls on the very brink of divine enlightenment.

Even Jesus faced this ultimate test when he ventured into the desert to open his sixth chakra. After forty days of fasting and isolation, His third eye finally opened, and the first creature to appear before him was *Satan*—intent on making a deal with Jesus and taking his soul in exchange.

The devil possesses the ability to change its appearance at will, using this power to craft illusions and deepen its deception. One of the devil's most common forms is Satan, the embodiment of chaos and destruction. However, rather than appearing as a monstrous entity, Satan manifests as a seemingly admirable, charming, and even beautiful being—a form designed to disarm and entice rather than instill fear.

The devil takes the form of Satan when it seeks to strike a deal and negotiate—a figure who whispers temptations with calm persuasion rather than brute force. In this form, it does not force its will upon you, nor does it openly reveal its darkness. Instead, it presents itself as a guide, an advisor, even a friend—appearing to offer wisdom, success, and power. It speaks in half-truths, planting seeds of doubt while subtly steering you toward decisions that lead to spiritual decay. This form of manipulation is the devil's greatest weapon. Rather than imposing suffering outright, it leads you to choose your own suffering.

When Satan appeared before Jesus in the desert, it first tempted him with the basic need for sustenance, saying, "If you are the Son of God, command these stones to become bread." Knowing Jesus was near death from hunger, Satan sought to exploit his physical weakness. Yet Jesus refused, responding, "It is written: Man shall not live on bread alone, but on every word that comes from the mouth of God."

When this failed, Satan tried to destroy him and take his life, daring him to test God's protection: "If you are the Son of God, throw yourself down, for it is written: He will command his angels concerning you." Steadfast and unwavering, Jesus replied, "It is also written: Do not put the Lord your God to the test."

Finally, when all else failed, Satan revealed its final temptation, offering Jesus the entire world—its kingdoms, power, and wealth—in exchange for his soul: "All this I will give you, if you bow down and worship me." Jesus, resolute in his faith, rejected the offer and declared, "Away from me, Satan! For it is written: Worship the Lord your God, and serve Him only."

In overcoming these trials, Jesus pierced through the final veil of illusion, stabilizing his consciousness at an incomprehensibly high state of awareness. Here, his soul and conscious mind merge into perfect unity, being reborn as a spirit.

This is the realm of magic, mages, and mysticism, where physical reality loosens its hold and the spiritual reality becomes tangible. This is where superhuman abilities become accessible in tangle reality. This is how he could perform so-called miracles. By elevating his awareness to the state of pure spirit, he gained access to his superpowers, bending the laws of physical reality.

It is no coincidence that humanity has always been drawn to stories of superhuman abilities, as seen in our collective fascination with superheroes and science fiction movies. This reflects a deeper yearning within us—to open the third eye and perceive a reality that transcends the limitations of ordinary existence.

Our natural fascination with experiencing mystical realms tempts some people to take shortcuts to the spiritual realm. Some try to access it by opening interdimensional portals by contacting mediums or fortune tellers, while others turn to hallucinogenic drugs. Both approaches are highly inadvisable without first purifying your heart and mind, as they can expose you to dark forces.

Drugs may offer you a glimpse to the multiverse, like watching a movie, but you will remain an outsider, unable to merge with the spiritual reality or gain its full wisdom. True enlightenment requires sobriety and a disciplined mind. The chakras must be opened in sequence, for each step builds upon the last. Without love from the fourth chakra and peace from the fifth, the third eye better not be opened through any other means. Enlightenment cannot be cheated; it is earned through unimaginably challenging inner work.

If you still feel compelled to experiment with hallucinogenic drugs, it's crucial to approach them with utmost caution and a sense of responsibility. First and foremost, avoid synthetic drugs. Nature provides you with portals to other realms—organic and far less harmful than the artificial portals opened by synthetic drugs. Even with natural substances, their use should never be for mere entertainment. Instead, they must be approached with intent for spiritual understanding or self-exploration, and only when you are ready to fully respect the profound nature of these experiences.

Prepare yourself by cleansing your body and mind for days or even weeks beforehand. This means refraining from unhealthy habits, purifying your thoughts, and grounding yourself in a positive mental state. The darker your internal state—whether it's physical toxicity or emotional turmoil—the more vulnerable you become to the influence of dark forces. These forces are drawn to chaos and imbalance, and substances that alter your perception can amplify their effects on you if you are not prepared.

The goal should never be indulgence or distraction, but an earnest pursuit of insight. Respect the power of what you're ingesting, and remember that the intention you carry will shape your experience. Approach with humility, clarity, and reverence to avoid opening doors to darkness you may not be ready to confront.

Worse yet are those who turn to gifted individuals with interdimensional abilities to open portals into unseen realms. If these gifted people have turned their divine gift into a business or use it to showcase their abilities and feed their egos, know this: dark forces are going to be present. The moment any material exchange is involved—money, status, or even flattery—dark forces seize the opportunity to infiltrate with all their might.

You may not sense their presence at all. These forces are insidious, creeping into your mind and emotions in subtle ways, affecting the way you feel and think. They infest your mental landscape, planting seeds of doubt, fear, or discontent. Cleansing yourself from their influence becomes a painstakingly difficult journey, one that can take years of effort to overcome.

The small amount of information or "help" you receive from such portals will never be worth the toll it takes on your being. The cost is far greater than the reward. These dark forces siphon your energy, disrupt your clarity, and anchor you deeper into chaos. Protect yourself and do not play around with forces you do not understand. Divine gifts are sacred and meant to guide, not to be exploited for personal or material gain. Trust only those individuals with interdimensional abilities who wield their gifts with pure intentions, free from ego and material entanglements.

The best thing to do is just stick with the path of enlightenment. It will take you much longer, but it is far safer. If you walk the path of enlightenment carefully, with a sober mind and pure intent, you will eventually be able to merge dimensions on your own and open your third eye. This will forever change your perception of reality.

When your third eye truly opens, the world as you know it will dissolve, replaced by a deeper, more vibrant truth. You will no longer experience life merely through the limited lens of your physical senses, but through the boundless perceptions of your spirit—senses far superior, senses previously hidden and unknown to you.

You will hear words that are never spoken aloud, whispers carried on the currents of energy that flow between realms. You will see the unseen, perceiving what lies beyond the veil of physical reality—the elegant dance of spirits, energies, and forces that weave the fabric of spiritual existence. You will no longer walk through this world alone; you will merge and mingle with spirits from dimensions once thought unreal and unreachable.

In this heightened state, you will realize the superpowers that lie dormant within you. These are not the powers of fantasy or illusion but the profound transcendence of earthly limitations. You will rise beyond the boundaries of time, space, and the physical body, stepping into the vast, eternal realm of higher reality. Here, your spirit's wisdom will guide you, and the boundaries between worlds will blur, leaving you free to experience existence in pure and infinite form.

Another group of people who enter multidimensional states are those who have had near-death experiences. Across the world, countless individuals have returned from the brink of death—or even returned from clinical death itself—with vivid recollections of otherworldly realms. Some descend into terrifying depths, witnessing suffering beyond human comprehension, where fear expands beyond infinity within them as they encounter demons and dark forces. Others, however, ascend to luminous realms just below the divine, where an overwhelming sense of love and peace embraces them, free from judgment or scrutiny. In these realms, they interact with the spirits of the departed family members, encounter angelic beings, and receive profound wisdom—insights about their own life stories and higher truths essential for their spiritual journey.

This is the very realm accessible through the awakening of the sixth chakra, the seat of higher vision and perception. Jesus frequently entered this state after overcoming Satan, gaining access to deeper divine truths. Muhammad, too, entered this state during the last 23 years of his life to communicate with Angel Gabriel. A few other sages and spiritual leaders have experienced this state. You, too, can step into this realm, provided you possess a burning desire to uncover the truth—a longing so intense that it pierces through the veil of illusion, opening the doors to higher consciousness.

If you reach this state and yearn to go even higher, you must fully transcend—you must break through the final barrier, a barrier even the devil cannot cross. To go beyond, you must enter the realm of pure divinity, where all concepts of duality dissolve, and infinity becomes your only truth. This is where the understanding of quinternity arises: the complete and boundless comprehension of infinity itself.

To truly comprehend the concept of quinternity requires a model of reality that twists and bends in ways far beyond conventional understanding. Its intricacies are so profound and multidimensional that even attempting to articulate it is an exercise fraught with limitations. Explaining quinternity would necessitate an entire book dedicated to its exploration, and even then, much of its essence would remain elusive, slipping through the gaps of written and spoken language.

Language, no matter how advanced or refined, is inherently bound by the constraints of linear thought and human perception. It cannot encapsulate the full breadth of this level of existence, which transcends the capacity of words to describe. This truth resists articulation because its nature is not something that can be fully grasped intellectually or rationalized logically. It exists in a realm that can only be understood through direct experience and deep introspection.

In this way, quinternity is a truth best described by silence and an understanding best expressed through stillness. To grasp its essence is not to explain it, but to sense it—to let go of the need for verbal comprehension and instead surrender to the profound knowing that arises from being fully present within its reality. It is a concept that reveals itself not through the chatter of the mind, not through the voice of the soul, but through the quiet resonance of your spirit.

When you truly grasp the nature of infinity, your understanding stretches beyond the confines of time and dimensions. You begin to perceive a reality that existed before time itself—a realm where the boundaries of separation dissolve, and every one thing is everything, and everything is one thing. In this state, all that exists is an interconnected whole. This is when you, as a fragment of consciousness, become one with the whole of consciousness.

When your awareness transcends these constructs and you see the oneness underlying all existence, you unlock the wisdom of quinternity—a state of understanding that embraces the infinite complexity of existence as a singular, harmonious truth.

At this stage, your spirit is granted entry into the divine realm, merging with the kingdom of God. This is the moment when the gates of heaven open to you. It is here that you awaken your seventh chakra. No longer do you see, hear, or perceive through your own limited understanding, nor even through the perception of your soul. Instead, you begin to perceive existence through the vision of the spirit—a Godly vision unfiltered by mortal boundaries. You step beyond multidimensional understanding into all-dimensional existence, entering a realm that comes closest to base reality, where all truths are unveiled, and all illusions fall away.

Here, the entire structure of reality becomes apparent to you. You no longer perceive yourself as an individual living within a finite world, but as an inseparable part of the infinite whole. Your physical body, material desires, and earthly life become so insignificant that they cease to hold any weight. Hunger, thirst, or pain lose their ability to cause suffering, for you transcend the very concept of suffering itself.

The emotions you experience in this state are beyond anything the material world can offer, beyond any human language, for they are pure and boundless. No metaphor, no earthly sensation can describe them. This is why silence becomes the only voice and stillness the only motion through which this truth can be understood.

In this state, you move beyond the limitations of humanity and into the boundless realm of divinity. Here, existence itself becomes an eternal act of understanding—a union with the infinite, where all dimensions, all perceptions, and all dualities collapse into a singular, infinite presence. You become not a seeker of truth but truth itself. You transcend.

Jesus was granted access to this elevated state of consciousness more frequently than perhaps anyone who has ever lived—so frequently that it is almost humanly impossible for the average person to sustain. This profound closeness to divine truth is why Jesus is often mistaken for God itself. He had come so near to the essence of the Creator, so deeply aligned with divine wisdom, that his followers confuse him with God. They see in him a reflection so pure, so untainted by the distortions of human perception, that they cannot distinguish between the messenger and the source.

However, even this exalted state of being is not beyond your reach. You, too, can ascend toward this level of awareness. You, too, can step beyond illusion and glimpse the true nature of reality for yourself. It requires an unwavering dedication to truth, a relentless pursuit of love, and the courage to transcend the fears and attachments that keep you bound to a lesser existence. Jesus was not merely a figure to be worshipped, but an example—an ultimate arbiter of humanity and a guidepost illuminating the path of enlightenment for those willing to walk it with sincerity and devotion.

To ascend and walk the path of enlightenment, you must follow each step in its proper order, for the journey is not one to rush. First, be humble. Understand that you are not better than anyone else, nor is anyone better than you. Even if you ascend to the highest levels of spirituality, it does not make you superior—it simply gives you a different experience of life. The moment a sense of superiority grips your heart, your ascent will halt. Always keep your heart and mind open to truth, for the truth you encounter may be greater than your own.

Next, be grateful—for everything. The good and the bad alike are gifts in your life. See the beauty in all things, even the challenges. Avoid complaints and ingratitude; do not wallow in pity for what you lack but rejoice in all that you have. Gratitude is the foundation of peace.

Enhance your intelligence to perceive the layers of reality that lie hidden behind masks, facades, deceptions, and falsehoods. Do not merely listen to the words that are spoken—attune yourself to the tone, the pauses, and the emotions behind them. Observe actions not just for what they achieve but for the intent that drives them. Train your mind to go beyond the surface, to recognize patterns and contradictions, and to uncover the underlying truths that often remain concealed. True intelligence lies in discerning the intention behind words and actions.

The only way to enlightenment is to seek truth, for every other concept emerges from it. Sacrifice anything and everything that stands between you and truth, even if it means leaving behind your most precious people and possessions. Truth demands a pure heart and clear mind.

Live in balance. Let neither your logic nor morality tip into imbalanced. Do not excel in one area of life while neglecting another. Strive to improve your physical reality while ascending on your spiritual journey. Nurture your body, mind, and soul simultaneously. Seek truth with compassion and understanding, not with resentment, hatred, or anger. Avoid justifying malevolence through seemingly righteous acts; revenge, even when disguised as justice, remains a force of darkness.

Strive for harmony within yourself: align your passive thoughts—the voice of your soul—with your active thinking. Allow your emotions, which are the sensations of the soul, align with your feelings. But be vigilant. The devil's manipulations are subtle; it will twist your thoughts and feelings to mislead you.

Know that you will never know everything. Even if you open your seventh chakra, parts of truth will forever elude you. The deeper your wisdom, the more you will realize how vast reality is—and how much of it lies beyond your comprehension. Keep your beliefs flexible; refine them constantly. Doubt is the fertile ground of progress, while certainty leads to stagnation.

Maintain balance in all things. Recognize the power of the devil, but know that your power—born of love—is greater. Understand that your suffering is not a punishment but a measure of your strength to overcome. Be honest with yourself to know who you truly are. Be honest with others to know who they are. Practice integrity; when you keep your word, you gain respect for yourself and earn the trust of others. In this way, you navigate the devil's den with the light ignited in your heart through honesty and integrity.

Balance solitude and connection. Spend time alone to know yourself deeply, and time with others to understand humanity. Do not fall into the trap of favoritism, which divides people and clouds judgment. Take no sides in worldly agendas—truth and justice are the only causes worth championing.

Strive for harmony between competition and cooperation. Be brave. Take risks. Face your fears, for fear is the greatest barrier to your dreams. Do not let it paralyze you. Instead, conquer fear with love, for love is the one energy in the universe that the devil respects. The devil knows it cannot overpower love. Live through love, and you will become stronger than the devil itself.

Let your love be unconditional. Love without expectation. Love for the sake of love itself. Sacrifice in the name of love. Forgive in the name of love. Release regrets and resentments. Allow love to cleanse your mind and heart, freeing you from your self-inflicted suffering. See the world through the lens of love.

Love must begin within. Love yourself first so you can understand how to love others—love your friends and even your enemies. If love is offered to you, receive it with an open heart, but never demand it. Do not depend on others as the source of love; generate it within yourself. Share it freely with the world, for the world needs your love more than anything. Overcome fear with love, for it is the only force that can conquer it. This is the greatest gift you can offer to the world in your lifetime—give love as abundantly as you can.

Take control of your life by taking responsibility for it. Everything and everyone that affects your life is, in some way, your responsibility. Act with good intention in all things. Do not act out of resentment or obligation; do it with love in your heart. Build bridges where others build walls. Open channels of communication, understanding, and compassion. Seek to understand others rather than fight them. Use empathy to feel their pain and take their suffering as your own. When you have the capacity to help, do so with grace and a smile.

Remember, we are all fragments of the same consciousness, and the more harmoniously we connect with one another, the greater we become. Be a drop of consciousness in the vast ocean, and an ocean of consciousness within a single drop.

Use quaternity concept to approach the mysteries of the world with humility and caution, avoiding absolute certainty in your discussions. Speaking with unwavering certainty about mysteries of life leads to misunderstanding, resentment, and division. Use quaternity as a balanced approach—understand where a topic falls within its four-step framework and align your level of certainty accordingly. Use it to remain grounded in reality, fostering open dialogue and mutual respect. Use quaternity as a tool to understand the vastness of knowledge while maintaining a sense of connection and understanding with others.

Be kind, not because you must, but because kindness reflects the light within you. Carry your responsibilities with pride, but do not let pride poison your heart. Keep your head high, but your gaze low—humility is the mark of wisdom. Be proud of your accomplishments, but never arrogant.

Above all, be yourself. Follow the path of your own heart and learn from your greatest teacher—the soul that dwells within you. Walk the path of enlightenment with courage and persistence. With every step forward, your suffering will dwindle until, at last, it ceases altogether.

There is no greater purpose in life than to walk this path. It is a journey of truth, love, and peace, one that will transform you and the world around you. With each step, you move closer to freedom, to understanding, and to the infinite light of truth that has always existed within you.

As for myself, I do not see myself as an enlightened guru or an awakened master. I consider myself a dark soldier of the light. My life began in the chaos of war, and my spiritual journey took root in the depths of hell. My relentless curiosity for knowledge led me down a perilous path. For the wisdom I sought, I sold my soul to the devil—and that I did. Once, I was cast into the abyss, the depths of hell, forced to witness the torment of a world so twisted and horrifying that it surpassed my worst imagination. In that hell, I experienced the depths of ultimate fear and despair.

When I returned, my entire being was tainted with darkness. I carried with me an unbearable weight—agony, hatred, anger, despair—every form of suffering imaginable. The idea of escaping it all, even through death, became a haunting whisper in my mind. I entertained thoughts of ending my life countless times, yet I was too much of a coward to act upon them. I was afraid that if I took my own life, I would be sent back to the hell I was desperately trying to escape. When you sell your soul to the devil, reclaiming it is not as simple as asking for it back. You must fight for it. And my soul had been trapped in the devil's den for so long that I questioned whether I still had one at all.

Desperate to escape, I turned to everything I could find. I dissected and deciphered religious texts, immersed myself in spiritual doctrines, and studied philosophies from every corner of the world, searching for a way out of my personal hell. But when you seek knowledge from the devil, what you receive is knowledge wrapped in darkness. You see not the truth itself, but the illusion that the lower realms of reality is built upon. You begin to see the matrix, the grand deception that binds humanity to the devil, and you realize just how impossible it seems to break free from it. The devil does not grant you insight into what lies beyond the illusion—only a deeper awareness of the trap itself.

With every sacred text I read, I saw devil's illusion. I saw how humanity had been manipulated, how noble ideas had been twisted into instruments of suffering, how peace and unity had been promised yet rarely delivered. It felt like slamming into dead ends at every corner, over and over again. And in those moments, I could hear the devil laughing, mocking me, knowing that I was lost in its labyrinth of deception, my soul buried beneath layers of darkness.

Yet, I held on to the small ember of hope still burning within me. I refused to let it die. Every night, I was plagued by nightmares of battling demons—sometimes I emerged victorious, but many times, I was devoured, waking in a state of panic and dread. My days were filled with torment, and my nights were haunted. I numbed myself constantly with whatever I could, just to momentarily silence the suffering.

But then, something changed. As I continued my search, I began to see light flickering through the cracks. Among the deceptions, I noticed fragments of truth embedded within religions and spirituality, hidden among the layers of illusion. I saw glimpses of purity within the teachings of spiritual leaders, scattered amidst the distortions. And so, I followed the light—wherever I could find it.

Slowly, my life began to improve. The more I followed the truth, the more I reclaimed my soul. The suffering that had once consumed me began to subside, piece by piece.

I am no more than a seeker—a wanderer determined to pursue the light of truth above all else. This path, though grueling, has filled me with a sense of joy and fulfillment that I had never known before. I am painfully aware of my own flaws, and every day, I continue to dance and wrestle with the darkness within me. Everything I have written in this book, I first wrote for myself. These are the words I tell myself, the wisdom I try to live by—though I fail often, and my progress is slow, sometimes excruciatingly so.

Yet, I press on. Because the suffering that once ruled my existence has now diminished a trillionfold. And if I can continue walking this path, step by step, then perhaps, just perhaps, I can one day emerge fully into the light and stay there. In the first phase of my spiritual journey, I learned the dark knowledge of the devil and the infinite depth of fear and despair. Now, I seek the luminous wisdom of the divine to completely end my suffering.

Still, the cost of reducing my suffering has been immense. I have sacrificed much—my career, my friends, my loved ones, and nearly all my earthly possessions. I have left behind everything I ever loved. Some of the people I cherished most no longer speak to me, simply because I chose to voice what I believed to be true, and they did not want to hear it. Some of those whom I deeply admired now believe I am destined for hell because I refuse to conform to their worldview. Most of those who remain in my life do not understand my purpose. Fewer than a handful of people are willing to engage with me in a discussion about raw truth, without filters. These are the very few who are my true companions in the path of enlightenment and do not run away when I share the insights of my journey with them.

For years, I wandered this earth, mostly alone, lost in the depths of my own darkness, searching aimlessly for truth. I have faced the devil and its temptations countless times, and many times, I have failed. Time and again, I have given in to my darker desires and struggled deeply with my weaknesses and shortcomings. Through the wrong choices I have made in my life, I have plunged to lower levels of awareness, forgetting all the blessing that I have in my life, and then doubt has gripped my heart, whispering that I have made no real progress—that perhaps I am deluding myself. In these moments of despair, I question whether the sacrifices I've made are worth the truths I am seeking. The allure of returning to a "normal" life—a life of safety, comfort, and familiarity—tempts me. When I see the cruelty and evil in this world, when I witness how humanity treats one another, I want to give up.

There are times when fear takes hold, blinding me to the light. I plunge into the depths of my own darkness, losing sight of the path ahead. In those moments, the devil brings me to my knees, leaving me on the brink of despair and madness. Yet, even in this darkness, a faint spark of light within me stirs. A fragment of memory surfaces—a realization that the agony I feel is not an external curse but the consequence of my own missteps. I remember the allure of temptations and desires that led me astray, the subtle traps I fell into, and the ignorance and arrogance I allowed to take hold.

As the devil pushes me down, I recognize his tactics and see through his deception. Something within me refuses to surrender. I recall the value of truth and love—the pillars that form the foundation of this path I have chosen. I remember how much suffering I endured in the past, how anger, hatred, and bitterness once consumed me, and how far I have come since stepping onto this journey. My mind, once a battlefield of torment, no longer suffers when I resist the pull of ignorance and arrogance. This realization reignites the light within me.

I rise again, defying the weight of adversity and the darkness that seek to consume me. As I stand, the light of truth returns, illuminating the path ahead. It reminds me why I have sacrificed so much and endured so many trials. My resolve is renewed, my determination fortified. I am reminded of the treasures that lie at the heart of this journey: unity with truth, love, peace, my soul, my spirit, the vast interconnected reality, and ultimately the Creator—the Source of all things. These are treasures beyond measure, far more valuable than any fleeting comfort or desire the devil might dangle before me. And so, I push forward, carrying the light of truth within me, step by step, closer to the divine.

When the light of truth fills my heart again, I feel weightless, as if I could soar beyond the confines of this material world. In those moments, I rise above the darkness, experiencing the serenity of higher awareness. My mind grows quiet, peaceful, and clear. I enter the state of bliss where there is no suffering. Sometimes, I can go for days, even weeks, in a complete state of bliss—filled with immense joy that words cannot describe—amidst daily struggles. I am reminded of how good it feels to live in the light of truth, and I resolve to never forget this feeling, to never give up.

As I tread the path of enlightenment, the moments when darkness takes hold have become increasingly rare, the devil's grip weaker, the durations shorter. The overwhelming despair that once consumed me has faded into something distant—no longer an all-encompassing abyss, but a passing shadow.

Long ago, I made a pact with the devil. I sought knowledge without wisdom, power without discipline, truth without love. And now, I must pay the price for my wrongdoing. But I fully accept this. Whatever the cost, I will gladly bear it for it means fully reclaiming my soul.

I am not yet free from suffering, nor do I claim to have reached the summit of enlightenment. But I see the path. I know where it leads. And for the first time in my life, I know my life's purpose and know where I am headed.

Nowadays, when I look around, when my eyes meet those of strangers, I see their suffering. It lingers in the way they walk, in the way their shoulders slump under invisible burdens, in the silent weight they carry in their gaze. I see pain hidden behind forced smiles, exhaustion disguised as determination. And it reminds me of how I used to feel—trapped in my own torment, chasing illusions, waiting for a tomorrow that never arrived.

I wish I could do something for the world to ease its suffering because I know how much it hurts. I see people running tirelessly toward the mirage of success, believing that just beyond the next milestone, happiness awaits them. Yet, tomorrow never delivers on its promises. The happy future they long for always remains just out of reach, an illusion that vanishes the moment they arrive, only to be replaced by a new goal, a new desire, a new chase.

And so they wait, always waiting—postponing their joy, delaying their peace—never realizing that happiness was never meant to be found in tomorrow. It was always meant to be lived today.

I shared my journey and insights with you in this book, hoping that some of my experiences may resonate with you and bring fulfillment to your life and ease your suffering. I have drawn upon concepts from various religions and spiritual traditions, piecing together fragments of understanding to create a cohesive model of reality. I believe each religion holds unique insights—Buddhism and Taoism best explain the energy levels of the spiritual realm, while the Abrahamic faiths describe spirits and moral understanding with greater clarity. Yet, I believe in neither all nor none of them, for every religion contains both truth and illusions. Since my sole pursuit is truth, I have endeavored to extract and combine the clearest truths from each tradition to create a framework that guides me forward.

I consider myself my own greatest critic and skeptic, constantly questioning, reevaluating, and refining my beliefs. I fully expect this model of reality to evolve, or perhaps even be entirely redone, as I continue on this path, based on uncovering truths that are currently beyond my understanding. I am not attached to this model, and I will discard it without hesitation if I come to understand that it is flawed or untrue. This journey is ongoing, and each step brings new insights that may reshape or redefine what I believe today. This is simply a step along the path, not the final destination.

I have learned this lesson from nature itself. Spiders spend hours, sometimes days, weaving intricate webs with meticulous precision. Yet, when the wind tears through their delicate strands or a careless passerby brushes their creation away, they do not mourn or cling to what was lost. If the web is salvageable, they repair it; if it is beyond saving, they simply weave a new one—without hesitation.

Birds do the same. They construct their nests with care, raising their young within them, only to leave them behind as the seasons change. If a nest remains intact and serves its purpose, some birds return to restore and reuse it. But if it has withered or been destroyed, they do not grieve for what is lost; instead, they gather new twigs and build again. And if the wisdom gained from their journey teaches them to build a better nest—one more suited to their needs—they do so without hesitation.

I do the same with my understanding of reality. If the hands of destiny shake the foundation of my beliefs, if the winds of truth unravel the strands of my thoughts, I will weave again, unafraid of letting go. Like the spider and the bird, I will not mourn the collapse of old constructs and beliefs. If what once stood can be restored with deeper understanding, I will repair it. But if wisdom demands that I rebuild, I will do so without hesitation—for every fall is merely an opportunity to construct something wiser, something truer.

With that said, do not take anything I have written in this book as the absolute truth. Analyze it for yourself. Question it. Dissect every idea, every concept, and ensure that what I have presented is not merely an illusion born from something I have yet to fully understand. The responsibility of discerning truth from falsehood is yours alone. I can only offer what I have learned and warn you of the dangers of this incomplete work and the lack of my understanding of truth.

I have done my best to be as honest as possible, to lay out the truth as I understand it today. But I am only a man—flawed, incomplete, and ever-evolving. My understanding is far from perfect, and I carry countless misunderstandings, many of which I have yet to even realize.

So do not follow my words blindly. Use your own wisdom, your own intuition, and your own reasoning. Take only what resonates as truth, and discard whatever does not hold up under scrutiny. If you find something valuable here, use it. If you find something flawed, refine it. Truth is not something handed to you—it is something you must seek for yourself. If even a single word in this book helps you make better choices, then my purpose of writing this book will have been fulfilled.

I have intentionally generalized and simplified the concepts in this book, knowing that they cannot be fully explored or contained within a single work. The subjects discussed here span vast and complex realms of thought, each deserving of its own exploration. My goal was not to overwhelm you with exhaustive details but to provide a basic framework that you can build upon in your own mind.

This book represents less than 10% of what I have written over the years. I have deleted most of my writings, stripping away excess words, refining ideas, and distilling them down in an effort to make the concepts as simple and accessible as possible. My goal was not to overwhelm or confuse, but to create clarity—to present only what is essential, leaving out what might distract from the core message.

Even so, I know that no matter how much I simplify, some of these concepts may still be challenging to grasp. That is the nature of truth—it is not something that can always be neatly packaged into words. Some truths must be felt, experienced, and lived to be fully understood.

I chose to weave these ideas together loosely, leaving spaces intentionally for you to fill with your own reflections and insights. This book is not meant to be a final word or an unchanging doctrine—it is a starting point, a seed planted in fertile ground. While the gaps in this model exist, they are purposeful. They are an invitation for you to engage with the concepts, to explore beyond what is written, and to arrive at your own understanding.

Ultimately, this book is not about handing you answers but about encouraging you to seek them for yourself. The bigger picture I have attempted to present here is merely a lens through which you might view the world and your place within it. It is my hope that this perspective serves as a guide, but the journey is yours to undertake, and the truth is yours to discover.

Much of the information I share comes from my own research and understanding, but some of it, I believe, has been gifted to me by superior beings from other realms. However, the information I receive is raw and unstructured, leaving me to interpret and decipher it alone. It arrives like a puzzle, and solving it is entirely my responsibility. Even if these insights are genuine, my interpretations are prone to flaws and misjudgments. Therefore, I urge you to question everything I have written here.

You might think I am delusional for claiming to have encountered higher beings and spiritual entities. Trust me, I ask myself the same question regularly. The line between reality and delusion becomes alarmingly thin when dimensions merge, and the experiences are so vast and unfamiliar that they defy comprehension.

Often, portals to higher realms of existence open unexpectedly. At least in my case, they are almost never premeditated. They catch me off guard, pulling me into an overwhelming experience that transcends my ordinary perception. In those moments, I am fully immersed, lost in a reality so vivid and profound that it feels more real than anything I have ever known. But when I return to lower states of awareness, the encounters slip through my fingers like fading dreams.

No matter how intense the experience, no matter how deeply it shakes my being, the return to ordinary consciousness always brings with it a sense of distance—as if what I glimpsed was not meant to be retained in its entirety. I try to hold on, to recall every detail, but much of it dissolves into the background of my mind, leaving only fragments behind. Yet, those fragments—subtle impressions, lingering emotions, flashes of insight—remain enough to change me, enough to remind me that there is more to existence than the narrow lens of daily life.

Beings from higher realms often do not communicate through physical senses. They bypass the eyes, ears, and mouth, connecting directly to the brain, heart, mind, and soul. They gain access to thoughts, memories, even those buried deep within the subconscious. The experience leaves you utterly exposed, unable to retreat into the privacy of your own mind. This connection blurs the boundary between external reality and internal perception, making it incredibly difficult to discern truth from illusion. I must constantly reassess and question my experiences, struggling to determine whether I am hearing my own thoughts or the voice of something beyond.

Some time ago, supernatural events began happening in my life with increasing frequency. They were subtle but undeniable, leaving me deeply unsettled as if reality itself was shifting in ways I could not understand. Then one night, a dream came to me—vivid and extraordinary, unlike anything I had ever experienced.

In the dream, I encountered two beings of immense power, their presence so overwhelming that fear gripped me, and I turned to run. But one of them called out, commanding me to stop. "We have something for you," they said, their voices calm but unyielding. "Something you have been waiting for, for a very long time." They invited me to sit with them at a table. Hesitant but curious, I took a chair and sat down. Then I realized they were beings of light, and a surge of joy filled my entire being.

Shortly after, I woke up, and the dream remained crystal clear in my mind, every detail etched vividly—every word, every character, every sensation. But more than the memory of the dream, I awoke filled with an overwhelming sense of ease and peace. It was as if every problem, every struggle I had ever carried, had been lifted. In its place was a powerful energy, indescribable in words, coursing through me. I was elated, not because of any external event, but because of the unshakable peace that now dwelled within me. I thought that was the message they had for me—the peace I had been searching for all this time. I was happy to finally sense that infinite, unshakable peace within me.

Days turned into weeks, and slowly, that peace began to fade. Not because it was gone, but because I didn't know how to hold onto it. The distractions and struggles of daily life pulled me back, as they often do. The dream, once so significant, started to lose its grip on me, its meaning blurred by the noise of the world.

Then, one morning, weeks later, I awoke with a peculiar sensation, unlike anything I'd ever known. It was a strange unease, but not unpleasant. It carried with it echoes of the peace from the dream, mingled with a sense of being somewhere else—not here on Earth. I do not know how to describe it; the sensation is unlike anything we have words for. All I can say is that it was peculiar beyond measure. I decided to take a walk outside. Something about the moment felt profoundly unusual.

While walking out in the open under the sunlight, I felt alienated from the world around me. Everything seemed so distant. For reasons I cannot explain, I looked up at the sky. And then it happened. In an instant, I was struck by what I can only describe as a flash of light—not a physical light, but something that struck my mind, heart, and body all at once. It was as though lightning had entered my being, yet I could also see its holographic image in the blue sky. It lasted only a fraction of a second before disappearing.

In that instant, I saw everything—the entirety of reality, from the simplest to the most complex, laid bare before me. I saw a tree, but within that tree, I saw the entire universe. Its branches cradled galaxies, its molecules shimmered like stars, and everything flowed together as one seamless whole.

And just as quickly as it came, the vision vanished. But it left me with one undeniable urge: I had to write. The urge was overwhelming, almost as if I had no choice. I had to write about what I had seen, what I had sensed. It was a paradox, because writing had always been my greatest struggle.

In high school, I repeatedly failed my language classes. In college, I continued to struggle with my English courses to the point where I nearly dropped out. My coworkers found endless joy in mocking my clumsy attempts at writing. And yet, here I was, driven by something far greater than my fears or insecurities, compelled to do the one thing I had always thought impossible—write a book.

This journey has taught me that spirituality is not about what you desire, but about what you are called to do. It is about surrendering your will to the path that life sets before you, even when it's unexpected or uncomfortable. I never wanted to be a writer, yet here I am, fulfilling a destiny I did not choose but have come to accept.

This book is my attempt to capture, in words, a fraction of what I experienced in that flash of light, in that blink of an eye. Years and thousands of hours have gone into recreating that fleeting vision, knowing full well that I can only understand and convey an infinitesimal glimpse of that picture.

I sincerely thank you for taking the time to read my book, and I truly hope you find it meaningful and useful in your own journey. In a strange yet beautiful way, as I write these words, I feel a connection to you, even though I have no idea who you are or when you will read these pages. Despite this lack of knowledge, the connection feels real—an unspoken bond that transcends time and space.

Though I sit here alone, penning these thoughts in solitude, I do not feel lonely. Instead, I feel deeply connected, as though these words are reaching out to you, bridging the gap between us. It is a reminder of the invisible threads that weave us into a shared fabric of reality, and in this moment, I find comfort in the sense of unity that connects us all together. Thank you for being a part of this shared experience, even if we may never meet.